THE FORTY-EIGHTERS ON POSSUM CREEK

THE FORTY-EIGHTERS ON POSSUM CREEK

A Texas Civil War Story

by

W.A. TRENCKMANN

Translated and Annotated by

JAMES KEARNEY

State ⬩ House Press

State House Press
at Schreiner University
Kerrville, TX
325-660-1752
www.mcwhiney.org

Cataloging-in-Publication Data

Names: Trenckmann, William A., 1859-1935, author.

[Die Lateiner am Possum Creek. English]

Title: The forty-eighters of Possum Creek: a Texas civil war story / William A. Trenckmann; translated and annotated by James C. Kearney.

Description: First edition. | Kerrville, TX: State House Press, 2020. | Includes bibliographical references.

Identifiers: ISBN 9781933337845 (softcover); ISBN 9781933337869 (e-book)

Subjects: LCSH: United States – History – Civil War, 1861-1865 – Fiction. | German Americans – Texas – History – 19th century – Fiction. | Texas – History – 1846-1950 – Fiction. | Kearney, James C., 1946-

Classification: LLC PT2532.T4 (print) | DDC 833.7

First edition 2020

Distributed by Texas A&M University Press Consortium
800-826-8911
www.tamupress.com

TABLE OF CONTENTS

ABBREVIATIONS

DBCAHS: Dolph Briscoe Center for American History Studies

HBT online: Handbook of Texas online

SWHQ: Southwestern Historical Quarterly

SBAt: Solms-Braunfels Archives (transcripts)

ACKNOWLEDGEMENTS

The author would like to acknowledge the very helpful comments and contributions of James Woodrick who has family connections to Millheim and who has done extensive research on the families and farmsteads of the original settlers; research that he has generously shared. I would also like to thank Dr. Walter Kamphoefner for his insightful comments and suggestions; as usual, always right on. Finally, I would like to thank the staff of the Briscoe Center for American History Studies at the University of Texas at Austin for their helpful assistance. The microfilm copies of W.A. Trenckmann's newspaper, *Das Bellville Wochenblatt* are housed there as well as other invaluable primary source materials.

INTRODUCTION

he Latin Farmers of Possum Creek; A Texas Civil War Story is a historical novel by W.A. Trenckmann that focuses on the life of one young man, Kuno Sartorius, who grows up and comes of age in a community of educated German immigrants during the waning months of the Civil War. Kuno is clearly modeled after the author's older brother Hugo Trenckmann, for the challenges Kuno faces in the novel are very similar to those faced by his older brother in real life. Trenckmann serialized the novel in his newspaper, *Das Bellville Wochenblatt* (The Bellville Weekly), beginning January 1908 and continuing on the back pages throughout the year. Born at Millheim in 1859, Trenckmann was only a small boy during the Civil War, but the tensions and hardships occasioned by the conflict, experienced acutely in his own family as well as in the wider German community, left an indelible impression upon him.

Trenckmann also wrote of these impressions in his memoirs that have recently been released in translation as *Preserving German Texas Identity: Reminiscences of William A. Trenckmann, 1859-1935* by two distinguished Texas historians, Drs. Walter L. Buenger and Walter D. Kamphoefner.[1] He also penned a short account of a memorable Christmas celebration in the midst of the war entitled "Weihnachtsfeier in trüber Zeit (Christmas in Troubled Times).[2] Clearly, these memories stayed with Trenckmann throughout for he returned to deal with them in literary form, employing both fiction and non-fiction, at different periods in his life.

"

In the novel, Possum Creek is the fictional name given to Millheim by the author. Millheim was never a town in the normal sense; it was rather a cluster of educated German immigrant families who set up small subsistence farmsteads in walking distance from one another along the west bank of Mill Creek in Austin County, Texas. To be sure, the community included in time a store, a doctor's office, a school, a community hall, and several small shops, but these venues were often adjuncts to the more or less self-sufficient farmsteads. There were about thirty families associated with the community in its heyday.[3] Many of the characters in the novel share unmistakable characteristics with real-life individuals from Millheim, but the author takes pains not to make the identities too obvious since at the time of its publication in 1908 many of these people were still alive.

Millheim's cluster of farmsteads stood on a picturesque elevation of the broad Mill Creek Valley, which traced a course from its headwaters forty miles to the northwest toward its debouchment into the Brazos River, just above present-day Stephen F. Austin State Park about eight miles to the southeast. To the south the community fronted the northern bulge of the expansive Bernardo prairie that filled the twenty-five-mile spread between the Brazos and Colorado River Valleys and included parts of Austin, Colorado, Brazoria, and Fort Bend counties. These topographical features play an important role in the story.

Millheim was always a sister community to Cat Spring, which is located about four miles to the southwest. Cat Spring numbers among the earliest German settlements in Texas. The large and extended von Roeder family settled it originally in 1834 on land grants they received when Texas was still part of Mexico. Because of the poor sandy soils around Cat Spring, Ludwig Kleberg, member of the extended von Roeder clan through marriage and a model for Grossenberg in the novel, was the first to relocate to Millheim where broad and fertile bottomlands offered better prospects for farming and where water and timber were more readily accessible. Many settlers from Cat Spring and from the Bernardo River to the west subsequently followed Kleberg's lead, including Andreas Trenckmann and his family. The establishment date for Millheim is

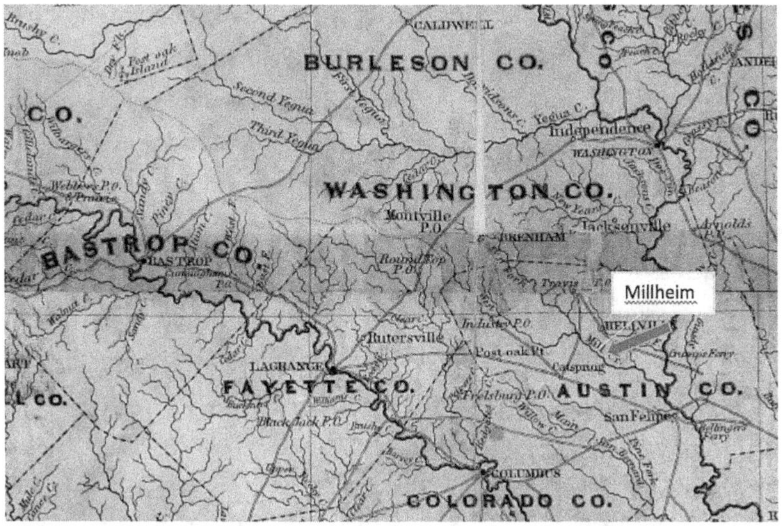

often given as 1845 or thereabouts.[4] The community of Collinsville in the novel serves as a stand-in for Cat Spring.

Millheim is one of the *Lateiner* communities in Texas, towns and communities where university-educated German immigrants tended to concentrate. The German name *Lateiner* came about because at the time knowledge of Latin was considered indispensable to any educated person. Unfortunately, the closest English equivalent, "Latinist," lacks the rich associations of the German term. The reader will quickly notice the prevalence of Latin words and phrases sprinkled throughout the novel, which reflects the classical grounding of most of the principle characters in the book. Charles Nagel, who also grew up in Millheim and subsequently became Secretary of Commerce in the Taft Administration, recalled that he had never known such a concentration of university-trained men in a single community.[5] These communities also produced an amazingly rich literature, of which this novel is but one example.

It is a curious fact that in Texas educated Germans associated with the Forty-Eighter migration—the wave of immigration following the European revolutions of 1848—tended to cluster into separate rural settlements where they often developed a community life that contrasted markedly with the more typical immigrant destinations like New Braunfels, Fredericksburg, and a host of smaller named communities, where the vast majority immigrants hailed from either agricultural or small trade backgrounds and whose education had been restricted to primary school or regulated apprenticeships. Thus, classes that were vertically stratified back home in Germany separated and spread out horizontally across the vastness of Texas. This pattern repeated itself nowhere else in North America to the degree it happened in Texas.

Organized religion played a noticeably reduced role in the *Lateiner* communities as a central and unifying community activity.[6] The residents of Millheim in fact voted on one occasion to exclude churches from their community on the grounds that they would be divisive. Accordingly, typical German social clubs [*Vereine*], such as gymnastic, literary, singing, and shooting clubs, played an expanded role in shaping community cohesion.[7] Rudolph Biesele in his study of the German settlements in Texas lists the *Lateiner* communities as Millheim in Austin County, Latium in Washington County, Bettina in Llano County, and Sisterdale and Tusculum in Kendall County.[8] But to this list we can also add neighboring Cat Spring, Comfort and Boerne in Kendall County, and Round Top in Fayette County. Opposition to slavery and secession, it should be noted, was always more strident in the *Lateiner* settlements in Texas than the other German communities.

The collision of the Forty-Eighters' democratic, republican, and freethinking ideals with the realities of secessionist Texas—the decision to resist or accommodate—forms one of the main themes of the novel. Herr Lüttenhoff, one of the principal characters in the novel, is obviously closely modeled after Trenckmann's father, who emigrated for political reasons following the failed German revolution of 1848. Accordingly, his father grew up in modest circumstances in the province of Brandenburg, but was a gifted student who by dint of hard work and self-discipline acquired a university education. Later, he became a schoolmaster at a private school in Magdeburg, where he rose to a position of modest affluence and prestige. Proscribed from teaching because of his political beliefs, the father decided to emigrate with his family to America in 1849 and to begin a new life near Cat Spring and later Millheim. Several long digressions in the novel highlight the circumstances that led educated Germans to leave their homeland during the period and the varied paths that led them to Texas as a final destination.

As an adolescent, W. A. Trenckmann attended the frontier school organized and supported by the residents of Millheim for whom education was always a high priority. The school's teacher, Gustav Maetze, was a powerful and positive influence on him throughout his life. The influence of a respected teacher, especially when this influence conflicts with that of the father, is one of the themes of the novel. Bolstered by his excellent primary education, Trenckmann enrolled in the first class at the newly established Texas A&M College and graduated as the school's first valedictorian in 1879. He thereafter began a career as an educator, first at the German language Hermann Academy at Frelsburg in Colorado County and later at Shelby in Austin County. He married Mathilde Miller on April 20, 1886.[9]

In 1891 he began publication of *Das Wochenblatt*, a German-language weekly newspaper in Bellville. This was part of a trend that saw an explosive proliferation of German-language newspapers in Texas and across the Midwest. He edited and published it continuously for over forty-two years, until its sale in 1933, but he continued to write for it until his death in 1935.[10] The paper soon gained a reputation as one of the more important voices of the German element in Texas in the post-Civil War period.

Throughout his long and distinguished career Trenckmann acted as a mediator, interpreter, and calm voice of understanding between the dominant Anglo culture and the substantial but minority German community. His balance gained him respect in both communities, which led to his election as a representative from Austin County in the Thirtieth Legislature in 1907. Thereafter, Trenckmann moved with his wife and four children from Bellville to Austin where he soon became an esteemed presence in the capital city's large German community and a civic leader in wider society as well. He served as a member and chairman of the board of directors of Texas A&M and was asked to become its president but did not accept. He also served as chairman of the board of directors of the Blind Institute (now the Texas School for the Blind and Visually Impaired). During this period Trenckmann also relocated his newspaper to Austin, where it grew beyond its regional scope and gained state-wide influence. The old Trenckmann building, where the paper was published, still stands on Guadalupe Street two blocks south of the university.

Trenckmann never shied away from controversy. He was sensitive to one of the most challenging dilemmas for all democracies, namely, how to reconcile the will of the majority with the rights of the minority. In keeping with this, Trenckmann vigorously opposed Sunday laws and Prohibition, both of which he considered examples of majority overreach and unnecessary infringements on personal freedoms. In several editorials written for the *Austin Statesman*, he argued eloquently and persuasively for the principle of academic freedom, the importance of free public education, and the right of new immigrants to retain their customs and language. He also took a firm stand against the Ku Klux Klan, anti-communist hysteria, and Know-Nothingism of all stripes.

Millheim, in contrast to the Hill Country *Lateiner* communities, was for many years an island of refined German culture, language, and tradition in a largely Anglo-American region dominated by the powerful slave-holding plantation owners who had settled up and down the Brazos River just to the east. Their large plantations, often with scores of slaves divided into field and domestic servants and grandiose, lavishly appointed mansions, set the tone socially, economically, and politically for the whole region. In contrast, the German farmers practically next door set up and farmed their modest farmsteads on a model using free labor reminiscent of the German system where paid farm laborers (*Knechte*), usually residing with their employers, augmented the labor of the farmer and his family.

They had left Germany, as Charles Nagel has noted, not because they disliked Germany and its traditions, but rather because they could no longer live under the all-encompassing *Obrigkeit* (authority) that oppressed and stifled them at every turn, and which they considered a betrayal of true German values.[11] They wanted to preserve the German language and German customs in their community even as they strove to be good American citizens. They saw no inconsistency in this, for the ideals they had supported in Germany were the same ideals that inspired the founding fathers and had found expression in the words of the Declaration of Independence and the U.S. Constitution.

The little community enjoyed an amazing amount of forbearance and independence in the decade prior to the outbreak of war. The Germans were left alone, for the most part, to go and do as they desired. Nor were they harassed for speaking German, as happened at a later date.[12] On the contrary, they were feted for their industriousness and the fact that they paid their bills on time. Moreover, many of them brought with them valuable skills acquired through the centuries old German apprentice system (*Zunftwesen*). German carpenters, music teachers, cabinetmakers, tailors, shoemakers, saddle and harness makers, etc., came to be highly prized in their new rural environment.

But this situation of mutual tolerance was bound to come to an end. The simple fact that most of the Germans farmed on the free labor model was cause enough for suspicion in the early stages of the conflict. The vote for secession exacerbated mutual distrust because it showed in an unmistakable and quantifiable way that the great majority of German settlers at Cat Spring and Millheim had remained loyal to the Union. Ninety-nine votes were cast against secession and only eight for at the Millheim-Cat Spring box.[13]

The situation worsened markedly, however, after the imposition and enforcement of conscript laws in April 1862.[14] Prior to this, the South had relied on volunteers or had called up militias, which at root were also voluntary. Thus, until the spring of 1862, those who were opposed to the war could simply sit out the conflict. With the imposition of the conscription laws, however, this became increasingly more difficult.

The Germans of South Central Texas reacted very negatively to the new draft laws. A flurry of alarmist reports documented in the *Official Records of the War of*

the Rebellion paint a picture of widespread disaffection bordering on insurrection in the South-Central Texas Counties of Austin, Fayette, Washington, and Colorado on the part of the German element. German settlers met secretly on several occasions in gatherings of 500 or more persons, if the reports in the Official Records are to be believed. A. J. Bell was the recruiting officer for Austin County at this time and it might be instructive to quote from his official report, not the least because Bell, under the pseudonym Captain Ringwell, plays a prominent role in the novel, where he is portrayed as corrupt, conniving, and self-serving:

> Enrolling Officer
>
> Industry, Austin County, Tex. November 28, 1862
>
> To Maj. J.P. Flewellen,
>
> Superintendent of Conscripts, Austin, Tex.:

> Sir: The above thirty-two names are all Germans, except four. They are remarkably stubborn, and I am satisfied they do not intent to submit to enrollment. I shall, therefore, need a force to bring them in, and as the militia nearly all sympathize with them, I cannot safely rely upon them and would suggest that a military force of at least one good company is placed under my orders, and to be well-supplied with provisions, or money to obtain them in the countryside, and to be mounted and well-armed.

> I deem it my duty in this connection to say that there is evidently a spirit of insubordination existing among the Germans in this region. I have it from the most reliable authority that they contemplate resistance to the conscript law as well as the contemplated draft. Sundry meetings have been held to concert measures of resistance . . . These meetings are largely attended—by 400 to 500 persons.

> J. Bell
>
> Enrolling Officer, Austin County, Texas[15]

This occurred at a time just as Major General J. Bankhead Magruder, overall commander of Texas, was attempting to expel Union forces from Galveston. Fearing a large-scale coastal invasion of Texas, Magruder had begun frantically taking steps to counter such a threat. The possibility of a home-grown insurrection, therefore, appeared doubly threatening. On January 5, 1863, Magruder signed Special Order N. 35, putting South-Central Texas under martial law and ordering various units to be dispatched to Columbus, La Grange and Bellville for the purpose of arresting the ringleaders and quelling the rebellion, which they quickly accomplished.

The behavior of his troops, however, was less than exemplary during this action. On more than one occasion, the troops roughed up wives and children of the men they were attempting to arrest, leading to further bitterness on the part of the families. On other occasions, it must be noted, the women themselves were the aggressors. In December of 1862, Bell reported that his conscript officer assigned to Industry (his brother) had been attacked by a mob of irate German mothers and wives, who drove him and his men from the town with brooms and pans, an incident that is referenced in the novel.

In truth, the Germans resolved in their gatherings to keep as low a profile as possible and try to stay neutral as best as they could. They emphasized that their reluctance to serve was grounded primarily in the concern that there was no safety net in place to help their families if the men were sent off to war. This is clearly stated in the petition delivered to Brigadier General W. G. Webb in La Grange in January 1863.[16] The petition was drafted after a large meeting held at Biegel's Store in Fayette County. It read as follows:

The measures taken by this government to protect this State against invasion are so far-reaching and serious in their consequences that they fill our minds with dread and apprehension.

The past has already taught us how regardlessly [sic.] the government and the county authorities have treated the families of those who have taken the field. We have been told that they would be cared for, and what, up to this point, has been done? They were furnished with small sums of paper money which is almost worthless and which has been refused by men for whose sake this war and its calamities were organized. . . .

Besides the duty of defending one's country, there is a higher and more sacred one—the duty of maintaining the families. What benefit is there in preserving the country while the families and inhabitants of the same, nay, even the army, are bound to perish in misery and starvation?

In view of the foregoing we take the liberty to hereby jointly declare that unless we obtain a guarantee that our families will be protected, not only against misery and starvation, but also against vexations from itinerant bands, we shall not be able to answer the call, and the consequences must be attributed to those who caused them.[17]

Instead of addressing their concerns, the military arrested the authors of the petition and all others over the three-county area who had been fingered as ringleaders. Curiously, since these meetings had all been organized and conducted before the imposition of martial law, the leaders were all turned over to civilian authorities, who promptly released them. One has to admit that here was a sense of due process at play on the part of all sides at the time that in retrospect appears quite extraordinary. Though the leaders suffered no draconian consequences for their perceived disloyalty, the imposition of martial law did have the desired effect: organized resistance to conscription collapsed in the German communities. Henceforth, the Home Guard devoted its manpower to hunting down die-hard draft evaders, intimidating their families, and preventing gatherings within the German settlements. It remained a tense situation that could easily have escalated into open conflict or a low-grade guerilla war similar to the one seen in the Hill Country settlements, but this never came to pass in South-Central Texas.

One episode in the novel in particular deals with the difficulties that the Germans faced under martial law. The Home Guard has been trying to catch a

German draft dodger, Herwisch, who has successfully hidden out in the brush for two years. He is captured, however, when he comes out of hiding for the funeral of his young daughter, who had succumbed to a virulent and lethal form of measles. The community is incensed by the circumstances of the arrest and several young hotheads, including solders on leave, conspire in a secret meeting to ambush the Home Guards and free Herwisch from his captors. Only with difficulty is Herr Lüttenhoff able to dissuade them from this course of action, which could have had disastrous consequences for the whole community. Trenckmann's own life story reflected this attitude of prudence and balance.

In light of the historical facts—the vote against secession, the clandestine meetings, the resistance to the Home Guard, the imposition of martial law, etc.—it is somewhat surprising to find in the novel the story of a community that is actually conflicted on the question of slavery and succession. There are those who are passionate in their belief that slavery is a great evil and a stain on the country. Herr Lüttenhoff, Kuno's private teacher and the father of Hedwig, embodies this point of view as well as the ex-university professor Winzig. Kuno's father, on the other hand, as well as the ex-cavalry officer Grossenberg, are both more practical in their attitude concerning slavery and more sympathetic to the Southern cause. Both see slavery as an evil necessary for the work of state development, and both feel that it will eventually wither away with time

"Texas German family leaving for Mexico" (print property of James C. Kearney)

once circumstances change. In line with this practical accommodation, Herr Sartorius, Kuno's father, has even acquired a slave as a cook for his wife and two other slaves to work on the farm; the only one in the community to own slaves.

The novel clearly underscores that the length of time these men have been in Texas has conditioned their beliefs: the longer they have been in Texas the more sympathetic their stance toward slavery and the Southern cause tends to be. The novel thus offers conflict along three axes: between father and son; between a father and his son's teacher; and between the old guard and the new.

A kind of uneasy truce exists among the principal characters in the novel. This is symbolized by the weekly Sunday afternoon card game of whist among the four above-mentioned men, who manage—sometimes with difficulty— to put aside their political and philosophical differences in order to enjoy an afternoon of refined fellowship over a game of whist. And similar to the card game, whenever a crisis arises, or an individual finds himself in trouble with the authorities, the community quickly pulls together to help their own. This is one of the chief purposes of the novel: to showcase a community spirit based on a deep consciousness of shared German heritage that, in the end, overrides all differences and holds the community together during difficult periods.

Here it is well to mention that a large literature has arisen concerning the attitude of the German settlers toward slavery and secession in Texas during the Civil War, especially in regard to the more spectacular incidents, such as the Battle of the Nueces, which took place between a group of sixty-four (largely) disaffected German Unionists from the Hill Country settlements seeking to make their way to Mexico and a larger contingent of Confederate forces, who overtook and ambushed them in a remote stretch of the Nueces in August 1862.[18] For the purposes of this introduction, let it be noted that scholars still disagree as to the true nature of German dissent, which has remained elusive. I argue that it has remained elusive precisely because German attitudes to slavery were more complicated and conflicted than normally portrayed. In other words, Trenckmann's novel more accurately portrays the conflicts of opinion regarding slavery within the German community than the picture of unanimity that previous historians have presented.

Exactly how to classify *Die Lateiner am Possum Creek; a Texas Story* as a work of literature remains problematic. Clearly, at the time it was written, 1908, it would have been considered first and foremost a historical romance since it contains a love story set in the waning months of the Civil War and continuing through the period of Reconstruction. The novel, however, is also clearly a *roman à clef,* which is the technical term used by literary historians to describe a novel, "about real life, overlaid with a façade of fiction [where] the fictitious names in the novel represent real people, and the 'key' is the relationship between the nonfiction and the fiction."[19] Though Trenckmann has shuffled the deck, so to speak, all of the principal fictional characters are composites who share features that can be unambiguously associated with real people. Likewise, nearly all the situations in the book relate to circumstances either experienced first-hand by the author or known to him through his family. These associations and similarities will be pointed out in footnotes, thus supplying the reader the key to the relationship between the fictional and the non-fictional elements in the story. Additionally, an appendix has been supplied as a handy reference outlining the principal real-life families of Millheim, where their homesteads were located, and how they relate to the fictional characters of *The Lateiner.*

To further complicate matters, the novel is also consciously patterned after the German *Bildungsroman,*[20] or "education novel," in which the youthful main character—in this case Kuno Sartorius—struggles to follow the right path and finally, after a number of false starts or wrong choices, develops into a mature and well-rounded *Mensch.* Despite all the fascinating digressions, the novel always returns to the central focus: a young man coming of age during the war who is forced to choose between his private teacher, Herr Lüttenhoff, who remains true to the Forty-Eighter ideals that had inspired him in Germany, and his own father, who evinces a much more practical attitude that has led him to a more sympathetic and tolerant attitude in respect to slavery and the Southern cause.

At this point it might also be mentioned that Kuno's adventures bring him into contact with an amazing collection of characters and panoply of vivid settings characteristic of the Texas Home Front, the Western Theater (Louisiana,

Arkansas, and East Texas), and Reconstruction. Trenckmann provides marvelous descriptions of the towns and communities, of the flora and fauna, of the roads, and, especially, of representative types from all walks and classes who inhabited the period, from rich plantation owners to dirt-poor squatters, from upright Jewish merchants to crooked speculators and schemers, from generals to common soldiers, and everything in between. The novel thus transports the reader back to another time and place in a way that only first-hand knowledge can do.

As the novel progress, it also becomes increasingly clear that the author has intended Kuno's journey as a kind of parable or roadmap: his personal dilemmas and hard choices dramatize the dilemmas and hard choices of the wider German immigrant community even as they suggest a path forward. This is especially true for that portion of the community from educated backgrounds, i.e., the *Lateiner.* These immigrants seek to preserve their cherished German traditions, culture, and language while fully engaging with the culture of their adopted homeland and becoming responsible citizens. Finding the correct balance, the story of Kuno seems to suggest, is a constant challenge that requires flexibility and, yes, modification of the original Forty-Eighter ideals that had so inspired his father's generation. Once again, the opening scene of the whist game clearly sets the stage for this thematic contour to the story. Trenckmann's own life story—a mixture of progressive idealism and practical realism, yet always evincing a calm voice for mutual understanding—seems entirely consistent with the character of Kuno Sartorius. Indeed, Kuno's story could be said to describe his attempt to find a kind of Hegelian synthesis between the two extremes represented by his father and his teacher. This is actually not so abstruse and far-fetched as it sounds: all educated Germans of the period would have been familiar with the Hegelian dialectic of thesis, antitheses, and synthesis, which was very much a current topic with not only philosophical but also social and political applications.

Toward the end of the second part of the novel another aspect unfolds to compliment the synthesis theme. Even as the great national drama of the American Civil War comes to an end and recedes into the past, new wars in

Europe, especially the series of wars fought by the Kingdom of Prussia against first Denmark, then Austria, and finally France—wars which paved the way for German unification under Prussian leadership in 1871—continue to rivet the attention of the immigrant German communities in North America.

These wars posed a particular dilemma for the *Lateiner* of Possum Creek: on the one hand, most could not help but feel pride in the astounding military successes of the Prussian armies in these conflicts; on the other hand, glorification of Prussia represented renunciation of the republican and equalitarian ideals that had motivated many of them to emigrate in the first place, for Prussia was an arch-conservative, aristocratic state that stood in complete opposition on all fronts to the democratic and republican ideals of 1848. The German farmers of Millheim and elsewhere across the state avidly followed the developments in Europe through the numerous German language newspapers that had proliferated throughout North America and Texas in the latter decades of the nineteenth century and now found their way into even the remotest households.

Trenckmann weaves German unification under Prussian hegemony into his story to produce a surprising *denouement* of all the threads of the narrative in the final chapter of Book Two. Kuno's military experience, it will be seen, makes him even more appreciative of the accomplishments achieved by his German countrymen on numerous fields of battle in Europe, but once again he finds himself torn between conflicting attitudes, especially as they relate to the freedpeople and Reconstruction, and it all comes to a head (and is resolved) in the final wedding scene when Hedwig and Kuno are linked in marriage and the assembled guests all join in a rousing version of "Deutschland, Deutschland über Alles" to celebrate Prussian victory over France in 1871.

In light of the foregoing discussion of the literary and thematic elements in the story, the title Trenckmann choose for his novel, *Die Lateiner on Possum Creek; a Texas Story,* and the fact that the title contains both German and English phrasing, begin to make sense. Kuno's journey of discovery and adaptation in a difficult period of Texas history stands for the journey of all *Lateiner* in Texas; and, by extension, for the struggle of every immigrant group and ethnicity as each is forced to find its own unique solution to the universal challenge that they all faced: how to remain true to the old while embracing the new.

A final note to the reader: the little community of Millheim (together with the sister community of Cat Spring) has produced more literature in nearly all genres—from novels to agricultural studies, from memoirs to plays—than perhaps any other community of comparable size in Texas. A full taste of this novel, not just as a rote narrative, but as an amazing window into another time and place, will be enhanced immensely by reference to some or all of this literature. A full bibliography has been provided of these works, but four stand out as indispensable, namely, *A Boy's Civil War Story*, by Charles Nagel; "The German Settlers of Millheim (Texas) before the Civil War," by Adalbert Regenbrecht; *Reminiscences of William A. Trenckmann, 1859-1935*, edited by Walter L. Buenger and Walter D. Kamphoefner; and *The Engelking Letters*, translated and edited from the German by Flora von Roeder.

James C. Kearney

EPISODES

Translator's Note

The story begins during the fall of 1864. The Civil War is entering its final stage and all but the most die-hard Southerners, of which many still remain, can see the writing on the wall: it is only a matter of time until the South collapses in total defeat, an utter catastrophe. Meanwhile, on the home front, life goes on and the common people are dealing with the multitude of hardships imposed by the war as best they can. With most of the adult men away at war (or hiding out in the brush from the "heel flies," as the home front conscription officers are pejoratively termed), small farmsteads that depend on free labor find everyday life especially trying since the plowing of the fields and the harvesting of the crops falls either to the women and children or to the generosity of neighbors. Even the most basic staples such as coffee, flour, and sugar are scarce or non-existent and families are forced to make do with whatever is at hand in creative ways.

*An astonishing percentage of university-trained men (**Lateiner**) settled at Millheim (Possum Creek[21] in the novel) in the 1840s and 1850s; men who in their previous lives in Germany had pursued professional careers: lawyers, educators, government bureaucrats, and the like who now lead the simple life of small farmers in Texas. Inspired by the democratic and republican ideals that swept Europe in the first half of the century and culminated in the failed 1848 revolutions in Germany, these families strive to maintain and uphold some vestige of the rich intellectual and cultural existence* *they once knew in Germany but voluntarily abandoned in exchange for the freedoms (and privations) they found on the Texas prairie.*

Most of the thirty or so German families that make up the community of Possum Creek in Austin County do not own slaves and not a few heads-of-household are openly strident in their opposition to slavery, an opposition threatening to bring down the wrath of the slave-holding class upon all. These men have transferred the idealism that once inspired them in Germany—and which was dashed by the collapse of the 1848 revolutions—to the new situation they have encountered in Texas: on the one hand, they cherish the freedoms they have found here, while on the other they regard slavery as a true stain on American democracy. They are embittered by the fanatical devotion to the institution of slavery on the part of many Southerners, which they regard as incomprehensible and unforgivable, and which has issued into a disastrous war they now all suffer from. In the story, Herr Lüttenhoff clearly embodies this attitude of disaffection.

Nevertheless, as becomes clear in the story, the community actually harbors a surprising diversity of opinion regarding slavery, secession, and the war. Other **Lateiner** *show themselves more tolerant of African American slavery and evince a more sympathetic stance on the War and the South's rationale for starting it. Herr Sartorius represents this point of view in the novel. He even owns four slaves himself, a fact that has ingratiated him among the Anglo slave-holding elite whose large plantations fill the vast river bottom of the Brazos River and its main tributaries only a few miles distant.*

And then there is the divide between parents and children. The children of these **Achtundvierziger** *(forty-eighters)—a term often used to describe this wave of idealistic German immigrants—are now coming of age, and many were either very small when their parents emigrated or are native born and have thus been shaped by their own Texas experiences more so than by the revolutionary ideals of their parents, which now appear to them distant in time and remote in place. But despite all these tensions and internal divisions, the* **Lateiner** *of Possum Creek consciously cultivate a vibrant community life based on their shared German heritage that transcends their differences, as difficult and awkward as this becomes at times. When the chips are down, however, the community always rallies to help their own.*

In the course of the story we see clearly how the war accelerates the process of acculturation and assimilation, which is seen to be both creative and destructive, both desirable and regrettable, as young men of military age are uprooted prematurely in large numbers from their rather isolated and self-contained communities and assigned, as the need dictates, to various Confederate military units and forced into the harrowing experience of war.

There is a linguistic contour to this process as well, for as the German settlers of Texas adapt to their new environment, for the German language, like its speakers, is compelled to change and adapt, which hastened its improbable transformation into a new dialect of German, a fascinating development in its own right that will be addressed in a later note. The novel, which takes place at the front end of this process, offers an important window into this transformation.

It is in this complex and self-contained world of the educated and free-thinking **Lateiner** *that Trenckmann's story unfolds; a world that he himself grew up into as a young man during the Civil War and Reconstruction years and which now he now attempts to celebrate in all its fullness. It is an extraordinary community, contrasting markedly even from most other German communities in the state: its members are educated and cultured, yet down-to-earth; of modest means, yet generous to a fault, individualistic, yet community-spirited; freethinking, but principled; principled, yet realistic; consciously German, but proudly American, because to be a good German, as Charles Nagel has put it, was to be a good American.*

The novel is also a classic coming-of-age tale, and our young hero, Kuno Sartorius, turning eighteen and facing conscription, is forced to choose between the idealism of his teacher, Herr Lüttenhoff, and the more practical and sympathetic stance of his father, Herr Sartorius. It is also a budding love story of two young playmates, Hedwig Lüttenhoff and Kuno Sartorius, as they emerge from adolescence to experience the awkwardness and wonder of first love.

NEIGHBORHOOD CHILDREN

It was a Sunday afternoon in the late fall of 1864. Above the forest that stretched to the north and east a pall of gray-blue smoke rose almost halfway up into the sky, concealing completely the *cross-timbers*,[22] that long, narrow strip of oak trees that otherwise marked the boundary of the broad prairie that stretched to the south and west toward the gulf. No rain had fallen since early July and the tall grass of the prairie was already as dry as if it were January. At a meeting of the German farmers of Possum Creek the previous Sunday, the word was passed around that at first sign of fire to the south, all the men should gather with their teams in order to plow a fire lane to hold the blaze in check, but their number was greatly reduced since most heads-of-household, whether by choice or compulsion, were away at war. Four years previously, a similar fire had burnt several wooden fences in the area and destroyed numerous haystacks and other things of value to the farmers. The day was oppressively humid and the smoke-reddened sun, which had already passed the noon meridian an hour ago, burned almost as hot as if it were August. At sundown, a narrow, black line of clouds appeared across the horizon to the north while the animals of the prairie moved in long lines toward the southeast in the direction of the canebrakes where they were accustomed to finding shelter from the cold as well as ample nourishment during the winter months. The night before, countless formations of cranes and geese passed high overhead heading south. With their incessant chattering and monotonous honking, they announced that the change in weather everyone was hoping for was close at hand. Ol' Achilles, the *factotum*[23] slave of Mr. Phillips, who owned a large plantation a few miles to the southeast in the Palmetto Creek bottom,[24] announced in the morning to everyone who cared to listen that the first genuine *norther*[25] would arrive before evening.

A deep stillness lay over the small German settlement of Possum Creek. This less than impressive name stubbornly persisted once it caught on; this despite the fact that seven years before, at a celebration for the opening of a bowling alley[26] in Bertrand's Store, the owner of the store had proposed naming the town

Charlottenhöhe, or "Charlotte Heights," in honor of his wife, and his proposal had been heartily agreed to over ample supplies of German beer from Bremen, no less.[27]

Meanwhile, at the farmstead of Herr Lüttenhoff, two children emerge from a large corncrib constructed of rough logs. Since these two play no small role in the story we are telling, we want to have a closer look at them. Hedwig, at fourteen years of age, is well developed for her age and an enormous bonnet shields her rich brown braids, her cheerful blue eyes, and her nicely tanned cheeks. As she skips along she hums a song to herself. Her eight-year-old brother Albert approaches with a slower and more deliberate gait. He has long legs for his age, possesses flaxen hair, is freckle-faced and bare-footed; his long face makes him appear more mature than his years and contrasts markedly with the countenance of his sister, which radiates a more carefree and cheerful attitude. Both have on their Sunday clothes, but Hedwig also has on a long, striped apron that is tied in the front and made from a discarded Gingham dress

"Scenes from rural life." Friedrich Richard Petri papers, [11949], The Dolph Briscoe Center for American History, The University of Texas at Austin.

of her mother. She is carrying a clutch of eggs in her apron that she and her brother had gathered from nests scattered around in the hayloft and horse stall. As she approached the backside of the family house, which was ringed by moss-laden live oaks, four of which were magnificent examples of their species, she broke off with her song and turned to her brother.

"It helped that we trapped the skunk[28] yesterday. Otherwise, he would have stolen all the eggs. The hens are laying a lot now; too bad no peddler is coming around to buy them."

This remark jarred Albert from his thoughts and he replied very perceptively:

"No matter, with the extra eggs mother can just bake that much more."

In response to Hedwig's objection, however, that there was no sugar in the house, he replied:

"Cakes made out of molasses or honey don't taste so bad either."

"You are right, Albert, especially if none of the others are around! But look at you! Covered from top to bottom with hay. I need to brush you off in case you meet up with the cows." And with this Hedwig began dusting off Albert straight away, who protested energetically:

"Don't whop me so hard, Hede. The cows won't bother me because 'the goat only bothers him who makes himself green,'[29] and hay is not green grass."

"Well, little philosopher, I see you have picked up another cute saying. But come along and help me water the straw flowers. It will help pass the long Sunday afternoon, and the flowers are in need of it."

"I can't do it now. They are playing whist[30] this afternoon and I have to keep the *Fidibus*[31] bowl filled."

"Well then, be off with you! Take the eggs along to the storage pantry but don't break them over your head like you did last time when you put your cap on without noticing the eggs inside. I will read you an Anderson fairy tale later."

Albert disappeared into the rear room of a long, narrow log structure that contained a kitchen, dining room, and storeroom.[32] The entire structure was joined to the main house by a covered walkway. Hedwig began to carefully ladle water out of the big barrel that hung from a rope for that purpose and soak the straw flowers as well as a pair of rose plants at the far end of the large

"Snake in the hen house." (Friedrich Richard Petri papers, [11949], The Dolph Briscoe Center for American History, The University of Texas at Austin.)

garden, which, despite the long drought, was in excellent shape due to the careful attention it had received. Dug wells were still a rarity in Texas and in dry periods it was necessary for the Lüttenhoff family to haul drinking water from a spring a mile away along Possum Creek. As she was doing this, she carried on a little conversation with herself. She gave vent to her displeasure that her good friend Kuno, son of the neighboring Sartorius family, had decided to spend the afternoon riding and hunting instead of keeping company with her. She had some important matters to discuss with him. A long, drawn out blast from a hunting horn, however, occasioned the following remark:

"That sounds like Kuno's horn. I bet he was not able to catch his pony and nothing has come of the hunt. And if that's the case, I'm going to have a good laugh at his expense." Leaning over the palisade-like garden fence, which was constructed out of thinly split *pickets* stuck firmly into the ground, she soon spied Kuno, who was leisurely striding up the sandy path in her direction, keeping close to the fence bordering the road all the while.

"Just wait, you sly Nimrod,"[33] she muttered to herself, "I'll give you a good scare." And with this she plucked some butter bean vines that still had dried hulls on them and then hid behind the fence where she awaited his approach. He was a tall, elongated lad in his eighteenth year, and on whose face a fuzz beard had recently emerged. He was clad in a coarse hunting suit without a jacket. He sported a powder horn, game bag, and hunting horn slung about his shoulders, wore a coonskin cap on his head to cover his dark locks, carried a shotgun on his shoulder, and in his other hand clutched a bridle for his mare Polly that he had the habit of catching and riding without a saddle. Hedwig's little surprise succeeded wonderfully: she tossed the vines with rattle beans over the fence, which landed neatly on Kuno's head. Startled, he ducked instinctively to the side, but quickly regained his wits and exclaimed, "I'll be thunderstruck if that isn't that little trickster Hedwig." He then quickly reached over the fence and grabbed Hedwig by her long locks and bonnet. As she strove to get loose, the somewhat precarious fence gave way under the onslaught. Kuno however maintained his grip and exclaimed:

"Just wait. You are going to get your comeuppance now, first from me and later a scolding from your father."

"Let loose you brute!" she exclaimed. "I thought that it was Bobby Phillips, but he is much too gallant to grab girls by the hair. I thought you were out hunting geese."

"That was my intention, and I have already bagged one, a big one, and I intend to pluck it. Ol' Achilles told me that up there at Elm Point the whole prairie is covered with geese, and he even saw a crane. I intended to get my Polly from the prairie and ride up there. I found her but she wouldn't let me catch her. Three times I approached with an ear of corn but each time at the last moment she turned tail and bolted. The last time she knocked the hat off my head and that made me so mad I fired a shot over her head in anger."

"I bet that made her stop!"

"Hardly, she took off and kept running until I couldn't see her anymore."

"Serves you right. *Festina lente*[34] your father would say while having a good laugh at your expense. Just wait a bit, he will be coming along shortly to play whist."

"Ah, you and your dumb Latin. Don't get a big head because you can recite your irregular verbs better than me. I'm ahead of you in math and geometry.

Your father is of the opinion that these subjects are much more important in America than the proper conjugation of *loquor*."[35]

"Well, so much for neglecting Latin; it doesn't seem to have made you a better shot; look at all the geese you have missed! But tell me, Kuno, aren't you supposed to be inducted into the army shortly, within a fortnight, and I wanted . . ."

"Not me; I'm heading for the brush; no intention of serving in the Confederate Army."

In the meantime, he had let loose of Hedwig's hair and both had worked to prop up the fence they had knocked down. Hedwig put her bonnet straight again and, to all appearances, her feisty spirit had mellowed somewhat. After a bit she resumed her speech:

"But to spend all your time in the brush, hunting and knocking about like Herwitsch and Müller; you find that preferable to going off to war like your brothers."

"Look Hede, you are clueless, so hold your tongue," he replied somewhat harshly. "What do you know about these matters that concern only men? And just so that you understand, I have given your father my word and hand of my own free will that I will not fight for slavery."

"Father has the best of intentions, but he is an old man and has different reasons than you for hating the Confederacy. The fact is you grew up here and I believe every upstanding young man has the duty to fight for his country when called upon. When I see the poor soldiers returning from the battlefields, ragged and malnourished, often crippled; when I see how they still perk up when they hear 'Dixie' playing, how proud they are of their generals, then I can't believe it is such a terrible cause for which they are fighting and suffering. And even if the South is compelled eventually to bow down, I can't get it in my head that you or anybody else have the right to hide out when others are going off to war and shedding blood for their country."

This little speech served only to fuel Kuno's growing annoyance and the color deepened in his brown face. But with a promise to himself to repay these unwelcome opinions in good measure at a later date, he changed the subject abruptly and continued:

"Have you heard the news already? Wolves killed and ate three calves at the Erkenbrechers right next to the pens last night?"

"What? Not a word. The poor calves."

"I hope they don't get one of yours. That cow you love so much, Toni, the one with the small calf with a white star in its face, I spotted her outside close to Live Oak pond, and there are lots of wolves around there."

"And you're just telling me that now, and you call yourself a brave hunter and bush warrior." And with that she ran into the house thinking to do something for her favorite cow and calf. Kuno, however, chuckled to himself while exclaiming, "Well, she will be right annoyed after she saddles up her horse and finds her Toni in short order munching on one of our hay stacks." With this thought he climbed over the fence and cut across the field for he hoped to avoid his father whom he feared would belittle him for the meager results of his outing.

THE DISTURBED WHIST GAME

Given the circumstances of the times, the Lüttenhoff house counted as a very respectable residence. It contained four rooms, two on each side of the breezeway.[36] The cracks between the logs had long since been filled with clay and straw and whitewashed with lime. The house was unusually tall for a log structure and offered a large attic space under the peak of the shingle roof.

In the front room on the left-hand side a large, powerfully built man with a dark head of hair and a full beard sat on a cowhide chair at a desk that had been cobbled together somewhat crudely by a native Texas cabinetmaker. Otherwise, the room was graced by several refined walnut furniture pieces from Europe. Also, two bookshelves had been built into the walls and filled with books to the ceiling. He had just set aside an American language newspaper, the *Weekly Telegraph*,[37] which was issued in the smallest possible format and printed on inferior gray paper. The deep furrows of consternation on his brow testified to the worries that this life had brought with it. In a low voice, he muttered to himself:

"The Battle of the Nueces, August 10, 1862." Author's collection.

"Thank God, Erwin's name is not on the list of those killed and wounded. That is one consolation at least. Even though he swore allegiance to the Confederacy against the express wishes of his father and has now risen in the ranks to become an officer, at least he is still alive. Unfortunately, the names of the enlisted personnel, the poor devils, don't even make it to the newspapers, or, if they do, they are often so bungled they are barely decipherable. But thousands have fallen at Cedar Creek[38] and Erwin must have been present at the battle for his colonel is included among the list of the fallen. One last valiant effort to break through the ever-tightening iron ring of encirclement around Richmond has collapsed; Early's army is exhausted and half destroyed.[39] Meanwhile, Sherman's powerful army pushes ever deeper into hapless Georgia, the grain basket of the South, marauding and laying waste as they move along. Every intelligent person must recognize that the last hope for Confederate victory has vanished, for the South is now split into three parts. But still they continue to fight, sacrificing needlessly ever more *hecatombs*[40] and foolishly devastating the land just because, in their stubborn blindness, the slave barons refuse to concede the inevitable.

"And now even Kuno has been summoned to join the army, perhaps to sacrifice his young life needlessly to this accursed cause. How I struggled the whole night with myself about this matter. How fervently Kuno reacted when he discovered the Union flag that I keep hidden in my desk. Was it the right thing to do then to use this opportunity to extract an oath from him to not fight against the Union?"

His monologue was soon interrupted by the sound of a deep bass voice that from the distance could be heard singing the last stanzas of "Zwei Grenadier zogen nach Frankreich."[41] Looking outside, he continued:

"There comes Sartorius.[42] He can still sing at least, but of all things, a song in praise of two ex-patriot soldiers of that Corsican butcher Napoleon. He is my closest neighbor, but I can scarcely comprehend how, as a German, he can sing a song of admiration for Napoleon or speak words favorable to the Secessionists for that matter." Nevertheless, Lüttenhoff stepped out onto the gallery in order to receive and greet his guest warmly.

Both men were almost the same stature, easily six feet tall. Both were also broad-shouldered, fit and trim, and of approximately the same age; in the latter half of their fifties. But the similarities ended there. Sartorius's dark black hair clung like a thin wreath around his pate, which was marked by the broad and impressive forehead of an intellectual. His brown eyes, which could alternatingly penetrate to the core or light up in satirical glee, contrasted with the blue-gray eyes and prominent eyelashes of Lüttenhoff. Likewise, his eagle beak nose and small, well-manicured hands stood in contrast to Lüttenhoff's very straight and regular nose and his large, heavily calloused hands.

They dressed differently too. Sartorius sported fine linen pants and a blue striped shirt, over which, oddly, he had put on an expensive, but well-worn Turkish night robe. Lüttenhoff, on the other hand, wore a snappy German Sunday coat, typical for the German bourgeoisie of the 1850s. Both wore the same sort of shoes that were standard for the period, coarse but sturdy, and made from kid leather. The difference, however, lay in the fact that Lüttenhoff's large feet occupied well-oiled and tended footwear, whereas the shoes for Sartorius's smaller feet actually creaked as he walked since they suffered from lack of both oil and shoeshine. Sartorius's carefully shaven face revealed nicely his aristocratic features; Lüttenhoff's deeply tanned countenance, in contrast, presented a true likeness of the resilient German peasant.

The course of their lives had differed as markedly as their outward appearances. Sartorius came from a prominent family who owned a large country estate and whose members typically had served as bureaucrats in the Prussian Rhineland. In accordance with family tradition, and without any kind of special encouragement, he had decided to study law, but apparently had devoted his energies more to the appreciation of domestic and French wines than to mastering the intricacies of Roman jurisprudence[43] and the Prussian legal tradition. A prominent scar on his forehead and a gash on his chin testified to certain difficulties in the past that he had obviously survived.

He had completed his stint as a *Referendar*[44] and even obtained a position as an *Assessor*[45] in the Prussian civil service. He had also taken the hand of the daughter of an impoverished German nobleman of ancient lineage in marriage. But in the end, he found the legal profession much too dry and uninteresting for his taste and, infatuated by the literature,[46] had decided to emigrate to Texas. Possessed of quite ample means, he had settled at Possum Creek where he purchased a farm and a large pasturage for the numerous livestock he had acquired. He also purchased four slaves, but recognizing they were dealing with a true *greenhorn*, the former owners had taken him to the cleaners in all these dealings. When he related the story, he often laughed about the matter himself.

Nor had he enjoyed a lot of success as a farmer and livestock breeder. He did not understand how to manage the slaves through a regimen of strict supervision and preferred instead to spend his time in his study reading newspapers and books, or receiving guests and paying visits, or in bowling, singing, and engaging in learned discussions. His wife, likewise, was more suited for the fashionable salon than the daily drudgery of the farm. The result of this double inattention was that the slaves were often left to their own devices as to when and where to spend their time and energy with the natural result that they often decided to do nothing.

Sartorius had gleaned his agricultural knowledge for the most part from the Latin and Greek classics, which he enjoyed perusing, and also from the *Brockhaus* encyclopedia.[47] His inclination to undertake grandiose and costly experiments would have long since led him and his family into financial ruin had not a string of serendipitous cash infusions arrived from Germany, the result of several inheritances. But his missteps had never seemed to dampen his good spirits and offered instead endless material for the peculiar brand of ironic and self-deprecating humor that he cultivated.

Lüttenhoff, on the other hand, was the son of a small and impoverished farmer from the Mark Brandenburg.[48] He had put himself through his studies only by means of severe self-discipline, paying his way largely by tutoring to other students on the side. He had earned high marks and later taken a position as an assistant teacher at a city school in a mid-sized German city where he had found in the daughter of a rather well-to-do baker his true love and life's partner.

Since his pronounced democratic and freethinking tendencies had found little sympathy among the provincial school administrators, he decided to open his own school, which quickly flourished due to his industriousness and his considerable talents as a teacher. Gaining the trust of his fellow citizens, he rose by degrees to a certain prominence in the city and, by means of a well-ordered and frugal lifestyle, attained a modest level of prosperity.

His actions in 1848 earned him initially a gold star in the eyes of the local power elite. As the captain of the home guard, he had intervened in a timely and decisive way to maintain order and suppress any excesses on the part of demonstrators in the city. He regarded the repressive reaction that later set in, however, as an unpardonable breach of confidence, and joined the ranks of those who refused to pay their taxes in protest.[49] In consequence, as the reaction deepened, he soon found it prudent to dispose of his assets in a most precipitous fashion, which led to significant losses, and hastily emigrate with his family to Texas.

But once arrived, he threw himself into his new life with great energy and enthusiasm. His petite but loyal and energetic wife adapted soon enough to the new circumstances in Texas and was a great help in all matters. Lüttenhoff did not shy away from the hard labor of the farm and found in his growing sons welcome assistance with the everyday chores and drudgery of farm life. As the son of a farmer himself, he also was better suited temperamentally for rural life than most of his fellow *Lateiner* farmers.

For all these reasons, he would have enjoyed considerably more success than actually came to him were it not for the fact that he held a little too stubbornly to the practices advocated in German and English agriculture publications, practices which were often ill-suited to the altered climate and dissimilar soils of Texas. Still, he found much satisfaction in this new life close to the land, though he felt duty-bound to serve double duty as a surrogate teacher to his own and other children of the neighborhood since no suitable German teacher could be found for the small community.[50] But within this ambience, characterized by pleasant and stimulating interaction with neighbors, a daily regimen of demanding but healthy physical work, and a deeply sustaining family life, the Lüttenhoff family passed nine happy years.

Then, however, the gathering agitation in favor of secession and the subsequent war injected much discord and unhappiness into this idyllic setting. Lüttenhoff was an uncompromising opponent of slavery and, similar to the majority of his fellow German emigrants in Texas, a loyal supporter of the Union. Since he was not one to keep his opinions to himself, he often found himself in disagreement with several of his German neighbors who owned slaves. He also incurred the unyielding hatred of ardent secessionists and had even found himself in peril of his life on occasion.

His oldest son Erwin, however, had come into frequent contact with the sons of Anglo-American neighbors during his duties as overseer of the family's livestock, and had come to hold completely different views. Father and son ceased being able to communicate and, in the end, Erwin volunteered to join the Southern army. This action appeared to the father, who was accustomed to complete and unquestioning obedience on the part of his children, as an unacceptable affront to him personally as well as an act of treason against the Union. His chagrin was so deep that he refused even to offer his son a word of farewell and considered him, by virtue of his defiance, banished from the family forever.

His second son Hugo, on the other hand, shared his views concerning slavery and secession completely and, although he bore an uncanny resemblance to his mother in his face, had in truth inherited the stubbornness of his father.

While on a trip to the Hill Country counties to buy sheep, he fell in with that unfortunate band of young German firebrands who had armed themselves and mounted an expedition to flee the state and join up with Union forces on the other side of the Rio Grande. As with all the other members, with the exception of one miserable traitor, his bones were soon left to bleach in a rugged and remote valley of the Nueces River.[51]

The parents had waited in vain for the return of their son and it took a long time before they received any definite knowledge of the affair. The father, so strongly partial to the Union cause, had himself rejected any thought of active resistance against the newly installed authorities. Instead, he had advised prudence, urging his fellow countrymen to yield to the reality of secession and to bear arms against the Union only as a last resort, and then only when compelled by threat of force. Still, he could not find it in his heart to be angry against his son for acting contrary to his advice. His deep sorrow was softened by an unmistakable pride that his son had sacrificed his young life willingly for his

"'Gaudemus Igitur,' German student drinking song." Author's collection.

convictions. The disobedience of his older son, it seems, had actually affected him more deeply than the death of Hugo.

For her part, his wife found consolation in her work, in the abiding love of her remaining children, and in the unshakeable conviction that her eldest son would return one day to be reconciled with his father and be welcomed back into the family fold. For the time being, however, Erwin's name was only rarely spoken for the wife understood how intensely her father had suffered from her son's stubborn defiance. She also realized that the act of trying to give expression to his feelings only deepened his anguish; she could only wait and hope.

Despite the great differences in background, Sartorius and Lüttenhoff had quickly become fast friends, and as such they were wise enough to avoid divisive questions of a political nature. Sartorius had settled in Texas much earlier and, as a result, had come around by and by to the point of view that slavery was a necessary evil for the South. Along with a small handful of other Germans from Possum Creek,[52] he had actually supported the growing sentiment for secession early on even though he was the first to admit that the South had slim prospects for success if it came to a fight since the North was so far superior in terms of manpower and resources.

After both had taken seats in the comfortable chamber that served also as Lüttenhoff's study, Sartorius remarked to his host:

"After an entire morning spent perusing old books, nothing is better than a good walk and a good walk always calls for a good song."

"I heard. Your favorite song."

"Please pardon me. That you, as a good German patriot, can stomach this song about as well as 'Dixie' or 'Bonnie Blue Flag'—I didn't think about that, so I ask your forgiveness. But my pipe went out while singing and I see that our little philosopher has brought around supplies for a refill." In short order the two men had tamped their long German pipes full of fresh tobacco from Lüttenhoff's canister, made available for that purpose, and securely lit them by means of steel, stone, and sponge.[53]

"Lüttenhoff, I'm afraid you have put a nasty bee in my Kuno's bonnet."

"In what way?"

"The boy fusses about Jefferson Davis as much as I used to rant and rave about Prince Metternich[54] when I was a student. What will happen when he reports for duty at Camp Magruder[55] in a couple of weeks?"

"Kuno is also my student, whom I love as if he were my own son, and he has responded better than any of the other students when I emphasize the importance of valuing human rights and freedom above all else. And since he loves freedom, how can he fight for slavery?"

"Those are your views and previously I would have expressed myself similarly. Indeed, I have all the respect for one who stands at the threshold of his sixties and still remains true to the ideals of his youth. But Kuno is my son and I have cherished the hope that one day he will play a more influential role in his new country than his elders, who will never be able to fully adjust and fit in. Did it not occur to you that by encouraging him to follow the example of Brutus and Andreas Hofer[56] you also might be bringing my fuzz-bearded hotspur into conflict with his own parents, who seek to be true to their beliefs as well, a situation that you know full well from first-hand experience and have suffered from yourself?"

"You may well be right in this, but you knew where I stood beforehand and must have anticipated that I could neither suppress nor hide my own convictions when in the company of your son."

"Yes, I concede I should have known. But when you took it upon yourself to school my youngest along with your own children, an arrangement that relieved me at once of all my worries concerning his education, my great joy blinded me to such a consequence. And if I failed to educate Kuno properly in these matters myself, then I have only my own laziness to thank, and additionally my own temperament, which renders me incapable of giving lessons to such an impulsive youngster; one who prefers to bum around with a hunting rifle and ask all kinds of awkward questions when one speaks with him. I am afraid it is too late now; the die has been cast and the youngster has come to regard you as the only authority he respects. I decided a while ago to let my children go their own way so that they could become proper Americans, and I stuck by this decision even though the results have not always been satisfactory; so, there is not a lot I can do to alter the present situation. But wait, I hear steps on the gallery; that has to be Grossenberg and Winzig, the two opposites.[57] We do not need to take up this subject again otherwise our game of whist will quickly turn as sour as vinegar.

The host opened the door for the two guests whom he had been expecting. The characterization "opposites" suited them perfectly, for one seldom encounters such a startling contrast as presented here by these two when seen standing side by side. Since both were not only necessary for the whist party, but also dyed-in-the-wool *Lateiner*, we need to have a closer look at them. Grossenberg was just slightly over five feet tall, stocky, with a somewhat puffy and rosy countenance. His incessantly blinking brown eyes had a humorous aspect to them while his ample belly and swollen, ruddy nose indicated that he was no stranger to either the pleasures of the table or of the bottle. Similar to Sartorius, he came from a family of bureaucrats, but he had decided to become a soldier and had served for a spell as a lieutenant in the Hussars[58] where he quickly gambled and caroused away his paternal inheritance. But one day he suffered such a catastrophic fall from his horse while on the exercise field that his right leg was broken in several places and had to be amputated. Now a cripple, he was forced to resign from the service, but this actually turned out to be a blessing in disguise since the accident served to mask an impending dishonorable discharge; and this because his financial situation had deteriorated to such a point that he was faced with imminent expulsion.

He arrived in Texas at the beginning of the 1840s after wandering around for a period of time through the middle and southern states, the whole time without a dollar to his name. In Texas, his luck took a turn for the better. The daughter of a well-to-do slaveholder, to whom he was offering music lessons, fell madly in love with the one-legged foreigner who had seen and experienced so much; a man who could carry on such a fascinating conversation, and who appeared to all the world to be a *grand seigneur*,[59] despite his wooden leg and hand-me-down clothing.

With no real knowledge of his character and relying on nothing but blind trust, she agreed to elope with him over the objections of her father, who was dead set against their romance, and had even threatened to shoot him. A sympathetic justice of the peace performed the marriage. With the help of the mother's intervention, however, the father eventually acquiesced to the *fait accompli* and welcomed the two back into the family.

The ex-lieutenant became the beneficiary of a quarter league[60] of land on Possum Creek and two slaves to boot. He built a house and engaged in horse-trading and practiced veterinary medicine on the side. He even was elected to the position of justice of the peace. He was well on his way to being *a made man,* but when his young and energetic wife died, followed shortly thereafter by their only daughter, matters took a turn for the worse for Grossenberg was never a fan of physical exertion and paid little attention to the business of running a farm.

After the death of his wife, he had brought over an unmarried sister to manage his household, who was quite unattractive, to say the least, and common in every other way. She was, however, well versed in the culinary arts, especially in respect to wild game, ragouts, and the likes, but she despised the slaves and did with them as she pleased. In the end, they were forced to sell them and they also found it necessary to peddle off tracts of the land piecemeal, as the need for money arose. Grossenberg did not seem to be much affected by any of this, continued to eat and drink in excess, and spent much of his time composing articles for both domestic and foreign publications.

He was well regarded by his neighbors because he had been in Texas for a very long time and was intimately familiar with all the ins and outs of the Texas legal system and often assisted his friends with advice. In addition, because of his easy way with words and his complete mastery of the American language, he was regarded as an excellent *raconteur* with a large stock of off-color stories, suitable for gentlemen's circles, and always a natural choice for *maître de plaiser*[61] at weddings and events of that sort. He had also been strongly in favor of secession, which had earned him warm supporters among the American planter class in whose *mansions* he was always a welcome guest.

In all respects, both inward and outward, Winzig was the opposite of Grossenberg. He stood better than six feet tall and was so thin the wind, it seems, could blow him over. While Grossenberg wore an unstylish coat and pants that had been hand sewn by his sister Albertine from coarse, pea-green cloth, together with a blue hickory shirt and a broad-brimmed, coarsely woven straw hat, Winzig walked around in a formal suit complete with coat and tie.

Except for the large wide-brimmed felt hat he wore, one could have easily mistaken him at first glance for a man of the cloth, but on closer inspection those in the know would have immediately recognized him as a quintessential German academic type, and an extreme form of it at that. His father had been a professor of philosophy at the University at Königsberg, of all places,[62] and had been favorably regarded in the widest circles of academia. Many of his close relatives, similarly, had counted among the elite *Koryphaen*[63] of German academic life in astronomy, ecclesiastical jurisprudence, and philology.

He, too, had studied philosophy for quite a few semesters but never to the neglect of the taverns or other aspects of German student life. He had also fought in several *Mensur* duels,[64] which had required a lot of pluck on his part, since he lacked the steady hand and confidence necessary to an accomplished swordsman; in short, he had enjoyed the life of a student to the fullest. Since mathematics was nearer and dearer to him than philosophy, he really did not bring a lot of enthusiasm to his chosen field of study. Still, in the end, he managed to earn his *doctor philosophiae*. But since he was more absent-minded than even the old professors and also suffered from a mild speech impediment, he turned out to be unsuited for the life of an academic. In 1858 he emigrated to Texas in order to live his life there, so he hoped, in a way that was compatible with his ideals.

Upon arrival in Texas, however, he found it necessary to put these ideals aside, at least for a while, because the daughter of an old *Lateiner* on Possum Creek, with whom he had taken quarters, took a liking to him and, before he knew it, he was a bridegroom and astonishingly did not forget to say *yes* during the marriage ceremony. Winzig threw himself into his new life as a farmer with unexpected dedication. Nobody ever laughed as hard at Possum Creek as at the sight of Winzig's first efforts at fieldwork. However, his young wife, who had come to Texas as a child, was exceptionally practical and down-to-earth, and soon took the reins in hand both in respect to running the household and also managing the farm.

From then on, everything seemed to run smoothly and according to plan until the movement to separate the South from the Union reared its ugly head. Winzig, who saw in the slaves his own unhappy brothers, and who agitated for the legal and spiritual liberation of the same, soon gained the reputation among the slave-holding class as a despised abolitionist. Only his love for his wife and his two small children, as well as Lüttenhoff's wise counsel, had prevented him from fleeing Texas and dedicating himself totally to the service of the Union, this despite the fact that he was thoroughly ill-suited to the life of a soldier.

As it turned out, he was one of the first to be conscripted into the Southern army.[65] He resisted tooth and nail, but was placed in irons and hauled away anyway. If his neighbors had not intervened on his behalf in a timely and energetic way, he might well have been shot for treason. As it turned out, he faced court-martial, but his "opposite" and most ardent opponent, Grossenberg, exploited a technicality in the proceedings to obtain an acquittal and he was eventually discharged as physically unfit for service. At the next local election, Grossenberg nominated Winzig for the position of constable to the communities of Possum Creek and Collinsville[66]—and this he justified with the tongue-in-cheek suggestion that his long legs would better enable him to catch up with horse thieves.

The proposal was accepted to hurrahs all around. At first Winzig was taken aback by the idea and protested, but he quickly saw that this was a well-intentioned ploy on the part of Grossenberg to keep him free from possible military service in the future and he willingly agreed. From then on, he contented himself with doing as much harm to the Confederacy as possible from behind the scenes by using his position as constable to aid deserters and to assist those who took to the brush to avoid conscription.

Since both were avid chess players, who regarded the game as the best of all remedies for the ills of the world, and who were the only ones in the community who truly understood the intricacies of the game, the two soon became inseparable. But if, heaven forbid, so much as a word about politics were uttered, the old feud between the two would erupt with renewed fury, the game would end abruptly, and Winzig would stomp out and head home, swearing to himself as he strode along on his long legs never to visit Grossenberg again and suffer the indignity of being mocked by someone who supported slavery. But in the end, the pleasures of the game and the satisfaction of besting an adversary seemed to prevail and would bring the two "opposites" back together again.

After the gentleman had exchanged greetings and cracked several jokes, Anna also entered the room whereupon Sartorius commented: "Gentlemen, behold, our pleasant hostess and mistress of the house! My wife extends her greetings to you as well. She wanted to come along but our Sally surprised us at noon with a new and festive dish. It tasted wonderful, similar to a young baked pig, but when Sally beamed with pride at my praise and announced it was, in fact, a possum that her youngster had recently caught; well, that was too much for my wife's nerves, and she retired for the day. That scoundrel Kuno, however, had no problem polishing of the dish with gusto in the kitchen."

Upon hearing the story, the petite blond housewife clasped her hands together in horror, and exclaimed:

"A baked opossum! How awful! That makes me glad that I don't have a black cook!"

"Yes, you can be happy about that," replied Sartorius, "but in truth she is quite a clever cook. You just can't be too nosy, and best not to look in the pot while she is cooking, because then she can turn right nasty. My wife gave up a long time ago and allows her to prepare whatever she likes and what we see is what we get. But certainly, what appears on the table qualifies as neither typical *Königsberger* nor Rhenish fare and, to make matters worse, her son Pompey is a shameless thief to boot."

At this, Lüttenhoff interjected, "Why then do you keep slaves? Aside from everything else, they don't seem to accomplish a lot in the way of work."

Whereupon Sartorius replied: "My God man, we all pay the price for our vanities. My wife couldn't stand to play second fiddle to the American planters and I looked forward to studying the slave question up close and firsthand. You are correct insofar as it does not seem that we Germans have the stomach for applying the whip often enough and so can't seem to get much out of the blacks. My Negros are almost as lazy as your Phillip whom you continue to pay even though he has been put out to pasture, so to speak, but that is a taboo subject, as well. I can see that Winzig is about to erupt with righteous indignity and the master of the house is barely able to contain himself as well."

Frau Lüttenhoff now requested that the gentlemen go ahead and seat themselves for coffee and cake. She wanted to hasten this part of the ritual along since she had plans to visit her neighbor, Frau Köhler, whose two young children had contracted measles while her husband lay sick in a field hospital. Her daughter had ridden out to check on her favorite cow that had just calved and she did not trust either Phillip or Albert to serve the coffee properly. In short order the elegant Meissen porcelain from Germany was set out to serve the cakes and coffee. As she began pouring the coffee from her beautiful porcelain coffee pot, Sartorius declined, but the Frau would not take no for an answer:

"No, no, Herr Sartorius you can't turn it down; this is real coffee, not Confederate coffee."

"Well then, no harm in having some real mocha. For breakfast, I continue drinking an awful concoction brewed from acorns, or corn, or sweet potatoes, or barley—often, I sometimes feel, at risk of my life—but I didn't want to jeopardize my Sunday afternoon with the likes of that and preferred rather to double up on my share of the cake." After a quick sip, he added, "It tastes wonderful! But tell me, how in the world did you manage to come by such an unheard-of luxury in *Charlottenhöhe* after three years of blockade?"

Frau Anna replied, "It is what is left over from the sack of coffee we all shared from Mexico. I saved back a portion for my husband, but he puts on a show as if he actually prefers sweet potato coffee, but I can tell he doesn't really care for it. But the children and I have actually developed a taste for the surrogate and it sits quite well with us."

At this Sartorius exclaimed in astonishment, "Unbelievable! Here it is November and you still have beans left over while we haven't seen a single one since last Easter; Sally, no doubt, pilfered the lion's share. But the same thought goes for the pastry: coffee cakes when there is not a pound of flour to be had for a thousand miles."

"Well, I have to disappoint you on that score; the coffee cake is actually made from corn meal, but only from the very fine meal that is obtained by grinding the corn when the kernels are crisp and well-dried. The difference is not as noticeable when one uses this kind of corn meal."

The brown coffee cakes were a big hit with the guests as well. Winzig turned to the housewife with the request: "You absolutely must give me the recipe so I can pass it along to my wife. She was in a tizzy today because there has been so little variety in our daily menu." The response that she would gladly write down the recipe and give it to her daughter Hedwig to give to Frau Winzig, occasioned a sarcastic observation on the part of Sartorius:

"See there Winzig; the truth is out about you. Our hostess knows very well that, while walking home, you are likely to work yourself into a such a lather about the sad decline of our German homeland that, forgetting yourself, you will be inclined to use the slip of paper with the precious recipe to light your pipe; something you already once did with your official appointment as constable. But don't we live in la-la land here? The mocha that some big shot in Constantinople once sent my father never tasted so pleasing; and then cake to boot. Truthfully Grossenberg wasn't so far off the mark with his description of Texas in the "*Tante Bos*" [67] as the land of everlasting springtime where splendid peaches, cherries, and apples, along with other nourishing southern fruits, thrive at all seasons of the year in such abundance that the wild pigs feasting on them become so fat they can't walk any more, and the exquisite flavor of their hams exceeds all other hams anywhere in the world, and you cannot dispose of a pound of sausage for even a penny because of the surfeit. Verily, that is the picture you painted, isn't it so neighbor Grossenberg?"

Grossenberg, however, parried this effusive sarcasm quite calmly and easily with the comeback, "In respect to the article in question, and others of a soberer and more considered nature, as well, I am quite proud. The pleasures of the hunt were always for me, a cripple with a peg leg, a pure delight, and, had I not succeeded in hoodwinking my friend Sartorius, and others as well, with my fairy tales about Texas, similar to how we entice children with tales of cookie mountains in la-la land, how much longer would I have had to wait in order to enjoy a civilized game of whist over coffee and cake?"

"No, I have never regretted it," replied Sartorius, "even on those occasions when I think back on apples, cherries, and oranges and have a bit of difficulty aligning your depictions of gentle breezes, mild days, and rejuvenating nighttime showers with the reality of the searing heat of July, or perpetually frost-free winters with the biting cold of January northers. The free and unfettered life where every superfluous luxury and convenience falls to the wayside, the generous hospitality that is everywhere practiced here—these features pleased me from the very first day I was here. And as fervently as I long to see the Rhine once again, the thought of returning remains out of the question. I think that is probably the situation for us all."

But at this Winzig sprang to his feet so abruptly that he spilled his coffee and exclaimed: "But if only it were a free country, free from the curse of slavery! But thank God, that will soon come to an end . . ."

Grossenberg also rose from his seat, but in a way that was not so rash, and after he had calmly and deliberately emptied his second cup of coffee stated: "That goes too far; what you said is treasonous . . ."

Sartorius, however, intervened in his sonorous bass: "Gentlemen, let us remain calm; and in respect to you, dear neighbor Winzig, honored protector of our humble hovels here, it is good that no one outside this circle heard what you said and that your loose talk can be contained within our group—but, the cards are waiting and the days are growing shorter."

Frau Anna quickly cleared the table, which was rearranged to serve as the card table. After the master of the house had placed and lit a wax candle in the silver candelabra that stood on the table next to the wall, and after Albert, who had been occupied in the kitchen with the dishes, resumed his station next to the *fidibus* bowl in order to repack and relight the pipes as required, and after the mistress of the house had taken her leave, the game began, where we will leave the gentlemen for the present.

But in the meantime, a wall of clouds spread quickly to cover the horizon. Several violent gusts of wind kicked up thick clouds of dust followed by a sudden downpour of rain. Then the wind rose to blow continuously from the northwest; the first norther of the fall had arrived. After a half an hour, the storm clouds passed and the sky was clear and crisp over the landscape.

The five o'clock hour had passed. The gentlemen had ended all small talk and were earnestly engaged in a critical evaluation concerning the course of the game and were discussing, in particular, how Winzig had incorrectly trumped, but by so doing had also inadvertently helped bring his partner Grossenberg into the minus column. Suddenly Frau Anna, hastily and visibly agitated, interrupted the gentlemen in their discussion with the question: "Has Hedwig been here?" When Lüttenhoff and Albert responded in the negative she exclaimed, "My God. The child has not returned yet and it will be dark in an hour! If only she has not fallen from her horse and had an accident."

"There is no danger of that," replied Grossenberg, "because she sits upon her horse Falada[68] with more assurance than any Amazon. At this moment, a knock was heard at the door whereupon Kuno entered with the news that a neighbor, Mr. Phillips, had arrived for a visit and that Sartorius needed to return home forthwith. Frau Lüttenhoff queried him immediately if he had seen Hedwig; that she had ridden off on her horse and hadn't returned yet. And when Sartorius interposed, "I met her at the creek where she turned and headed to the right," Kuno turned pale and cried out:

"She rode to the right and I thought for sure she would take the Collinsville road as usual and find her cow at her normal place by our hay stack and be annoyed that I sent her off on a wild goose chase."

At this Sartorius interrupted his son with the remark, "You shameless trickster, what kind of mischief have you caused with your impulsiveness? Who knows where Hedwig has headed off to. Even Lüttenhoff, who normally was so composed and difficult to upset, was visibly shaken by the turn of events. Kuno quickly went to Frau Lüttenhoff and said:

"I will go hunt for her right away and I will find her. But first I will get my horn and my dog Pluto; he will find her for sure." With this he took to his heels and left the house. Frau Anna stepped out into the breezeway and called for the hired hand Phillip. She received no answer but the unmistakable sounds of a snoring man announced how the loyal employee was wont to spend his Sunday afternoons. He finally reacted and slowly came down the ladder from the half room above, rubbed his eyes, and inquired if it were time to feed already, and upon the directive of the mistress of the house that he needed to saddle the gray right away, he replied:

"What, me, saddle the gray, this evening?"

When the command was repeated, he responded somewhat incredulously and in protest: "But he ain't had no saddle on in a good while!"

But after Frau Anna hastily explained to him that Hedwig had ridden out and not returned, and her husband wanted to go look for her, the normally staid and worthy man suddenly became agitated, "What the... Our gal ain't come back; I need to go saddle up the gray," and with this turned on his heels and headed for the stall where he applied bridle and saddle to the old, long-legged gray by the name of Charley faster than he had ever done before.

In the meantime, Lüttenhoff returned to the room with a lantern where the guests, visibly agitated, stood discussing the gravity of the situation. He excused himself for his sudden departure.

Frau Anna had to remind him to take off his night jacket and put on a warmer coat and then wrapped a thick shawl around his neck and shoulders. After giving his wife a farewell hug, he swung himself into the saddle rode off into the dusk at a fast trot. Sartorius, however, who had maintained his composure, spoke to Frau Anna:

"I will return home also and get my horse. I am sure Mr. Phillips will want to join us and press his Negroes into the search as well. Pompey will alert the entire neighborhood to the situation, but first we will need to hold a small council of war and then, within a half an hour, we can begin a systematic search of the whole area. You can be reassured that we will find and bring back your daughter, safe and unharmed, to your arms. For sure the stormy weather has caused your Hedwig to lose her way on the prairie.

With the words, "I want to help as well," Winzig started to leave, but was fortunately held up by Sartorius before he could depart.

"Stop, that won't do," he said, "you can't find your way around in the bright sunshine much less at night and we don't need to divide our people searching for you as well. Grossenberg, keep Winzig here by the coattails if necessary and deliver him to his wife at home."

The men soon disappeared from view behind the neighboring sand hill. Frau Anna, who rarely if ever stayed idle for long, stood for a long time at the farm gate staring into the distance with dry eyes. Albert, however, had snuggled up to his mother, and looking up into her face, asked her with some hesitation in his voice:

"Mother, can I also help in the search for Hedwig?"

"No, Albert," she replied, "you cannot go out by yourself; your father would not permit you to leave me here alone."

"I thought as much," replied Albert, "otherwise, I would already be gone. Dear mother, don't be so sad; our Hedwig will be back shortly."

Frau Anna folded her hands and as the tears began to flow, spoke from the depths of her heart, "May God grant it."

Mother and son stood embraced for a long, long time until the mother, righted herself and said:

"Come Albert, you need to look after the animals now and I need to clean up. The activity will help me to forget my sorrows."

WAR COUNCIL AND SEARCH

Sartorius kept his word and Pompey did his duty by alerting the neighborhood quickly to the situation. Twilight descended and as the bright disk of the full moon lifted above the horizon, about twenty men from the neighborhood gathered on the porch of his spacious double-chambered log house. Since the younger members were away in the army, it was older men for the most part. Still, a couple of younger men, who were home on furlough, had joined the party. Those gathered held their war council by the light of candles that had been placed inside wine bottles. The planter Mr. Phillips, who cultivated friendly relations with his German neighbors on Possum Creek, had already struck out for his home in his large buggy in order to marshal the slaves under his and his overseer's direction to patrol the area to the southeast. With ten men to assist him, Sartorius undertook to scout the prairie to the west. The others had responsibility for the area to the north, but in this they had the fortuitous help of *Long Mike*, actually Michael Schmidt, but the nickname Mike, given to him by his buddies while in the ranger service, had stuck. He looked the part of an adventurer: tall, lean, and sinewy, with large owl eyes that had a yellow cast to them and a mop of red hair. A red woolen Mexican serape was draped over his shoulders in a picturesque fashion. He had just returned from the war zone in Louisiana in order to—as he stated—chop some wood for the winter and do a little plowing. Whether he had a pass to do this or not, no one seemed to know or care, and Mike was no friend of superfluous questions. All in all, he was a straight shooter who never intentionally harmed a flea, but if anyone wronged him, they better watch out, because Mike was as proficient with six-shooter and Bowie knife as he was with his massive fists. He had taken a shine to Lüttenhoff's Hedwig, who liked to visit his little wife and bring along treats when she was

"Feeding the cows." Friedrich Richard Petri papers, [11947], The Dolph Briscoe Center for American History, The University of Texas at Austin.

under the weather and snuggle and play with their small children. He was firmly resolved to bring her home safe and sound as soon as possible. The other neighbors were no less steady in their resolve, not only because the parents were held in high regard by everyone in the community, but also because Hedwig had endeared herself to practically everyone, far and wide, by her friendliness and innate cheerfulness. Soon the men mounted their horses that were tied to the front fence. In the meantime, the torches fashioned from kindling and lit by the slaves imparted to the scene a warlike and romantic picture. Nearly all had armed themselves, several with German shotguns and others with cavalry carbines, while others carried Enfield[69] muskets. Some wore gray Confederate uniforms, and one even sported the blue coat of a Union officer, a trophy from the war. A few simply had wool blankets against the cold. Some sat astride good horses; others rode small Mexican ponies, or even mules. They then departed accompanied by a pack of baying hounds. After a sufficient lapse, nocturnal tranquility returned to the log cabins and outbuildings in the valley of Possum Creek and extended to the hills on either side. But in the houses below, anxiety and concern held sway. The wives and children who had remained behind exchanged anxious doubts in hushed tones as to whether Hedwig would return to her parent's house alive and healthy.

At Lüttenhoff's house, however, Frau Anna passed the hours in utter anguish. A neighbor's wife, who had come over for a spell to comfort her, had to return home to be with her small children. The clear night air carried the nocturnal sounds for miles, it seemed. Standing on the porch, she heard the men ride off on their horses into the night; heard the blowing of horns; waited, waited in vain for the signal that she had been found: four shots; two after long pauses, two in quick succession. Albert stayed all the while by her side, attempting to console and comfort her with tender words and by stroking her hand. She finally took a seat on the horsehair sofa inside with Albert next to her only to jump up and rush to the window to better hear with each faint echo of dogs baying, or horns blowing, or wolves howling. In such a state of tortuous worry, she passed the endless night.

HEDWIG IN THE FOREST

Hedwig did indeed take a turn to the right instead of following the usual country road that led past the Sartorius place. She was riding the small, fine-boned sorrel mare Falada, who had a preponderance of mustang blood and who was tame as a kitten, of an easy gait, but capable of all sorts of mischief, which only served to amuse so experienced a rider as Hedwig. Heading towards the north, midway between the settlement and the forest, one hill stood out considerably higher than the rest and was known as the "iron hill" because of the iron oxide gravel that covered it. Hedwig headed straight for this landmark in the hope of possibly spotting her pet from the top of the hill on the way back home. She was disappointed in this hope and nowhere in the distance was an animal to be seen, because the cattle had instinctively sought protection in the forest or returned to the shelter of the farms.

Now she gave her brave little pony her head and galloped out on the prairie in the direction of the pond where Kuno said he had seen her cow. Soon her keen young eyes spotted a small herd of cattle together with calves in the vicinity of the pond next to two large, wide-spreading live oak trees for which the pond had been named. After narrowing the distance, she noticed that one of the cows was agitated and charging forward with her horns lowered and all the while bellowing as if threatened by an enemy. When she approached within a couple of hundred feet, a large flock of wild ducks, all black except for white spots on their wings,[70] arose from the reeds surrounding the almost dried-up pond while simultaneously a pair of large, gray wolves trotted off in the direction of the forest. But it wasn't Hedwig's pet cow Toni putting up the valiant fight with the sneaky predators to save her newborn calf, but rather a cow belonging to their neighbor Köhler. Hedwig felt duty-bound to try and drive cow and calf back in the direction of the settlement where they could reach the safety of their home pasture. This took a lot of time since young calves are not that easy to drive and the black line that covered the horizon spread with such rapidity that the young girl recognized a storm was brewing and fast approaching. Once she felt they had moved far enough away from the pond, she turned her horse back in the direction of the forest, but with a more westerly bearing than before, and urged her horse to a gallop. Once there, she quickly skirted the edge of the forest until she arrived at a familiar trail next to a natural draw and entered the forest at this point. Hedwig knew a large spring was at the head of this draw, not too far in the distance, under some willow trees, where she hoped to locate her missing animal. She did not intend to venture further under any circumstances because this forest, a good twenty miles in breadth, stretched clear across the county. Even adults avoided the forest, while its haunts appeared mysterious and frightening to the children of Possum Creek. From deep within its depths came bears, wildcats, panthers, as well as the larger and the more aggressive lobo wolves that were responsible on occasion for severe losses to the livestock of the farmers. Redskins had emerged from these forests thirty years prior to kill and scalp the first German pioneer in the area and to kidnap his wife and children.[71] A few years earlier, runaway slaves had sought refuge in the forest only to venture out from time to time to plunder the smoke houses of the settlers of Possum Creek, to kill their livestock, steal their horses, and even, on occasion, to waylay and rob sojourners along the public road. This

"German woman riding sidesaddle." Friedrich Richard Petri papers, [detail from 11950], The Dolph Briscoe Center for American History, The University of Texas at Austin.

situation persisted until a group of resolute men under the leadership of "Long Mike" entered the forest with a pack of bloodhounds. When they returned three days later, they calmly reported that the runaways would not be a problem any longer. In recent times, however, those men who hoped to avoid the clutches of the conscript hunters,[72] the so-called heel flies, took refuge in the brush, as they termed it, but related that when they penetrated even deeper into the forest, they had encountered armed and dangerous looking men on several occasions, who quickly disappeared without a word as if they had they had some reason to steer clear of human company. The general consensus was that a band of desperados had hidden in the forest and had spared the settlement of Possum Creek so as not to draw attention to themselves.

As she approached, she startled a big buck that fled the spring in big bounds where he was watering, but her Toni was not to be seen. Hedwig wanted to turn back but she thought she heard the bleating of a calf in the distance to the left where thick brush covered the rise. She decided to make one last search although the storm clouds were gathering in an ever more ominous manner. She found it difficult to make her way forward because the annual fires that once helped to clear out the underbrush had not burned this area in recent memory and yaupon,[73] scrub oaks, and thorny vines had grown up to form an impenetrable thicket. Finally, Hedwig gave up, convinced that her cow could not have ventured so deep in the woods, and started to retrace her steps when all at once a strong north wind arose, shaking and rocking the treetops violently, scattering dried leaves, moss balls, and dead branches to the forest floor, followed by a cold downpour.

The young girl found shelter under a large, leaning post-oak tree. The rain continued to fall for a good while and Hedwig grew anxious that it would continue until nightfall overtook her. When the clouds finally began to clear, she sprang quickly into the saddle. The rain had washed away the tracks of her horse but she felt confident that she could retrace her way. Soon it appeared to her that the forest had become even thicker and more impenetrable. Thorns and dewberry vines clawed at her riding clothes. The wet bushes she pushed aside soaked her thoroughly and finally, in order to make progress, she found it necessary to dismount and lead her mare by the reins. Then the forest opened up somewhat and she spotted a small draw and thought it was the one she was looking for, but, alas, no spring, no meadow. She was forced to concede that she had lost her way.

Now she tried to orient herself to the sun and strike a path due south where she was bound to come to the prairie. But once again, she encountered a thicket so dense and formidable that it was impossible to maintain her bearing, which in any case was made doubly difficult by the fact that trees still had leaves in their canopies and were heavily laden with moss, all of which obscured the rapidly setting sun. Often, she found it necessary to get down on all fours and push aside the thorny vines in order to clear a path for her mare. Then suddenly she noticed a hoof print and the footprint of a person only to recognize that it was her own horse and her own track; she had made a full circle.

At this, the plucky child lost her composure somewhat. Soaked to the bone, she hastily pressed forward, still leading her horse by the reins, but only succeeded in becoming even more disoriented. An hour passed in this way without ever reaching the edge of the forest. And then with darkness falling, with the howl of wolves and the hooting of owls sounding from all quarters, it seemed, the mare Falada, who had already shown signs of restlessness, suddenly set back on her hind legs, jerking the reins from Hedwig's grip and bolted at a full run to quickly disappear from sight of her mistress. Hedwig was now all alone, hopelessly lost in the fearsome forest as darkness rapidly enveloped her.

Her first impulse had been to run after her pony, but then she remembered Kuno's recent and unfortunate experience with his Polly. She also recalled how her good companion had once explained to her that the best thing to do when you get lost is to sit down and regain your composure because, otherwise, you just become more confused and wander around in circles until, as often happens, you lose it completely. She decided to stop and wait until the moon arose, improving her prospects for holding a course to the south toward the prairie. Sitting on the fallen trunk of a tree, pulling her thick riding coat over her shoulders, she waited while the lengthening shadows of swiftly approaching night advanced over the landscape. Slowly her rapidly beating heart settled back into a normal rhythm and she calmed down. The barking and howling of the wolves, the hooting of the owls, and plaintive cry of the whippoorwill, as well as the many other creepy and unnerving nocturnal sounds that interrupted the solitude of the forest, sounds that would have scared any city brat half to death, only occasioned a mild discomfort on her part, for they were noises with which she was intimately familiar.

From time to time she heard the snapping of a dry twig close by caused by the misstep of a slinking four-footed night prowler, and her fears wanted to return, but with cold-blooded resolve, she determined to stay put and consoled herself with the thought that it was probably only a raccoon or fat possum. Her biggest worry was for her parents because she knew they would be beside themselves with worry and fear for her well-being. It took a long time for the moon to rise, but concern for her parents compelled her to resume her wanderings by the first dim light of its beams, but this time with slow and deliberate steps. She quickly realized, however, that it was even harder to strike and hold a steady course by the faint light of the moon than by daylight.

She finally reached a sand hill that was open enough to allow a clear view of the night sky. After much effort, she was able to pick out the North Star from among the thousands of sparkling stars in the firmament. It offered her a confident but temporary bearing for she soon lost it from sight. Finally, she stumbled upon a footpath that was barely perceptible and decided to follow it in the hope it had been beaten out by cattle and would lead to the open spaces, but it turned out instead to be an old Indian trail that only led deeper into the forest.

The hours passed in aimless meandering. It is a curious fact about wandering around during the nighttime hours. The friendly, welcoming night that poets often praise can assume a very unfriendly face, especially in a dark forest, and become, as the saying goes, friend of neither man nor beast: our phantasies conjure up apparitions of monsters, dragons, spooks, and vampires at every turn, and even dumb animals become more anxious and wary as soon as the sun goes down. The moonlight casts ghostly shadows and a knobby, moss covered oak tree or a fire-blackened stump of a long dead tree can take on an eerie and frightful silhouette.

The twig that snaps under our foot, the tree limb that groans as it rubs against another, the shrill call of a nocturnal bird, can often curdle the blood of even a self-assured and resolute man accustomed to such wanderings. Small wonder then that the composure that Hedwig had managed to achieve after much internal struggle began to falter. In the uncertain light her unease increased markedly as she realized that the character of the wooded landscape was becoming ever more unfamiliar and stranger. The hills were now steeper and rockier and were for the most part covered by live oaks rather than post oaks. Occasionally she encountered stands of mountain cedar that in places formed dense thickets even though the forest in general was thinning out.

Once the height of the moon indicated midnight, Hedwig, by now fully exhausted, sank down next to the trunk of a gigantic oak on the edge of a small clearing. Her limbs were depleted and her courage had faded as well. "My dear, dear mother; my dear good father," she whispered with trembling lips. It struck her that she couldn't allow herself to sit too long since it had grown steadily cooler and she might perish from exposure, but by continuing her wandering she also ran the danger of straying ever further from familiar ground.

Then she recalled what she had often read in children's books given to her by her parents, especially those by Christoph von Schmid,[74] stories about how children in danger, Rosa von Tannenburg or the good Fridolin, for example, always turned to prayer when they found themselves in danger, and their pleas were invariably answered. Although her parents were definitely religious, her father had gotten into a disagreement concerning the increasingly pietistic[75] turn of his church and, as a consequence, had avoided raising his children in any one confession. The majority of the Latin farmers in Possum Creek, however, were Freethinkers,[76] and though Lüttenhoff often tried to shield them, his children often overheard sarcastic remarks about the papacy and things of this nature.

Hedwig had never prayed, nor ever even heard a prayer, but still she knew that both her mother and father believed in an omnipotent and benevolent Deity, and she determined to beseech His help in her hour of need. Rising and turning her gaze toward the starry firmament above, she spoke loud and distinctly: "Dear God, I don't know if you also listen to those who do not go to church, but I believe you must. I would ask of you to comfort my dear mother and father until I can return to be with them again." This request to a higher authority seemed to bring a measure of relief to her, and she set about to resume her journey.

Just at this point she once again sensed the presence of a stalking animal and heard a cry that sent a shudder through her being; a noise that almost sounded like the crying of a small child, and one often described to her; she realized in horror that it must be a panther, of all the predators common to Texas, the most fearsome, and this panther had been following her the whole night, waiting for the opportunity to attack her and tear her limb from limb. And then the trembling girl heard a soft noise and could clearly make out in the dim light of the woods a pair of large eyes that glowed like phosphorous.

With the cry, "Help, father, Kuno, help me!" she instinctively fled in the direction of the path across the opening and into the forest where she stumbled over the roots of a tree, fell, and hit the ground so hard that she was left momentarily stunned. The marauder took up the chase, springing after her in large bounds, but it abruptly changed course and exited into the brush to the side. Her forehead bloodied by the fall, Hedwig roused herself to resume her flight, but just at this moment she picked up the sound of a voice singing the old student song "*Gaudeamus igitur, juvenes dum sumus* . . ."[77] and though the voice was quite gruff, it had the ring of salvation, and crying for help once again, she stumbled in the direction of the singing by some unknown person trudging through the forest.

In a moment, the wanderer was at her side and quickly heard her account of the danger that had threatened her and with the cry, "Aye, such a hussy!" quickly unlimbered the musket slung over his back with the intention of punishing the malefactor. The predator, however, had quietly disappeared and the man set about consoling and comforting the frightened child.

ROBBERS' NEST OR KNIGHTS' CASTLE?

With the firm resolve to find Hedwig—and if unable to do so, or in the event that some misfortune had befallen her, then to never return again—Kuno left the house of his beloved schoolmaster. Returning to his own home, he quickly exchanged his Sunday suit for his leather-hunting outfit, filled his hunting canteen with mustang wine,[78] and put a large piece of corn bread in the pocket of his hunting pouch. Sally, the black and corpulent cook, who was at that moment busy stewing and cooking in various pots and pans in preparation of a sumptuous meal for the honored guests that evening, watched in amazement. But in response to her nosy queries, she only received the reply that the young *"massa"* would not be present for dinner and probably would only return much later.

But after he had slung his father's rifle over his shoulders and saddled his mare Polly, who, in the meantime, had returned to the barn in search of corn where she stood quietly munching as if the previous altercation had never occurred, an overpowering urge to say farewell to his mother suddenly overcame him, something that the youngster, so accustomed to unfettered liberty to go and act as he pleased, often neglected to do. He found her in the rocking chair in front of a flickering fire of the chimney in the comfortable living room, speaking with Mr. Phillips. With a quick kiss on the lips and a hasty good-bye to the fretting mother, the son was gone.

Sensing his services would soon be needed, Pluto, the large black and brown bloodhound, strained at the leash, and leaped with joy when his master released him from the chain. Kuno had already departed at a gallop before his father appeared and only slowed down to a trot now and then so as not to tire out his dog too quickly, who was a bastard mixture of a Scottish deerhound and a common bloodhound.

Before it was totally dark, Kuno had reached the prairie between the settlement and the woods and had convinced himself by the deep but narrow hoof prints he picked out at the edge of the pond, still visible despite the rain, that

Hedwig had ridden this way. Certain now that the maiden must have strayed into the forest and gotten lost, he headed his horse into the woods. With the aid of his hunting lantern, he was able to pick out the faint imprint of Falada's small hoof prints in the moist clay at the edge of the spring, which confirmed that his hunch had been correct. It was a tiresome piece of detective work, made the more so by the fact that the lantern kept blowing out and had to be laboriously relit each time with sponge and stone.

After hours of fruitless search, he finally located Hedwig's fresh footprints and those of her horse, now being led by the reins. The hound, sensing what was expected of him, took up the scent trail so quickly that his master could barely keep up with him. Soon he found the spot where Falada had set back and torn loose, and his heart skipped a beat when Pluto suddenly let out an angry growl after picking up the fresh scent of the large panther.

Kuno knew that, unless provoked, panthers (more precisely, jaguars) only attacked humans on rare occasions, but this thought only gave him slight comfort. In the attempt to hurriedly follow her tracks, Kuno often lost the trail at those places where the young girl had made her way through dense undergrowth, and

"Shack in the woods." Friedrich Richard Petri papers, [detail from 11950],
The Dolph Briscoe Center for American History, The University of Texas at Austin.

each time it took precious time to relocate the trail. Apprehension for his young companion and playmate and the thought that a dangerous animal was stalking her, however, continued to replenish his youthful vigor and to drive him ever onward without rest, only pausing now and then to blow his horn in the hope that the sound would reach Hedwig's ear.

When he found the spot where Hedwig had called upon divine assistance, the day was already beginning to dawn. At this point, the hound, which had hurried ahead, suddenly turned tail and, growling angrily, beat a hasty retreat to the safety of his master. Not twenty paces in front of him, a large ashen predator with bright spots slowly arose. Here next to the trunk of a large fallen tree, the big cat was awaiting the return of the prey that had eluded him. The animal now turned to the side and seemed to be contemplating whether or not to flee. Kuno's finger, however, was already on the trigger of his rifle, which erupted with the detonation of the shot.

The startled animal jerked around as if intending to charge, but then collapsed to the ground and began thrashing, its claws tearing furiously at the forest floor, only to expire on its side shortly thereafter. With his rifle at the ready, Kuno cautiously approached the animal, and judged that it was easily over four feet long, an unusually large female. Kuno saw that his shot had entered next to the ear and passed through the brain. Pluto now regained his courage and sprang at the large cat and acted as if he wanted to tear it to pieces.

Kuno had bagged quite a few deer in his short life, and even wild cats and mountain lions on occasion, but never before a jaguar. Pride in his kill led him momentarily to forget Hedwig. He set his horn to his lips to blow a farewell tribute to the queen of the forest. But then as he espied the unmistaken footprint of a large man next to that of Hedwig, he quickly regretted his reckless outburst. Who knew what new danger for Hedwig this sign of a human might signify; indeed, the thought of a stranger in this forest might be something more to fear than the stalking night-predator intent on ambush that now lay dead at his feet.

From now on, extreme caution was the watchword. Taking pains to be exact, he reloaded the discharged barrel of his shotgun with a slug that had been greased carefully with deer tallow and then reassured himself that his long, sharp Bowie knife was safely in the deerskin sheath on his belt. He put collar and leash back on his hound and kept him close by his side so that he would not rashly betray their presence. In a couple hundred yards he crossed a small stream even as the sun began to turn the tops of the trees a bright scarlet. On a gentle rise on the other side of the stream the large trees of the forest gave way to a thicket of young oak trees, thorn bushes, and vines, such as often reclaim land previously cleared but since neglected.

Once at the crown of the hill, however, close by a gulley that carried the runoff from the hill, Kuno spotted an old, gray shingle roof of a log cabin that was itself partially hidden and fairly overgrown with shrubs and brush. Kuno had heard about this place often enough; that here in the forest unwelcome guests, perhaps robbers and outlaws, possessed a hideout, a hidden cabin that years before, even before Texas became a republic, had been erected by a squatter and then abandoned.

Carefully he made his way along the twisting and overgrown path, still following the two tracks, in the direction of the cabin. Soon it stood there before him, within shooting distance. The undergrowth had recently been cleared and partially burned in front of the cabin in order to offer an unobstructed view. To the rear, however, the forest seemed undisturbed by the hand of man. The house appeared to consist of only one large room and was obviously quite old since it contained no windows as such, only slits and an old chimney made of logs and mortar that leaned so badly to one side it threatened to separate from the rest of the building. A large bonfire such as wayfarers often build crackled and popped under one of the trees.

Nearby under a huge and ancient live oak Kuno spotted a hammock, made from ropes and a wool blanket, attached to the limbs of the tree. Next to that Kuno saw a tall man with a buffalo hide wrapped around his shoulders who was looking intently in the direction from which Kuno came. The thought struck Kuno: this must be the robbers' nest. His next thought was, what should I do? But no sooner asked than his heart supplied the answer: die I must, if even the smallest harm has come to her. With a determination and eagerness for battle akin to a soldier marching in lockstep at double time with hundreds of his comrades towards an enemy stronghold, there to face an entrenched enemy and to run the risk of death or injury at any moment, he marched straight toward the stranger but with his rifle steady and at the ready.

The stranger, however, did not appear to have a weapon and placed his hand before his mouth as if to signal that he should remain quiet. Once he had approached closer, he addressed Kuno softly and in broken speech, as if the act of speaking were difficult for him. "You must be looking for Hedwig Lüttenhoff, who strayed into the forest and got lost yesterday evening? Be reassured, she is ok, but she has suffered a terrible fright since a predator stalked her and threatened to tear her limb from limb in the night. She has fallen into a deep sleep now that will help her to recover.

The stranger wore a wide-brimmed slouch hat and had very long hair that was almost entirely white. His long beard, in contrast, was still totally black. A pronounced hawk's beak stuck out from his sunken face that had an unhealthy, sallow look. His dark eyes, likewise, glistened with a fever-like luster, revealing, indeed, someone who was seriously ill. It was the face of a man that any enemy would do well to fear, but not the face of a robber or someone who shied from the light of day. Kuno's misgivings lessened and he willingly grasped the bony, ice-cold hand extended to him by the man who still possessed the firm grip of someone who once was very stout.

Sensing the great concern and anxiety on the part of the young man for the well-being of the missing girl, the stranger quickly added, "If you would like, you can see her." He led Kuno to the door of the log cabin and gently lifted the wooden latch. Through the crack in the door Kuno could make out a rather spacious but low-ceilinged room that was illuminated solely by the faint light filtering through various slots made for shooting and other cracks in the walls. He noticed many objects hanging on the walls that under other circumstances would have aroused his curiosity. Rifles and shotguns, curved sabers and stiletto daggers, sundry articles of military attire, some impressive deer antlers and the large, outstretched pelt of a mountain lion hung from various pegs along the walls. The floor, constructed of rough-hewn beams, was covered with the hides of a bear and several other predators as well.

But Kuno's eyes were only looking for Hedwig and he spied her lying upon a bear hide stretched over a crudely constructed bed frame in the back corner of the room; and to all appearances, lost in a deep and replenishing sleep. Her hands were folded as if in prayer and she lay upon a magnificent, multi-colored wool blanket such as the Indians in Mexico are accustomed to weaving. Her cheeks were flushed and her thick, brown locks fell to either side of the narrow pallet and only a slight wound on her forehead testified to the ordeal she had just gone through.

Taking a deep breath, Kuno gently closed the door and tiptoeing behind his host followed him to his hammock where the man collapsed as if totally exhausted. His breath appeared to be labored, but at a sign he seated himself on a stump close by but did not venture to ask any further questions. After he had recovered somewhat, the man spoke:

"My good companion was going to check his lines in the creek when he came upon your sister as she was crying for help in the forest. He went back into the forest before daybreak to retrieve any fish he might have caught so that he could prepare a good breakfast for our young guest. He will be returning shortly and then, after the two of you have been restored somewhat, he will guide you back to a place you recognize and can continue on your own. I know that you come from the German settlement but my companion cannot accompany you that far, and I have to ask you to remain silent about the mysterious forest dwellers you have discovered here."

Kuno promised absolute silence, but also reported that Hedwig was not his sister, but rather the daughter of his school teacher, and that he was responsible himself for Hedwig's ordeal due to his irresponsible and foolish prank. The stranger, who appeared to have recovered somewhat, was obviously pleased with his young guest and continued to speak with him on a variety of topics. Kuno gained such confidence in the man that he ventured to ask if he might actually be permitted to return to join the group here at the hideaway deep in the forest so as to avoid conscription. In so doing, he also remarked how he had always wanted to lead a hermit's life in the style of Robison Crusoe and to live solely from hunting and fishing.

At this the stranger raised himself from his place of repose and addressed Kuno very earnestly. "Young man I assume that it is not because of cowardice that you are attempting to avoid military service, but rather because you condemn Secession. Personally, I am not well enough acquainted with the circumstances that led to the traumatic separation of the South from the Union and to this horrible war to form an opinion as to whether this step was anything more or less than the failed attempt of a group of young but genuinely patriotic hotspurs. But as one who has willingly parted from his fatherland because of his own deep convictions and who will now die as a homeless and despised expatriate on foreign soil, let me offer a piece of advice: do not follow through on what you are now contemplating. Your country might be poorly governed, or you might believe this to be the case, but it remains nonetheless your country. It is better to go along with your compatriots in a bad cause than to become a man without a country, which is what has happened to me.

"Embrace your homeland! Your precious homeland . . ."[79]

At this, his voice, which had unintentionally risen in pitch, broke, but Kuno, deeply moved, completed Attinghausen's admonition to Ullrich von Rudenz:

"Here lie the roots of your strength;

There in a foreign land you are alone."

The two then fell silent until footsteps announced the arrival of his companion. He was a rather thinly built man of medium height who looked to be in his middle thirties. He wore a green hunting frock that had seen its better days, and a similarly battered pair of blue service trousers tucked into a large pair of riding boots for his feet. Slung over his back he had a small caliber carbine. In his hand, he held a wooden stick with a fork fashioned from a tree branch that had been inserted through the mouth of a very nice "blue cat,"[80] approximately eight pounds in weight, which he carried at the end of the stick and which he had caught during the night on a trotline he kept in a nearby stream. He greeted Kuno heartily and then set about preparing breakfast.

In the meantime, he kept up a conversation with the sick man in the French language of which Kuno knew not a word; a language that the two seemed to use exclusively among themselves. But he could pick out from the exchange that the sick man called the man who had just returned "Eginhard." Kuno offered to help Eginhard but he appeared to be quite adept in the preparation of wild game and was in no need of help.

In short order the fish had been skinned and salted; small pieces of bacon cracked and popped in the pan set over the coals of the fire and from a tin coffee pot the smell of stout coffee filled the air and showed that the forest dwellers, at least in respect to this beloved morning drink, were better furnished than the housewives of Possum Creek. Despite this activity, Eginhart found time to rattle off a barrage of questions at Kuno, who attempted to answer them willingly and truthfully. After a while, however, the reaction to all the excitement set in and, as he sat on the block of wood, he found himself nodding off while his answers drifted into incoherence.

At this moment, the latch at the door of the log cabin lifted and Hedwig stepped outside. Her first glance fell upon her dozing playmate and she yelled "Kuno, Kuno!" and as he stood up with a start and still half befuddled, she threw her arms around his neck, now crying, now laughing. It took a few moments before Kuno came to his senses enough to realize that he now held a vibrant young woman in his arms, the same Hedwig with whom only a few years before he had even traded blows on occasion, and that strangers were witnessing this embarrassing spectacle. His own youthful awkwardness led him to try to gently disengage from her encircling arms. Finally, Hedwig stepped back and the two now both turned red as beets and looked away ashamedly, as if they had both been caught in the act of something quite naughty. Deeply moved by the scene, tears moistened the eyes of the sick man in the hammock and, in a gesture of respect, he quickly turned his head aside, as if to signal that he had not observed the spontaneous outburst of joy on the part of the young couple.

In the meantime, Eginhard had gone back into the log cabin in order to retrieve tableware. He returned to drape a less-than-spotless linen tablecloth over a crude table made from discarded pallets. He also set out three tin plates, cups, and forks. He then placed small pieces of cold cornbread, hard and brittle like Mexican tortillas, on the table. Finally came the main course, the perfectly cooked fish, taken from the pan at just the right moment when the meat begins to separate from the bone. The only regret was that the frying pan had to double as a serving dish. The sick man did not join in the meal. The young guests, however, did not need to be asked twice and quickly took their places and joined in. The host followed suit and praised the wine in Kuno's canteen so favorably that Kuno implored him to empty the contents into his cup and he happily complied.

But before the last bite had been consumed, Hedwig expressed the strong desire to return home as soon as possible. Eginhard made ready to accompany them as guide but first he provided his sick comrade with fresh drinking water from a nearby spring and placed a pot with cacao on the coals of the fire that were now covered in ashes. Deeply moved by the scene, the two young people took their leave from the sick man and began their return trip home.

THE STORY OF THE BANISHED

Their guide estimated that they had at least ten miles to travel before they reached the edge of the forest in the vicinity of the settlement, and since they had occasionally to detour around impenetrable thickets, it would require at least four hours to complete the journey. Eginhard von Seiffert, their leader, carried a pocket compass that insured they would not lose their way. But it soon became apparent that both Hedwig and Kuno were suffering the ill effects of the previous night's ordeal and both were not a little bit sore and weary as they began their journey. Although the north wind had settled, it was still quite cool, yet refreshing for walking, and soon their joints began to limber.

After they had walked a spell, it became clear their guide could no longer contain his silence concerning himself and his comrade. The words came out in a rush as he related to the young people under his care the full story of both his companion and himself, while constantly insisting that he was not betraying anything of a confidential nature, which could only be allowed to come to light at a later date during quieter times. His speech was that of an educated person, but occasionally he would transpose the consonants b and p, which suggested that his cradle years had been spent in beautiful Saxony.[81]

The one forest dweller will soon depart this world and our story, but the other will play an important role to the very end, and although counts and barons were not exactly a rarity in Texas at the time, we need to outline as much of their life stories as is necessary to justify to our discerning readers the somewhat sensational title affixed to this chapter.

Ernst Eberhard Count of Scharfenegg was the youngest son of a noble family of ancient lineage, originally from Brandenburg, but later transplanted to East Prussia. His grandfather had served under "Old Fritz"[82] with distinction; his father had suffered the humiliation of Jena[83] and lost a leg a Ligny.[84] Absolute obedience to and reverence for the ruling family of Prussia was the first commandment in his father's house, and the son, whose mother died soon after his birth, grew up with the conviction that the true calling of a young nobleman was to proudly don the uniform, to fight and, if necessary, to die for the greater glory of Prussia. Although inclined to daydreaming, he graduated from a military prep school and later from the Prussian cadet training academy at Lichterfelde[85] and soon found himself a snappy lieutenant in the feudal Guards Cuirassiers;[86] a strikingly handsome officer, the spoiled favorite among the ladies, but nonetheless proficient in his duties; a man all believed to be standing at the threshold of a stellar career. His eldest brother, destined to become the major of the regiment, had long since taken over the business side of the family estate; the second brother had risen to be an official in the higher bureaucracy of the state; three sisters had married men with noble names; but Ernst Eberhard, the youngest pup in the litter, was the unapologetic favorite of the old father, who already imagined him as a future Field Marshall, the son most likely to advance the standing of the family name even higher in the glorious annals of Prussia history. But there was a fly in the ointment that would spoil all these hopes and aspirations.

The young officer was inclined to spend a lot of time in the home of his aunt who lived in the ancient Prussian coronation city of Königsberg[87] and was the widow of a German diplomat of the middle echelon. There he had come into contact with German men of learning who spoke of other matters besides military life or the local race track and who had adopted attitudes and expressed ideas that were highly likely to appear heretical to the mind of a noble cuirassier, especially in respect to politics.

Frederick William the Fourth[88] occupied the throne of Prussia at that time. His coronation as King of Prussia in 1840 had been greeted throughout Germany with great enthusiasm because he was seen as the harbinger of better times to come. In the seven years of his reign, however, this monarch had disappointed sorely. To be sure, he gave many fine speeches, both in respect to form and content, which had inspired his loyal subjects with all sorts of hopes and possibilities, but it all remained in the realm of empty talk. After a certain point, the previous optimism began to fade and was replaced by widespread grumbling.

Then on April 7, 1847, it came to pass that the "romantic on the throne" opened the Prussian State Assembly with full medieval pomp and circumstance, and, adopting his most striking romantic posture, held a speech whose essence was contained in the formulation, "that there was not a power on the face of the earth capable of compelling him to exchange the natural relationship between king and subject for a mundane, constitutional arrangement and that he would never surrender to the belief that a page of scribbled words could supplant the divinely ordained hierarchy of God above and country below, a new-fangled providence, as it were, to replace the venerable, time-honored relationships of the past." This speech aroused widespread dissatisfaction among all classes and levels of society, even among former loyal supporters, and since at this time free speech and expression did not automatically lead to a cell in the local citadel, expressions of discontent soon gained a wide currency.

The above might explain, but not excuse, how at an informal dinner where ample supplies of champagne had loosened tongues that a lieutenant from an ancient noble house came to characterize the above speech as "rubbish."[89] A Prussian officer cannot be permitted to entertain such a thought about his supreme commander much less express it, and a very unpleasant scene followed shortly in the officers' mess when three of his comrades, who had gotten wind of the unfortunate remark, confronted him with a challenge and demand for satisfaction. Thankfully, however, it did not actually reach the point of a duel.

His commanding officer, a man previously well disposed toward him, placed him under house arrest and summoned him to his office the following morning. He informed him that such an insult to the majesty of the sovereign actually warranted a court martial, but because of the long and distinguished record of service of his father and other family members, he would forego this in lieu of an immediate discharge, which was more of a remission than he deserved. Ernst Eberhard, Count of Scharfenegg, was thereby summarily dismissed from the military, which, in the final analysis, was for a Prussian officer schooled and trained to uphold his honor above all else, a punishment not much better than facing a firing squad.

Under these circumstances, his former comrades felt obliged to withdraw their demand for satisfaction, since his disgrace rendered him incapable of supplying such. This was perhaps not all that difficult for them to do since the challenged officer enjoyed the reputation as not only the best horseman in the regiment, but also as the best shot with a pistol. His father almost suffered a stroke when he heard the news. He ordered the portrait of his son burned, and created a scene with his pastor when he refused to expunge the name of his

"Street battle in Berlin, 1848." Author's collection.

son from the church records. He then directed his second-born son to disburse 2,000 *Thaler* to the errant brother under the condition that he leave the country immediately never to return.

Henceforth, Ernst Eberhard's name could never be mentioned in the presence of the father. His brother, the *Assessor,* carried out his task fully in the spirit of his father's wishes, but Ernst Eberhard threw the money on the floor in disgust and ordered his brother to leave the apartment at once where he had sequestered himself in sullen isolation to brood over his precipitous fall from grace since the unfortunate incident at the dinner table.

Soon thereafter he antagonized the family further by moving to Berlin where he attempted to earn his bread by menial labor, something almost inconceivable for a titled ex-lieutenant of the Prussian military. But worse was to come. On March 18[th,] the following year, when it seemed as if a new day was about to dawn for Germany,[90] he fought alongside Polish refugees, cobblers, and tailors on the barricades of Berlin. All this notwithstanding, no one felt more keenly the humiliation of his king, who had been compelled to bow before the elemental eruption of discontent and anger on the part of his subjects, than this disgraced ex-lieutenant.

But then, to the further chagrin of his relatives, he actually joined up with the wicked democrats for a spell, fighting alongside Mierolawski[91] the following year in the Palatinate. After Mierolawski's defeat and surrender, he found himself banished to Switzerland along with thousands of his comrades without any means to exist and incapable (and also unwilling) to take up any sort of new bourgeois existence.

Like so many refugees from Germany at the time, he soon entered French military service and by the fall of 1849 found himself in Algiers where he witnessed the destruction of the brave Marabout defenders at Zou-Zian.[92] Thereafter, and once again an officer, he took part in the campaign against the Kabyles.[93] All the while, during his free time, he occupied himself in hunting, which soon developed into a passion. After peace had prevailed for an extended period, he applied for a transfer in order to participate in the Crimean War,[94] and after Sebastopol had fallen, he served under the French flag in the China campaign.[95] In all these actions he distinguished himself through his reckless contempt for death in the face of danger; but he emerged throughout untouched by the bullets that flew all around him. Finally, with the rank of major, he returned to France.

In Paris, he received the news that one of his close relatives in Germany had remembered him. It was his aunt in Königsberg, who had died shortly before. In her last will and testament, she decreed that the earnings from her not insignificant estate should go to her nephew, who had been so unceremoniously disgraced and dismissed, for the span of his lifetime, but, thereafter, the principal should be used for charitable purposes. Ernst Eberhard, however, wanted not a single *Thaler* from the country where he had been disgraced, and so renounced this inheritance in favor of the poor orphans for whom the bulk of the inheritance was to fall after his death, and returned to Algeria.

In the ruins of an old Roman city, not far from El Goela,[96] it came to pass that this man who had sunk so low in the eyes of the world and his fellow humans found a real friend and true comrade until the end. Eginhard von Seiffert's coat of arms was still brand new. His grandfather had been the owner of a soap, hair oil, and pomade company and in this well-smelling profession, had become a rich man and was honored with the title *Kommerzienrat*.[97] His oldest son subsequently expanded the business and enlarged the family fortune to the point he could afford to purchase an estate that included a villa with forest and meadows. He also acquired two sons-in-law from the nobility and even obtained an inheritable title for himself in recognition of his services (in both meanings of this word).

The only son of the somewhat vain first Baron von Seiffert was groomed for even greater renown as a future statesman and was assigned an appropriate course of study to this end. For his part, he would have much preferred to be a forester since he enjoyed nothing more than wandering around through the green woods of the estate with a shotgun slung over his shoulder during his free time. Still, as an obedient son, he submitted to the program set out for him and managed, barely, by the skin of his teeth, to get through the *Gymnasium* and obtain admission to the university. But once there, he relished the free and unfettered life he encountered, and passed the first two (and only) semesters carefree and happy, as behooved a newly titled and well-heeled *Coleurstudent*.[98]

Then his father died unexpectedly and hardly had his body been committed to the grave when it came to light that a couple of disastrous speculations combined with the excesses of the two blue-blooded sons-in-law had decimated the family fortune. After the estate, the country house, and the warehouse had all been liquidated to pay off creditors, Eberhard only had enough left over to cover his student debts and to spend eight dissolute weeks in Paris living life to the hilt.

After his resources were completely exhausted, he came face to face with the abyss and had ample opportunity for thoroughly studying all its horrors. In short order, his pocket watch, fancy wardrobe, and other valuables made their way to the pawn shop and with what he obtained therefrom was able to survive for a couple of months more in cheap flop houses. As the New Year approached, he exchanged his last possession of any worth, a nice warm fur coat, at the *mont-de-piété*[99] for a loan, and with this, the realization finally struck home that the care-free life of *Seine-Babel*[100] was not for someone with empty pockets and a rumbling stomach.

Homeless, chilled to the bone, and hungry, he wandered one clear, bitter cold night onto the *pont de invalids*,[101] with the intention of putting an end to his suffering by drowning himself. As fate would have it, however, the Seine was practically frozen over, which frustrated his intent. The bridge was even colder than the street, and though half-frozen, he continued his wanderings and finally ended up in a cheap wine bar where he hoped to warm himself a bit.

But at the very moment when the bartender sought to have him thrown out, a recruiter stepped forward and invited the young man to join him in a glass of *Glühwein*.[102] He then proceeded to tell him how nice life in the *grande armée* was; Eginhard shook his hand in agreement; accepted a small advance with which he used to drink himself into a stupor, and, soon thereafter, found himself on the way to Algiers as a *Chasseur d'Afrique*.[103]

Six months later Count Scharfenegg, now a major, found him while on a hunting expedition in the desert, languishing deathly ill in a filthy, vermin-infested corridor that once had been the dining hall of a Roman villa, but now served as a field hospital for the French forces in the area. He lay in a delirium caused by high fever, loudly ranting alternatively in French and German, and occasionally in his native Low Saxon. "Inflammation of the brain; in twenty-four hours, he is done for," opined the rather poorly trained medic assigned to the ward. Scharfenegg, who had acquired much practical medical experience during his many campaigns, did not accept the validity of the diagnosis and asked permission to take his countryman under his care, which was quickly granted.

With the help of cold compresses, it was easy enough to bring down the fever, but the sick man was so weakened in body and spirit by his ordeal that it required months of constant attention to restore him to full health. From that point on, the two men, who had both seen their lives dramatically altered by precipitous changes in fate, remained inseparable companions. They shared a tent, took their meals together, hunted together, and, in their off time, conducted archeological investigations among the old Roman and Moorish ruins that littered the landscape of North Africa in abundance. The count's modest personal savings, which he had only managed to accumulate on the salary of a major due to his own thrifty habits, was always available to his young friend, who repaid the sacrifices of the older one with genuine faithfulness and dedication.

By 1862 peace reigned in Africa and the two decided to join the expedition to Mexico[104] in order to experience another part of the world. In July of 1863 under Forey[105] they marched with the French expeditionary force into Mexico City, this ancient, memory-laden imperial capitol of the former Aztec empire. Soon thereafter, however, after the noble but ill-fated Maximilian was hailed as new emperor by an assembly of notables, the two left the service. It had become clear to Scharfenegg that the French occupation could only be sustained by brutal repression of the Mexican people, a people who yearned for freedom and who were striving for an independent national identity; he wanted no part of it.

For his part, Seiffert had no firm opinions separate from his companion, and so went along with the decision. The two then travelled for a while across the country, taking time out to examine Aztec temples and other antiquities. During a hunting diversion to the Cayman Islands, however, the count fell seriously ill. His companion was now able to pay him back in full for his former generosity, and he did so with alacrity.

From this point on, Seiffert, who had been the protégé, took the lead in all matters, because it soon became clear that the continual hardship and deprivations the count had endured as a military man had seriously undermined his health, especially in regard to his heart, which now caused him constant pain. After he was halfway restored, the two travelled to Monterrey where a German doctor, a refugee from Texas, diagnosed Scharfenegg's ailment as advanced heart disease and recommended that he move to a colder climate.

Scharfenegg, who held out little hope of recovery, yielded to Seiffert's insistence that they leave Mexico. His condition, as well as an outbreak of yellow fever that was as raging in all coastal cities at the time, precluded travel by sea, so they decided to risk an overland journey. At the time, the situation was very unsettled in Northern Mexico and Southern Texas alike, because Juarez[106] and his followers had fled there to escape the French.

Accompanied by a Mexican guide and two pack mules, which allowed them to camp off the beaten path, they managed to make it into Texas by horseback, and eventually to the small town of New London[107] on the Colorado River somewhat west of the wooded area where they now found themselves. Here an official, who suspected them of being spies, detained them. When they finally disabused him of his suspicions by presenting their papers, the Count's health took a turn for the worse and he lay at the point of death in miserable quarters for several weeks.

Then he improved somewhat, but his condition precluded a continuation of the trip, and their monetary resources were seriously depleted by the exorbitant prices they had to spend for bare necessities in Texas. But he yearned to be back in nature and no longer confined to his bed, and upon the suggestion of Seiffert, who had scouted the area thoroughly during several hunting outings, they moved into the abandoned log cabin Seiffert had discovered in the forest and, after some effort, managed to make it more or less habitable.

With Scharfenegg, however, things quickly took a downhill slide, and soon he could not even manage to hold a gun in his hands and languished day and night in his hammock where he could breathe more freely than in the house. In October, the Mexican, Mozo Jesus Cortez, upon whose true and loyal service they had relied, disappeared during a mild, moonlit night along with the horses and pack mules that had been hobbled and allowed to graze on a nearby forest meadow.

It apparently had not set well with him that he had been asked to do menial labor such as clearing away the underbrush in the vicinity of the cabin. Scharfenegg, normally easily aroused, greeted the news passively with the remark: "I will have no further use for the animals in any case." From that point on, Seiffert attended his friend alone, taking care of all his needs. With his shotgun and fishing pole, he supplied them amply with wild game and fish and, when necessary, made the long trek back into the aforementioned village to obtain such necessities as were available there.

They were well aware that there was a German settlement nearby, but they avoided coming into contact with the inhabitants of the same because Scharfenegg harbored an almost irrational fear of meeting countrymen who might pass on word of his untimely demise to his relatives in Old Germany. During the long nights when he lay sleepless in his hammock due to the oppressive und unrelenting angina he was suffering, he related for the first time to his comrade his full life story and gave him a glimpse into his innermost soul.

THE RETURN TRIP—TWO CONSOLATION VISITS

While Seiffert was speaking with barely a pause, they covered about half the distance to the edge of the forest. Kuno listened intently to the story of the unfortunate man who had made such an impression upon him and who was able, in just a few brief words, to alter his earlier resolve and firm intention.

Hedwig's attentiveness, on the other hand, had been diverted by the thought that her parents and younger brother were waiting anxiously for some word of her as the long hours ticked by.

Just as they crested a high, sandy hill covered with a low scrub brush, which permitted a panoramic view of the surrounding landscape, they heard the far off and faint sound of a French horn to the east, which could only be the personal instrument of the cabinetmaker Frohmann; the first indication that friends and good neighbors were in the vicinity and looking for them. Trembling with excitement, she grasped the hand of her young companion, who was walking next to her. Kuno consulted briefly with the guide whereupon he fired off two shots from Seiffert's carbine, a breechloader, with a minute's pause in between, and then two shots in rapid succession from his own shotgun, the signal for "found."

Numerous horn blasts followed; the shots had indeed been heard. Seiffert prepared to take his leave, but it was if he could not bring himself to separate from them. Alternating between imploring them not to speak about that which he had told them and wishing them all the best, he finally tore himself loose and had just disappeared from view behind the crest of the hill when the sound of horses' hooves and loud voices in the distance became evident. Kuno fired off another shot in order to better mark the direction, and then the young man and girl stood next to one another in silence for a couple of minutes, until Kuno turned to Hedwig and said: "Hedwig, I am going to make myself available for military service and not hide out in the brush."

"Thank God," whispered Hedwig with a smile on her lips which were flushed from excitement. Leading the group, Hedwig's father was the first to break into the clearing. Hedwig wanted to rush forward to greet him, but her feet refused to budge. In a moment, the father was at her side and, speechless, held the child in his arms whom only shortly before he had come to fear was lost forever.

In the meantime, the others arrived and quickly dismounted to offer their greetings. *Long Mike* had to blink his eyes rapidly and clear his throat a couple of times to deal with the touching scene unfolding before them. He finally gave vent to his feelings with a loud Texas battle yell, the same one that had struck fear into the hearts of many a Yankee on countless battlefields across the South. Thereupon, a powerful and spontaneous *hurrah* erupted from the throats of the old-timers and youngsters alike, who now had been searching for Hedwig for eighteen straight hours, and then everybody, at Mike's suggestion, fired off their muskets, shotguns, and revolvers in a joyful salvo despite the rarity and expense of powder and lead in anno 1864 Texas.

Only one failed to discharge his weapon, namely the tailor Hansjakob Muerly, but he went shooting from the saddle himself into the soft sand below. Despite his own humpback and lack of equestrian skills, the good master of the needle had insisted on taking part in the search for Lüttenhof's "*Maidli*,"[108] but only managed to get on and off his mount with difficulty, and when the salvo was fired his stubborn yellow *jenny*[109] had not yet allowed him to dismount. At the report of the guns and the billowing of the smoke, however, she panicked and bucked him off straightway, head over heels, and attempted to flee, but was quickly caught by members of the party. They then unceremoniously reinserted into his saddle the master tailor, who, remarkably, had suffered not a whit from the unfortunate incident. And all this took place, it seemed, before the last echo from the salvo had fallen silent.

The father, who in the meantime had regained his composure, wanted to take his protégé Kuno into his arms in an embrace of gratitude and joy, but Kuno pulled away from his gesture, muttering something indistinct beneath his breath as he did so. But he could not prevent the others from shaking his hand so vigorously that his own hand began to hurt. "Well done! said his father, beaming with pride. One of the men had in the meantime led Hedwig's Falada by the bridle up to the couple. Hedwig quickly mounted and the party commenced the ride back to the settlement. Two young men from among them spurred their horses ahead to bring the good news back to the mother as fast as possible.

In response to the many questions put to them during the trip back home, Kuno only replied in as brief a way as possible that he had found her asleep at daybreak in a dilapidated cabin many miles further to the northwest. Kuno, who in the meantime had ridden double behind Long Mike, found his own Polly at the spring where he had left her and was greeted by friendly neighs. The party then continued on their way at a quick trot. At the edge of the forest a second salvo announced to the settlement that Hedwig had been found, alive and unharmed. Then the party split up, each returning to his own home after Lüttenhoff had thanked them profusely for his help.

On the ride back, Kuno and Hedwig heard the story about how the group under Michel Schmid's leadership, which Lüttenhoff had also joined up with, had searched the region between the settlement and the creek for a good fifteen miles upstream until midnight. Then they followed the edge of the forest until they came to the large forested stream that crisscrossed the county from the northwest to the southeast without encountering any sign.

Finally, one member of the party who was in the know took a detour toward an almost impenetrable thorn thicket and at its edge gave a cry that was an imitation of the gray horned owl. The same owl call came as a reply and in a few minutes a tall, emaciated man emerged from the thicket, cautiously and suspiciously. It was Herwitch, the fugitive who sought refuge here when he felt threatened by the home guard, which wanted very much to catch him and put him in a Confederate uniform.

He slept on a moss bed in a crude structure, similar to a hog shed, but erected for the purpose of trapping wild turkeys. It was a square structure of tree logs with a roof of branches and dried moss. When he recognized his good friend, he shared with him that both he and his fellow fugitive Müller had heard the neighing of a horse around midnight. They had built a fire and wiled away the time in a game of sixty-six about halfway between the turkey stall where Herwitch stayed and Müller's own forest palace. With this added intelligence, the search was extended in the direction indicated and, after a little bit, the tracks of a horse were discovered, and a little thereafter, Hedwig's mare.

The animal, which had been raised on a plantation on the other side of Palmetto Creek, had most likely headed instinctively in that direction, but an iron stirrup on the saddle had gotten stuck in a tree limb in a way that trapped the animal. Nobody said so out loud but when the horse was found everyone suspected the worst and expected to find Hedwig close-by, either dead or seriously injured. Whispering silently or not speaking at all, the men formed a long line as the day began to break and moved to the northwest searching every square foot long the way.

It is difficult enough being a member of a search party that expects to find something terrible. But it is even harder and crueler when one is forced to wait and remain confined to one place, all the while expecting to hear what one dreads the most. After a sleepless and tortured night in which the flames of hope weakened with each tick of the pendulum of the old cuckoo clock until finally they were but a dull glow, the morning finally arrived which would bring the anxious mother certainty, be it good or bad.

Hedwig's mother prepared breakfast mechanically while Phillip and Albert saw to the chores at the cow pen. She was not able to swallow a bite, and probably for the first time since she had assumed the management of the household, her trembling hands caused her to spill the canister of brown liquid on her tablecloth, which they termed coffee simply for appearances' sake. Albert only took a couple of bites himself, and for the first and last time neglected to fill his bowl with seconds from his favorite dish, which was a concoction of cottage cheese, cream, and cinnamon with syrup as a sweetener.

Then guests began arriving: first, Winzig and his wife. Since he was not able to take part in the search for his neighbor's daughter, Winzig wanted at least to comfort the mother, for whom he had a very high regard, but due to the fact that he was not very adept in such matters he brought along his wife Minna, who had arranged for her small children to stay with the nearby grandparents. When Frau Lüttenhoff came out to the gate with unsteady steps to greet her visitors, it was obvious from the shocked expression that she feared the worst; that they were the harbingers of terrible news: "Is this a condolence visit such as one receives upon the death of a loved one?" her eyes seemed to ask.

Noticing this, Winzig's whole idea of being cheerful and comforting quickly faded and, as is often the case in such situations, he began muttering incoherently.

"German settlers going for a visit." Friedrich Richard Petri papers, [10669],
The Dolph Briscoe Center for American History, The University of Texas at Austin.

Finally (and wisely), he yielded the task to his wife, who had a much more down-to-earth and basic understanding of how to handle the situation. After a few well-placed and tactful words of hope, spoken from the heart, she began to divert the conversation to everyday matters of household management and then whisked Frau Lüttenhoff off to the kitchen and pantry, ostensibly to seek her advice. She also had the presence of mind not to relieve her of all her household responsibilities. In the meantime, Winzig smoked one pipeful after another in Lüttenhoff's study and became absorbed in a complicated trigonometry problem as a means to divert his own concerns.

Grossenberg showed up a little later. His sister Albertine, despite all exhortations, had adamantly refused to come along since she could not tolerate emotional situations. The man who normally was never at a loss for words searched in vain for something cheerful to say, and soon excused himself with the claim that official matters required his presence at the county seat several miles away.

About eleven o'clock in the morning, to the accompaniment of much hollering and whip popping, a hack pulled by a big black horse and a small white jenny arrived at the gate. Mismatched as they were, the animals shared one thing in common: namely, one could count all their ribs and, indeed, inspect their whole skeletal structure. It required in consequence of their emaciated condition continuous exhortations both by tongue and whip to keep them moving, even at a slow gait.

The vehicle was a two-seater and the masterwork of the wagon maker Christian Hilfreich of Collinsville and constructed after a pattern he often used. The wooden parts, accordingly, had once been lacquered a shiny black, but only small patches of this remained. There could be little doubt as to who sat in the vehicle since strangers were a rare occurrence in this remote settlement. Its inhabitants, as well as those in the surrounding area, usually travelled by ox cart, or even sled; occasionally, in a light field wagon pulled by a team of horses. There were only three *classy* conveyances in the vicinity: Colonel Phillip's Parisian Landau,[110] Sartorious' ambulance, and the two-seater of the salesman Bertrand. "That must be Bertrand!" cried out Albert to his mother, who was in the act of filling up the large firewood box in the kitchen. A tortured look spread over her relaxed face as she took off her apron and prepared to go out and greet her guest.

In the meantime, Herr Bertrand had stepped down and tied his horses, but with his wife it was not so simple a maneuver because she was the one lady in Possum Creek who made a pretense of being outfitted according to the latest Parisian fashion. The *chignon*[111] hair-do she sported as a first necessity did not cause her any problems, but the crinoline dress[112] she wore—one suspected it had been fashioned out of light barrel hoops—was another matter, for it billowed out in a way that frustrated her attempt to climb over the rather high sides of the coach and to reach the stool placed at the foot of the coach by her husband. Finally, she succeeded through an opportune hop, but would have fallen flat on her face had not Frau Lüttenhoff intervened in a timely fashion to assist her. Both were attired in festive black and let loose with such a stream of words that Frau Anna had no need to say anything as she showed them into her house.

※

Translator's Note

At this point the author flashes forward many years, presumably to 1908 when Trenckmann serialized his novel. Trenckmann places himself in his study in the process of typing the manuscript and is interrupted by his daughter, who eagerly reads each page as it emerges from the typewriter and who has become impatiently curious about the fate of Hedwig. This technique of shifting from a third-person to a first-person narrative first came into vogue in the nineteenth century among French novelists. Trenckmann studied the French language while a student at Texas A&M and apparently was well-read in contemporary French literature and, presumably, adopted the technique from them. Despite his knowledge and appreciation of the French language and literature, Trenckmann evinces a definite anti-French bias in his story. In this section, he introduces a French couple, the Bertrands, who have settled among the **Lateiner** *at Possum Creek and, as he clearly states, they are destined to become the villains of the story, which becomes clear only in book two. The Bertrands are a pure invention on the part of the author; there is no indication in the records that a prototype for such a couple existed in the historical Millheim. The couple embodies all the superficial flightiness and shallowness which German preju-dices at the time associated with the French. This was all conditioned, of course, by the stunning military victory of Prussia over France in 1871, which paved the way for German unification under Prussian leadership. This turn of events is actually an important backdrop to this story on several scores: Prussian victory swelled the hearts of many Germans with pride, both at home and abroad, while reinforcing certain prejudices concerning the French; it also represented in a certain sense the death of the democratic and republican ideals that had inspired many educated Germans to emigrate to the Texas before and after the failed revolutions of 1848. In the general enthusiasm and national pride that followed Prussia's military successes, the old idealism was largely swept aside. Prussia represented the old aristocratic order, pure and undiluted, and it was very difficult to both admire Prussia and be critical her at the same time. The evolution of Forty-Eighters' ideals as they confront the realities of Texas (slavery, secession) and then respond to the changing political circumstances in Europe (German unification under Prussia hegemony) becomes one of the driving motifs of the book, with* *different characters embodying different responses. The introduction of the Bertrands into the story becomes a convenient platform on the part of Trenckmann for joining these two threads of the story in an immediate way. We also sense an unmistakable sympathy for military experience as an accelerator of personal development and an admiration for those who have experienced the intense camaraderie of battle.*

"But Papa, tell us first about Hedwig's return and reunion before you introduce us to the Bertrands!"—With these words my oldest daughter interpellates[113] me. Among many other admirable traits, she exhibits an unbounded thirst for knowledge and loves to browse my library. In this respect, she is a chip off the old block. This trait, plus the fact she is a clever baker and occasional assistant during the posting of bills, allows her certain privileges; for example, the right to examine each page of the *Lateiner* as soon as it emerges from the typewriter. Many of my readers will concur in her assessment that the introduction of several of the characters in the preceding chapter has been rather long-winded, but I cannot accede to her request.

The Bertrands occupy a rather central place in this story. Every person knowledgeable about literature recognizes that an author always takes pains to describe the arch-villain of his story. . . . The old *Lateiner* of Possum Creek and their children, as well as those non-intellectual types who also made their home there, were, in spite of many eccentricities and weaknesses, across the board uniformly upstanding and decent people at core. The one exception was this married couple. They stood out from the rest by the extreme measure to which that evil spirit which to a small degree exists in us all possessed them. It is important, therefore, that we deal with them in a thorough manner, and not push them unceremoniously to the side in order to hasten Hedwig's return to her mothers' arms.

Incidentally, in respect to official and civic status, Bertrand occupied a special niche in Possum Creek and the immediate surrounding countryside. He was not only our postmaster and storekeeper, but he was also the only one in the community who had the right to be addressed by a bona fide military title, namely *Colonel*. The postmaster position was an exceedingly important in a place where the postal rider only arrived once every fortnight. The store, though, left much to be desired, with a small inventory to begin with that gradually dwindled down during the war years to a mere three stoneware crocks, a large supply of sewing needles, and one barrel of whiskey, which never seemed run dry while tasting ever more suspiciously of pepper and tobacco. To be sure, Mr. Phillips, who owned the nearby Acadia Plantation, was also often addressed as *Colonel*; a habit that was customary at the time for most rich or otherwise well-regarded Southerners who had attained their fiftieth year and who had no other claim to a title. Bertrand, however, possessed an official letter that confirmed he had been designated *Colonel of the Home Guard*, which in common parlance was usually referred to disparagingly as the *featherbed brigade*.

According to local gossip, he had his last keg of Geneva brandy to thank for the position, which had been completely emptied on the occasion of his being chosen. The fact of the matter was that Bertrand had been *Americanized* much faster than his cohorts and that he come to realize that certain goals and ends

"Woman on horse." Friedrich Richard Petri papers, [detail from 11950], The Dolph Briscoe Center for American History, The University of Texas at Austin.

could be achieved much quicker and more efficaciously by means of the free and generous dispensing of brandy and other spirits. But there you had it, he was now a real *colonel*, and a mere week after his being so designated, in the name of local defense, rode out at the head of his regiment, a good eighty in number, all worthy heads of household, for the purpose of practicing the drills necessary to achieve military competency. The brave defenders marched beyond Palmetto Creek and ventured a full ten miles further as far as Camp Hardeman.[114] The entire contingent, composed of men from both Possum Creek and Collinsville, packed all the provisions needed for the excursion in the numerous wagons that accompanied them. They also packed their feather mattresses and wool blankets, each according to his own, since it was already late into the fall. For their part, the Possum Creek denizens did not forget their long pipes either.

A few accompanied the trip without any sort of firearm. The wagon maker Helferich, for instance, presented a long liverwurst sausage in place of a weapon during the first dress formation where all lined up in rows and columns to present arms. The wagon maker offered the explanation that it was the only thing in his house that bore any resemblance to a deadly weapon. Less than amused at this prank that smacked of insubordination, our stern colonel gave orders to have the perpetrator thrown in chains,[115] but when no one stepped forward to carry out his order, he had to content himself with confiscating the offending sausage. The camp was set to last a full three weeks, and in respect to these three weeks, one continued to hear tall tales and humorous anecdotes from the inhabitants of Possum Creek for a full twenty to thirty years thereafter.

Just about everyone had brought along an ample supply of provisions: slabs of bacon and hunks of smoked meat, hams and sausages, clay crocks full of butter, corn meal, and sweet potatoes, and all the necessary pots, pans, and dishes to properly prepare these things. Here and there one provided a haunch of venison to be grilled on a skewer or a brace of tasty prairie chickens, which existed in such abundance that one could practically knock them dead with his hat toward sundown in the blackjack[116] groves along the edge of the camp. And for all his shortcomings, Bertrand certainly understood how to prepare a sumptuous fricassee therefrom.

For his part, Bertrand had attempted to be a strict disciplinarian in the beginning but, upon realizing the futility of such a course, had quickly adjusted his own attitude and adopted a more lenient tone. Drills were conducted every morning and afternoon. The men formed up somewhat clumsily into squads of four, each with a former Prussian soldier as drill instructor, with all commands issued, to no one's surprise, according to the dictates of the Prussian drill book.

Over the course of the stay, however, the time spent in drill grew ever shorter. In the evenings, after everyone had eaten, the men sat around the campfires playing tarot,[117] or solitaire, or giving speeches, or playing all sorts of practical jokes on one another. Frohmann would take out his instrument and strike up a tune, now happy, now sad, while the poultry farmer from Krähwinkel[118] and the cabinetmaker Pannewitz took turns playing their harmonicas—playing in unison was out of the question, since the first preferred up-tempo selections that Pannewitz could not follow—brisk polkas, Rhenish dance tunes, galops,[119] and the like.

Many of the assembled gentlemen could not resist the urge to dance, especially if the canteen being passed around was not yet empty. The tailor Müry maintained to the end of his days that these three weeks had been the happiest and most carefree of his life, and we believed him, because we knew that the master tailor's good wife ran a very strict household and quickly saw to it that her wayward spouse, who had grown to be quite lax in his habits during his weeks in camp, was properly retrained upon returning so as to once again toe the line in respect to spousal obedience and household order.

One beautiful, clear night toward the end of the three weeks a strong norther blew in upsetting most of the tents in camp, and since it was quickly followed by a cold rain, many in the camp came down with nasty colds in spite of their feather beds and woolen blankets. This *malheur* plus the fact that most of the rations were exhausted and Christmas was not that far off were seen as a sign from above that it was time to stop playing soldier and return home. Bertrand, who had not lost a single man during the campout—an extraordinary accomplishment among Southern colonels of the period—quickly led his men across the Palmetto and dismissed them on the left bank of the same. Since the supply wagons were now considerably lighter, all those who were coughing and wheezing and suffering runny noses, or who otherwise had not run afoul of their superiors, were allowed to ride in the wagons, which was considerably less strenuous than the march up had been.

Concerning Bertrand's birthplace and ancestry, little in the way of hard facts was known. He often referred to himself as the son of an emigrant family of noble French lineage that stood in direct line to the famous medieval troubadour Bertran du Born.[120] He also maintained that the famous Napoleonic officer, Henri Gatien du Bertrand,[121] descended from an impoverished branch of the same house. He hinted that he had occupied a rather high administrative position *over there*, but that his firm intention to emigrate had finally moved him to resign. Sartorius, who had a fine nose for such things, maintained that certain habits and mannerisms suggested strongly that he had once been, in reality, a court stenographer. He and his wife Charlotte had arrived at Possum Creek with numerous large trunks on an ox wagon and had inquired straightaway if any plantations were for sale in the vicinity. Land speculators were soon enough alert to the newly arrived *greenhorn*, but beat a hasty retreat once that discovered he was *de facto* penniless; also, the good farmer who quartered the new arrivals had a rude surprise and found himself holding the bag for the expense of feeding them.

But mother luck soon smiled upon him. He managed to parcel off and sell on commission two whole leagues of land belonging to a Mr. Richardson in New Orleans to various farmers and recent immigrants in the vicinity. The titles to the tracts of land were, in Grossenberg's considered opinion, a little more than suspect, but Bertrand, who was a born salesman, managed to pull off the sales. The commissions, no doubt, were very substantial. Soon thereafter he purchased property at the west end of the settlement and opened a store to the great delight of the locals who previous to this had been forced to travel fifteen miles to Collinsville in order to procure basic necessities. Over time, however, his inventory shrank noticeably, and many locals suspected this was because he paid his suppliers with IOUs rather than cash.

Mrs. Bertrand's life story was even more mysterious than that of her *cher Achille*. She was said to have confided to an intimate friend that she was the illegitimate daughter of a Prussian prince and a French opera singer. But in any case, she was well versed about court life, knowledgeable about the lives of many officers, and was quite talented musically. She played the piano and could sing many love songs (and even better roundelays[122]) to the accompaniment of a mandolin. Moreover, she could perform the Tarantella[123] as well as several Spanish and gypsy dances with a refined elegance that suggested many years of practice.

Soon after her arrival in the community she had demonstrated her dancing abilities at a birthday party in honor of the master of the house at the home of Sartorius. After the birthday meal had been cleared, the mood of the celebrants had become noticeably more animated, whereupon she took the opportunity to perform a lively dance to the obvious delight of the gentlemen, who applauded energetically, and to the noticeable consternation of the ladies, who rumpled their noses in disapproval. As she concluded the dance, entirely exhausted by the effort, Grossenberg leaned over to his neighbor and whispered somewhat derisively, "It would have been a true pleasure to have seen her dance thirty years ago, but even today she would create a furor in the *Brockenszene* in *Faust*."[124] The snide remark eventually reached the ears of Frau Bertrand, which gave rise to a never-ending feud between the Bertrands and the less-than-charitable Grossenberg.

Owing to their refined manners and social skills, the *Lateiner* welcomed the two with open arms into the community, especially in the beginning. Over time, however, an accumulation of ill will caused Monsieur and Madame Bertrand to gradually fall from favor among the locals. The rumor began to spread that the thoroughly refined married couple behaved quite differently toward one another at home than in public where they were in the habit of addressing one another with such affectations as *"chere Charlotte,"* or *"mon ange,"* or *"mon cher Achille."* Indeed, within the sanctity of their own four walls, shocking scenes of domestic violence apparently played out on a regular basis such that Possum Creek had never experienced before; not even among the Moravians,[125] a man and wife, tenant farmers and neighbors to the Bertrands, a couple so poor that they often took turns pulling the wooden plow to till their field. Bertrand's face often showed the unmistakable signs of fingernail scratches and the rumor spread that the large supply of kitchen stoneware which he had procured for the store and housed in an ox shed had rapidly diminished due to the fact that she was in the regular habit of practicing her skill at tossing plates and bowls with her husband as the target. The fifteen-year-old daughter of an impoverished widow, who had taken a position as a household maid for Madame Bertrand, ran away back to her mother after only a few weeks of service. The poor child was full of horror stories: they had had not given her enough to eat; she had been beaten with the broom; and finally, at risk of being attacked herself, had taken to her heels in the midst of a particularly violent episode, namely, Herr Bertrand set upon his wife with a large bullwhip in consequence of a disagreement whereupon the wife pulled a dagger and chased him from the house. *Long Mike* had once witnessed a scene where Madame Bertrand, who was both taller and stronger than her husband, had chased her spouse from the house into the store where he barred the door behind him to escape her wrath. In consequence, he christened her the *hellcat*, which seemed to fit her better than any German term.

Despite all this, however, Bertrand came to exert a marked influence in the community. In addition to being a storekeeper and postmaster, he was also someone who possessed an unusual gift of gab and ability to persuade—and this facility in someone who otherwise was rather nondescript. Having fallen out of favor with the *Lateiner*, he took pains to ingratiate himself among the non-*Lateiner*—the day-workers, carpenters, and the like—and he did this by railing against the supposed haughtiness of the educated. Only Winzig continued to stand up for Bertrand for a while. And this because at the beginning of the war, Bertrand presented himself like a dedicated Unionist, and used every opportunity to hold fiery, nay, poisonous speeches against the corrupt slave drivers and misguided rebels and their German stooges—and by this he meant Grossenberg and Sartorius. Yes, on occasion he even spoke of *armed resistance*, but when he did so, it was always on the side and in confidence. Such talk, however, led Winzig to view Bertrand as an ally and, consequently, to dismiss the nasty stories concerning him and his wife as uncharitable gossip. But when Bertrand suddenly did an about face and began to curry favor among the Confederate power elite by passing himself off as an ardent secessionist with an eye toward obtaining an official appointment, Winzig was through with him as well. Indeed, Bertrand's turncoat opportunism was so disgusting to him that upon hearing Albert's announcement that someone was approaching the Lüttenhoff house, which shook him from his reveries, and upon realizing who the new arrivals were, he beat a hasty retreat through a side door across the dogtrot and out into the backyard in order to avoid having to exchange pleasantries with the couple.

To complete the picture of the Bertrand and his spouse we need to mention that he was short with black-hair and black eyes. With the exception that she was a full head taller, the same description applied to his wife. Bertrand was a good fifty years of age, and ample make-up on the cheeks of his wife could not hide the fact that she was not much younger. The two also had distinguished themselves by the fact that they had the habit of timing their visits to neighbors in such a way as to insure they would receive an invitation for a meal. Madame Charlotte thought that cooking was beneath the dignity of a cultivated lady and it was said that she often passed the whole day sitting in her rocking chair reading stories by Paul de Kock[126] and Eugene Sue[127] while never lifting a finger toward the household chores. Her husband, on the other hand, definitely had a talent for the culinary arts, but he had little interest in practicing it at home.

The Bertrand visit had barely lasted ten minutes before Frau Winzig urgently sought out her husband, who was standing at the garden fence lost in thought, and informed him that he absolutely needed to try to come back in and somehow hasten the departure of the Bertrands. This was because Madame Bertrand, who was dominating the conversation, had begun, after the obligatory condolences, to relate stories about terrible things that were happening to young girls in Berlin and, despite all efforts on the part of Frau Winzig to divert her, had persisted in pursuing this inappropriate theme. Frau Winzig could clearly see by her nervous reaction that the woman of the household would not be able to withstand her flood of words for very long before she suffered a breakdown. Only Winzig could help in this matter; he was quickly summoned and more than willing to take up the *fight against the dragon*. With long strides he marched back into the house and, after a short and courteous greeting, proceeded to inform the Bertrands in Latin—it was not that long ago that he had composed learned disputations in the language of Cicero—that Frau Lüttenhoff's troubled state of mind absolutely required the avoidance of excitable speeches and required, furthermore, a shortening of their visit. Winzig noticed right away, and Sartorius confirmed his suspicions, that Bertrand understood not a word of what had been said to him since his Latin consisted of only a few set quotes that he had memorized. Winzig then attempted to restate his speech in French. French, of course, enjoys the reputation of being a language wherein it is possible to phrase unpleasant matters in a way that is courteous and inoffensive, but Winzig's mastery of French from his *Gymnasium*[128] days did not extend to this degree of subtlety and refinement. The result was that what he said came across rather heavy-handed and blunt. Bertrand understood right away what Winzig had requested of him but threw it back in his face that he was an uncouth *lourdaud*.[129] Taking his wife by the arm, he said, "Come Charlotte, we do not have to put up with these insults!" and the two stormed out of the house without a word of farewell.

All breathed a sigh of relief once the two had left. The well-meaning Phillip, however, attempted as a gesture of courtesy to assist Madame Bertrand into her coach, but his awkward efforts only earned him the remark, "You clumsy jackass!" He returned to his wooden abode shaking his head, not having a clue as to what he had done wrong.

A few minutes later a couple of riders galloped up to the gate waving their hats excitedly, but before they even had had time to dismount, a second volley from the search party proclaimed the good news. Frau Lüttenhoff attempted to rush forward to greet the messengers, but her feet did not want to bear her weight, and she was forced to receive the good tidings seated on her couch. She regained her composure soon enough, though, and insisted that the messengers refresh themselves with food and drink. As soon as they had departed, she hurried into her kitchen in order to tidy up, but Frau Winzig would hear none of it, so she quickly retired to the privacy of her room in order to give thanks to her Creator.

In just a little while Albert's young eyes spotted father and sister topping the nearby hill at a trot. He wanted to run toward them but the mother bid him, "Stay with me!" and, with his aid and support, walked to the gate. Sobbing and laughing, Hedwig soon enough was in her mother's arms, which she did not want to leave for a long time. But she finally did in order to throw her arms around her father, and Lüttenhoff had to more carry than lead her into the house. But after a few more kisses and queries, Hedwig turned to her mother with the remark, "But now I have to go see if my sitting hen has hatched her new chicks yet; you have probably forgotten to check on her, and with these words rushed out to check the corn crib. At once all anxiety and worry vanished from the mother: she was sure now that her child had suffered no harm. Soon thereafter, Frau Minna stepped inside and announced that dinner was served.

"Jakob Kuechler on horseback." Friedrich Richard Petri papers, [03142],
The Dolph Briscoe Center for American History, The University of Texas at Austin.

But before she could be implored to stay, Winzig and his wife took their leave with the justification that they could not remain any longer because they needed to see after their children. They had not wanted to disturb the joyfully reunited in their hour of happiness.

KUNO PREPARES FOR WAR

Kuno was welcomed back home like a *triumphator*.[130] Old Ned declared pompously that he had known all along that his young *massa* would be the right one to rescue Hedwig from her peril. Sally fell into an endless stream of praise to her and Kuno's maker, while Pompey grinned from ear to ear and began turning a whole series of somersaults for joy. The youngster had never before received from his mother such a happy and fervent welcome. She kissed and caressed him and expressed her pride so openly that Kuno was not quite sure what to make of it since, heretofore, he had not been accustomed to such overt displays of affection; the sort of extra warmth that often falls to the benefit of the last born but had been withheld from him. Frau Sartorius's features, her small feet, and well-manicured hands betrayed her aristocratic origins.[131] She must have been quite an attractive woman at one time, but she had grown very thin, and her fine features displayed the unmistakable signs of physical suffering.

Due to his intellectual vigor, his breath of knowledge, and his sharp wit, Sartorius dominated his wife to the degree that his wishes and beliefs had become the unquestioned standard for her. We have already noted his opinions concerning the education of the youth. He believed strongly in complete freedom of choice, even for children, and also was keen on the fact that his children not be in any way overly spoiled or sissified. On most occasions Sartorius was uncommonly tender and considerate toward his wife, but whenever Frau Sartorius betrayed a tendency to pamper her two oldest sons, something she was accustomed to do from her own upbringing, her husband would invariably intervene, usually by ironic comments rather than overt criticism, but he nonetheless made his disapproval quite clear to his wife. He often declared that should they be blessed with a daughter, then the mother could raise her entirely according to her own conceptions, and the mother had hoped ardently that she would be blessed with a daughter.

When, alas, her third child, and also her last, turned out to be a boy, it was a bitter disappointment that took her years to overcome. She remained sick for a long time after his birth with the result that his care fell almost exclusively into the hands of old Sally, and she, who had her shortcomings to be sure, came to love the child as almost a demigod, waited on him hand and foot, and allowed him the freedom to do and behave as he pleased. The mother's health had improved markedly after a couple of years, but by then her son had become almost estranged from her and his behavior at times so willful and alarming that the poor woman, who was still weakened by the effects of her long illness, did not know where to begin, and continued to defer interest in his upbringing.

But for all of this her mother's love never ebbed, and when her son and husband had disappeared from the house the previous evening not to return the entire night, she had grown ever more anxious and her worries had been aggravated by the ceaseless lamentations of Sally. That her son had said good-bye with a kiss and a *fare-thee-well* was something she was quite unaccustomed to receiving when he took off on one of his extended hunting jaunts. As the sleepless hours ticked by, the realization struck her that he must be anticipating some sort of danger or extraordinary situation: perhaps he was contemplating suicide if it turned out that something dreadful had happened to the neighbor's daughter due to his foolishness; perhaps Lüttenhoff, whose views in respect to the Civil War were well-known and disapproved by her, had convinced him to flee the state to avoid conscription; the thoughts flew through her head like apparitions and caused her anxious nightmares once she finally dozed off even as the day began to break. Thus her joy was all the more heightened when father and son returned safely to hearth and home and she learned from her husband all that Kuno had risked and accomplished. Kuno was so completely and utterly exhausted by the physical exertions and emotional rollercoaster he had undergone that he could barely find his way to his bed after having a bite to eat. His mother helped him to undress and became concerned when he failed to wake up in the evening. Her husband reassured her in the meantime that this was nature's way of restoring what had been neglected and overdone, and that their son would wake from his deep sleep refreshed and renewed.

And so it was. Upon waking up at the first morning blast of the horn announcing breakfast, Kuno rubbed his eyes in astonishment and took a few moments to gather his wits. In his dreams, he had relived the adventures of the preceding night, often through distorted and sometimes frightful apparitions, but in every one he had felt the warmth of Hedwig's arms wrapped around his neck. When he finally came to his senses completely, he realized that Hedwig must now be safely in her own home, and as he began dressing himself, could not help but whistle a little congratulatory tune in the thought that this had come about due to his own pluck and determination. But his moment of self-satisfaction was cut short when he realized that he was faced with two serious tasks. He stopped whistling and went to straightaway to the breakfast table.

He took care of the first task with a simple request while chowing down on a stack of cornmeal battercakes topped with honey, which the old mammy had prepared especially for him. "Monday in a fortnight is enlistment day and I need a new pair of boots because my old ones are worn out."

At this, the surprised and delighted father, looked at his son and replied: "Certainly, my son; you can put in an order with our local bootmaker for what you need and I will take care of it. I am very happy that you are making preparations. I was afraid . . . well, everything is in order now."

"I am not happy about going off to war," replied Kuno, "and not only because the cause is hopeless, but also because secession is, in my opinion, an appalling mistake. But I have been called up and I intend to show up and do my duty."

The mother was not a little shocked by this revelation, which would be seen as heretical by the flinty-eyed supporters of secession in Possum Creek, and she explained to her son that slavery was a natural and necessary condition; that the South was fighting for its freedom; and that every good Southerner should be eager and proud to sacrifice his blood and goods for his country. When Kuno attempted to defend his position, his father intervened with a jovial aside and diverted the conversation to another topic.

Kuno prepared to leave after breakfast because the altered situation required that he appear before his teacher and tell him personally that he had changed his mind. Frau Sartorius in the meantime threw herself feverishly into outfitting her son for his departure to the field of action and to equip him in a manner that was appropriate to his social standing.[132]

Kuno set off on foot and just as he cleared the shallow creek with one bound from which the community took its name and landed under the large sycamore tree that marked the crossing he noticed someone approaching on foot with long strides from the opposite direction. He recognized right away that it was Herr Lüttenhoff and his first temptation was to hide himself in the thick bushes, but he said to himself, "It has to be done," and proceeded to walk in the direction of his teacher. His teacher greeted him very warmly and offered his thanks once more and explained that he had just been on his way to the Sartorius house to see for himself if Kuno had recovered from the effects of this exertions and had woken up as refreshed and renewed as Hedwig. Slowly and softly, Kuno replied:

"Herr Lüttenhoff, I I was just coming over to see you, to tell you in person that I intend to report to duty and that I cannot keep my word to you.

At this, Lüttenhoff regarded Kuno in stunned amazement, as if he had not heard correctly, and half turned his side to him. But then, he faced his student squarely, and, with a hard look in his eye, said:

"I give you your pledge back; I never heard it. It is probably better this way and will doubtless please your father. For your parent's sake, I earnestly hope that you return safely from the war." He spoke these words slowly and without emphasis as if he had strained to utter them. Kuno blanched upon hearing his teacher switch to the formal *Sie*, since he had always addressed him with *du* before.[133] From the expression on his face and from the icy tone of strained courteousness to his words, he felt the full impact of his disapproval more forcibly than any spoken reproach could have brought about. He could not answer, said simply *adieu*, and turned to make his way back. For a second it seemed as if Lüttenhoff wanted to call him back, but checked himself, did an about face, and retraced his steps back home, heavy of heart and weary of bearing.

As soon as Kuno arrived back home, he mounted one of his father's workhorses in order to ride over to the shoemaker Wohlfahrt for the purpose of having his feet measured for a new pair of war boots. The die was now cast and all bridges burned. There was no turning back.

The weather had changed during the night. A damp and perceptively cooler southeast wind had blown in bringing with it a gray, overcast sky to replace the clear and sunny weather they had briefly enjoyed. It began to rain and the wind drove the drizzle with such force that Kuno was soon wet through and through. He hardly noticed it though since the thought burned inside of him like a fire that his teacher, whom he so revered and loved, had censured him so severely without giving him opportunity to justify himself.

Possum Creek's shoemaker lived alone on top of a steep and barren sand hill not far from the store. When he announced his presence, a snarling and barking dog, who was chained to the fence, answered his "hallo." Kuno quickly dismounted and climbed over the fence by means of a couple of wood blocks that took the place of a missing gate and quickly noticed that thick smoke was wafting out every crack in the house, and after knocking energetically on the door several times to no avail, he turned the latch and entered. After the smoke and soot had dissipated somewhat due to the open door, he noticed Wohlfahrt's excessively tall frame standing next to a parlor stove that also served as a cook stove, frantically trying to rescue his midday meal from ruin, coughing and wheezing mightily as he did so. The pot on the overly stoked stove that contained his noon meal of pea soup and bacon had overflowed onto the red-hot surface. After he had scraped the last nasty remnants of the foul-smelling char from the stovetop, he turned to Kuno and explained to him that it was necessary to keep the house warm in order to keep his shoemaker's tar pliable.

He then continued: "I once read that shoemakers are a strange lot compared to their fellow human beings. Poets or philosophers, pietists[134] or anarchists, worry warts or practical jokers. But that is not always the case. Among my colleagues in the trade, I know many who are down-to-earth, solid, and like everybody else."

But Wohlfahrt was certainly an odd bird himself, and something of a philosopher to boot. He had travelled extensively as a journeyman,[135] and had not only spent time in Gross-Wanzleben and Halberstadt,[136] but also had plied his trade in Magdeburg, Bonn, and Strasburg. He was quite proud of his worthy trade and often declared that neither Prince Eugene[137] nor Napoleon would have won so many battles if they had had amateurs for their personal shoemakers. Pride in his craft had also driven him to Texas. In Germany—so he explained to his friends while striking his hammer against a leather scrap with such force that it almost parted—we are in a bind. As master craftsmen, we are not allowed to marry the daughters of the simple wage-earning class, but when an honorable shoemaker approaches the haughty daughters of the town elite with a sincere marriage proposal, they rumple their noses in disgust. In consequence, he packed up his shoemaker tools and his unfinished work and swam across the big herring lake to America where everyone was free and equal; to a place where it would be possible for even a shoemaker to marry the daughter of a king or count, if such a thing were to be found over there. He landed happily at Possum Creek but met with disappointment in his marital expectations. In the 1850s, eligible women and widows were a great rarity in Texas and much in demand. When an emigrant ship landed in Galveston, German men, young and old alike, arrived from the interior and crowded the landing dock, some waiting for days and weeks, in the hope that a rosy-cheeked German maid might show some inclination to share a log cabin and thus relieve the suitor from the everyday burden of button-sewing, darning, ironing, cooking, cleaning up pots and dishes, and all other the domestic tasks that were a veritable plague for a single man. Wohlfahrt, who in any case was anything but Apollo, always seemed to arrive too late. To be sure, the dreadful war had created a surfeit of widows and stranded brides-to-be, a situation that had improved his marriage prospects considerably, but by this point he had become a confirmed bachelor.

He was already over fifty, but he held stubbornly to the belief that the cut-off age for military eligibility was sure to be raised,[138] and he was too soft-hearted to want to consciously risk adding to the growing number of widows and poor orphans, and so preferred to manage his household alone.

Wohlfahrt was even taller than Sartorius and Winzug, but his bent over posture made him look shorter than he was. His body was fully encased in a buttoned-up overcoat of dark and coarse homespun wool that extended down to his feet. His bald head was always covered with a brown felt hat from which here and there a lock of straw blond hair dangled. His workshop, which also served as kitchen and bedroom—the second room in the cabin remained shut off for the future Frau Shoemaker—was kept painfully clean, as if a cleaning room. Despite his warm coat and hat, he was constantly shivering, and there was a good reason for this. He had arrived in the summer and in order to take advantage of the breezes constructed his house on the top of a hill and, contrary to the usual practice of using closely fitted timbers and plastered walls, preferred logs with large gaps so that the fresh air could freely circulate.

After Kuno had announced his purpose, Wohlfahrt replied, "Yes, things are what they are, but it is still dumb; I wish I could have Davis and all the other miscreants in Richmond under my hammer just for once. I would pound the tar out of them until they make peace, and make it before I get called up," and

Ellersly Plantation House. Author's collection.

with that he gave a mighty blow with his hammer to a piece of sole leather. After Kuno had specified to him that he wanted his boots made out of stout and pliable cowhide, not calf leather, and with thick soles, he replied approvingly:

"Well, well, I never thought I would hear something so sensible from the mouth of a *Lateiner*. Quality, waterproof boots and a trustworthy attitude are the basic attributes of any good soldier." Pointing to a pair of delicately worked and finely polished boots made from calf leather hanging on the wall, and with decorative stitching on the uppers, he continued: "There, I made a pair for Mr. Phillips's son with very high heels and red leather and with a very tight fit. To begin with, when he rides up for the first time, they are going to laugh themselves silly, and then his legs will be cold, and then when he dismounts and tries to walk, his feet will kill him. But that is how it is with a young romantic, but it is still dumb beyond belief."

Kuno seconded these insightful observations, especially the remarks concerning Bobby Phillips, and garnered thereby the complete approbation of the master shoemaker. After taking very careful measurements and promising to have the boots finished in three days, the master asked Kuno to pay his respects to his father and let him off with the warning not to make a fool of himself and not to wear stockings in the field, but rather to wrap his feet in foot towels, a much healthier and more militarily acceptable practice,[139] and that he should always form up in the second row, because the Yankees' muskets would not shoot through more than one cadaver at a time.

Wohlfahrt's down-to-earth advice together with his observation that Bobby Phillips was also about to enter the army diverted Kuno's thoughts in a less worrisome direction. After spending time in the over-heated shoemaker's cabin, he felt the chill of the fresh air keenly. He put the spurs to his pony and, as he galloped across the hill, the thought struck him that it must be a magnificent feeling to charge headlong toward an enemy's position, saber in hand, in company with hundreds or thousands of brave comrades.

When he arrived at his home, he saw Mr. Phillips's buggy parked next to the gate, where old Ned and Pompey, the colonel's gray-headed *Factotum*, who now for some time had also served as the colonel's coachman, were both busily removing the harness from the two large dapple-gray horses and feeding them. Despite highly polished silver buckles, the harness appeared to be old and almost worn-out, while the lacquer on the coach was entirely missing in places. Both horses, similarly, also betrayed clearly that corn was in short supply in their master's barn.

It was time for the noon meal; Kuno changed clothes very quickly and then entered the dining room where he found his parents in a conversation with Mr. Phillips. Their guest was small of stature and rather slight of build; his hair almost completely white although he had not yet reached his sixtieth year. He wore a suit made of fine gray cloth. A large diamond sparkled on his stiffened and dazzlingly white linen shirtfront,[140] while diamond studs graced his cuffs. His pale, sharply featured, and beardless face, together with gray eyes that were partially obscured under enormous eyebrows and that had a dreamy aspect seemed to better fit the picture of a diplomat of the old school than the stereotypical image of a Southern planter. A thoroughly obliging personality complimented his diplomat's face. He greeted Kuno warmly and proceeded to lavish such excessive praise on the young man for his courage and resourcefulness during the search for Hedwig that Kuno blushed and grew increasingly ill at ease. His father had always been sparse in his praise, while Lüttenhoff, out of fear of making his children vain, went to the other extreme in avoiding praise altogether; it was natural, therefore, that Kuno felt awkward, even annoyed about such complements. He began to suspect that Mr. Phillips was making fun of him. But he was wrong in this. When he lavished praise to the point it bordered on flattery then he did so with one purpose in mind, namely to bring joy to people he held in esteem; but it must be said he always took delight when they paid him back in kind, although he occasionally barked up the wrong tree in this regard.[141] He turned to Kuno and said:

"I hear that you are getting ready to enter the army. My son Robert Emmett also did not want to wait until he was conscripted. He hoped to join a year ago and I was only able to dissuade him from doing so with great effort. But I can no longer talk him out of it since he turns eighteen in January. That is actually the reason I have come today because, for the benefit of Mrs. Phillips as well as for myself, it would be a great pleasure and reassurance were our son to count such a upstanding and reliable young man as yourself as his tent mate and loyal comrade. Robert Emmett intends to join the First Texas Cavalry Regiment[142] and will take along Cicero, who could serve you as well."

Kuno, who just a half an hour before had enthused about being in the cavalry, replied tersely, "I have decided to join an infantry regiment and I do not need a servant." Frau Sartorius, who was on the point of thanking Mr. Phillips for the honor and advantages that would come to her son as a result of this offer, was angered by the tone of her son's refusal, which had a distinct hint of rudeness to it. For his part, Sartorius wanted to avoid an unpleasant scene and quickly interjected, "Yes, you see Colonel, my oldest son took my best horse off to the war and by and by needed another four; my second son requested three horses; and now the one sits in a prison in Ohio since the fall of Vicksburg while the other one is afoot somewhere in Louisiana. Nothing, of course, would be too great a sacrifice for our country, but still I must admit that I would be thankful for any consideration my youngest son shows me in regard to my greatly reduced stand of horses and my diminished pocketbook."

"Quite right, and I am firmly convinced that your son will continue to distinguish himself equally on foot, just as he has done the last few days, answered Mr. Phillips in a diplomatic manner and in such a way as to side-step the delicate subject at hand. During the meal, he related how he had paid a visit to Lüttenhoff in the morning to congratulate the family on the happy turn of events in respect to their daughter and to inquire about Hedwig's well-being.

"The girl blooms like a rose and one cannot look at her and detect any ill-effects from her recent perils. She is a young heroine. It is rare to encounter a young woman so gracious, charming, and courteous and, at the same time, so courageous and resolute; one has to admire her. Her parents appear to be recovering more slowly from the anxieties of the ordeal than she, and Lüttenhoff, especially, looks shaken to the core and unusually reserved and dejected."

The praise for Hedwig did not seem to Kuno to be at all exaggerated and caused him to view Mr. Phillips in a better light. That his praise might have contained a hidden barb directed at him, escaped him completely but not his father. Soon thereafter, Mr. Phillips departed the noon meal since the intermittent showers had grown in frequency and intensity and any hope for a quick clearing in the weather had vanished. No sooner had he departed than Frau Sartorius began to reproach Kuno for the abrupt and discourteous way he had responded to their guest's generous offer, to whit to have Kuno as the mess mate to the only son of the richest, most respected, and most educated man of the community—Herr Lüttenhoff excepted, of course. Sartorius felt compelled to concur with his wife that it was inappropriate to turn down such a generous offer so brusquely. Only a few days before Kuno would have accepted such a reproach without a peep of protest and without making any effort to defend himself, but the events of the last few days had not passed him by without a trace. So instead of holding his tongue in quiet resentment, he explained to his parents while the rain beat noisily against the windowpanes in the parlor, which in spite of being early afternoon, was half-darkened by the overcast weather, of his first meeting with Bobby Phillips, which he remembered as clearly as if it were yesterday.

Since this concerns a feud among boys and Kuno's version, although completely sincere, could not expected to be completely impartial, it is necessary that we take over the role of narrator at this point.

It was on a beautiful, clear January day almost seven years previous when the two brothers Kuno and Albrecht, who actually answered to the name of Muller, both under the nominal oversight of their live-in house and music teacher, Gottfried Misslich, mounted their horses. Three days before one of Mr. Phillips's slaves outfitted in a servant's uniform had delivered a letter containing an invitation to attend the tenth birthday celebration of young Robert Emmett Phillips. Herr Sartorius was away on business at the time and Frau Phillips was not a little proud of the fact that her sons had received an invitation. On previous occasions the talk had swirled around for weeks prior to such an event for only the sons and daughters of the most prominent families received invitations while the celebrations themselves exceeded in grandiosity anything else of a similar nature in the whole area. In consequence, she had taken great pains to outfit her sons appropriately and had reminded their teacher pointedly upon departure to see to it that Albrecht and Kuno deported themselves correctly and courteously during the celebration.

Gottfried Misslich did not look forward to his task and mounted his gray mare with a heavy sigh. He would rather herd cats than keep watch over his two young charges on such an outing. He was the son of a sexton from Mecklenburg who by dint of great personal sacrifice and discipline had managed to study theology and had advanced as far as a *Kandidat*.[143] Then as he awaited a pastorate, the worst scenario that could possibly befall an impoverished and unattractive candidate transpired: he fell madly in love with the pretty but portly daughter of a local Mecklenburg estate holder who happened to be his future patron and, in consequence, had seen all his aspirations in respect to both his candidacy and the young woman go up in smoke, and so he chose to emigrate. Sartorius discovered him in very distressed circumstances. Instead of shepherding souls he had become a lowly sheepherder in Texas for a well-to-do farmer who, in spite of the fact that he was a close countryman of Misslich, had little respect for his lofty educational attainments. And so it came to pass that the farmer drove him away, heaping insult and scorn upon the "wretch of a preacher" because the poor soul, totally absorbed one day in the study of his Greek edition of the New Testament, had failed to notice that wolves had made off with several of the four-footed creatures in his charge. Sartorius took pity on him and brought him under his care. He found it amusing that the young man had an unbelievable appetite which never seemed to wane, even in his beneficiary's household where hearty portions of tasty fare were the norm. At the time Grossenberg counted not only as the most pronounced gourmet but also as the biggest glutton in the whole county, but he could not hold a candle to the hollow-cheeked theologian. Sartorius remarked to his wife that whereas many seek to drown their sorrows in drink, Misslich appeared to seek relief from life's disappointments solely through the consumption of excessive amounts of food. He soon discovered, however, that Misslich was also accomplished musically, and was, in fact, a master flutist, whereupon he promoted him straightaway from freeloader to private tutor. Alas, with this promotion began a period of incessant suffering and conflict for the theologian. Rudolph, Sartorius's fourteen-year-old son, called "walnut" by his mother and "doctor" by his father and everyone else, rebelled right away against the tedious and boring schoolmaster who, it must be admitted, had not one iota of aptitude for the pedagogical profession. The doctor played so many practical jokes on his teacher that he was eventually exempted from his lessons. Muller (Adelbert) showed an interest in learning how to play the flute but Latin and German grammar were not to his liking, and even the small Kuno, who otherwise was so hungry to learn, soon discovered more pleasure in aggravating his teacher than in learning from him.

In the morning on the day before Bobby Phillips's birthday party a light snow had accompanied an otherwise mild cold snap. Most of the snow had melted but here and there patches of the rare precipitation had collected along fencerows and under trees. The boys rode their nimble ponies this way and that looking for accumulations sufficient to make snowballs (or better yet ice balls) with which to pelt one another. When Misslich tried to intervene with the warning that they were going to soil their party attire, he ended up on more than one occasion in the line of fire and on the receiving end of the frozen projectiles. Then, when a long-eared *mule rabbit*[144] busted from his hiding place, the two boys took up the chase behind the fleet-footed creature, racing past their teacher and out onto the wide prairie in hot pursuit. They did not follow him for very long but kept up their line of travel across the prairie in the direction of the Acadia Plantation and the large mansion that was barely discernible in the distance. They soon came upon a grove of trees and brush next to a small creek where they hid themselves from the bespectacled eyes of their teacher. Muller then suggested they turn their coats inside out, wind moss around their shoulders, and when their mentor arrived, charge him suddenly from both sides while letting out blood-curdling yells. He would surely believe that wild Indians were after his scalp and get a good fright. Kuno, however, protested and even convinced his brothers to ride back in the direction of their teacher so that he would not lose his way.

They soon espied him in the distance and he was a sight to behold; a picture to arouse real pity. His mare had bolted and attempted to follow the other horses on her own, whereby her rider soon lost his stirrups as well as all control of the animal. He only managed to stay aboard by clinging for dear life to the saddle horn. His large black hat had flown off his head at the start of his perilous ride and landed in a mud puddle somewhere to the rear. Young boys are not normally moved to take pity when something strikes them as ridiculous and laughable, but in this case, let it be noted to their credit, both Kuno and Muller withheld their laughter and even rushed to help the unfortunate man regain his stirrups and thereafter backtracked to recover his lost hat. For the rest of the trip they behaved with more consideration. This altered behavior was due in no small part to the sobering realization that the party they were about to attend was indeed a weighty affair.

The mansion was eight miles distant from Possum Creek, a large imposing two-story edifice constructed entirely of wood and painted a dazzling white.[145] Wide verandas, both above and below, accented the sides and the rear. It stood atop the last hill before the Palmetto Creek bottom and was separated from the flat prairie to the front by a small valley through which a narrow and wooded stream flowed. In front and well to the right stood a good twenty single-story brick houses of one or two rooms each, arranged in two neat rows. A brick factory on the plantation had supplied the material for the houses. These were the Negro quarters. Behind these stood a collection of barns and sheds. To the left was located a large peach orchard, the largest and finest far and wide. Select large shade trees that had been spared by the forester's ax surrounded the house itself. A large horse pasture filled with many magnificent animals was situated to the rear of the house in the direction of the forest while a well-organized plantation of over two thousand acres stretched out across the creek bottom below, a bottom blessed with the finest alluvial soil of a reddish cast. A large and imposing gate in the fence that enclosed the plantation stood open and the boys and their teacher rode through and then along a long avenue lined with catalpa trees,[146] silver poplars,[147] and pines that led from the gate to the mansion. A row of coaches stood parked in front of the green picket fence that enclosed the house while two young Negro servants dressed in pale blue jackets with mother of pearl buttons walked forward to greet them and to help Misslich dismount. They then led their ponies to the horse barn to feed them. Old Pompey led them into the house and the boys had but little time to admire the painstakingly manicured yard that surrounded the house before they were ushered up the front steps where the lady of the house dressed in a splendid silk gown awaited her guests. Due to a recurrence of rheumatism, Mr. Phillips was indisposed and confined to his room. Mrs. Phillips greeted them and then introduced them to a row of finely attired ladies and gentlemen who were promenading around the front veranda. Kuno thought he detected a smirk on the mouths of several of the attendees, which was most likely due to the rather stiff deportment of the boys and the stilted English of their teacher, which the Americans could barely understand. Mrs. Emmett indicated to the boys that they should follow her into Robert Emmett's playroom where a good twenty boys and girls had gathered, most of a similar age to the birthday boy, and all outfitted in the finest clothing. They were the children of rich planters, lawyers, and government officials and all were crowding around Bobby, who was showing them all the expensive birthday presents he had received. Bobby Phillips was just a month younger than Kuno, a slender, attractive youngster with long blond curls, blue eyes, and fine white hands. His penetrating blue eyes could assume an unbelievable arrogant and haughty cast while his white hands were known on occasion to let the whip fall across the faces of his black servants. As the only son of the rich plantation couple, and one who only appeared after a long period of childlessness, he had been unbelievably spoiled and coddled by his mother, and even the otherwise sensible father had allowed his offspring free rein to do as he pleased. The slaves trembled before their young *Massa*, though they still worshipped him. Likewise, his tutors as well as the German gardener—Mr. Phillips liked to employ Germans for his service—deferred to his mood swings and felt compelled to bend to his will in all matters.

Bobby acknowledged the new arrivals only with a nod of the head. The two congratulated him on his birthday as their mother had instructed them to do, and then turned to interact with the other children. Soon thereafter, Pompey entered and announced that the birthday table was ready. The music instructor, a French lady, played a march in the dining hall while the children lined up and paraded by twos into the room led by Bobby, who escorted a charming planter's daughter on his arm, to take their places at the table. To both Kuno and Muller's great joy, neither was assigned a young lady to escort, so they brought up the rear of the procession.

The beautifully painted walls of the large dining hall were almost completely covered by long garlands made of evergreen vines and holly branches that had been interwoven in a most artistic way. On a long table covered with a snowflake patterned damask stood several large crystal bowls filled with roses, tulips, and violets, as well as other flowers unknown to the children that had been grown in the plantation's greenhouse. Other dishes contained oranges, bananas, or red-cheeked apples—the apples sent by a relative in distant Tennessee especially for the occasion. Still others offered wonderfully arranged salads, sweet cakes, and jellies. A huge porcelain dish in the center of the table contained a roasted pig with stuffed and baked turkeys at either end. The place settings were solid silver while the plates, bowls, and cups were of the finest French porcelain, all with floral designs. Although the household of their parents was not exactly impoverished, the two German boys had never imagined that such fairy-tale luxury existed. The lady of the house indicated that the children should take their seats while the black servants removed the sumptuous roasts to the large mahogany sideboard where it could be carved and offered for serving. Bobby Phillips, however, did not make a move to sit down. When his mother repeated her directive, her son announced in a loud enough voice that Sartorius's sons, who were standing in awe and admiration of all the splendor and excess at the far end, could clearly hear:

"I will not sit down to eat at the same table with the two small Dutchmen.[148] If you expect me to eat here they have to sit at a separate table." Mrs. Phillips, who did not share her husband's fondness for their German neighbors and who had only agreed under protest to invite the children of Sartorius even though he owned slaves and his wife did not work in the kitchen, was nevertheless clearly mortified by this outburst of willful rudeness on the part of her fair-haired darling, but she also realized that any attempt to counter him would be useless. She quickly ordered a small table to be brought from the card parlor and set up and prepared for the German boys next to the grand piano that had been brought into the dining hall for the occasion. She then invited Misslich to the piano and he gladly accepted, happy for the opportunity to be able to play on such an impressive instrument. The children took their seats and soon the room was filled with the happy sounds of childish banter and laughter. Bobby appeared unusually animated and his mother and the other guests took note of his clever remarks and witticisms. Nobody listened to Misslich's lovely playing and no one paid any attention to the small Dutchmen seated at their own table in the corner next to the piano. Seemingly unperturbed by what had transpired, Muller started in on the portions that had been served to him by the dutiful black servants. Kuno, however, despite all exhortations, refused to take a single bite. Only for a brief instant did his youthful sweet tooth overrule his smoldering resentment, and that was when, for dessert, the servants brought out plump, red strawberries that were bedded in fresh snow and generously sprinkled with sugar. Up to this point he had only had heard of such a sumptuous delicacy from his parents and so could not resist the temptation to plop a single berry in his mouth, but he quickly spat it out into his handkerchief and then covertly deposited it on the floor. He even refused to taste the seductively aromatic pineapple punch, which was being served at the end of the table from an enormous silver punch bowl into the fine crystal glasses of the children. "Are you crazy?" Muller asked his brother in a hushed voice as he emptied a second glass. But for Kuno, all these pleasures only served to heighten his chagrin.

Once finished, the children moved from the table to the large garden in order to admire the greenhouse flowers and strawberries as well as the magnificent fruit still hanging on the orange trees from which the protective cloths had been lifted. In the meantime, the large table in the dining room was cleared and set anew for the adult guests and even the many of the slaves had gathered under a neighboring shed to enjoy a share of the birthday feast. Once the tour of the garden was completed, Bobby, who had shown himself to be very adroit as escort and guide, had his personal servant Cicero, a half-grown mulatto, bring out a tame raccoon on a chain leash.

To the delight of the children, the clever animal performed all sorts of tricks. Then Cicero was asked to dance a jig for the assembled guests in the garden house with the vine roof using bones in his hands in the place of castanets to keep time while he danced, and he did it well, as only a *darky* can. Bobby threw him a gold coin and several of the children followed with silver coins that served as his applause. Finally, Bobby turned to Kuno, whom, up to this point he had not graced with a single word. "Well, now two coons have danced, the gray, four-legged one and the yellow one with two legs. We call you a *coon*,[149] or something like that as well, and now you need to show us what you can do." With this insult, all the chagrin that Kuno had heretofore suppressed broke loose, and as if a dam had burst, he replied: "You are a liar and if I dance you are going to dance with me." In a split second the dance was underway, but it did not last very long. Several fisticuffs were exchanged and Bobby was soon stretched out on the ground with Kuno on top of him pounding him mercilessly until the blood came out of his nose and lip to stain his starched white shirt and fashionable clothing until Muller pulled his brother from him. Instantly, Bobby jumped up and grabbed a spade that lay nearby and swung it at Kuno who had not moved from the spot and would have hit him in the head with it, had not Muller grabbed his arm just in the nick of time. At this, Cicero wanted to spring to the aid of his young master but Muller, whose reserve had suddenly disappeared, and who possessed an uncanny strength for a person of his years, gave a stomach kick to the mulatto of such force that he fell like a sack of meal into the starting bed of potted plants, breaking several into pieces.

"Let the hound dogs loose and set them after the damned Dutchmen!" cried out Bobby with a foaming mouth. At this, Bobby's cousin, who was a good four years older and the son of a lawyer from the nearby county seat, placed himself between the two and declared that among young gentlemen only a fair fight was proper, even with *Dutchmen.* He then quickly hustled Bobby back into the house so he could be cleaned up and given a change of clothes.

The other children followed the two excitedly into the house. Though still in a defensive posture with sleeves rolled up, as if expecting a renewed attack, Muller and Kuno seized the opportunity, like two fleeing deer, to make a dash for the stall where they quickly threw their saddles on their ponies and, in a flash, were off. At the big entrance Muller took time to say, "You did well, you little squirt," an acknowledgement that filled Kuno with youthful pride.

Mrs. Phillips and her guests, who in the meantime had taken their seats at the big dining table, had not noticed the fight outside. Neither had the Negros at their festive table. The lady of the house, however, must subsequently have received a report of the affair for her visits to Frau Sartorius abruptly ended. Her husband, on the other hand, most likely never heard a word about it. He continued to associate with the *Lateiner,* and especially with Sartorius, whom he continued to hold in high regard for his many talents, and especially for his broad facility in world literature and world history. He was curious why every time he invited his wife along for a leisure jaunt to Possum Creek, she was either indisposed or otherwise excused herself from the trip, but he never looked further into the matter. Her station in life as a FFV member (association of the preeminent Virginia colonial families),[150] as well as being his wife, gave Mrs. Phillips the unquestionable privilege of her moods.

At age twenty, Phillips, originally from South Carolina, and on his mother's side from Huguenot stock, had journeyed to Paris where he spent many months in order to acquire French habits and culture. While there, he met a young English writer who had travelled extensively through Germany and had related to him many fascinating facts about the "Land of poets and philosophers." In consequence, he decided to spend a couple of months travelling in Germany before returning to the United States. Despite the sad political circumstances that prevailed in Germany at the time and despite his complete ignorance of the language, the young American saw a lot there that had impressed him. He was very proud of the fact that he had been introduced to the great poet Johann Wolfgang von Goethe[151] and the old "Prince of the Arts and Literature" had honored him with a hearty handshake.

⋅⊷⊶✦⊷⊶⋅

After their hasty retreat from the birthday celebration, Kuno and Muller rode aimlessly back and forth across the prairie for a good while since they did not want to arrive back home prematurely. Finally, Kuno was so overcome by hunger that he could no longer resist heading for home and the dinner table. When they reached the house, they found their mother sequestered in a dark room due to a severe migraine attack, and since their father was also away on a trip, they were spared the possibility of awkward questions for the time being. Grateful for this, they did not seem to demonstrate proper sympathy for their mother's indisposition. Later, it must be said, Muller reported the events at the birthday party in such an artful manner that the parents remained completely ignorant of what truly transpired.

However, as if recompense for not evincing enough sympathy for their mother's misery, the two suffered many pangs of conscious and anxiety that evening concerning their teacher, whom they had abandoned and left in the lurch in such an idiotic way. When he did not appear for supper at the usual hour—something that had never happened before—they feared that he had gotten lost and considered whether they should ride out to meet him. But before they could arrive at a decision, Misslich was happily delivered by his mare; the animal had not forgotten the way to the feed trough. Instead of acting incensed over the behavior of his charges, he behaved as if in the best of moods while accomplishing an astounding feat on the cold pork that had been laid out before him by Sally. After he had stilled his hunger, he played nostalgic songs on his flute until midnight, which he often did when in a good mood. After Sartorius had returned the following day, he explained that he had recognized his true calling in life. If he could not serve as a preacher to lead the heathens in America to salvation, and if nature had not endowed him with the proper attributes to be a successful teacher, then he could serve in another capacity, namely as a pioneer for higher civilization in America, helping to lead American cultural philistines,[152] who often prefer Negro dance music and French operatic melodies to Bach and Hayden, into the sacred halls of true musical appreciation. Sartorius assured him of his support in this calling and by means of his and Mr. Phillips's warm recommendations, he obtained a position a couple of weeks later in a newly established college. In his endeavor to instill in the minds and ears of the daughters of rich plantation owners proper understanding and appreciation for the laws of harmony, he suffered many a sad setback, but still he achieved much of substance as well. Muller and Kuno, however, were now rid of their live-in teacher and regretted it not in the least.

KUNO RECEIVES A DIFFICULT TASK

In the night after Kuno's confession, it rained buckets without interruption, as if to make up in one night for all that had been lacking in the fall. The following morning brought little change in the weather pattern. Even though the sun would make a modest attempt to peek through the dull, overcast sky now and then, the rains would quickly resume. Small streams began to build in the fields and the usually sluggish Possum Creek overflowed its banks and took with it the split rail fences, while the flat prairie became a huge sea with only clumps of grass visible here and there. Kuno, out of sorts and impatient, sat the whole day long in the house doing geometry lessons or translating the great General Julius Caesar's commentaries concerning his battle with Ariovistus,[153] both fitting tutorials for a soon-to-be warrior.

In the evening, as a welcome diversion, he had to swim his Polly across the swollen stream in order to drive the milk cows, still standing on the far bank bellowing for their calves, a couple of miles upstream. Here it was possible to cross and he was able to herd them back safely into their pen by nightfall.

When the rain continued the following morning, he could no longer contain his impatience. Without a saddle and with his shotgun in its canvas scabbard, he rode out onto the prairie in order to bag as many ducks and geese as possible, which he had seen flying over in endless formations from the gallery of the house. But lady luck did not smile on him here either. Because of the long dry spell, the grass was short and the small ponds had swollen to large lakes making the ducks unreachable while the wild geese, which had gathered in enormous flocks on the occasional knolls where there was still dry land, could spy the approaching hunter from a thousand paces and took to flight before he could get within shooting range. After hours of toil and effort, he could only claim one meager gray duck as a reward. The sun finally came out and Kuno rode home dripping wet and in a foul mood. There he found his father in bed suffering from a severe backache and impatiently awaiting his return. An hour before a Negro had brought him a letter from Major Bolton,[154] a slave dealer in Pine Valley.[155] Bolton, who was said to be very rich and a sly trader to boot, had purchased a large herd of steers from Sartorius in the spring for a small down payment for delivery to the troops in Louisiana. Shortly thereafter, Bolton bought fourteen bales of cotton, Sartorius's entire harvest of three years, which he intended to transport to Mexico to sell for Mexican gold. For the outstanding debt, which amounted to $2,200, he had offered a promissory note that specified payment in gold.[156] Bolton had written him that due to pressing business, he had to return to Mexico on Sunday of the coming week. But first he wanted to dispose of his debt and invited Sartorius personally to come pick it up, or to send a reliable representative, since he did not trust such a large amount of money to a Negro. "What to do? asked Sartorius, "I am lying flat on my back here and I have just recently heard disturbing reports about Bolton that make me very uneasy. How can I be sure that I will ever get my money if he takes it with him over the border? I am sure Lüttenhoff would gladly take care of the matter for me, but I do not want to impose upon him with such a request . . .

"So, let me take care of it father," interrupted Kuno, "I can ride over to Pine Valley and fetch your gold."

Sartorius looked intensely into his son's face and after careful deliberation, replied: "Well, why not; up to now you haven't worried yourself much with money matters, but you are old enough now, and as far as the danger, that should be minimal. And someone who can rescue a damsel in distress is certainly capable of saving my golden fox." After a short deliberation, it was decided to borrow Grossenberg's large red horse for this trip of sixty miles, there and back, over boggy ground and across swollen streams. Such a journey would be asking too much of Polly or any other of Sartorius's horses. While Kuno hastily ate his lunch, and readied himself for the coming trip, Pompey fetched the horse, a magnificent golden red stallion, sixteen hands high, and around one o'clock, Kuno swung into the saddle. He secured his saddle bag and a woolen blanket to the saddle while, around his waist, he fastened a strong leather belt to serve as a money pouch. He then placed his father's freshly loaded percussion cap six-shooter into the shaft of his boot.

"I do not believe that the trip will be dangerous, since robbery in these parts is practically unknown, but if somebody does try to waylay you, shoot to kill, and then put the spurs to your horse. But remember, you are more valuable to your parents than any thousand dollars."

When Kuno arrived at Palmetto Creek, he found the whole creek bottom to be a swirling sea of murky flood water. When he nevertheless attempted to cross, he was warned by the Irish postal rider, who had made camp on a nearby rise to wait out the flood, that the current was much too strong for even the strongest horse to counter. And, in truth, Kuno could tell from the speed of the large tree trunks that were being swept along by the force of the flood waters that the warning was well-founded. He rode a further ten miles upstream before he found a suitable place to swim his horse across without undo danger. But the detour cost him an additional two hours and he had arrived in an area that was completely unknown to him. Taking his chances, he struck out on a little travelled road that appeared to be heading in the correct direction. It led him mostly through wooded areas; then through a couple of clearings; then into the woods again, where the road finally shrunk to a small path, probably made by a sled or drag of some sort. The sun was beginning to bend low and Kuno did not want to backtrack and loose valuable time, so he took a bearing to the south knowing he would eventually have to cross the main road,[157] but realizing full well that he would most likely be forced to spend a wet, miserable night in the woods.

As the last glow of day faded above the treetops, he suddenly heard the barking of dogs, a welcome surprise after so long a period of silence broken only by the occasional squawk of a crow or other natural sounds of the forest.

Spurring his horse on, he soon overtook a hunter. He was a tall, gaunt man with a coonskin cap on his head and ragged clothes on his body. The three scrawny hounds accompanying the hunter set upon Kuno in a rage, but quickly retreated at the command of their master.

A quick question and answer session soon revealed that the hunter was named Sandy McIver, and that he lived in a nearby clearing with his family, and that he would gladly offer the lost wayfarer shelter for the night. Kuno dismounted and accompanied the hunter on foot and discovered that he had ventured out in the afternoon in hopes of bagging a wild pig to improve the monotony of his daily fare. They soon reached a clearing that was only a couple of acres in size. In the middle was a log cabin surrounded by a brush fence. The cabin reminded Kuno strongly of the *Ritterburg*,[158] the cabin in the woods where Hedwig had found refuge: a single-room blockhouse with a dilapidated lean-to for a kitchen. With McIver's "Hallo!" the entire family spilled out of the house and ran out to the fence—a wife with a baby in arm and a good twelve children of all sizes, all barefoot and red-haired, all clothed like ragamuffins, especially the younger ones—in order to greet their father and his guest. The children stared at Kuno as if they had never seen anybody but *mammy* and *daddy* before, but they finally took turns shaking his hand. Madame McIver took her corn cob pipe out of her snuff-blackened teeth long enough to assure her guest that it would be an honor to have him as a guest in her house. Kuno's horse received a couple of ears of corn—McIver had probably never heard of hay—and that was a big sacrifice because his entire store of corn, which was supposed to last the family until summer, consisted of only a few meager bushels.

After a half hour supper was served by the light of a burning cedar torch on the front gallery, and in two shifts, since the rough-hewn log table was not big enough to accommodate all at one seating. As guest of honor, Kuno received a fork along with the man of the house. More forks and knives were lacking, but more were not needed since fried bacon as well as *hoe cake*[159] straight from the frying pan can be easily consumed without either. After the hard ride, both tasted wonderful to Kuno and soon thereafter he was treated to the complete life story of the McIver family, which was related to him in a dialect that was a curious mixture of Scottish brogue and Georgia *cracker*. The family, according to Sandy, had come to Texas because it had gotten too crowded in Georgia.

After the table had been cleared and Kuno was able to have a good look at the interior of the one room cabin by the light of the fireplace fire and the cedar torch. He counted a total of fifteen heads and came to the quick conclusion that the prospect of finding space for his nighttime quarters was limited. In the rather large room there was one sizeable bedstead with a rocking cradle for the baby next to it. After his host had listened for a spell in amazement to Kuno's description of the daily life and goings on at Possum Creek, he began to yawn. Kuno took this as a cue to arise and announce that, with their permission, he would make his bed with his woolen blanket outside on the gallery since space was so limited inside.

"Nothing doing," his host was quick to reply, "my hounds are pretty dumb; they might forget that I introduced you to them and attack you in the night. Besides the night air is really unhealthy and will give you the fever and shakes. You are our guest and will spend the night in a good bed."

"Yes, but I cannot deprive you and Mrs. McIver of your bed!"

"That will all be *fixed*,"[160] replied McIver and so it was. In an instant, a couple of sacks of corn husks were spread upon the floor and blankets laid over them for the McIver children. Then the back half of the room was partitioned for the children by means of two sheets of canvas tent cloth that were strung across the room.

"So, and now before bed we need to have a drink of water out on the gallery," said McIver.

When he returned with Kuno, the room was dark—the fire in the chimney had long since died out—and McIver, leading his guest by the hand, said: "So take your coat and boots off and lay down here next to me on the edge of the bed; my wife is already in bed."

Kuno did as he was bid, and it soon seemed to him as if the bed were much narrower than he remembered, or that McIver had grown much broader. After a quarter of an hour the whole family had fallen into a deep sleep; only Kuno remained wide awake in the dodgy, smoke-blackened room as he listened in amazement to a regular concert of snoring; a cacophony of sounds that included the full register of tones, the most notable aspect of which was that a regular duet seemed to arise from his own bed; immediately next to him, a deep bass; a little further over, sharp nasal tones; now simultaneous, now alternating, like antiphony, but nonetheless harmonic. Finally, it became clear to him that in the *four-poster* his host as well as his honorable lady were enjoying the sleep of the righteous. With this thought, he fell fast asleep and did not wake again until the first light of day when one of the small McIver boys started to raise an unholy racket because his mother had insisted that he wash himself in honor of their guest. Red shafts of light pouring through the cracks in the walls brought the traveler back to life and reminded him of his task. He was in a similar frame of mind as Saint Maurice[161] as he hurried in order to save his friend and guarantor from the hangman's noose, and insisted that he had to leave forthwith. Mrs. McIver and her Lord Master insisted that he share a festive breakfast of pork ribs with them, but he explained to them that he was in a hurry and had packed provisions for the trip. Only with effort was he able to separate from the good-hearted and well-meaning couple. At the very end, he almost spoiled all the good will with a crass affront to Texas etiquette. In deference to their obvious poverty, he had asked how much he owed them for their hospitality.

"I am a poor devil but I am still a gentleman. It would take a *Dutchman* to offer a poor white man money who had freely shared shelter for the night and food to eat," he replied, obviously annoyed.

Kuno quickly apologized and, in consideration of his youthful innocence, his apology was accepted. Then, after he had said his final goodbyes, and had shaken everybody's hand, and had promised to visit them again when in the neighborhood, he departed at a brisk trot. McIver had told him that by following the slide trail for ten miles or so he would reach the major road[162] that led to Leesburg,[163] New Mobile,[164] and the neighboring Pine Valley.[165] He ate his sausage bread and hard-boiled eggs in the saddle. He soon arrived on a broad, *hog wallow prairie*[166] that brought him to the designated road that led to Leesburg, a rather large settlement. He saw only a few people out and about, only women and children at the houses, and a few Negros working in the fields. The houses and the fences were in ill-repair and the fields only partially cultivated. The soil was a sticky, black gumbo and the roads in such a deplorable state that his horse could only proceed at a walk. By the time both the sun and his stomach had convinced him that it was close to noon, he had left the settlement far behind, and since his horse was sorely in need of rest, he decided to pause a while under a grove of post oak trees where his horse could graze on dry mesquite grass while he partook of his provisions and enjoyed a drink of water from a nearby pond. After a half hour's rest, he swung back into the saddle and resumed his journey.

Soon the land began to slope down into a broad river bottom while the road itself skirted the edge of a dense forest that bordered the river for many miles. It must have been around three o'clock when he arrived at the river itself at the place where a ferry boat was supposed to transport him across the river, but the ferry was nowhere to be seen; only the thick ropes that stretched across the river to mark its path. The river itself was almost bank full with flood waters, very swift and chocolate-brown in color. At the sight, Kuno felt even more like the poor Maurice, but his spirits sank even lower when, after several *halloos*, a gigantic, one-eyed Negro emerged from the nearby shanty to inform him that he was the ferryman and that around noon, just after he had transported a couple

Liendo Plantation House. Author's collection.

of wagons across the river, the raft, along with its accompanying canoe, had torn loose and floated away, most likely lodging against an obstacle somewhere downstream, and that he intended to look for it the following day and try to retrieve it. The Negro declared, moreover, that any attempt to swim the river would be akin to suicide; that the numerous tree trunks and debris carried along by the fast-moving current presented a real hazard to anyone attempting to cross.

The Negro then retreated to his cabin. Kuno dismounted and looked dejectedly at the flood waters, and even though he was tempted to risk a crossing, he recalled the farewell words of his father and hesitated. The sun sank ever lower and Kuno still wavered. With less than a half hour's daylight left, Kuno noticed that although the river was still rising, it was now totally free of logs and debris, and that this was probably due to the formation of a *raft*[167] further upstream. He hesitated no longer. With difficulty, he coaxed his horse down the steep and slippery bank to the water's edge. As a precaution, he took off his clothes and wrapped them carefully in his wool blanket and then tied the bundle securely to the back of his saddle. With a final word of encouragement, the horse took to the water, Kuno at his side with one hand on the saddle horn. The river was a good hundred paces wide at this point but the current was so unexpectedly swift that the youngster and his plucky horse were quickly swept much further downstream than they had hoped to a place where the steep river bank made it completely impossible to gain a foothold on *terra firma*. As Kuno attempted to climb the slippery bank by carefully holding on to exposed tree roots, a gigantic mass of earth broke loose from the river bank next to him and collapsed into the river with such force that it almost jarred him loose from his handhold. He then noticed that a large elm tree that had stood behind the eroded spot was beginning to quaver precariously and threatened to topple over, as if to follow the collapsed earth into the river. His horse snorted anxiously and swam further downstream, while Kuno, now fully mindful of the danger posed by a bank collapse, prudently followed him.

A hundred paces further downstream and around a sharp bend, Kuno spotted a suitable place to attempt a landing and at his yell the clever horse also swam for the spot. They soon both found themselves safe and sound on the soft red soil of the forest floor. Soon thereafter, they heard a gentle creak followed by a massive crash: the huge elm tree where they had first attempted a landing had given way along with a large chunk of riverbank and both had plunged into the river. Deeply mindful of the fate they had narrowly avoided, Kuno was shaken to his core. But there was little time to pause and reflect. Luckily, his clothes had remained dry. He quickly got dressed and soon was back in the saddle. According to the directions that had been given to him, he took the road to the right with the cheerful prospect of arriving at his goal on schedule.

Bolton's plantation was the first of a dozen or so large slave farms along the right bank of the river. Kuno arrived around sunset at the outer fence of the same, a split rail fence that in places had completely fallen down. It was not even necessary to open the entrance gate because it too lay off to the side on the ground. The field was a veritable wilderness in which the fresh growth from the roots of the felled trees had grown in places into an impenetrable thicket. As Kuno proceeded along the road, he became aware of a furious racket of barking of dogs mixed with the anxious bleating of a cow in the distance, and then the whole commotion approached him in a frenzy through the undergrowth amid the loud snapping of dried branches and parting undergrowth, as if a wild hunt were underway. A dozen or so gaunt and half-wild cur dogs emerged from the bushes in pursuit of a young cow. The leader of the pack had seized the young animal by the lower jaw, others by the neck and legs, and the animal was near to collapsing. Only with effort was Kuno able to drive the dogs from the prey they had so wanted to tear to shreds. He then struck a course toward the large, two-story *mansion* that had come into view. No smoke wafted from the large chimney and many panes were missing from the windows; the doors were all boarded shut.

After repeated *halloos*, a smallish, bald-headed man eventually emerged from a neighboring building and asked what his pleasure might be. It was Bolton, who had taken up residence in the house of his *overseer*.[168] After Kuno informed him of who he was, Bolton's facial expression betrayed momentarily bewilderment and revealed little that suggested a welcoming surprise. Still, he greeted Kuno courteously, and reiterated often how fondly he regarded his father, and how much he admired Kuno for carrying out his task punctually under such precarious circumstances.

"Your ride, however, was unnecessary," he stated.

"This morning, as a precaution, I dispatched my *overseer* Jackson by wagon, because I feared the river would continue to rise and become impassable. I gave him orders to take the long detour to Possum Creek in order to deliver the promised gold. You can't imagine how happy I am, however, to make the acquaintance of such a brave young man; the son of my good friend Sartorius, and I insist that you spend a couple of days with me. My quarters are, to be sure, pretty cramped since the mansion has been closed down, but we can make it comfortable enough for you."

The invitation sounded sincere and Kuno found little reason to doubt Bolton's explanation. Nevertheless, there was something about the man that made him uneasy despite his pretty words and friendly manner. Bolton was of middle stature with beginning indications of an expanding midriff, while his portly red face and bald head, sporting a band of short-cropped, fox-red hair, would have allowed him to pass easily for a wealthy and self-satisfied *bonvivant* were it not for his abnormally small blue eyes and short eyelashes that imparted to his countenance an unmistakable impression of both duplicity and cruelty.

Kuno, however, could not turn down the invitation to spend the night. At a shrill whistle by Bolton, a young mulatto appeared who looked very unkempt and who behaved unnaturally servile, as if recently chastised, or even whipped. He led his horse away while Bolton showed his guest into the *overseer's* house where he fetched a large stoneware pitcher out of a trunk and poured Kuno a glass of whiskey. Kuno refused the offer and resolutely resisted Bolton's efforts to persuade him to change his mind. After some time, an old Negress brought the evening meal for the two men and even though the plate and napkin set out for him were less than inviting, the hungry youngster found the roasted possum, corn bread, and coffee very much to his liking. After the meal, Bolton declared that he had an urgent task to perform and after showing the young man his bed for the night, shut the door and disappeared into the darkness. Kuno was exhausted and quickly fell asleep despite the fact that—as became all too clear the next morning—hordes of bedbugs had feasted overnight on his young body. After a breakfast of bacon, cornbread, and coffee, Kuno explained that he could not afford to tarry any longer. His host relented and Kuno set out on the return trip home laden with well-wishes from Bolton for his father and family.

As he approached the river, he noticed, off to the left over a rise, the white spire of a little church shimmering in the distance. That had to be New Mobile, the county seat, and Kuno, who had seen so little of the world, decided to take a slight detour to have a look. Upon arriving, he found that it resembled his own county seat, even as one egg does another: sandy, neglected streets, scarcely forty residences, but a few surrounded by pretty, well-tended gardens; in the center of town, a large bare plaza, the *courthouse square*, and in the middle of it, a large blockhouse for a courthouse; and off to one side, a smaller building with strong iron bars over narrow windows: the jail. Businesses fronted two sides of the courthouse, but nearly all of them had their doors closed. Kuno had just about seen enough and was ready to resume his ride when he noticed an old man dressed in a festive black suit on the gallery of the only business establishment that had two stories. He appeared to be checking on the weather. He greeted Kuno very courteously at which Kuno spontaneously exclaimed, "That is surly Old Man Levi!"

Hearing this, the old man roused himself, approached Kuno, and said: "Well, who could that be there who speaks German? That has to be Kuno Sartorius, the selfsame who once found poor Levi's purse and returned it to him. No, what a pleasure to see him here before my door! My God, how happy my little Rebecca will be to see the young gentleman! Dismount, young Sir, I will go get my Rebecca."

At the time, Solomon Levi was a unique and genuine character known far and wide across the land. With nothing but a backpack, he had travelled the width and breadth of the state peddling his household goods, then later with a large covered wagon full of his wares. Often, he had found overnight quarters at the Sartorius home, a welcome guest, because although he was doubtless a shrewd businessman, he was also an intelligent and brave man. Sartorius loved to engage in long conversations with the old *peddler* who seemed to know more about what was going on in the state than anyone else.

Kuno had not seen him for several years. He had stopped travelling, as he later related to Kuno, and located in New Mobile where he could set up shop and where he could also collect the money that many of the local plantations owed him. Rebecca, a small wrinkled woman similarly dressed in her finest clothes in honor of the holiday, came and greeted Kuno warmly, who then had to follow the old couple into their living quarters, which occupied the second story of the building, where he was offered a glass of strong, sweet wine to drink and some cake to eat. Everything he saw in the room testified to comfort and affluence.

After he had related what had brought him to Pine Valley, Levi clapped his hands together over his head and exclaimed:

"For crying out loud! Such a crook—Rebecca go to the kitchen; the goose needs to go in the oven!" Mrs. Levi disappeared at once and the old man had Kuno relate once again exactly his mission and precisely how Bolton had received him; then he said:

"I have always said it, the *Lateiner* are good, upright people, but they are not businessmen, and anyone can swindle them out of their hard-earned money. Your father won't get a single red penny of what is owed him. *Mister* Bolton did not send his wagon to Possum Creek but rather to Austin. I even gave Jackson some letters to deliver there. Bolton is the biggest crook in the whole state, and once some semblance of order is restored to the country, things are going to get hot for him, and so his man has been sent to Mexico with a sack full of gold never to return, and Bolton will never come back either. And for the likes of someone like that, the young Sir whose father is such a fine, upstanding man and whose mother is such a noble wife, almost drowned crossing the swollen river."

On his own and without knowing exactly why, Kuno had developed a great mistrust for Bolton. Nevertheless, he was thunderstruck by this revelation and implored Levi, whom he fully trusted, to advise him how to best deal with the situation.

"Let me think about it awhile," said Levi while twirling the gray locks that spilled out from underneath his felted headpiece. He then proceeded to pace up and down the room, all the while muttering incoherently to himself, to the point that Kuno grew impatient. Finally, he asked Kuno to show him the promissory notes and after he had carefully examined them with the help of his golden rimmed glasses, he began to rub his hands together in a self-satisfied way, and said:

"I know now what we can do. You dear father always said that Levi is a wise Jew, and he spoke with the old *peddler* like he was one of his own; your good mother let a Jew sit at her table and offered him Kosher fare, and now I will show you that I really am wise. Mr. Kuno, I would like you to look out the window for a short while and hold your ears shut."

Kuno did as instructed though it was an odd request, but his hearing was so keen that he could clearly distinguish that Levi had shuffled a ladder into the room below and that he had fumbled around on it for a spell until gold coins started falling from the ceiling onto the floor below. Then Levi returned, closed the door, carefully pulled the curtains to, and then began emptying his pockets of ten- and twenty-dollar gold pieces, which he then proceeded to count out to the astonished Kuno the full amount of the note.

"But this can't be!" exclaimed Kuno, "I know you are a rich man, but you do not owe my father any money, and my father never accepts charity."

"Hold your horses, young man; it would never occur to me to give Herr Sartorius something for free. And I am not so rich after all, but I do have a bit of money in the house. Mr. Bolton has been pestering me this whole week to buy his plantation so that he has more hard cash on hand. We reached a deal the day before yesterday and he wanted his money right away. I told him I didn't have so much money in the house and that he should come again the following day. Yesterday, I put him off until Sunday when I assured him we could get all the paperwork straight. He cursed and said I was only trying to trick him and wangle a better deal, but he begrudgingly agreed to the postponement. So, when he shows up tomorrow, I will give him the money, minus, of course, the value of the note, which I will hand over to him. He will curse and protest, but in the end, he will have no choice but to take the money and go about his way. And now, young man, count the money for yourself, put it away, and don't let it be known to anyone that Ol' Levi has so much money in his house, and my Rebecca neither, because she is always suspicious and overly cautious, and will not understand why I have made a business deal without a *Rebbe*."[169]

Upon realizing that the wise old Jew had found a way to extricate his father from his dilemma without himself suffering any loss, it was if a heavy burden had lifted from his heart. Full of gratitude he took Levi by the hand, but Levi admonished him sternly:

"First count the money out and put it away; then offer your thanks!" Kuno counted the coins, put them in his money pouch and thought to himself that even money can become a burden at times. He then handed over the note to Levi. At this moment, Frau Rebecca returned to the room from the kitchen and announced that the goose was done to perfection and that Kuno had to help them enjoy it.

"The young man cannot wait if he still intends to get his money from the *Gannef*.[170] Besides my bones are telling me that cold weather will be arriving tomorrow. Fetch him another piece of cake and a spot of wine. I will go along with him and see to it that he makes it safely across the river."

With this he hurried to the stable behind his building and had his Negro slave saddle up his two fine mules. In a short while the three were underway in the direction of the river, but very slowly, because it appeared that despite the soft coverlet that Levi had put over his saddle, the riding caused him discomfort. Arriving at the location of the ferry, they discovered that the ferryman had not been able to retrieve the ferry proper, but had managed to rescue the canoe, which he had in place and ready for service. Once again, Kuno thanked Levi profusely for his generosity. Before he climbed into the boat, Levi said to him in German:

"My slave tells me he saw Bolton's black horse tied in the bushes a short distance downstream. I'll wager that he is hiding there to see if you made it across the river safely. It is good that he knows nothing, and will know nothing until Sunday, then we will trust everything to Him."

Soon Kuno sat in the canoe leading his horse by a long rope until they arrived safely on the other bank. Kuno shouted one last farewell in a clear voice to the good man on the other side of the river, and trotted away. He spent the following night at the house of a family acquaintance, a planter, who had often enjoyed the hospitality of his father in the past. He had to travel at a much slower pace on the return trip owing to the fact that his loyal horse had been much fatigued by the exertions of the trip.

He arrived at home around evening time on Sunday, and just as Levi had prophesized, a fresh *norther* began blowing with full cheeks, bringing an event filled week to a successful completion for the young man.

THE UNWILLING RECRUIT

Not everyone who resisted fighting for the Confederate cause or who preferred hiding out in the brush or leaving the country to willingly presenting themselves at the recruitment office were motivated by loyalty to the Union, or hatred of slavery, or idealistic convictions of a similar nature. Joseph Herwisch, to take an example, whom the *conscript* hunters had continually pursued for over two years, had never asked himself whether he should fight under the banner of the Stars and Stripes or under the blood-red battle flag of the Confederacy; he was simply someone for whom war was unthinkable and who, in his entire life, had never fired a weapon. He had a wife at home who was almost neurotic in her devotion to her three small children. The oldest of these, Mändelchen,[171] had been a hapless cripple since her third year, the result of a nasty fall from a hayloft, whence the child had attempted to follow her father. The father was painfully attached with every fiber of his being to this unfortunate child who remained patiently on her bed, day in and day out, playing with her puppets or arranging her gravel pebbles, and who reacted with such genuine appreciation to every kind word or encouraging gesture.

Upon receiving a summons to fight for a cause that had already cost so much human life and about which he was completely detached and neutral, he decided to take to the *brush* instead, which is to say, he decided to hide out in the deepest recesses of the forest to avoid the levies of the local officials. Many others attempted to follow his example, but all with the exception of himself and his companion and fellow draft evader, Jörg Müller, had either eventually been caught or had come to some sort of accommodation with the local *recruiting officer*, either as a result of outright bribery, or as a result of voluntarily turning themselves in, in which case the officer was inclined to look the other way and accept all sorts of fanciful excuses sworn to by the delinquents.

Several expeditions had been mounted to snare the two draft dodgers, but thanks to Herwisch's fleetness and Müller's cunning, they had always managed to escape with their hides intact. Müller, who had never taken much to hard work, rather enjoyed his exile, while his wife was satisfied, so she maintained, with not having to cook for her ne'er-do-well husband. Herwisch, however, worried himself sick about his wife and little children. Often, on those nights when the air was clear and the sky bright, he would steal back home to visit his loved ones and, with plow, axe and hoe, take care of the most pressing tasks of the homestead before the morning gray warned him to flight. But for several months now he had not risked the trip because the more critical the manpower shortages of the South had grown over against the numerical superiority of the North, the more aggressive the *"heel flies"* in Texas had become in mounting sweeps to round up *conscripts*.

"Captain Ringwell must be in a financial bind again, since he is so keen to mount these sweeps," opined those who were well acquainted with the recruiting officer. A few days after Kuno's return ride, the sad news swept through the settlement that Herwisch's oldest daughter, the small Amanda, was dying. The measles raged in many families in the area at the time, and often in a very virulent form. Herwisch's young children appeared to have weathered the disease all right, but his daughter had not exhibited the usual symptoms, and had succumbed instead to a high fever that produced a delirium in which she constantly called out for her beloved *pappy*. The anxious mother finally called upon Frau Lüttenhoff, the most trusted nurse and confidant to all the sick and distressed in the settlement, to come to her assistance. It took only a quick look at the normally pale complexion of the young sufferer, which had now turned an unnatural brownish-red and a brief listen to her labored and congested breathing, to grasp the seriousness of the situation. After a few words of consolation, she quickly returned home and dispatched her husband to Collinsville to fetch a doctor as soon as possible. Thereafter, she hurried back to the sickbed of the child.

Lüttenhoff had intercepted the physician, Dr. Bretthauer, a Swiss surgeon whose rude bedside manner was often more pronounced than his abilities as a doctor, while making rounds in the vicinity, and contrary to the usual situation, he found him sober, but, as customary, in a sour mood. He was, however, willing to pay a visit and soon thereafter found himself in the humble bedroom of the young victim. He examined the patient, felt her pulse, mumbled incomprehensibly to himself through the stubble of his beard and finally announced in a very direct and untactful manner:

"'Hops and malt'[172] won't do any good at this point. Why do people wait to summon the doctor when they need the undertaker instead? The little girl will not survive until sundown, and for the pitiful little creature, that will be the best for her."

And without another word, he tramped out of the house and disappeared. Bretthauer's prognosis proved to be correct. Only a few hours later the grieving mother threw herself upon the lifeless form of her child. The poor woman had known very little in her life except constant worry and hard work. For the last three years, she had lived with never-ending anxiety concerning her husband, and often, in moments of deepest despair, had said to herself that it would be better if death would come and free her hopelessly crippled daughter from her present suffering and from all earthly misery, as well. Now that the Grim Reaper[173] had so unexpectedly come to liberate her, she was frozen in grief, and Frau Lüttenhoff and the other ladies of the neighborhood tried in vain to console her as they went about the business of disrobing the young girl and dressing her in her funeral attire, which came from Frau Anna's linen closet. After it had become fully dark outside, one suddenly heard the disturbed cries that marsh snipes make when frightened from their nests and forced to take flight. Startled out of her state of frozen grief, Frau Herwisch rushed outside and began striking the wash basin that was outside the door. Soon thereafter, the women inside could hear the sounds of loud weeping and one could clearly discern the voice of a man as well.

"Don't cry so hard, my dear Gustav, our Mandelchen is much better off now."

At this Frau Lüttenhoff remarked:_

"The poor father has been summoned. Let us go. Our work is done and now we want to leave the couple alone to deal with their grief and pain, and let us stay silent as we leave."

The neighboring women returned with first light the following morning to help place and properly situate the child in the wooden coffin that a carpenter had hastily put together overnight, and also to receive directions from the parents concerning arrangements for the burial. Frau Herwisch was now more composed and requested that the burial take place as soon as possible under the large live oak where the child's grandfather was also buried. She had one further wish:

"If it might be possible to fetch Pastor Langjochen so that he could speak a couple of words over our departed Amanda?"

Soon the small body was resting in the coffin, white straw flowers from Frau Lüttenhoff's garden neatly arranged on her breast. During this period, the bedroom had remained closed and locked and the men outside could pick out a gentle sobbing. They departed the house without further questions.

It was close to midday when the small Franzel ran up to his mother in the kitchen.

"Look Mommy," he cried, "there are many people outside coming to see the body of my sister."

At this, Frau Herwisch rushed to the kitchen window and spied a large group of mounted men approaching her house from all sides, their rifle muzzles sparkling in the sun, and heard the barking of blood hounds being led on the leash.

"Max and Joseph, come here quick! The conscription officers are here to get my Joseph!" she stammered as she rushed into the living room where the coffin had been set up for the wake to warn her husband and urge him to try to hide himself as quickly as possible. Joseph, who did not want to leave the side of his beloved daughter until she was committed to the earth, looked around in dazed confusion, noticed the riders and the four-legged human hunters, and considered that perhaps he might be able to hide himself under the coffin. Frau Herwisch, however, quickly called her children inside, fetched the axe from the woodpile, and stationed herself in front of the door, as if to defend her husband with all her frail might. In the meantime, Joseph had regained his wits and rushed to the window to observe the movements of the *heel flies*, who, as a first step, had surrounded the small *corn crib* and proceeded to search it thoroughly with loaded weapons at the ready. Then two men approached, one with a saber slung from his side—it was the head of the recruiting office, Captain Ringwell—who called out loudly:

"In the name of the Confederate States of America and the law, open the door!"

"Cow and Hunting Scene." Friedrich Richard Petri papers, [11948], The Dolph Briscoe Center for American History, The University of Texas at Austin.

Resistance would have been completely useless, even if Herwisch were the sort to try it, and any attempt at flight, equally hopeless, since the forest along Possum Creek was a good half-mile distant. Nevertheless, all he could think about was making a run for it. With his weathered right hand, he stroked the folded hands of his child one last time, called out a farewell to his wife, and in a split second exited the back door of the house. Heeding neither commands to stop nor threats to shoot, he lit out at a full run across the open field, his tall frame bent over, making a bee line for the nearest woods, and his pace was only increased by the shots that were fired his way. The shots, incidentally, were not intended to hit their target, because Ringwell had had made it very clear to his *boys* that they were not to kill or cripple Herwisch; that they could hound him to their heart's desire, but he needed to remain alive and sound of limb.

"The bum has already caused me enough trouble, and he's not going to end up lying in bed and sitting out the war with a lame leg, especially since I already have ruined my best horse chasing after him. They'll break him of his habit of running away soon enough in the army."

Hezekiah Ringwell was head of an office that caused a lot of people to loathe and despise him. By virtue of his official position and authority, he had assumed the title of *captain*, but in truth, he was anything but a tyrant; actually, a sympathetic sort at root who enjoyed playing practical jokes. In addition to what the Americans called *an itching palm*, he possessed many other character defects such as a strong penchant for brandy, whiskey, rum, port, and all other forms of alcoholic beverages known to him, a passion for gambling on horse races, and an addiction to playing poker with more gusto than luck. The result of all this was that he found himself in constant financial embarrassment, and those who possessed money or other financial resources, and who were not, as Winzig was, too conscientious to consider bribery, found it an easy matter to avoid their service obligations. Recently, because his financial woes had once again become acute, he had made the rounds afresh of all who were subject to conscription and, under the pretext of new orders from his superiors, extorted whatever additional money he could get. His constant companion on these forays was his younger brother, Houston Ringwell, a totally dissolute character, and a German, Ferdinand Schmeier, who owned a small store at Live Oak Hill near Collinsville. Because Ringwell was his best customer at the brandy barrel he kept there, he had also been spared conscription, and had assumed the despicable role as both blood hound and snitch on his own fellow countrymen. And it often transpired that the recruiting officials not only accepted bribes on their forays into the countryside, but often also helped themselves to chickens, young calves, and pigs at the farmsteads they visited. Ringwell was especially annoyed at Herwisch, who had cost him so much time and energy with little to show for it either in bribery or booty. However, when Herwisch made his break and his brother yelled for the Negros to set loose the hounds, Ringwell had quickly countermanded the order.

"We can catch the bum in spite of his long legs and we don't want to cause bad blood by letting the dogs loose on a white man like we would a *nigger*," he said.

"*Nigger* or *Dutchman*, what's the difference?" his brother replied. The dogs, however, while pulling frantically at their leashes and barking furiously, remained tied.

As long as he remained over plowed land that was still somewhat boggy from the recent rains, the fleet-footed fugitive stayed ahead of his pursuers, easily reaching the fence and leaping over it in one clean bound, but once upon the prairie, his pursuers soon caught up to him and surrounded him. He made a vain attempt to break through but an expert throw of a *lasso* snared him and his feet were jerked out from under him. Others quickly tied his hands behind his back. He was manhandled to his feet, but was so exhausted and out of breath from his exertions that he could barely stand. His breast was heaving like it would burst, and he looked for all the world like a crazy man. With blows from canes and quirts, he was forced to walk between two riders with the *lasso* still securely fixed around his body as far as the *fenz*[174] that enclosed his farm. Once there, he stammered out the wish in German that he be able to return to his house for one last farewell to his loved ones. Schmeier translated and the *captain* was inclined to grant the request, but his brother protested.

"If we allow that we are going to have trouble with his wife for sure," he said. "It is better if we get him out of here right away."

"Yea, I reckon you have already had your share of trouble with German wives and won't forget it anytime soon."[175]

The comment touched a sore wound for his brother. A few months before Houston Ringwell and one assistant had attempted to arrest a German citizen of Collinsville during the night who had overstayed his leave and who lay sick in bed. When he knocked on the door and no one answered, he broke the latch and forced his way into the house whereupon two scantily clad women, one the wife and the other the mother-in-law of the sick man, threw themselves upon him, relieved him of his pistol, and then attacked him with fingernails and broom, scratching and thrashing him so severely that he refused to be seen in public until his injuries healed. Only with effort could his companion restrain him from shooting at the women once he escaped to the outside, an act that, had he followed through, would have forever covered him with shame and humiliation.

"Still," Captain Ringwell continued, "you have a good point there; the shots will certainly have been heard, and since the matter doesn't look too pretty here, it is highly likely that we would have trouble, if not with the wife, then with the neighbors. Let's get out of here!"

When Herwisch heard that his request had not been granted, he struggled with all his might to free himself, but in vain, and the rope that bound him only cut deeper into his wrists. With curses and strikes from a cane, he was placed on a horse behind a Negro and for further security, his feet were tied together under the belly of the horse, and as he sat there in silence, incapable of moving a limb, his bloodshot eyes bespoke now plainly not fear but blind hatred, and they did so with a ferocity that justified the added measures. Ringwell and his men quickly departed though not in the direction of the county seat but rather toward Collinsville.

Soon thereafter, a couple of the neighbors came running up who only a short time before had prepared the gravesite and had been on the way back home when they heard the shots. They found Frau Herwisch, her frightened child by her side, lying unconscious on the back steps of the house, bleeding profusely from a wound on the back of her head. They quickly carried her into the house and placed her on the bed and then splashed water on her face and washed her wound, which was not deep and had been caused solely by the fall. Soon thereafter, Herr Lüttenhoff and his wife arrived and several others as well. After a short while the poor wife began to come to her senses, and she commenced right away to wail:

"Help Maria and Joseph, they wanted to take my Seppl[176] away."

She had stepped outside and had witnessed how her husband was chased like a wild animal and when he finally fell to the ground, she had fainted, fell and struck her head on the steps.

The body of the young girl was to be interred at three o'clock in the afternoon. Despite a raw southeast wind, only young children and the unwell from a very wide circumference were missing for the burial ceremony, for the news of what had taken place had spread with the speed of the wind to all the homes of the community. One could easily see both anger and sympathy in the faces of the men and women who had gathered at the house and farmstead. The question made the rounds: "Who was the scoundrel who informed Ringwell where he could catch Herwisch for sure?" Only one person came forth with an answer: Bertrand.

"In all of Possum Creek only one person is missing, and that is Grossenberg and we know that Grossenberg came home late last night." Bertrand phrased his statement in such a way that it was clearly accusatory, and several in the crowd, remembering that Grossenberg had often castigated draft dodgers as cowards and traitors, accepted the accusation as proven, and began to curse the missing man. The majority, however, and certainly those who knew Grossenberg well, characterized such accusations as nonsense, while Winzig, clearly agitated and angry, denounced them as pure infamy.

Just as the casket was closed, Pastor Langjochen arrived, riding a sled with a chair affixed thereto, pulled at a maddeningly slow tempo by a span of oxen despite the fact that the good pastor was attempting to urge the beasts to a faster pace by poking at them with a long stick, something that was quite out of character for their master. He was not clad in priestly garb, but rather attired simply in multiple darned and patched farmer's clothes; he possessed neither church nor congregation, but anyone who saw him could mistake him for none other than a man of the cloth. In the Old Country, he had once made a name for himself in a large city as a well-regarded *Kanzelredner.*[177] However, his original research as well as his own speculations had led him to results that did not mesh well with the accepted attitudes of the *Kultusminsterium*[178] and its members. He was offered friendly advice with the suggestion that he show a little more deference and tact and not sabotage a promising career, but in answer they received only responses with an Old-Testament flavor, which is to say, direct and unadorned. He continued to preach after a manner that was consistent with his heartfelt convictions, and his church was always packed with worshipers. The powers that be, however, increasingly attempted to throttle him, until finally, in spite of his wife's unholy protestations against his stubborn willfulness, he laid aside his vestments, resigned his office, and emigrated across the sea where, once settled as a farmer in the wooded area near Krähwinkel,[179] he provided for his family in an upright but exceedingly humble fashion. Several members of the community had attempted to persuade him to offer regular church services, and had promised to build a church to this end, but he replied that he had taken a vow to never preach for money again. Nevertheless, when circumstances called for it, he always made himself readily available to offer either words of admonition or consolation, a true comforter of the soul. The people loved and adored him, and even the unbelievers among the *Lateiner* held this genuine priest of love in high regard. As the leader of an excellent double quartet in quieter times, he had also gained general approval. In spite of his decidedly taciturn nature, he was sincerely congenial when in society and always took pleasure in the happiness and good fortune of his fellows.

Whoever saw him standing at the graveside today in his heavily mended coat, bent over, the long strands of already graying hair blowing in the wind, could not fail to be reminded of the disciples of Jesus, who ventured forth to the various lands to spread the teachings of the One from Nazareth among all peoples and classes. To begin with, he spoke softly and haltingly, as if suppressing with difficulty strong emotions from within. Then, in the deepest, most heartfelt tones, he admonished the mother, who was near to collapsing, and only kept upright by two other women at her side, not to lose faith in the Father of all widows and orphans, without whose will the smallest sparrow could not fall from the roof; whose ways were unfathomable to man, and who often allowed a beautiful happiness to bloom and unfold from the deepest depths of despair. And then as he mentioned her spouse, his voice swelled to new strength:

"Our God is a God of forgiveness and compassion. He reads the hearts of men and sees in all our doings our true purposes. He is able to forgive those who tear a grieving father away from the body of his child, men for whom even a place of death is not hallowed ground; he can also forgive the one who betrayed Joseph Herwisch, even though we are not able to do so and must recoil in horror before one who has shamed all of humanity by such an act.

Thus spoke the respected Man of God, and eyes that before had been moistened with tears now shone with righteous anger, and hands that had been folded in prayer, now clenched into tight fists.

With tender words of consolation, words of hope for a better day, when peace would heal the wounds of a long and bitter war, Langjochen closed his remarks. The women accompanied the grieving mother into her house. A group of men, however, remained for a while a short distance from the gravesite, speaking excitedly among themselves, until they too finally dispersed.

A CONSPIRACY AND WHAT BECAME OF IT

This day, so sad for Possum Creek, also brought a bitter disappointment in the evening for the young Albert Lüttenhoff. It was his birthday and, according to his father's determination, he was to receive on that day the key to the library, that treasure trove containing the knowledge of millennia. The father had come to the opinion that it was wrong to force children onto a treadmill of regimented study before their eighth year; that when given free rein to develop both mentally and physically beforehand, they would progress even more rapidly thereafter. Albert, however, had been accelerated in his development by constant interaction with older and more serious people. He was also exceptionally bright for his age and, for a long time now, had longed fervently for the day when he could decipher for himself all the strange symbols and begin the process of exploring the pages contained between the covers of the many books, both large and small, without having to wait for either his sister or his parents to find the time and inclination to read aloud to him. But the evening found the father so out of sorts that he declared it would be out of the question to begin the first lesson and, after the evening meal, where he barely ate a bite, retired to his study and lost himself in a weighty pedagogical study. To counter a decision of the father was out of the question even for the youngest and most pampered child in the Lüttenhoff household; only with effort was he able to hold back the tears that were beginning to well up in his eyes, while both mother and sister attempted to console the dejected birthday child; the mother with the promise of cracking all the pecans he had gathered and topping the planned Christmas cakes with them; the sister with the offer to read him his favorite fairy tale, the story of the twelve swan brothers and their sister from the book of fairy tales by Hans Christian Anderson.

Mr. Phillips had observed correctly: Lüttenhoff had seemed very despondent since the episode with Hedwig. Kuno's broken vow—and this is the only way he could construe Kuno's sudden change of mind—had hit him like a blow to the face by the hand of a loved one. He had locked him in his heart almost as if he were his own son, this promising and capable young man, whose eagerness and enthusiasm often swept his teacher along and who, in many respects, reminded him of his second eldest son, the one who had been murdered way out there in the wilds of West Texas. To be sure, he had looked hard to find mitigating circumstances, but he always came back to a central thought that he could not escape: "He gave me his word freely and openly, and broke it offering neither excuse nor explanation." Today, however, he had witnessed how a fellow countryman had been hunted down and torn from the casket of his child, a man who had done exactly what Kuno would have needed to do to avoid service in the army. The episode forced him to confront the question: "Was it not a mistake and an injustice on my part that I accepted his vow outright without advising him against a decision that would necessarily bring him into conflict with the laws of the land?" Such self-doubt, alas, only served to strengthen his bitterness toward his once beloved student; so it is with human nature.

It must have been around eight o'clock when from outside a hearty "Hallo" could be heard. The whole collection of dogs—Pluto, Diana, and the younger pups—began barking furiously. Lüttenhoff rushed outside and, as he did so, fetched the leather whip with the heavy lead handle—formerly known as the "Death Dealer"—from the saddle hanger on the wall of the outside gallery. Frau Anna and the children also rushed out on the gallery, fearing danger for spouse and father, but when she recognized the voice of the caller, she returned with her children into the house, fully reassured.

It was Peter Kägel at the *gate*, formerly a respected citizen of Mecklenburg, a man straight as an arrow, solid and capable in all ways. In the early years, he had worked for Lüttenhoff until he had saved up enough money to send for his wife and set up his own farm. He also established and operated the local horse gin and mill, an occupation that qualified him for deferment from military service.[180] He conducted all his affairs with such frugality and attention to detail that Lüttenhoff had prophesized that one day he would become the Croesus[181] of Possum Creek. His deep admiration and respect for Lüttenhoff, whom he had always been able to rely on for honest and straightforward advice, was touching.

"Herr Lüttenhoff, you must come quickly if we are to avoid a great calamity! he said in a voice that was clearly agitated, and then continued in great haste, falling into his native Low German dialect:[182]

"A group of our people with *Long Mike* in the lead have sworn to free Herwisch this very night, and if the conscriptors don't stand aside, then they are going to kill them too, my God, not good, as much as I would like to see the poor man set free, but they will only end up facing the devil's revenge!"[183]

"Have the people then taken leave of their senses? replied Lüttenhoff, "If they carry through with this, then we will see vicious reprisals with little distinction between the innocent and guilty. There are people enough who are just looking for the opportunity to murder and burn out the Unionists, and especially Unionists among the Germans.

"I have told them the same thing, interjected Kägel, "but they don't want to listen to me and called me a scaredy-cat and a fear monger instead, and then I thought, there is only one person who can help, my old boss Lüttenhoff. They are planning on rendezvousing this very evening near Leibock's place on the Collinsville *rot*.[184] There is no time to lose. I have brought along my *Bossy* so you don't have to catch and saddle your own horse."

Lüttenhoff hurried back into the house to grab a couple of things and to inform his wife briefly that he felt compelled to accompany Kägel in a very serious matter. She should not grow anxious, he insisted, if he only returned very late in the night; there was no danger to him personally. Frau Anna knew very well that there was no sense in trying to dissuade her husband when he felt strongly that his sense of duty demanded action. She implored him, at the very least, to take along a firearm, but he turned this request down, since he saw no use for it. Then he gave her and the children a farewell kiss, and departed in haste with Kägel into the night.

A half an hour later, they arrived at the rendezvous, a place where three large live oaks stood in a small depression of a large sand hill not far from the Collinsville Road. The clouds being driven across the sky by a rising southeasterly wind only permitted a few stars to peek through now and then. Still, Peter's sharp eyes picked out the group of men already gathered; some on horseback, others dismounted.

"Who goes there?" came a sharp command.

"It is me Lüttenhoff, your neighbor and friend, and Peter Kägel is with me. We have come to advise against what you are planning, which will only bring calamity and misfortune to you and your families.

This declaration was followed by a few moments of murmuring and hushed discussion, whereupon a very tall man came up to them, a man who did not need to open his mouth in order to be recognized, and who was universally known as *Long Mike*.

"Herr Luttenhoff," he said, "we all know that you mean well, but you are wasting your time here. It is best if you ride back home and pretend you have neither heard nor seen anything. We are going to free Herwisch tonight because we can't stand the thought of a German being *getrietet*[185] like a dog. And if we have to *killen* a few of the *rowdies* in the process, so be it, because they earned it, the way they treated poor Herwisch and his wife and children."

"Mike is right," seconded several voices in the group.

"People, be reasonable, replied Lüttenhoff. "I understand your anger. But you cannot forget that you are breaking the law, and that the punishment for forcibly freeing conscripts is death.

"They have got to catch us before they can hang us, and they won't find that so easy, and now we don't want to waste any more time with useless talk," answered a short man with a hoarse voice. It was the tanner, Franz Gerloff, who often, after a stiff drink or two, liked to brag how he had once shot to kill during the street battles in Vienna.[186]

"At least let me hear what you are planning on doing, Lüttenhoff continued, "You know that I will never betray you!

"*Well,* we have *plenty* of time and it won't do any harm to hear out a man who has more *sense* in his little finger than most people have in their heads," spoke *Mike.*

He explained then the plan of attack. It was known that Ringwell had ridden to Collinsville with his band in order to arrest a couple of men eligible for service who had just returned from Mexico. These men, however, had been forewarned and had made their escape. The band then returned to Schmeier's place where they had gathered around the brandy barrel, as usual, and it was to be expected that they would not resume the ride to the county seat before midnight, most of them inebriated by this point. The plan was to jump them at the *crossing* on Palmetto Creek and relieve them of their captive.

"*They won't be able to help themselves,*" explained Mike, "We have eleven men and they only have five, since Schmeier doesn't like to go out after dark, and the two darkies don't count. The older Ringwell will be full as a *tick,* and his brother Houston is a *coward.* I can take care of a half a dozen of the sort by myself," explained *Mike,* who had a tendency to such swagger.

"They will never recognize us since we have masks for everyone that we will tie before our eyes and if someone betrays us, then he knows what to expect," added Gerloff.

"Well then, that is your plan. Disguised like assassins, under the protection of darkness, you sons of German soil intend to waylay duly authorized officials, who—although in an inhumane, brutal fashion—were still in the final analysis doing their duty. And make no mistake about it, you are putting yourselves in a situation where in all likelihood you will have no choice but to kill the men you ambush. If only one of them offers resistance, if only one of you is recognized, then you will have to do away with the whole lot, including the Negros, so that no one remains to identify you before the judge. Then you will also have to bury the bodies deep in the forest and cover your tracks well enough that they don't betray you. And even if you succeed in all of this, how are you going to face your wives and children with such a bloodguilt on your consciousness. "Spilled blood cries to the heavens,"[187] and "Nothing is spun so fine that it doesn't come to light,"[188] sayings you all learned in school. And even if you get away with it, you will have your own conscious to live with. But that's not the end of it, not only you, but also your children, your wives, and all your neighbors will be called to account for this act. The same people who would have gladly driven all of the immigrants out of the country ten years before will at the slightest provocation turn their hatred upon us, burn out our farmsteads, and drive us from hearth and home. So, take heed of what it will mean for all of us if blood is spilled on the Palmetto because of your misguided anger and outrage. I have given you my word that that I will keep silent, but now I regret it, in which case I would already be underway to warn Ringwell."

So spoke Lüttenhoff in a voice, resolute and firm, and those who heard him have since come to the opinion that he was a born preacher who had missed his true calling.

At all events, his speech struck a chord. To be sure, Gerloff continued to mutter about spineless second-guessing and sanctimonious yammering,[189] but others were heard to say, "Yes, this is correct," or "Shedding blood, that would not be good," while the cabinet maker Frohman stated unequivocally, "Herr Lüttenhoff is right, and I want nothing more to do with it. Several amongst them, however, with Gerloff at the lead, attempted to sneak off, but in a thunderous voice, *Mike* ordered them back.

"*Süre, Mister* Lüttenhoff is right and we have been genuine *fools* because we haven't *konsidert* the matter fully. For my part, I don't aim to become a murderer, even though, I have to admit, I have whittled a couple of notches in my *rifle* for them that had to bite the dust in a *fair fight*. We need to go back home and keep our mouths shut. But at the very least, we want to do something to help out *Misses* Herwisch and her kids. Tomorrow I will go over and plow her *patch* and when I am finished I will return to the front so that I don't do anything more stupid here; all the rest of you can help her with getting her fields in shape and *fixin* her *fenz* and *meinden*[190] that she has something in her *smokehouse* and *pantry*. And now let's give, "*Three cheers and a tiger*"[191] because he has *ge-seeft*[192] us all. But we don't want to make any unnecessary *fuss*. And now back home, *forward, march!*"

This time there was no dissent. Kägel accompanied Lüttenhoff on his return home so he wouldn't lose the way since, in the meantime, it had grown much darker. Once arrived, he found his wife and children still awake by the light of a tallow lamp. She had found consolation in reading aloud to the children passages from Zschokke's *Hours of Devotion*,[193] failing to notice in the meantime that the hour for putting the children to bed, otherwise so punctually observed, had passed. With an expression more cheerful than she had seen in weeks, Lüttenhoff entered, and after he had given all a warm hug, exclaimed, Thanks be to God! Everything turned out all right, and now, children, off to bed with you, and you Albert, get a good night's sleep, because we want to start with your reading lessons first thing in the morning!

It only became clear to the conspirators the following morning what a disaster had been averted due to Lüttenhoff's timely *sermon*. Hezekiah Ringwell, it turns out, had returned with his prisoner escorted by a sizeable number of reinforcements. A Confederate captain and a dozen mounted troops on leave from the western counties, all armed, had stopped at Schmeier's place to take their supper. When the captain saw that Ringwell was drunk, he ordered him to accompany him back to the county seat, and to serve as a guide to himself and his people.

TAKING HIS LEAVE

If the hours had slipped by at a snail's pace for Kuno before, they suddenly seemed to sprout wings and fly by unbelievably fast during his few remaining days at home. The shoemaker Wohlfahrt had outdone himself: he actually had the commissioned boots finished by the appointed day; a promptness that normally ran contrary to the professional code of the sons of Crispins.[194] Along with the boots, Kuno also received many practical suggestions for their proper upkeep and use.

Kuno immediately put the new cowhide boots to a thorough test. After first rubbing deer tallow into the leather, he went on a long ride. He had decided that a careful and methodical inspection of his father's livestock holdings would be a worthwhile endeavor. His sizeable herd of cattle grazed along Possum Creek and on both sides of Palmetto Creek, but the great majority ranged across the vast prairie that stretched between the two big river drainages.[195]

Soon after the beginning of the war, Sartorius had entrusted the oversight of the cattle far from the *settlement* to a well-known livestock manager. His name was Jacob Ehrlich and his first impression was that of a simpleton, but in order to avoid saying that, people often called him direct and honest, a trait suggested by the literal meaning of his name.[196] But he was certainly clever enough to avoid service in the army, and it did not cost him a lot, just a fat calf now and then for Ringwell's kitchen.

For his oversight duties, Ehrlich was supposed to receive every fourth calf, which he was required to brand. Kuno was forced to conclude during his three-day tour that the calves selected by the honest herdsman for his own must have been considerably hardier than those left to his father. Among the younger stock on the *flat* prairie, the "S" *brand* appeared only occasionally, while the "JE" *brand* was as common as the sand along the sea and the younger cows and heifers appeared to carry the latter brand almost exclusively.

What he found was not wholly unexpected, but the scale of it exceeded his worst fears. Otherwise, the cattle were in good shape despite the fact that the long drought had left the grass very short. Their curiosity aroused at the unaccustomed sight of a solitary rider, six- and seven-year-old longhorn steers, many as fat as if they had been fed grain, would often approach and surround Kuno, bellowing and snorting, until he waved his hat or let out a yell, at which point they turned tail and stampeded off causing the ground to reverberate with the force of their hooves.

Kuno had brought his shotgun along and used it to his pleasure to bag wild fowl which he roasted over the evening fire, rounding out his simple fare of bacon and bread. At every patch of standing water along the way, large flocks of wild ducks and occasionally geese took to wing and arose into the sky. Under the *pin oaks*[197] that bordered the small streams, countless ducks competed with prairie chickens[198] for the acorn mast. Deer he encountered in abundance, often in herds of twenty or more, but precisely because of their numbers, offered little opportunity for a clean shot.

On the trip back home, however, when he was a scant ten miles from home, his hunter's luck changed. He was attempting to stalk some wild ducks he had heard quacking in a pond skirted by a lush growth of reeds and tall grass when a splendid six-pointer sprang up in front of him. The startled animal regarded him in astonishment for a split second before turning tail in panicked flight. But before his white flag[199] could disappear into the undergrowth, a shot cracked from the barrel of the shotgun, and the animal fell mortally wounded to the ground. Because the added weight would have been too much for Polly on the remaining journey, Kuno only dressed out the hams and prized backstraps[200] to bring back home.

Once home, his mother greeted him with the gentle reproach that it was unfortunate that he had spent so much of his precious time that remained out hunting rather than at his parents' house. Kuno explained to her what had been his real purpose, but his mother demurred:

"What is so important about the cattle that I have to do without my boy for so long?"

"My boy," how sweet this sounded to Kuno's ear, an ear unaccustomed to such tenderness on the part of his mother. Like most young men of his age, he hated endearments, but to be called "my boy" by his mother, that was something that he could live with, and for the remaining days of his stay in the family house, a bond strengthened between mother and son that was substantial and touching. The mother was all love and admiration for her son, whose new-found maturity had filled her with pride and happiness. The mother's small shortcomings, well-known to Kuno, only reinforced his love, for which he now gave full expression.

Kuno found his father on the road to recovery from his back ailment, but still irritable because of the prolonged period of enforced idleness in his room, as if under house arrest. Kuno's report in respect to the misappropriation of livestock did not seem to concern the father all that much.

"Well then, Jacob Ehrlich, despite his long ears and flowing mane, is not so dumb after all, and has worn the donkey mask only as a disguise. The Texas climate, it appears, can breed *smartness* even in the poorest of soils. But there is nothing we can do about it since I am no good as a cowman, and my Negros are even less suited, and if I replace Jacob's contract with another one, the odds are ten to one, when all is said and done, that we won't have a single calf left on the prairie with our brand on it, because the problem will just shift from the one to the other. But I am very glad nevertheless that you took it upon yourself to have a thorough look, and all the more so since you had just rescued my bag of gold from the clutches of that sly old fox Bolton. By the way, Kuno, what has happened between you and Lüttenhoff?

"What do you mean?"

"He came by yesterday with his wife and children on their rounds visiting the sick and repaying visits. Frau Anna expressed her sincere thanks for all you did during the rescue of Hedwig, but complained that you had not shown your face at their house since the event. However, Lüttenhoff, who otherwise has taken such a keen interest in you, seemed to shy away from even mentioning your name, except for when he said his goodbyes, at which point he did express the hope that you will return no worse for the wear in the very near future—he fully expects, as you well know, that the Confederacy will completely collapse any day now."

"For the sake of the parents!" added Kuno in the spirit of his teacher's words, whom he had so ardently hoped to put out of his mind. But in order to avoid his father's question, he suddenly saw himself in urgent need of looking after his horse.

Kuno happened to meet Michel Schmidt on a ride to the post office the next day and found out from him that he intended to end his much-prolonged furlough the following morning and return to his regiment. He invited Kuno to accompany him if he could be ready to depart by then, an offer Kuno was more than happy to accept. Michel served in a cavalry regiment that was stationed in North Louisiana, and had returned home on a fine Yankee horse expropriated from the enemy. But because the authorities had confiscated his *iron grey*, a favorite mount he had brought along from the farm for his own use in the war, along with all the horses of his regiment, in order to save the Confederate canons from Bank's advancing bluecoats,[201] he had resolved never again to bring a good horse into the war zone.

"Being afoot is not for me," he said, "but I have a couple of *scrub ponies* out on the prairie, one for me and one for you. We can ride them until we are far enough along and then turn them loose to find their own way back to their home *range*, which the two nags will easily do if somebody doesn't appropriate them along the way."

This well-intentioned suggestion suited Kuno quite well for although he was a good walker he still felt much more at home on the back of a horse, and had secretly dreaded the long march to the front. With words of thanks sealed with a handshake, he took his leave from *Long Mike*, a person who, especially among the young men of Possum Creek, had earned a lot of respect and admiration.

Back at the house, Kuno carefully examined his field gear once again. He then undertook a march around the perimeter of the farm. He found several spots where *riders*[202] had passed through the split rail fence and failed to replace the *rails*, leaving them on the ground. He carefully returned them to their *stakes*, fuming inwardly at the neglect of the Negroes, who were the most likely culprits. Finally, he struck a straight course in order to have one final look at this narrowly bounded world, which he called home, where every tree, every *gully*, and every body of water held a personal memory.

As a ten-year-old, there on the small pond between the sand hills, he had bagged his first wild game. From the gallery of the house he had noticed a flock of wild ducks settle on the pond. Since his father was not at home, and without a second thought, he took his father's fine, double-barreled English shotgun from the corner behind the writing desk where it was kept and ventured out for the hunt. He stalked the ducks slowly and carefully, paying little heed to the grass burrs[203] digging into his flesh that Winzig had sarcastically termed *Texas forget-me-nots*.

Using tall clumps of grass as cover, he finally maneuvered his way into shooting range. But as the young upstart raised the heavy shotgun to fire, he began to quiver in excitement, and it took a long time before he was finally able to bring a couple of the black heads,[204] who had concealed themselves along the edges of the pond, into his sights. And then his finger squeezed the trigger, and the percussion cap went *snap*—a misfire—and the entire flock, their point bird in the lead, lifted from the pond and flew away unscathed. However, one small bird remained at the far end of the pond, a duck, most likely.

To return empty-handed would be intolerable, and so Kuno resumed the stalk, took aim, and this time the weapon actually responded with a sharp report, and—wonder of wonders—the bird flapped once and the water began to stain red. But when Kuno stood on the banks and rolled up his pant legs to wade in and fetch his prize, the duck, only wounded, quickly dove under the water. With his bare arms and feet, he fumbled around in the ice-cold water, until he could finally locate the injured bird, which now appeared rather small and meager in his hands. It was not a duck, after all, rather a small blue water hen,[205] but still, how the heart of this young hunter beat with pride at his catch. All the more his bitterness when, later, Old Sally positively refused to cook the bird because, so she said, it stunk to high heaven and was completely inedible; this disappointment bitterer even than the chamomile tea he was forced to swallow as a remedy to the thorough wetting and chilling he had received on his first big hunt.

Over there, under a stand of *black jacks*,[206] he had bagged his first prairie chicken (and since then quite a lot more), and from the numerous fishing holes on the upper reaches of Possum Creek he had caught his first *cat-fish* and sun perch. He had often sat under the small waterfall, absorbing the full force of the water and, in later years, had often allowed himself to be swept along by the current over the fall into the foaming waters of the basin below, which had been carved out over time by the stream. Further downstream, under the willow trees, he together with Muller, and later by himself, in order to gain more volume for their swimming hole, had worked himself to the bone with axe, spade, and hoe building a dam, which unfortunately had been swept away by the next flood.

The stream and a small ribbon forest separated his father's holding from Lüttenhoff's field. There were but few trees here that he had not climbed at one time or another, partly out of the sheer pleasure and partly to prove to himself that he could reach their tops and, at other times, to shake down mulberries, wild plums, pecans, and the like for Hedwig or Albert, waiting below. And how often had he waded in the small eddies of water along the creek in order to churn up the water to the point that the water snakes poked their heads out of the water along the banks where they could be pummeled with stones or beaten with sticks until killed—a sport that Hedwig would have nothing to do with, because, so she maintained, it was gruesome and cruel, but which from Kuno's perspective, was justified because of his innate fear of snakes.

There, where a wall of yellow clay speckled with white flecks formed the bank of the creek, an episode had once played out that had left him red with shame. Together with Hedwig, he had spent a hot afternoon in one May picking *dew berries*[207] along the fences, up on the small hills, and, finally, along the creek until the two had finally filled their large wooden pails to the brim with the sweet black berries. Hedwig sat resting on a large grape vine that served as a swing while she sampled the berries, shoving one after the other into her lips that were already stained a dark blue by the fruit.

Meanwhile Kuno, leaning against the bank, was soothing his feet in the water, which had been scratched by the thorny vines. He suddenly turned very pale and let out a yelp of fright while grabbing frantically at his back with both hands, performing the most amazing acrobatic feats as he did so, but unable to reach the spot he groping for. Finally, he shouted in desperation to Hedwig, who was watching in stunned amazement at the sight unfolding below: "A snake has crawled down my neck and is biting me dead!"

At this, Hedwig sprang down to him in one quick motion, knocking over and spilling Kuno's dewberries into the stream, and, with no thought for her own safety, grappled for the unseen assailant under Kuno's blue shirt, and upon seizing it, squeezed it so hard that it finally ceased wiggling. She then yanked it out from under his shirt, but alas, it was only a large but harmless crayfish that had crawled out of his hole in the creek bank that had caused Kuno such a fright and had brought Hedwig to the rescue.

Seeing the creature, she broke out in a fit of laughter, and continued to laugh even harder after Kuno, obviously chagrined and embarrassed, called her a dumb goose and scolded her for spilling his berries into the stream. She then generously offered to share her berries, which Kuno naturally felt compelled to turn down. She did not, however, breath a word of the adventure to others, which was tactful on her part, but she had no qualms about bringing the story up whenever Kuno began mocking the fairer sex for their fear of snakes.

Today, Kuno had only one thought about the affair: "She is a brave girl, after all, and considering how afraid she is of snakes, that was really a much braver action than my night ride," and then he whispered to himself as an afterthought, "and I wonder if I will ever see her again?"

Lost in thought, he continued his walk along the fence in the direction of the Lüttenhoff household rather than toward his home, as if on the way to his lessons.

"There you are! I knew that you would at the very least stop by to bid us adieu," came a clear voice all at once from the other side of the fence.

Looking up, he spied Hedwig's *bonnet*, and thereunder her two bright, clear eyes that he had not seen for an eternity, so it seemed.

"I was not on the way to your house, just taking a stroll along the fence," he replied rather brusquely.

"Yes, I know, you are angry at my father and he at you, and the whole thing makes me so sad. But I wanted to see you before you go off to war and have been waiting over an hour for you. When I saw you begin your tour, I knew you would come this way."

With this Hedwig reached her right hand through the *rider*[208] and the top *rail* of the fence, and Kuno took her hand and squeezed it firmly and earnestly, as if they were old war buddies who had not seen each other in years.

"And Kuno, I really wanted to give you something that I made myself, and didn't know what to do, and then I decided to knit you two woolen socks so that you won't catch cold. I also spun the yarn myself, and it is nice and smooth, but as you know, I am not that good at knitting, but this time I didn't drop any stitches, and hopefully they will fit and you won't make fun of me."

She spouted these words out in a great gush and then quickly reached into her pocket and handed Kuno a small packet through the fence.

"Thanks so very much for this Hedwig," he replied with such a tone of sincere gratitude that his mother would have approved had she heard him, but more he could not bring himself to say at the moment.

"And so, take care, Kuno, and return home safe and sound as soon as possible. Things will turn out ok between you and my father soon enough, you will see—and think about us now and then—and now I have to go. Take care! And with these words, the girl ran back home. Kuno stood for a while, watching his youthful companion, and the feeling overtook him that something important from this farewell had gone missing, but he could not put his finger on what it was. He had never allowed himself to imagine that a farewell could tug at one's heart so wonderfully and make one's throat feel tight. Then he turned and headed home at a quick pace. As he started up the hill on the other side of Possum Creek, Kuno had to turn around for one last look at the Lüttenhoff homestead. Hedwig stood on the gallery, waving her handkerchief, before disappearing inside. Take care, dear Hedwig! Kuno cried out at the top of his lungs, but thankfully none was able to hear him except for the *mule rabbit* that was startled from his place of concealment under a nearby clump of grass and bounded away in fright.

Sally had put together a genuine celebratory feast for Kuno's farewell meal in which the venison backstrap, marinated in vinegar, served as the main course. Kuno's father also serendipitously managed to discover a bottle of Rüdesheimer[209] in his wine case. Later, Kuno's mother refused to let him leave her side, and gently caressed his hands as he sat next to her side, while his father artfully drew upon his rich store of experiences to recall just those memories that helped to cheer her up even as they helped to lessen the strong emotions of the occasion. Here and there he also offered practical and cautionary advice on a number of points to his son, but he did so as comrade rather than as father.

Translator's Note

After the Battle of Yellow Bayou in April 1864, the last battle in General Bank's disastrous Red River campaign, the situation in Louisiana and Arkansas developed into a stalemate. The Confederate generals had no choice but to hold and maintain large armies in reserve in Louisiana, southern Arkansas, and eastern Texas in the event that Union forces should decide to renew the offensive either in Louisiana or Northern Arkansas, or attempt to reoccupy Galveston in Texas. Many of the men were fresh recruits, but the majority now languishing in these camps were seasoned veterans who had experienced heavy combat and hardship either in the New Mexico campaign, the Siege of Vicksburg, or in the various battles associated with the Red River campaign in Louisiana and Arkansas during the spring of 1864. But now the soldiers' main enemies were boredom, hunger, cold, and disease. The Confederate government, by this point, **de facto** *bankrupt, could not adequately feed, clothe, or quarter the thousands of troops and horses found in numerous encampments and forts, large and small, spread* *across Louisiana, Arkansas, and Texas. Deserters and soldiers who simply took leave on their own initiative (AWOL) were rampant but, by and large, the penalties for such derelictions were not harsh, and usually amounted to some regimen of extended duty. Most units were forced to forage the countryside to supplement their meager rations, and in this regard the cavalry units had a distinct advantage as they could sweep far afield on their foraging expeditions. Woe be it to any stray cow, pig, or chicken they encountered.[210] This situation, of course, did not endear them to the local farmers, especially small family farmsteads, who found their livestock and crops under constant threat of confiscation or outright theft, and if they were paid at all for expropriations, it was in Confederate paper currency, which was essentially worthless by this point. Many of the large plantations, on the other hand, seemed to have fared better because the influence and standing of their owners insulated them from the marauding troops. Some of these plantations, like the fictional Fairview Plantation, as we will discover in the course of the narrative, attempted to maintain, as islands of plenty in a sea of deprivation and misery, the gay and privileged lifestyle characteristic of the* **antebellum** *period. Meanwhile, because the great majority of the troops suffered from various degrees of malnutrition and exposure, they became very susceptible to the deadly diseases the period-ically ravaged the camps: typhus, cholera, and yellow fever. By the final count, therefore, many more of the troops succumbed to disease than to the shot and shell of the enemy. It is into this situation that Kuno Sartorius now enters.*

KUNO WANTS TO JOIN HIS REGIMENT

Nine days have elapsed. We find Kuno alongside a deeply rutted military road that leads from Linden in Cass County[211] into Arkansas. It is a clear and starry winter night. The ground is covered with a layer of sleet that fell the night before. The sleet also hangs from the limbs of the *pine* trees as well as from the long strands of moss that drape the oak trees interspersed among the pines. Four men, Michel Schmidt and three others, sit warming themselves around a bright fire skillfully put together out of oak and hickory branches. They are all returning to their units after time spent on leave. The fire casts glowing sparks high above the narrow, sleet-covered opening of their small campsite nestled so quaintly among the sea of trees. Schmidt and his comrades have talked late into the night about their war experiences and debated how long the war might continue. They know that Lee cannot hold Richmond much longer against the Grant's mighty army even though the Southern newspapers strain to paint the situation in a more favorable light. In twenty-four hours, so they write, matters will improve, while the troops stationed in southern Arkansas and northern Louisiana should make a push to northern Arkansas, perhaps as far as Missouri.

Kuno lay to the side of the fire on a bed made of pine needles, wrapped in his cozy wool blanket, in order to get some rest from the long foot march they had just put behind them. The other three men were from Sibley's Brigade, likewise returning from leave, but hauling provisions from Bell County,[212] their home county, in a wagon drawn by two mules. They had overtaken them at this spot and invited the two to accompany them. Two days previous, Michel and Kuno had by choice exchanged their real horses for the "shoemaker's horse."[213]

After fording the Sabine on their horses, they had encountered two men, dressed in ragged gray uniforms, camped on the other side. The one who carried his arm in a sling had shoes on his feet; the other was barefoot; both seemed utterly exhausted. Michel recognized them both right away as fellow soldiers who served in another company of his regiment, Franz Macek and his brother-in-law, Joseph Saha,[214] both from Collinsville. He found out that Saha, as a result of carelessness on the part of another soldier, had received a wound from an Enfield rifle in his upper arm, which had shattered the bone.

He had been removed to a small hospital in a small forest town in Arkansas where his situation became dire and he barely escaped death due to infection and fever. He recovered somewhat but the wound would not heal properly; the arm remained stiff and, finally, a sympathetic doctor obtained a pass for both him and his brother-in-law, who was to accompany him on his journey back home.

They had been underway for five days now, but in their pitiful condition could only make slow progress, and here at the Sabine, they had laid up for several hours, waiting for an opportunity to cross the river. They were undernourished to the point of starvation. Their English deficient to non-existent, they had no luck in securing food from the settlements along the way, which in any case had little to offer. Neither had they had much luck foraging. The convalescent, especially, did not look like he would ever be able to survive the return march home.

Schmidt put an end to their miseries when he explained to the exhausted wayfarers that they would do him a favor by riding the two horses back home, that is back to Collinsville, since from where they were now the horses could only find their way to the home *range* with difficulty. The two men exhausted themselves in thanks to "Pan Meik,"[215] and when Kuno offered them a couple of silver coins from his generously filled money sack that his father had given him to secure food along the way—and, yes, silver is a language everyone understands—and when Michel added a little cornbread and bacon from his provisions to boot, their thanks knew no bounds. The two actually later delivered the horses at Possum Creek and continued on their way to Collinsville on foot. Kuno and Michel, however, bravely continued their march for two days until the forage wagon caught up with them.

As Kuno lay next to the fire listening alternately to the talk of the men and the sounds of the forest creaking and groaning under the weight of the sleet and ice that had clung to the branches and boughs, the events of the past several days passed by in front of him: he relived taking leave from his father, who was only able to mask his feelings by cracking jokes, and saying goodbye to his mother, who gave full vent to her emotions in a flood of tears. Then his audience with Captain Ringwell, to whom he was required to report. In disgust, Kuno recalled the early morning hour of his meeting with this thoroughly corrupt and self-serving man, who had inquired so disingenuously in honey-sweet words about his *"good German friends on Possum Creek.* Then he thought about the long ride, for the most part through endless forests, occasionally passing through small settlements and towns, and then he fell asleep and dreamed of all sorts of things, including Hedwig Lüttenhoff.

A loud "Hallo" and the snorting of horses aroused him from his slumbers. Michel Schmidt's tall figure arose from the fire, which was still burning bright, and as he did so he threw more dry wood onto the blaze. Two riders pulled up next to the fire and, to his astonishment, he recognized through his still sleep-filled eyes Bobby Phillip's yellow manservant, Horace, and then, as the fire illuminated the face of the other rider, he saw that it was none other than his favorite enemy, Robert Emmet Phillips, although now, because he was obviously cold, tired, and out of sorts, he bore scant resemblance to his usual haughty self.

With the help of his Negro, he dismounted stiffly from his horse, and took a place next to the fire, wrapping himself in his blanket. Horace had to pull his boots from his swollen feet while his master groaned and complained—aha, that is Wohlfahrt's tight calf leather—thought Kuno to himself, taking secret pleasure in his discomfort. For his assistance, Horace received only curses and a kick in gratitude.

Kuno started to get up and greet his neighbor's son, but he thought better of it. Under the circumstances, such a reunion would be awkward, to say the least, so he pretended to be asleep in his bed and, later on, was glad that he had done so.

After he has warmed himself a bit, Bobby explained that he had departed Arcadia in Arkansas where his cousin, Lieutenant DeBray, commanded a company in order to report to his own assigned company, which was bivouacked twenty miles to the south near New Camp on the Red River, but the *dumb Nigger* had not paid attention and they had missed their turn. When Michel explained to him that Kuno Sartorius was asleep just a few paces from the fire and suggested that they share the camping place for the night, Bobby quickly retorted:

"No, we have to press on: I don't like to camp out in the open and, in any case, certainly not together with Kuno Sartorius."

With that, he had Horace help him put his boots back on, then both mounted their horses and rode off into the night. Kuno called after them: *"Good night Bobby!"* but received no reply and, soon thereafter, fell back asleep.

The next morning was clear, cold, and very still. After a very meager breakfast, the march was continued and two hours later—so declared Schmidt—they crossed the Texas border into Arkansas. The next morning the driver used his whip generously to keep his two mules to a quick pace and a little past noon the wagon overtook four riders driving two scrawny steers along in front of them—apparently soldiers out foraging although only one from the group wore a Confederate uniform. The uniformed one had slung a large, blue blanket over his shoulders, which offered a most picturesque feature. He was a large, portly man with a red beard, red face, and a still redder nose, and he sat astride a pony so small that his stirrups almost reached to the ground, and so scrawny that one feared it might break under the weight of its rider. The rider, however, called out in a veritable lion's voice to the approaching wagon in very broken English:

"For God's sake, boys, stop popping that whip! Do you want to frighten our lovely fattened steers? You can see for yourselves that our nags are a bit too drawn to even strike a trot."

"*Holy Moses*, there is the *Major*," called out Michel Schmidt, visibly excited. He leapt from the wagon and headed straight for the man he had addressed as "*Major.*"

The *Major*, so labeled because of his enormous body size,[216] was actually named Ferdinand Klösel, and was also a *Lateiner* although, to be sure, not from Possum Creek, but rather from Amacitia[217] on the eastern branch of Palmetto Creek, a small *settlement* comprised of only a half a dozen families but one hundred percent *Lateiner* in makeup.

He had attended more semesters at the university than even Winzig but had never completed his doctorate. He sported a face full of dueling scars[218] and was roundly recognized for his deep bass voice, also for being the life of local taverns and for cheering up many a household on the Texas frontier during his visits. He was a bachelor who had joined the army of his own free will although still a citizen of Germany and a man of considerable means.

He had joined the army because, so he stated, life had become intolerably boring on his miserable little farmstead[219] after all his close friends from neighboring families had been called away to the flag. The entire brigade—excluding the officers, of course—envied Company F for their irrepressible and happy-go-lucky *bon vivant* who, whether in camp or combat; whether hot or cold, or whether stationary or on the move, was always ready with a cheerful song or an amusing story.

He was also legendary for the daring acts of bravado he had pulled off. On a lark, he had once fetched a shiny brass canteen, which was now passing from mouth to mouth, from an open field that was being furiously bombarded by the enemy from behind the protection of a distant rose hedge. Oblivious to the shells hissing over and past, he had ridden his horse nonchalantly at a slow trot across the field to fetch the canteen. On a bet, he had also stolen the pony that he was now riding from behind the picket lines of the enemy because, so he stated, he wanted an animal "that a man could mount and dismount without running the risk of breaking his neck in the process." But through all of this he had emerged untouched except for a couple of telltale signs of bullet holes in his blanket.

Klösel now solemnly dismounted from his horse, shook Michel's hand heartily and spoke:

"Hallo, *Long Mike*. You are returning to the devil's kitchen, you know. 'Old Blücher'[220] has been cursing a blue streak for six weeks now about you AWOL-ers[221] and is going to have you court-martialed for sure. And, wretched soul, returning on foot no less when we are so in need of horses that can jump fences when we are out foraging. You would have done better to stay home and rock your little ones in their cribs. The old man is going to eat you alive; hide, hair, and all."

"Quit talking *nonsense*" replied Michel unperturbed. "The *captain* will be happy when one of his *fellows* comes back who can *distinguish* between a fat calf and a bag of bones. *I'll bet you* the entire five pounds of rolling tobacco that I have brought along, the best *ge-raised* along Possum Creek, and a half dozen *twists*,[222] to boot, against your worn-out riding boots that you bought off 'Old Blücher' for five hundred *greybacks*[223] that I won't get more than two extra duty assignments as punishment because he will be glad to have me back."

"Boy, being among the *Lateiner,* you didn't learn to speak something better than this pathetic mishmash?[224]—but I'll pass on the bet, because anybody around here who has real tobacco, well, he will be able to coax the devil to dance to his tune, and our *captain*, right along, as well. But don't give him all of it; otherwise you'll be hanged and quartered by the rest of us. We haven't had anything decent in our pipes for a long-time; only some of that miserable Louisiana perique[225] now and then, or some of that half-green stuff they grow in the *piney woods* out here. And now, old boy, cheers!"

And with that Klösel pulled the stopper from his nicely silver-plated field canteen, which was amply filled, and passed it around so that everyone got a turn, and even Kuno felt obliged to take a drink. After he had taken a nice swig, which went down like fire, he was introduced by Schmidt, and was warmly greeted by the *Major* with a handshake so firm it caused his knuckles to crack. It turned out that he knew Kuno's father quite well. Upon finding out that Kuno had received orders to join the 2nd company of an infantry regiment, which was stationed near Ft. Lynn[226] not far from the Red River, Klösel related to the astonished young man that had his regiment had marched south already three weeks ago to reinforce coastal defenses somewhere in the vicinity of Sabine Pass.[227] Walker's Cavalry Division[228] had cleaned up South Arkansas so thoroughly, Klösel continued, that not a single clodhopper[229] could be found there.

"And by the way, *boy*," he added—he greeted everybody in this way, even those well up in years—"you are fortunate. I've heard tell that Lake Sabine is full to the brim with all sorts of oysters and gamefish. I wish we could be reassigned there instead of languishing here till we're all skeletons. Why, with a little better grub we would get up the courage to charge and capture those Yankee gunboats on horseback, no less."

With this he looked down so dejectedly at his well-fed corpus, as if he weighed less than a hundred pounds, when in reality he weighed over 250 pounds, that everybody had to laugh.

"Just take a nice, slow march south in the direction of Sabine pass," Michel added, "and if you take your time and aren't in too much of a *hurry*, with a little luck, the war will be over by the time you get there. I doubt if you would *object* to that."

To end his entry into the war in this way, however, was not what Kuno had in mind.

"I have been ordered to go to Fort Lynn and, unless I receive orders to the contrary, I intend to go there," he replied.

"It might be best to discuss the matter with 'Old Blücher,' added Klösel, "He always knows as well as a *judge advocate* what is the proper thing to in such cases."

"Well, I guess so," agreed Michel, "but that wouldn't *suit* me. I would make myself scarce for so long until the *Old Man* got good and worked up."

"Well, *Long Mike*, you won't have to wait long for that. For a week now he has been growling like a bear who's gotten nothing but bee stings and not a single drop of honey. And he's got good reasons for it, too, because the day before yesterday he got word that we have to withdraw even further—Abrahamsohn leaked the news—and to fall back always raises his bile. And today he had the crazy idea to hold a *cavalry drill,* but when his *mother-in-law*[230] reported to him that at best three of our seventy horses could trot more than a hundred steps at a time, then he really turned green with exasperation and mumbled something in his beard about the pathetic care and dreadful neglect of the horses. Finally, we got our allotment of three new recruits from Texas. But because Corporal O'Brien couldn't get anywhere with them, he undertook their training for himself, and the poor souls had to practice the *about face* for a full hour, and then surrender their heels one after the other to endless drills of *double time, single file,* and the likes. And then, to top it all off, he cut himself while shaving. You couldn't arrive at a worse time, and if I were you, I'd turn around right here and now and beat a path back to Possum Creek. My eyes haven't seen anything."

"'Well, *he's not going to have me shot in any case,*" replied Michel, but this time with a little less conviction in his voice.

An hour later they arrived at the *camp* of Company F, which occupied a clearing in the forest next to the major military road. The individual companies that made up the entire regiment as well as the cavalry division were strung out alongside the road since there was no enemy activity in the vicinity and since provisions for the troops in the very sparsely populated region, and especially fodder for the horses, was very hard to come by. The camp of Company F consisted of seven worn and ragged tents and a run-down blockhouse that served as the quarters for the cavalry and other officers.

With pride, Michel Schmidt assured his travel companions that in the entire regiment no other company was so keen on strict military discipline and exemplary camp hygiene as that of Old Blücher. Guards, in the meantime, allowed the wagon to pass and the three men from Bell County continued on their journey while Michel and Kuno walked toward the tents where here and there fires had already been lit to cook the evening meal of bean soup, prepared in large field pots, and corn bread, baked in *skillets*.

Michel was greeted warmly all around by his comrades but several of them made half-hearted jokes to the effect that he had better prepare himself for what was coming, and the suggestion was clear enough. He led Kuno to the last tent in the row and introduced him to his *mess mates* for the evening. First Sergeant Bohne was among them. While it was customary to call the ranking sergeant the "Company Mother," in Bohne's case, the men had taken to calling him the "Mother-in-law," since, as a former Perleberger[231] schoolmaster, he loved to give long and weighty sermons on the subject of morality to his subordinates, and especially to new recruits. But actually, other than that, he was a capable soldier and anything but a curmudgeon. He greeted Kuno very amiably and then he and Michel had a long conversation in hushed tones to themselves, but the word *captain* could be clearly discerned which indicated that the private chat could only be about the upcoming audience with his commanding officer.

After it was over, Michel began his "last walk," but held himself ramrod straight with hands "on the pant seams" strictly according to Prussian regulations and *Hardee's Tactics*.[232] Kuno, meanwhile, stayed behind engaged in obligatory small talk and getting to know his mess mates better, but all the while not a little concerned about how things were going with his best friend and comrade.

After a full half hour, Michel came back at double-time and with an obviously relieved countenance. To the storm of questions directed his way, he replied:

"'S all right, boys, the Old Man is a *trump*, and you'll hear the rest tomorrow, and now *tend* to it that after this *scare* my body gets something put into it. And you, Kuno, come along with me; the *captain* wants to see you."

Civil War Battle in Louisiana. Author's collection.

On the way to the *cabin* of the commanding officer Michel, however, opened up to Kuno:

"*Lucky* for me that the Major didn't take me up on the bet; otherwise, I would be out my tobacco. Do you suppose the captain would accept even one pipe full of tobacco as a *present*? *Not on your life*! He bought a full pound from me and gave me a half dollar in payment, and said, if he were to accept any tobacco without paying for it then he would not be able to assign me four weeks of *special gun duty*, and I think to myself, the devil himself couldn't *fix* some of these old Enfields and Yankee *carbines*. At any rate, I guess I will get off with eight days' *arrest* and about the same number of *extra tours*. He didn't *kick* too much about the missing horse either, because, after all, they confiscated mine earlier, and the *company* has a couple of nags left over from the last *raid* they made on the Yankees. I bet I will get worn out buzzard meat for a mount. Well, *never mind*, I can *stand* it. He's just too German and too upright, but *bully* for the Old Man, nevertheless."

With some trepidation Kuno entered the domicile of the stern and exacting cavalry officer. The man standing before him, however, bore little resemblance to the picture he had imagined. His appearance recalled in no way the image of the storied Prussian Field Marshal von Blücher. He resembled rather a cloistered academic: small to middle in stature; thin, blond, with a narrow, smooth-shaven face and with eyes so fine they were almost feminine in appearance. His bearing, however, was thoroughly military, and Krusius his family name who had studied chemistry *over there,*" had also been a reserve officer of an entire brigade and had often been consulted by his superiors on technicalities concerning strategy and tactics.[233] In normal conversations reserved, in a military situation his voice was razor-sharp, his directives, clear and concise. A half dozen years later his men would have no doubt more appropriately baptized him "Moltke"[234] rather than Blücher. The simple room with no hallway that served as quarters for himself and his two lieutenants was kept as neat and tidy as a cleaning room. On a table cobbled together from rough lumber lay writing material and a stack of books, mostly about chemistry and mathematics, but also several German classics were stacked among them. On the wall hung various weapons and a violin.

Krusius arose, greeted the young recruit warmly, and then had Kuno explain his situation, after which, he stated:

"You did the right thing by continuing on to where you were directed and not marching off into the blue toward Sabine Pass even though your regiment, together with the ranking officers of your brigade, who were stationed here in the vicinity, did indeed break camp and depart. I will give you a letter addressed to Brigadier General Mullins,[235] who is now serving as inspector-general of our army. He is scheduled to inspect Camp Sidney Johnston[236] at Yellow Bayou[237] tomorrow. He will be able to issue you new orders. In the meantime, I would like to get to know you better. I have pressing official duties to take care of at the moment, so I would like to invite you to call on me this evening—and you Schmidt, I expect you as well since you are free this evening."

At this Michel and Kuno were dismissed.

That evening after supper Kuno got to know another side of the cavalry officer, a side that was less military and more social. In informal gatherings, he came across as a highly educated man who deported himself easily and congenially. When he arrived at the *cabin,* Kuno found the two lieutenants, Davis and Schneckenburger, already there, together with Bohne, Klösel, and a half dozen others, all Germans, with the one exception of Corporal O'Brien who, in the meantime according to Klösel, had transformed himself into an entirely acceptable *Dutchman*. The men seated themselves around the room on crates, field stools, and an improvised bench. To his consternation, Kuno found himself seated next to the captain in the center of the circle because he was the guest of honor. The majority of those present had relatives or friends from Possum Creek and were eager to receive as much detailed information concerning their situations as he could provide. After he had overcome his initial (and quite understandable) reserve, he answered their inquiries with such freshness and insight that Klösel echoed an opinion shared by all when he declared:

"Verily, you are a new and improved version of your father. The old saying that the apple does not fall far from the tree certainly holds true in your case, though for me the saying does not apply: my father, you see, was a *genuine professor*, and I, well, I'm just the *Major*."

Then the conversation turned inevitably to war experiences whereby Lieutenant Davis, O'Brien, Klösel, and Bohne did most of the talking. During the course of the conversation Kuno began to get a conception of what Company F had endured in nearly four years of conflict: first with the bold expedition to New Mexico and then in various actions in Louisiana and Arkansas. He experienced vicariously the battles of Val Verde, Glorieta,[238] and then of Mansfield[239] and Pleasant Hill.[240]

He heard how at the Battle of Val Verde Colonel Green[241] had inspired his faltering squadrons to mount a general attack by holding up the example of the "Green Germans," who cast aside their useless lances and fell upon the enemy artillery and infantry positions with their revolvers as if *going to a dance*. And they heard Green shout: Look at the brave German boys over there and don't let them shame you! He saw Major Büchel[242] who, even though realizing he and his men would be needlessly sacrificed in the senseless attack, fearlessly charge the *plum thicket*, which was brimming with enemy weapons, only to fall from his horse mortally wounded. He saw his men openly weeping for their fallen leader, and heard them cursing their drunken general,[243] who had sacrificed him and so many of his brave men with his reckless order to attack.

He heard about daring cavalry raids and attacks, about hilarious escapades both in battle and on the march. He heard about Klösel's bold deeds and also about *Long Mike's* masterful talent for capturing turkeys and chickens from a slumbering farmstead while arousing the alarm of neither dog nor fowl. It was not the first time that he had listened to soldiers, but here in the field in the hut with a fire flickering in the chimney, in the circle of so many who had been there, it all sounded so much more real and compelling. It began to weigh on him that he had chosen to be an infantryman. For him, there would not be any of these dashing rides through the countryside. Even Klösel's words of consolation: Be glad you won't have to share the little bit of food you get with your horse, helped but little to nudge him beyond this sense of regret.

But at the same time it became quite clear to him as he sat listening to riveting accounts of bloody battles, and hearing recollections of unmentionable suffering, or sharing in the laughter at amusing anecdotes of soldierly tomfooleries, all from the lips of men from otherwise so utterly different spheres, men who hailed from dissimilar social backgrounds and were of different ages—all this brought home to him that nothing binds men together more strongly; that nothing unmasks what's truly beneath the skin and clothes of a man so thoroughly and quickly as a wartime experience.

Wasn't the most celebrated hero of the regiment a simple tailor, shy and deferential, who according to O'Brien, wasn't able to walk a straight line because he always needed to excuse himself to everyone he encountered for even being on the same planet. But still, all of the regular guys had valued the shy tailor Haase even before he had, as weak as he was, heroically retrieved a severely wounded comrade from a fox hole and brought him to safety when shrapnel from exploding shells threatened to tear him to shreds at any moment; in the final analysis, despite his deferential nature, a man willing to risk his life without a second thought to save another.

Then Krusius fetched a large mug from a corner of the room. In a tin pot in the fireplace in which the water was already boiling from the heat of the coals, a stout rum punch was quickly brewed and three *tin cups* filled with the strong concoction made the rounds of the assembled soldiers. Soon thereafter, the bugler blew *taps*, and Krusius announced:

"Let us continue here for another hour *boys*, but for no longer. Our young guest here needs to undertake a long march tomorrow and our long lost and rediscovered *Mike* has a lot of extra work to perform in the near future. They both need a good night's sleep. But we want to make merry for a little while yet."

And merry they were. First Lieutenant Hiram Davis, who actually was named David, and was called Abrahamson behind his back, was an excellent comic impersonator, and his skits, delivered in either Berliner or Saxon dialect, were, according to *Long Mike* simply not to *beat*. He was a small fellow and hard to pin down, but still a good soldier and a real go-getter like all Jews, even the baptized ones, and just for the reason that no one trusts them, explained Klösel and then left his post next to the rum pot long enough in order to sing the nice song from Angely's Paris in Pommern:[244]

Heyman Levi is my name
And my home is Meseritz;
My mother is Judith Esther,
Sarah Blümchen my sister,
Gumperz Levi is my father
Purveyors next to the Meseritz Theater,
If it's all the same to you.

He sang it in a very comical way but deliberately off key in order to annoy Levi, but he seemed to take no offense who, instead, picked up right away with Mielchen's song from the same play, where she sings of her love for her beautiful Michel, but as he did so, he looked so tenderly and maidenly at *Long Mike* that he turned red as a beet with embarrassment. Then it was Second Lieutenant Schneckenburger's turn, a man who reminded Kuno strongly of Winzig because of his height, the cut of his features, and his shock of coal-black hair. He fetched his beloved violin from the wall and commenced playing, alternating between sad and sentimental German folksongs and lively waltzes and polkas. Schneckenburger also sang in a very deep bass voice, *"im tiefen Keller sitz' ich hier bei einem Fass voll Reben.*"[245] Next up, Sergeant O'Brien sang the old Irish melody, "The harp that hangs in Lara's Halls"[246] and then "Coming thro' the Rye."[247] During the interludes the tin cups continued to circulate among the men until, finally, Krusius, glancing at his pocket watch, announced with a sigh:

"It's after eleven o'clock *boys* and a good soldier needs his sleep when he can get it. Gentlemen, I wish you all a good night." Everyone would have gladly stayed longer, but the *captain*'s word was law in Company F.

Unaccustomed to such a stout alcoholic drink, Kuno was right tipsy when he stepped out into the cold and moonlit night and had to be steadied and helped along by the sure hand of Michel Schmidt. When he looked up into the firmament above, his naked eye could discern a lot more than the usual six thousand stars, which appeared to be hopping and dancing around the smiling man in the moon. He did not awaken the next morning until the first rays of light penetrated the poorly patched tear in his tent and shone brightly on his face and Bohne roused him with the announcement, "Breakfast is ready!"

Michel Schmidt, however, was already away at duty, and Kuno did not see him again until he was back at home after many long months in the service. The breakfast *mess* was the best served up and laid out before the men by the 'mother-in-law' in a very long time. An evening like the one we had last night needs to be followed by something just as special, proclaimed Klösel, who served as chief cook and master of supplies. To the great satisfaction of his mess mates, he had prepared biscuits from pure, unadulterated wheat flour rather than the usual *corn dodgers*[248] and additionally had fried bacon instead of tough cuts of beef, while, best of all, he had brought real coffee beans from a secret reserve for the morning drink. To be sure, they were not able to fill the *tin cups* full to the brim, since the secret stash of beans was somewhat limited, but the brown drink was savored with all the more *gusto* in small sips just for that reason.

Soon thereafter Kuno began his long march to Yellow Bayou with Krusius' letter in his breast pocket, completely alone in a strange land, which wasn't exactly comforting to him. Thoroughly weary from the exertion, he arrived about four o'clock in the afternoon at his goal, a large encampment in the vicinity of a small town in which only two companies of cavalry remained. Upon asking, he was shown to a large, agreeable tent that served as the main headquarters where he was supposed to find General Mullins. A Negro man lounging in front of the tent informed him, however, that the general could not be disturbed at the moment; he needed to come back in the morning.

When Kuno returned the next day, he met a young officer with lieutenant's insignia in a fine uniform, who had just dismounted from his horse and was whistling a nice tune to himself. Kuno recognized him right away as none other than Clarence DeBray, Bobby Phillip's cousin, whom he had only seen from a distance since their first meeting at the unforgettable birthday party, and the recollection of those events made this encounter quite awkward.

After he had told him his name, the young officer greeted him in the most cordial way:

"I am very glad to see you because you are the first *Dutchman* I ever learned to respect after you gave that mama's boy cousin of mine a thorough thrashing. Since then, however, I have gotten to know a lot of brave Germans. Are you here as a new recruit? That would make me happy because we can use people like you here."

Visibly relieved to hear these words, Kuno hastily explained his dilemma to the lieutenant. DeBray reassured him that he would take care of the matter personally and together the two walked over to the headquarters tent. Lieutenant DeBray waved the Negro aside, who apparently held the position of gatekeeper, with a slight gesture of his hand, and entered the tent. After a short pause, he called for Kuno to step inside the tent which he immediately noticed was outfitted in a relatively luxurious manner. Kuno found the general, two other officers and a civilian, the plantation owner Delaroche, seated around a small table upon which several half-filled and empty whiskey glasses stood; also, a pack of playing cards that had been in service for a long time, and before each of the gentlemen, small piles of red and white grains of corn along with stacks of gold and silver coins. As unexperienced as Kuno was, he still had the wherewithal to recognize that he had chosen a very inauspicious time to have

Foraging. Author's collection.

his audience since no one wants to be interrupted during an intense game of poker, and especially not a high-ranking officer by a recruit. General Mullin's reddened countenance suggested that he was already in a sour mood as he made a half-hearted attempt to assume some semblance of military propriety in order to hear Kuno's report and accept the letter from Captain Krusius. After the thinking about the matter for a good while, he spoke:

"Well, yes, that is a situation. Captain Krusius is my friend and I will have to consider the matter. Come by again tomorrow, young man."

With this, Lieutenant DeBray interjected:

"With your permission, General, could I suggest that I bring the young man into my company. *Company* A is very weak at the moment since eight men are on leave and two are in the hospital, and we can put him to good use. He is a brave, young man from one of the finest families in Texas and I am convinced he will be of great service to us here—you would be satisfied with this arrangement Mr. Sartorius?"

Kuno was very pleased with the suggestion because Lieutenant DeBray had won him over heart and soul in a flash. General Mullins was obviously also happy with the suggestion because it quickly disposed of a bothersome distraction. He asked for Kuno's papers straightway, walked over to another table with writing material, crossed out and added, and after a minute Kuno was dismissed. He was quite glad to know where he finally belonged; a *private* in

Company A of Walker's Division and a soldier serving under the friendly and charming Lieutenant DeBray, who himself had seen the light of day for the first time not far from Possum Creek.

KUNO'S CAREER AS A SOLDIER

During his tenure as a soldier, Kuno experienced neither bloody battles nor other war-related adventures. For that, he had turned eighteen too late. And even though in the short span of five months until the end of the war he never wore a uniform, never laid eyes on an enemy soldier with the exception of a couple of hundred prisoners, and never heard the rattle of muskets, except for the occasional target practice, or shots fired to dispatch a chance stray pig or calf; still, during these five months, this young man, who had been uprooted from his self-contained world among the *Lateiner* on Possum Creek, experienced much that contributed to his spiritual and intellectual development.

With few exceptions, Company Eight was made up of very young Texans who came from the southwestern portion of the state[249] and who belonged to the interesting species called *cowboy*, young men who had already spent half of their lives in the saddle, and even without saddles, could cling to their mounts as tightly as a squirrel does to his oak tree limb, who could hit the bull's eye with either revolver or carbine, and who were always showing off daring tricks and feats of horsemanship or otherwise playing practical jokes on one another, and whose wild Rebel yells during several attacks had put Yankees to flight whose ears were unaccustomed to such ear-splitting and infernal shrieks.

Always willing to follow their young Lieutenant DeBray, a man they idolized in matters they deemed important, they were good soldiers in this regard. But strict discipline and punctual obedience were as alien to them as the New York skyline, and their officers acted wisely in this regard by not being overly demanding. Only a few had regular uniforms and since the young men were not very adept with needle and thread, and showed little inclination to learn about these things, preferring instead to repair their clothes with leather thongs, their outfits were often more picturesque than presentable.

But in respect to footwear, they were exceptionally well equipped. Every man had a good pair of riding boots on his feet together with heavy and sharp Mexican spurs. They also appeared to be well-fed, having put their finely-honed foraging skills to good use, so that even in this sparsely settled region, already exhausted by several large-scale troop movements, they had suffered little deprivation. There was, therefore, such an excess of youthful energy and enthusiasm on their part that they often filled the endless hours of inactivity with wrestling matches and other such activities requiring strenuous physical exertion.

Happy-go-lucky and friendly as these former cattle herders were, young men molded by their lives on the vast prairies, the young German who had dropped so unexpectedly in their midst had a tough go of it in the beginning. They could see right away that he was German since his deficiencies in pronunciation gave him away and, for a German at the time, there was no other name but *Dutchman,* and the poorest and most ignorant *native* of English, Scottish, or Irish descent felt it his birthright to make fun of any *Dutchman.* The *cowboys* offered no exception to this prejudice, but it did not take long for Kuno to earn their respect.

After supper, as Kuno sat around the fire on a mild December night, his five tent mates and another half dozen curious onlookers plied him with all sorts of ridiculous questions, for instance, where he had left his wooden shoes, whether the German girls, like Indian squaws, carried all the gear and had to pull the plows in the fields, and whether Germans ran the danger of splitting open from consuming too much beer and sauerkraut? But as they asked him these things, they put on such a good front of being earnest and genuinely curious that Kuno was unsure whether they were just playing him for a fool or really were so ignorant.

At first, he answered their questions in a forthright manner whereby they nodded their heads seriously only to follow up with even more preposterous questions. Finally, realizing the game they were playing, he announced that he saw no purpose in answering such absurd questions and retired to the tent to get some sleep while the young men outside reveled in the sport they had made of him.

An hour may well have passed when he awoke from his troubled slumbers to overhear soft whispering in the tent, and since it was relatively bright within, he saw his tent mates quietly arise and wrap themselves in their blankets. "They have got something up their sleeves for sure and will be sorely mistaken if they think they can pull something over on me," Kuno swore to himself inwardly, while awaiting whatever they had in mind for him.

He did not have long to wait. They grouped themselves around him on their knees and suddenly one of them gave his big toe a tug while at the same moment he heard a sharp sound of rattling on the floor of the tent that could only come from a rattlesnake, and anyone who has ever ventured too near to one of these dangerous reptiles and heard their warning buzz will react instinctively and immediately. Kuno even flinched momentarily, and all the more so after a long, fat, cold something that had the touch and feel of a real snake was pulled over his bedding and over his neck while the rattling continued. At the same time, the specters that were wrapped in blankets up to their heads, and that were making grunting sounds, arose like ghosts all around his bed. Kuno, however, had the presence of mind to realize right away there would be no snakes visiting tents in December and grabbed the long whatever with both hands, which in reality was the skin of an enormous water moccasin that had been stuffed with cotton, and slung it away from him but, luckily or unluckily, the flying form wrapped itself around the neck of one of his tormentors; the victim reacting with a shriek of horror and dropping both his blanket and the rattles, which were, as it turned out, from a real rattlesnake after all. In a flash, everybody retreated to their spots in the tent and pretended to be asleep. Kuno did the same and began, as if dreaming, to call out loudly: "Somebody come and drive the dumb jackasses out of the tent who are fumbling around looking for rattlesnakes in the middle of winter!"

At this, a chorus of chuckles could be heard from the beds until finally the oldest among the group, Jack Duff, spoke up: "*Bully for the Dutchman*, and now we want to let him get a good night's sleep, and anybody that bothers him will have to answer to me."

At a later date, it should be mentioned, Jack faithfully kept his word. His tent mates were soon all fast asleep but Kuno lay awake a long time as he mulled over with some resentment the inhospitable reception he had received and the practical joke they had tried to play on him—and practical jokes of this nature were something new to him.

The following morning his mess mates were sociable enough and commented favorably about Kuno's skill in preparing breakfast and also that the *newbie* refused to have his appetite spoiled by the many tasteless jokes concerning the meat.

After breakfast, the first sergeant, *Shoots* by name, took Kuno under his wing in order to select a mount from among the half dozen or so kept by the company as extras. The animals, which had their front feet bound together with *hobbles* and were grazing on a neighboring meadow, were driven in front of them. They had not received a lot of care. As was to be expected in wintertime, most had shaggy, unkempt coats while three among them were so poor that they appeared destined for the buzzards in the not too distant future.

The best-looking among them, a large, sorrel horse, had been raised some-where in Yankee land, but was blind as a bat, a fact Kuno recognized right away; the strong and seemingly well-nourished gray, he judged as too old and lazy for a young rider. That left only the *paint*, a true Spanish *mustang*, or *bronco* from West Texas, a critter that sported a dirty white coat with large brown spots on his shoulders and rump, and, although not fat, was still powerful and spirited.

"The *paint* is a real good animal," advised on of the bystanders.

"Yea, he's right pious and can run like *hell*" chimed in another and, as if on cue, the whole company gathered in the meantime to see the show, and all, it seemed, had something good to say about the *paint*.

"You need to try him out right away in order to see if his gait pleases you or if you would rather have the gray," opined another.

"I have every intention of doing that," answered Kuno. He then placed a heavy Spanish saddle with an enormous saddle horn on the critter's back, cinched the front and back gurts tight, whereby the animal laid his ears back and nipped at him, but then he stood there as innocent as a lamb, as if nothing in the world could upset him. Kuno then freed the hobbles from his front feet with one quick motion.

His fellow soldiers observed this process with rapt attention and they whispered softly among each other: "Hey, we are going to have a lot of fun with this," and one of the fellows ran quickly in the direction of the officers' tent so that these could also enjoy the coming spectacle.

Kuno, who had enjoyed in *Long Mike* an unsurpassed master in the art of *"horse-breaking,"* laid his hand on the critter's rump, who was attempting to always move sideways and away from him, caressed him along his back in a calming way, and then mounted the *paint* in one quick motion. Simultaneously, the horse reared up and gave a mighty kick but when his rider remained in the saddle he continued to employ every maneuver known to a true *mustang, bucking* and *pitching* for a full ten minutes. But it was all to no avail; the legs of the young rider had an ironclad clamp on his body and whenever the mustang loosened up momentarily from his wild jumps, the young rider raked him with his sharp Mexican spurs, bringing blood to his flanks. But even a *bronco* of this caliber will tire after a while, and the critter adopted another tactic: after standing completely still for a couple of seconds, he took off at a full run in a straight line for a couple of hundred paces and then came to a sudden stop, as if he had hit a wall. But even with his trick Kuno did not fly head over heels into the sand, but rather spurred him on anew and drove him around in circles.

"Bully for the *Dutchman!"* cried his *cowboy* comrades as Kuno rode back to them in a full gallop.

"I've got him now!" said Kuno triumphantly, but he had spoken a bit too soon. For as soon as he had begun to feel somewhat confidant and loosened the grip of his legs slightly, the animal suddenly turned sharply to the side in order to come to a sudden stop once again. This time the rider flew over the saddle horn and onto the neck of the horse but not to the ground and a split second later he was again in the saddle, spurring his horse on, and riding at all gaits: the full run, gallop, trot, and slow walk in a circle. When he finally dismounted from the quivering and sweat covered animal, very sore to be sure in all his joints, and gave it a friendly pat on the head and neck, the paint was totally conquered, and likewise Company A; all prejudices against the young recruit vanished because anyone who could ride such a formidable *bronco* had to be in the opinion of these people *an all right guy*. From that point on the entire company was not a little proud of our young *Dutchman*, and this word became in their circle rather a token of respect than a mark of scorn.

Kuno's paint went on to become well-known as an unusually easy trotter and for his excellent cantor, and as a horse you could not *ride into the ground*, even with heavy service and minimal feed. Kuno found out later that his *paint* had already unseated half the company since his original owner had fallen at the Battle of Mansfield. To be sure, several had managed to ride the unruly animal, but he had counted as too unreliable to be anyone's regular mount. Still, the men valued him highly just for the purpose of providing entertainment for, just like Kuno, every new recruit was persuaded to try his hand at riding him. Hence, he was retained among the company's horses during all their redeployments.

Kuno also found out that he was not the only German in the company and that he had a fellow countryman in the stern *mother* of the company, Sergeant Shoots. In the afternoons, the sergeant took it upon himself to provide the first military training for the new recruit. He was a large man of stocky build with a bull neck and black hair. He sported a bodkin beard[250] and had enormous bushy eyebrows. His military bearing, however, was somewhat diminished by his large stump nose and gentle blue eyes. He spoke very good English but his pronunciation did not have the softness of native Southerners. It was much harder and he rolled his "Rs" in a way that no native was capable of doing.

Terry's Texas Rangers. Author's collection.

Kuno mastered the horse gaiting drills, the massaging, and handling exercises easily enough. As his training progressed, however, three others were brought over for *squad drill,* whereby Kuno earned a few choice remarks, but his squad mates even more, because they did not take the unwelcome drills seriously enough. Kuno was startled when, during one of these drills, a very loud "*Himmelkrrreuzdonnerrrwetterr!*"[251] erupted from under the black mustache of the exasperated drillmaster.

Later, while carefully cleaning and oiling the Enfield carbine that had been issued to him, the sergeant stepped in for a look, laid his hand on his shoulder, and spoke: "One sees right away what a German is. Takes matters seriously and doesn't act so dumb during the exercises like those Texas rowdies who can aggravate a man to death."

"You are also German, *Herr* Shooter. I could tell that from your '*Donnerwetter*' at the drilling."

"Yes, that is to say I am half Polish. My mother was from Częstochowa[252] and I was born at Rosenberg.[253] My real name is really Schuette but the ignoramuses over here can't pronounce it and always butcher it. I got so irritated that I transferred to another regiment where I re-baptized myself 'Shooter.' I served eight years with the Silesian Dragoons across the water and the captain of cavalry always said that I was his best non-commissioned officer, and now I have to march along with these *cowboy* clowns who don't want to learn anything."

"And learning means, to my way of thinking" he added, "looking for cover behind every tree and gopher mound while riding and *fighting*; something these hotspurs don't understand. They have no fear, not even of the devil, much less of the devil's mother-in-law, or of me, for that matter. And my mother-in-law, just so you should know, is the one who drove this Prussian sergeant out of Germany."

It did not take long for Kuno to be fully informed about the life story of the good sergeant and even more so about the character traits of his wretched mother-in-law, whose incessant nagging and scolding had driven him to Texas, and who, according to his depiction, fit perfectly the picture of a witch from Grimms' Fairy Tales.[254]

In Texas, Shooter had tried his hand at farming for a couple of years, but when the Civil War broke out, he felt compelled to join up even though, as he stated, "personally, the history of it had nothing to do with me," and then he added wistfully:

"Who knows how things will turn out, because if peace comes and I send for my Pinchen[255] from Gross-Krotoschau,[256] the devil might convince the old bitty to also make the journey over the big water to America."

The old sergeant, however, took consolation in the belief that the war was nowhere near its conclusion.

"Naturally the large armies can no longer be maintained in the field as they have been, and the sooner they disband, the better. The Yankees will, of course, march across the entire land thereafter, but then the battle will really commence in earnest. With 10,000 men like my *boys*, dispersed in small bands across Texas, Louisiana, and Mississippi, we can keep the Yankees at bay for another ten years. We need only to scuttle the dumb idea that we have to face the enemy in open terrain in large set-piece battles, or to try to occupy and hold cities; that costs too many men and we need every man. We should operate in small troops, today on foot, tomorrow by horse, harassing the enemy at every turn, and when we catch him with his guard down, falling upon him like a violent Texas storm. When the exalted generals, of which we have six times more than we need, finally come to their senses, then the Northerners will never get their way with us."

It is often the case that a common sergeant thinks he knows more than a field marshal and, in truth, the good man may not have been too far off the mark with his suggestions and insights, but it was very fortunate that the South's generals and their men were of a different mind and decided, instead, not to continue the fight by means of a guerilla war.

Kuno listened attentively to his disputation but was clever enough not raise any objections and so remained the declared favorite of the sergeant. But the two only spoke German with one another when they were by themselves.

Shooter devoted a lot of time and energy to his young charge's military training and under his guidance Kuno progressed rapidly. According to his theories, regular military drills and exercises were completely superfluous and a waste of time; the only skills that mattered for a soldier were to be able to shoot straight and to know how to seek cover, but having the heart of a true Prussian sergeant, he also longed after full-dress parades and after people who could perform the manual of arms properly. He was, therefore, not a little proud of the fact that Kuno made such rapid progress. He was ready for guard duty after just eight days, and after two weeks he was held up as a model soldier to his comrades, and no one seemed to begrudge him the honor of the best drilled soldier in the company.

In the meantime, Lieutenant DeBray had not bothered much about Kuno, except that when he made the rounds he always had a kind word, as he did for all his troops and, more often than not, a humorous comment.

One Sunday afternoon Kuno had remained in the tent reading Tacitus[257] while all of his other comrades had gathered outside around Bill Bee for their amusement on this day of rest. Bill was imitating a sermon by a Negro preacher and had mastered Southern Negro plantation dialect to perfection. His camp mates had joined in the fun by pretending to be the excited and worshipful black congregation.[258] While this was going on outside, the lieutenant unexpectedly entered Kuno's tent. Kuno immediately sprang to attention and saluted his superior. DeBray sat down next to him and asked him what he was reading. He seemed quite astonished that the young recruit was practicing his Latin, and tried to translate a passage from the book himself, but was not able to get very far, which caused him to be all the more impressed that Kuno was able to easily translate the passage into English.

It became clear in the process that both men had learned differing pro-nunciations, which made it almost impossible to follow one another.[259] He explained to Kuno then that he had studied Latin at Houston College[260] for several semesters, including grammar, Virgil, Caesar, and for a long time he had also had a German instructor by the name of Misslich, who also pronounced the words of the old Roman texts the same way as did Kuno. He did not get very far in Latin, however, since like the majority of his classmates he always had his *pony*[261] in his pocket ready for surreptitious use, rendering the task of translating decidedly easier. In Horace,[262] however, there were many poems designed to be morally uplifting, and difficult to fake in translation. Winzig was the first to catch on to the fact that the students were cheating using *'ponies.'*

"That had to be our earlier private instructor, Gottfried Misslich. I am still ashamed to the depths of my soul when I think about him. My brother and I made life so miserable for the good man," responded Kuno, thereby giving the impetus for a more intimate conversation.

The lieutenant told of many nasty tricks that the young men and even the young ladies had played on the unfortunate German professor, and many so hilarious, that Kuno had to chuckle in spite of his sympathy for his countryman, who had been the butt of so many practical jokes on the part of the impudent students, both boys and girls, at Houston College.

Then the conversation turned to Bobby Phillips birthday party where they had seen each other for the first time. By the time DeBray had taken his leave from Kuno after an hour of friendly conversation, he had won over the heart of the young recruit totally. Since at that time neither official regulations nor custom stood in the way of friendships between officers and enlisted men, a close relationship developed quickly between the two.

In many respects this was fortuitous for Kuno. His fellow *cowboy* soldiers were certainly brave, but still they were rough around the edges. Not a few of them had succumbed to strong drink although they could only indulge this habit on rare occasion, since the army had long since ceased to pay the soldiers; not even in Confederate currency, which by now had become practically worthless. They had a passion for playing cards: poker, seven-up, and monte,[263] although for the reason named above the only thing they could wager was either nut shells or IOUs against future wages. Owing to a special order of the company, saddles, spurs, horses, and gear were off-limits to betting. Despite such limitations, the games often ended up in heated argument that threatened to end in bloodshed. When they were not gambling, the men spent their free time at wrestling or boxing, activities that Kuno liked to join in from time to time (and he did not fair badly either), or they liked to sing their favorite songs at the top of their lungs, songs like: *Bonny Blue Flag, The Texas Ranger, Little Brown Jug,*[264] etc., and others that cannot be reproduced in print.

As friendly as they now treated Kuno, he was not able to develop a rapport beyond a certain point, and this even extended to the good-hearted and upright first sergeant, who was only attracted to military matters, and had no interest in literature, music, or art. In this respect, Lieutenant DeBray was an entirely different man, and for a youngster like Kuno Sartorius, a rather dangerous liaison.

Clarence DeBray was only twenty-two years old at the time but already much more experienced in the ways of the world than many men much older than he. His father, *Judge* DeBray, was the most respected lawyer in the town which served as the county seat[265] for Possum Creek, and he was said to be very rich. Clarence, the only son from his first marriage, which had come to a premature ending due to death, had been unbelievably spoiled from early childhood on; from his father, from the house slaves, and from the private caretakers that had been engaged from time to time to help in his upbringing. Already by the age of twelve he had the earned the reputation as the most insufferable ne'er-do-well in the town.

In the meantime, the father remarried and partially to mollify his new wife and partly because his private tutors, both male and female, were at their wits' end in dealing with the wayward youth, his father sent him off as a boarder to the newly established college. There he found an even wider field for his arrogance and misbehavior. He was suspended several times because of his antics and finally expelled because of a prank he had thought up and orchestrated directed at the headmaster of the institute, Dr. Cawthon.

Cawthon was a preacher by profession and his extreme predilection for piety led his irreverent charges to christen him the *"Creeping Jesus."* After every morning devotional, he was want to hold a long-winded and sanctimonious sermon on the subject of morality to the great annoyance of the students, who were impatiently awaiting their morning breakfast. And one fine morning while in best form, striding back and forth across the rostrum, as was his habit, he was just at the point in his homily where he elevated his voice to a thunderous pitch to drive home his point when, with a sudden *crack* that reverberated across the room, the good headmaster disappeared from sight into the depths below to the astonishment of his students.

Under the rostrum there was a cellar and, from its depths, one could perceive sounds that resembled anything but the goodly words of a preacher's benediction. It later came to light that Cawthon had plunged into a large barrel full of brown sugar that had been especially placed there so that, upon falling, he would not hurt himself badly. A most embarrassing investigation immediately followed whereupon it soon came to light that only a few days before DeBray had borrowed a saw from a carpenter, and that one of the female students, who boarded in a dormitory opposite of the headmaster's house, had seen him at night by light of the full moon accompanied by his closest friend and accomplice in all his other practical jokes sliding down a lightning rod[266] from one of the windows in the *chapel*. That was the last straw and Clarence was sent back home to his father. It did not take long, however, before his new wife laid down an ultimatum: either she or this paragon of mischief had to go, whereupon his father sent him off to stay with relatives in New Orleans.

He was satisfied to remain there for a full half year there but thereafter was shipped off to a military academy in Virginia, which was well-known and highly praised throughout the entire Southland. At this time, many of the most talented and highly regarded instructors worked at the academy, among others Stonewall Jackson,[267] who garnered so much fame at a later date.

He fared much better here, applying himself to his studies and excelling in military exercises. Most of the students at this institute were the offspring of the most respected and well-to-do families in Virginia; students who, similar to the young Texan, had more money to spend than was salutary for their education; who ran up expenses, and who were always eager for opportune pranks and mischief.

When the war broke out, the vast majority of the students joined the army straightaway, and so too did Clarence DeBray. He took part in many of the famous battles of Virginia until, after a year and a half, he received news from Texas that brought him home; news that his father had suffered a severe stroke. He found his father sick with little hope of full recovery, out of sorts with the world, and with his finances in complete disarray, but faithfully cared for by his young wife.

After his condition improved somewhat, he returned to the army, but since the enemy now had blockaded the Mississippi, he could not return to his old unit in Virginia and chose, instead, to join the Texas cavalry regiment where we now find him. Because of his bravery he had received an early promotion to lieutenant, and only his impetuousness and rashness had prevented him from achieving an even higher rank. But now that he had command of a full company, his conduct had been above reproach, he had sworn off alcohol completely, and had earned general approbation as a decisive and thoroughly reliable officer.

All in all, the situation was such that Lieutenant DeBray was in a position to exert a powerful influence over a young man like Kuno Sartorius, who, even though in some ways still immature, perceived within himself an unmistakable affinity with the older man: their blood, it seemed to him, flowed in the same vein. The flippant side of his nature, which often came out freely and spontaneously, was always tempered by a measured sense of humor and such endearing charm that it never gave cause for offense. In the close relationship that developed with the older, so much more experienced and accomplished man, new and startling perspectives on the world and life opened up for Kuno.

DeBray was especially amused by the fact that even though Kuno was eighteen years old, he was such a chaste Joseph, who seemed to know nothing about the female sex except for what he had read in books. When telling stories about various romantic adventures that he had experienced himself or heard tell from his friends, Kuno would sometimes interject in a way that betrayed his naiveté, which occasioned sarcastic remarks from DeBray, such as: Are you really so clueless? Kuno would then feel deeply ashamed of his own ignorance even as his own phantasy was strongly stimulated by all the novelty and seductiveness that paraded before his mind's eye.

When DeBray discovered that Kuno had never experienced any kind of social interaction with young women of the same age (without knowing quite the reason why, Kuno never breathed a word of his chummy childhood relationship with Hedwig Lüttenhoff), he announced one day:

"It is high time that you learn something about the fairer sex, about how they really are and not as angels with carefully folded wings. I have visited *Colonel*

Delaroche on a couple of occasions and have an invitation for tomorrow evening at the Fairview Plantation. The *Colonel* has three grown daughters, all full of life and all naturally very *respectable*. They are just the ones to give you exposure into one of society's most refined skills, namely the art of *flirting*, and in this they are all well-versed." Naturally Kuno wanted none of it, but DeBray would not take no for an answer, and the visit was a done deal.

Translator's Note

In the following section, Kuno comes into serious contact with fashionable society, Southern belles, and evangelical Christianity for the first time. The section provides the reader an informative window into the social morays of plantation society and into the Southern frame of mind that so self-righteously and fanatically upheld the Southern cause. In respect to religion, one of the characteristics of the **Lateiner** *that has come in for much comment and mis-understanding over the years is given literary expression in this scene, namely the a-religious, freethinking aspect to their communities. I refer the reader back to note 76 about German freethinkers, which references the scene where Hedwig finds herself hopelessly lost and threatened in the forest and, feeling the urge to offer a prayer in her distress, confesses she has never before actually heard a prayer offered. Methodism was in its heyday at the time and was being vigorously advocated by an army of dedicated itinerant preacher-proselytizers who organized "camp meetings" to further their mission as they traveled around. The unabashed emotionalism and group enthusiasm, often typical of these meetings, was something entirely new and exotic to the German immigrants who arrived in Texas in the mid-nineteenth century, whether nominally religious or not. German protestant services, especially, whether Old-Lutheran or reformed, tended to be somber and weighty affairs, characterized by awe, reserve, and gravitas. Heinrich von Struve, among other Texas Germans of the period, commented on such "camp meetings," and seemed to regard them as exotic as if he had discovered some strange ritual in the heart of Africa. (See, "Das Camp-Meeting," in: Struve,* **Ein Lebensbild,** *80–90.)*

THE LIEUTENANT'S CONVERSION

The following night Kuno experienced for the first time in his young life anxieties concerning proper grooming and toiletry. His natural vanity, common to all young people his age, was suddenly aroused from its slumbers by the realization that in three days he would find himself in the company of three young, pretty, and lively American *ladies.* Up to this point he had always felt most at ease in his simple but sturdy and practical hunting outfit, and always considered it to be unnecessary torment when his mother insisted that he take pains to groom himself during festive occasions. Now he was oppressed by the thought that he had only brought along one coat, the one he now had on. Although almost new, the cloth was *homespun* and had been died a dark brown with sumac; practical but definitely not appropriate attire for high society. He was also worried that his boots, basic and serviceable as they were, would seem out of place in an elegant *parlor.* His tent mates soon noticed that something was bothering him and teased him for being homesick for Possum Creek or for missing his mother's home cooking.

He had wanted to report for sick call the next morning, but since not even one finger was ailing, he finally decided in his distress to look up his friend, the lieutenant, whom he found lying on his bed smoking a self-rolled cigarette, and share his apprehensions. The lieutenant laughed out loud and told him that Southern ladies knew full well that brave soldiers fighting for their homeland could not always be expected to show up dressed in full gala and would pay little heed to how he was attired.

Back in his tent and with no more to be done about it, Kuno began to groom himself as best he could, even as a few uncharitable thoughts about his close friend's lack of empathy crept into his mind. He was glad that his *mess mates* were away, either on duty or out practicing throwing their bowie knifes at a target affixed to a tree, while he attempted to make himself presentable for salon society. He gave his coat a systematic pounding, oiled his boots thoroughly, managing to impart a faint shine by means of a rag and plenty of elbow grease, brushed his curly hair as smoothly as possible, put on a pair of finely creased linen pants, which his mother had given him to take along against his wishes, tied a colorful tie around his neck and, although the mirror distorted his appearance, felt his self-confidence somewhat lifted by these actions. But when the lieutenant came by at ten o'clock to fetch him, his spirits once again took a nose dive. The lieutenant had donned a tailored parade uniform and otherwise was decked out in the complete gala of a fashionable 1864 *dandy*.

Fairview Plantation was about ten miles distant from the *camp*. But the lieutenant's fine-boned palomino and Kuno's *paint*, now trotting and now cantering, managed to get them there in an hour. Along the way Lieutenant DeBray whistled one happy tune after the other while Kuno's thoughts turned back to Possum Creek. The sight of the wool socks that Hedwig had presented him had fed his reverie, and he wondered why it was that he had not received a single letter from home. Finally, DeBray ceased his whistling in order to give his companion a few choice pointers on how to conduct himself

"You don't need to worry yourself about the girls," he said. "You will be good friends in ten minutes. You won't see much of the old Delaroche either. When he is at home, he is always occupied with some new system whereby he will be sure to win at the next big poker game, and is always glad not to be disturbed during these mental exercises. His mother, however, Madame Marcelline, rules the roost at Fairview and you need to try to stay on her good side. She is a reserved old lady but she has her peculiarities. Above all, never refer to this place as Fairview Plantation; to her it is always Place Bellevue, because she is a confirmed Francophile. And then you must never let on that you are not a dyed-in-the-wool secessionist because she hates Yankees with a passion and believes that slavery was instituted by God Himself, and any doubt about it qualifies as blasphemy. Also, you must not mention New Orleans, because that will remind her of her hatred for 'spoons' Butler,[268] who once threatened to have any woman in the city publicly whipped who insulted a blue uniform. She still longs to see Butler drawn and quartered in punishment for his unchivalrous attitudes, and when she is provoked by his memory, she starts to say things that are not very pretty. Pay her a couple of nice compliments, and act as if you think she is the mother of the pretty young girls and you will win her over completely and, in short order, she will bring out a plate full of the finest sweets as a reward."

"Not much hope for me," sighed Kuno to himself as he once again bemoaned this anything but voluntary outing even more than before. Soon thereafter, the pine forest opened up to reveal a large plantation of many thousands of acres. The entire area was encircled by impenetrable rose hedges which only permitted intermittent glimpses of the large field, which was mostly fallow.

Then the manor house came into view, a large, almost castle-like *mansion*, surrounded on all sides by wide verandas. It was situated upon a sandy elevation next to a small, half-moon shaped lake whose clear waters reflected perfectly the outstretched limbs of the patriarchal live oaks. A highly ornate wrought iron fence surrounded the house and enclosed a well-maintained lawn that had been landscaped with trees and shrubbery. The lawn also featured two stone fountains with large water basins, but they appeared to have been out of action for a long time and the fountains were dry.

They were received by a mulatto in a blue frock and long stockings in front of the large entrance that was covered with ivy; their horses were led off by Negro boys to the stall and, as they approached the foyer, a young brunette damsel, perhaps twenty years of age and dressed in a white woolen dress, came out to greet them.

"That is *Miss* Louisiana, the eldest daughter," whispered DeBray to his companion, and then introduced Kuno to her with many flattering comments about his person. *Miss* Louisiana did not suppress her delight at the long-awaited visit which, as she stated, came at a time when she found herself alone to the world and bored to tears. She then thanked the lieutenant for giving her the opportunity to get to know such a valiant and cultured young warrior for the good cause. They then walked up the broad steps leading up to the main entrance. On either side were a series of plaster pedestals that were handsome enough even though the tooth of time had left its mark on them.

Once inside, they were ushered in the direction of Madame Marcelline's boudoir by their garrulous hostess, the nicest place for casual conversation, so she maintained. Kuno's boots almost slipped out from under him as he crossed the smooth, well-polished floor of the corridor, but once inside Madame Marcelline's domain, he found the room furnished with a thick Brussels carpet. With a gesture, 'Mamzelle' Louisiana indicated that DeBray should take a seat in an ornate rocking chair with cane webbing, but Kuno was to sit next to her on a high-backed and upholstered tête-à-tête,[269] and he would have much preferred to march headlong against the Yankees than to occupy this position.

While a steady stream of words gushed from the red lips of the young lady, interrupted only now and then by a casual remark from the lieutenant, Kuno's eyes, which he did not want to hold glued to the floor, glided around the room; to the walls that had been covered with a pale blue silk; to the statuettes of Adonis and Venus; to various glass vases and other such decorative knick-knacks on the mantle and tables; to the broad windows hung with magnificent lace curtains; then finally to Miss Louisiana. His glance brushed her small feet, wedged in sapphire encrusted slippers that emerged from under the hem of her dress, and then passed to his own feet, which appeared to have swollen to enormous proportions in their cowhide leather boots. He would have liked to hide them, but where? And then his hands! His well-tanned hands were long like his father's, and strongly built with pronounced knuckles and joints, and truly the inside of his index finger, despite a careful washing, appeared almost black, the result of oiling his Enfield musket.

Normally he had the habit of putting his hands in his pockets, but that wouldn't do here. Mortified, he took out his handkerchief and began twisting it in his hands. He threw a glance in the direction of his friend, who was trying to draw him into the conversation, and had the distinct impression that he fully realized how awkward the situation was for him but appeared to be relishing his embarrassment. Then he thought to himself: "Well, if that is how things are, let them be like that," and, with this, he folded his handkerchief neatly, put it back in his pocket, and spread out his rough hands on his knees so that they were in plain view.

"Papa rode out with the *overseer* this morning," explained *Mamzelle* Louisiana, "and my sisters, Alabama and Georgia—Georgia is the youngest of the twins, and we really wanted to baptize her Texas, but that sounds too harsh for a girl's name—anyway, she went along with cousin Ruth to look in on our small Hannibal, daughter of our old Africa, who broke three ribs recently—but it just occurred to me that I have completely forgotten to tell you that our puritan cousin—Alabama always calls her that—Ruth Mullins is her real name—she has been visiting us here at Fairview already for a week now. Her father died six months ago up there in the mountains of West Virginia; the little village in the mountains where she was the school mistress was burned to the ground by the soldiers, and she finally decided to come join us here, like *grand maman* wanted all along. But I think it would have been better if she had stayed up there with the *Yankees.* Ruth is terribly educated and understands astronomy and grammar and geology and she can recite the multiplication table backwards and forwards, and I just don't know how much learning can occupy the head of one young lady. What she would really like us to do is convert us all to be Methodists, and she has already started trying; she even wanted to teach the small Negros—just like they were capable of learning anything—but *grand maman* wouldn't allow it— and, I'll be, there they are now! Excuse me a minute, I will go out to greet them."

With that she was gone like a whirlwind and DeBray and Kuno followed at a more leisurely pace. A large, enclosed coach pulled by four white horses pulled up in front of the entrance. An enormous, coal-black coachman, decked out in livery like all the house servants, occupied the driver's seat. Two cute girls— judging from their resemblance to Louisiana, the sisters Alabama and Georgia— were the first to emerge from the conveyance. They were so remarkably identical in appearance that Alabama always had to wear red ribbons, or accoutrements of that nature, while Georgia wore pink in order to avoid embarrassing mistakes in identity. They were both barely seventeen years old and were small and delicate of frame like Louisiana, but not nearly as talkative. Then an older lady climbed out of the coach dressed in an austere black silk dress, the grandmother Madame Marcelline. She was approaching her seventieth year and the hair under her black bonnet was white as snow, her face deeply wrinkled, but her black eyes still sparkled brightly and her step, lively and elastic for a person her age. The last to emerge was the cousin about whom Louisiana had spoken. A starker contrast as between Ruth Mullins and her relatives would be hard to imagine. While the ones were small and delicate with curly, dark brunette hair, Ruth Mullins was tall and slender for her sex with a full head of ash blond hair that was held together under a thick hair net. Her simple mourning dress also stood in contrast to the brightly colored attire of her relatives. Her more earnest and reserved nature, likewise, contrasted with the easy cheerfulness and exuberance of her cousins, a trait that seemed to characterize many Southern women, while her peach red cheeks, colored by a more northerly clime, diverged from the darker tint of the three brunettes. She resembled them in one point only: her eyes were also dark, but of a soft brown hue, not black.

After the obligatory greetings and introductions, the two guests were ushered into the salon, in its way just as elegantly outfitted as the boudoir. The ladies excused themselves in order to take their toilette before the noon meal while the gentlemen remained alone. The lieutenant used the opportunity to kid and laugh at his charge for his excessive modesty and to announce to him that, henceforth, he intended to always bring him along so that he would learn to overcome his shyness. Then he explained what he had found out concerning the tragic circumstances of the pretty young cousin from West Virginia.

Her father had come to Northern Louisiana as an itinerate Methodist preacher some years before and had aroused a lot of attention there because of his rhetorical skills. His presence had also stirred the hearts of many a young lady. The only daughter of the Delaroche house had fallen madly in love with him and, despite differences in belief and opposition on the part of the mother, she became the wife of the pious and eloquent but thoroughly impoverished missionary. She followed him up north, sharing with him all the hardships and deprivations that fell to the lot of a *circuit rider*, but this rich daughter of a Louisiana creole planter was never heard to utter a word of complaint. Still, in the end, she died of homesickness for her native state of Louisiana while in the mountains of West Virginia. Her spouse was left with a ten-year-old daughter who accompanied him on all his travels. The father devoted much care and attention to her upbringing and education and after his health had finally been undermined by the daily exertions and hardships attendant to his calling, she accepted the position of a teacher in a small rural school and took care of him until he died. She had endured much bitter suffering and had experienced all of the horrors of the war years that had befallen her home state. She was a true heroine who seemed to idolize her grandmother even though her father had despised the woman and her own views concerning slavery and other matters were so utterly at odds with those of her grandmother.

Soon Mr. Delaroche, who had just returned from his ride, joined his guests. He was a small, corpulent man whose bulging eyes and flushed countenance—the effects of an excessive fondness for alcoholic spirits—did not offer an altogether favorable impression. He did not speak a lot but compensated for this deficiency with spicy anecdotes that tickled the fancy of Lieutenant DeBray, who responded with thunderous laughter. Then Madame Marcelline returned with her granddaughters. No longer in black, she now had on a white silk dress with a long trail. Around her heavily powdered and shriveled neck she wore a magnificent pearl necklace and pinned on her breast a likeness of the savior. The two twins were now also dressed in white, and likewise Louisiana; Ruth, however, now as before, appeared in a modest black dress.

Madame Marcelline engaged Kuno right away in conversation but was very astonished to find out that Kuno was not fluent in French. She firmly believed that all educated foreigners could (or should) understand and speak French. She explained that she herself had been born in Louisiana but her parents had arrived as refugees from France to escape the guillotine. Still, she had always regarded *"La Belle France"* as her true homeland. She complained bitterly that her too granddaughters only spoke French poorly, and reluctantly, because since their move from New Iberia to North Louisiana they found themselves only among English speakers.

Then a black servant appeared to announce that the table had been set. Lieutenant DeBray gallantly offered Madame Marcelline his arm to lead her into the dining hall; Delaroche accompanied his oldest daughter. But before Kuno could take stock of the situation, Ruth Mullins slender figure was standing by his side and she whispered to him: "According to the silly custom that prevails here, you will have to accompany me to the table as if a single girl could not find her way there by herself." And then her hand lay in his arm, and the youth called himself lucky that it had fallen to him to accompany the *puritan* rather than one of the all too chatty and exuberant twins.

The dining hall was also stylishly appointed with a pair of quite tasteful paintings by French masters that Kuno would have gladly given a closer inspection. The seating order had him placed next to Madame Marcelline, considered to be the seat of honor, and since he was now able to dredge up a few crumbs of French from that period in his childhood when the portly and jovial Alsatian lady, Mademoiselle Becker, had spent a couple of months in his parents' house as a private teacher, a situation cut short, by the way, by a rich German bachelor who snatched her away for his wife. But with these tidbits of French he was able to secure her good wishes without the necessity of employing the disingenuous flatteries suggested earlier by his companion. The meal had been excellently prepared, although the meat dishes seemed a little too spicy for Kuno's taste; table conversation was lively throughout with the service between the various courses, flawless. Kuno took his time eating while his female table companion, taking notice of his uncertainty, discretely whispered helpful hints to help him avoid the many pitfalls associated with exotic dishes and unfamiliar table manners and, in the process, revealed herself as being a true helper in a time of need. Meanwhile, it seemed to Kuno as if the lieutenant were spending more time looking at Ruth than his own table companion, Miss Louisiana, who was seated opposite of him. At the conclusion of the meal, *Grand Maman* gave her black cellar master a directive. He quickly disappeared and in short order reappeared with two large bottles from the cellar.

"Champagne," cried out the sisters in joy and the lieutenant was quick to add that it was due to his solicitude that Madame Marcelline had discovered, once again, the very last bottles of vintage 1860; if he had not brought along Kuno with his *merci* and other such tidbits of French, this meal, fit for the Gods, would not have been crowned at the end with real champagne. The girls nodded their approval, the corks popped, and the guests savored their drinks from tapered champagne glasses. Only Ruth Mullins, who had also not touched her red wine, spurned the bubbly beverage. Kuno, however, experienced for the first time the delightfully prickly effect that the drink exercises upon the nerves; his reserve vanished and he completely forgot his large cowhide boots and his blackened index finger.

Afterwards, the party adjourned to the salon where the young women gathered around him, plying him with questions and requests. Under this onslaught his newfound courage soon abandoned him. "Kuno, you are tipsy and are going to make a fool of yourself for sure," he said to himself and retreated back into his old reticence. Sensing his mood swing, the young teacher came to his rescue once again. She invited him to sit with her, showed him photographs, and inquired in a tactful way about his home and family life and Kuno, who in the meantime had gained a rock-solid trust in her, cheerfully answered all her questions.

But when he let slip that he did not belong to a church, had never attended a church service, and was not even baptized, then Ruth recoiled in horror and fear for the young man's soul and resolved, as the true daughter of her father, that henceforth it would be her mission to convert the young heathen, whom divine fate had placed in her path. The situation became awkward for Kuno and he would gladly have gladly exchanged the gravity of the present discussion and the turn it had taken for the more lighthearted tone of the lieutenant and his circle.

He was in the act of relating one amusing anecdote after the next and was in fine form. He found an appreciative audience in the young ladies and also in the grandmother, who had foregone her customary afternoon nap. Kuno's escapades as a new recruit in Company B provided fertile material for several anecdotes, which he shamelessly embellished to accent the comical aspect of the situations. Throughout, however, Kuno got the distinct impression that it was all for the benefit of Ruth Mullins. But she was not to be diverted from her new-found resolve to convert Kuno to Christianity, until finally the lieutenant invited all to make music.

Louisiana and Alabama called for their instruments, a guitar and a mandolin, while Madame Delaroche agreed to accompany them on the magnificent concert piano that occupied a prominent place in the salon. Mr. Delaroche, who had been seated in a recliner and, as it appeared, struggling to keep his eyes open, arose and excused himself for the remainder of the afternoon with the announcement that he had pressing business to take care of. His mother, obviously annoyed, called out to him with a few words in French, the gist of which was that he ought to stay, but he excused himself nevertheless.

Then the two young ladies played a couple of duets from memory, light pieces from a French opera. They followed these with "Way down upon the Sewanee River"[270] whereby Lieutenant DeBray and Georgia joined in to sing the text. This was followed by a Strauss waltz which seemed to restore Madame Marcelline to her previous good spirits. She was keeping time to the beat with such enthusiasm that DeBray felt obligated to ask her for a dance. She did not decline and danced more gracefully and nimbly than one would expect from someone her age while the small granddaughter Georgia looked longingly over at Kuno, as if she expected an invitation from him, but Kuno was as ignorant about dancing as he was about religion and so could not satisfy her expectations in this regard.

After the music had begun and the grandmother had taken to the dance floor, Ruth walked over to the window with a flush of exasperation on her cheeks. When the music ended DeBray accompanied his partner, who did not appear to be at all fatigued by her exertions, back to her seat. He then called for the young teacher to favor them with a song for the cousins had let it be known that she had a wonderful voice. At first, she demurred with the pretext that she was not in the mood, but after the others also insisted, she walked quickly over to the piano and, accompanying herself, sang in a wonderfully sweet alto voice, "Nearer my God to Thee."[271] Upon finishing the song, a reverent mood held the audience in silence as the she arose from the piano with a deep sigh and, therewith, the improvised concert came to an end.

The two twins now commandeered Kuno, showing him in turn their canaries, the hot house, and their needlework. Then they led him out into the garden, and soon he was taking turn shooting the crossbow at a target and since he had practiced with the bow often as a boy, in this skill, at least, he could show himself to be the master. Soon the elder one also came into the garden and, since the day was warm, the four played a game of croquet, a game where Kuno deported himself as a willing student.

When the time finally arrived for their departure, he had come to feel really at home among these light-hearted and gracious people to which a friendly star had led him. His lieutenant, however, acted unusually silent and introspective on the return ride home. There was no whistling as on the morning's ride and, finally, he turned and asked Kuno outright, what exactly it was that *Miss* Ruth had to say to him during their seemingly long and intense conversation? And when Kuno confessed that this exchange could be attributed solely to the fact that she had discovered he was a heathen, he replied in exasperation: "Well, I guess I'm the jackass for being baptized!"

Before taking their leave Madame Marcelline and her granddaughters insisted that the Lieutenant and Kuno Sartorius join in the twins seventeenth birthday celebration. A few days later, Kuno gladly took them up on their offer, but this time his expectations were sorely disappointed. Kuno and the lieutenant found the festive house filled with guests, for the most part wives and daughters of the surrounding planters, but also including a collection of officers stationed in various camps in a twenty-mile radius.

To his amazement Kuno noticed that Inspector-General Mullins, the officer who had appeared to spend an inordinately long time at Yellow Bayou, was among them. As the only *private*, and in civilian clothes to boot, he felt awkward and out of place among so many with epaulettes on their shoulders, and it bothered him not a little that the strange women paid him, the simple recruit, so little heed while lavishing all their attention upon the officers. As hostesses, the Delaroche sisters were completely absorbed by their responsibilities and their social obligations to their guests and found, consequently, little extra time to devote to Kuno, while the grandmother seemed scattered and in a foul mood. When General Mullins wanted to make a case for being related to Ruth Mullins by virtue of their similar last names, the grandmother cut him short with the terse statement that Ruth was the daughter of a preacher, a genuinely pious man, who disliked nothing more than gamblers and drunkards. At this the eminent inspector-general choose to quickly disengage from the conversation.

The noon meal was fabulous and seemed not to suffer in any way from the shortages which the blockade had also imposed on well-to-do families. Those people for whom cost was not a consideration could, it turned out, easily obtain anything their hearts desired from the numerous smugglers in New Orleans.[272] There were, however, no alcoholic spirits served on this occasion.

After the noon meal, the guests enjoyed music and dancing. This time a one-legged mulatto played the violin: Virginia reels, quadrilles, polkas and waltzes; all without the benefit of notes and never missing a beat.[273] The young people devoted themselves energetically to dancing and had a lot of fun in the process, but Madame Marcelline withdrew from the festivities with the excuse that she was suffering from a migraine attack and, soon thereafter, the master of the house and General Mullins likewise both excused themselves. Ruth Mullins and Kuno, as the only non-dancers in the crowd, found themselves standing next to one another as a matter of course and, since the loud and festive atmosphere of the dancers had begun to grate on the young woman, they soon retired to the outside veranda. Ruth, who seemed to have momentarily forgotten her intention of converting Kuno, spoke simply and without affectation to the young guest. When he remarked about how gracefully her cousin Louisiana danced, she replied:

Seeing how carefree and happy my cousin seems on the surface, one could scarcely believe what pain and distress she carries in her heart. She cried the whole night long and never got a wink of sleep. Yesterday evening a letter came bearing the dreadful news that her fiancé, Captain Hunter, who has already suffered three serious wounds, is lying close to death in a Richmond hospital due to an inflammation of the lungs that he contracted from constant exposure to ice and snow while in the defensive trenches around the city. He may well be dead by now since he is said to have a rather weak constitution. At first, Louisiana wanted to hurry to his bedside, but after her grandmother made it clear to her that under the present circumstances that would be impossible, she swore a solemn oath to join a convent, should he not return. It is really painful for me because she really does love him fervently, but I can't comprehend how she can now put on such a cheerful front, laughing and dancing like she didn't have a care in the world, and all so as not to spoil the festive atmosphere for her sisters and the enjoyment of their guests. And, honestly, I can't fathom how anyone, just to forget their own sorrows, would voluntarily bury themselves in a convent and devote themselves to a life of fasting and detachment rather than dedicating themselves to the betterment of their fellow human beings in an active way.

With this report Kuno gained a new respect for the eldest daughter of the house who had come across so shallow at first but who now revealed by her reactions that she had a hidden side, one of deep emotions and firm resolve; qualities that no one would have suspected. It also drove home to him how wrong it is to make snap judgments of people based on externalities.

Their discussion was soon disturbed by an unwelcome altercation, and they were forced to witness a most unsavory exchange. In one of the antechambers that belonged to the realm of the gentlemen of the house, they suddenly heard the shrill voice of a woman and then could make out the sounds of chairs being slammed. Soon thereafter Madame Marcelline emerged on the veranda followed by her son and General Mullins. The face of the old woman was contorted in rage and in a shrill voice she called to a slave:

"Saddle the horse of General Mullins immediately, Anatole! The gentleman wishes to depart. And I wish to never have as a guest of Bellevue again someone whose sole purpose is to plunder his hosts."

Without noticing that this scene had witnesses, the energetic old lady fastened the nominal master of the plantation by the arm, who stood there as meekly as if he were a statuette of a poodle, and drug him back into the house, no doubt to deliver a stern lecture and give him a good dressing down, while the general hastily departed on his horse at a full gallop without any further adieus. Ruth Mullins, however, used the occasion to deliver a pointed lecture on the evils of gambling and seemed genuinely pleased that Kuno nodded his complete agreement with her point of view. Soon thereafter, they were once again interrupted, this time by Lieutenant DeBray, who came out on the veranda to join them and who addressed the young teacher in a sarcastic tone:

"Ah, just as I figured, *Miss* Ruth, busy at work with your efforts to convert my young friend. Don't lose heart if he comes across a bit stubborn. He is not nearly so naïve as he sometimes lets on, and that he has good tastes, well, the proof of that stands before us. And, if you are finished with him now, maybe you will be so good as to expend some effort on me.

"In order to rescue you, Lieutenant, it would doubtless require the rollout of more heavy artillery than is available to a young maiden. I have always heard it said that it is easier to convert a genuine heathen of pure heart than to redeem a baptized Christian who strays habitually from the path of righteousness."

"Well if that is what missionaries believe, it must be true *Miss* Ruth Mullins, because they certainly understand their trade better than anyone else. I can only congratulate my dear young friend Kuno Sartorius that no one less than your esteemed self and not some old and grey-bearded evangelist has undertaken the salvation of his soul. And not a few would envy him this preference even though such pretty lips seem ill-shaped to properly describe all of Hell's many torments below; much better suited to paint the wonders of Heaven above."

"Gentlemen, let us return to the salon," she replied, ignoring his sarcasm. "When there is music and dancing, it is never the best time to discuss scripture. Moreover, it has turned downright cool out here."

"Really biting cold, my teeth are beginning to chatter," the lieutenant added sarcastically.

The three then returned to the salon. Kuno began to wonder about the barely concealed tension that had become obvious in the recent exchange between the two, both people whom he had grown fond of. The improvised ball continued and the officers and young ladies danced with such zeal and dedication as if they feared never to be able to take part in such pleasurable affair again. Kuno was also very surprised when he observed that not only the gentlemen but also two of the ladies adjourned in the pauses between dances to immodestly roll their own cigarettes and smoke. They delicately rolled them with their tender fingers out of corn husks and finely cut but exceedingly strong perique tobacco. But for the remainder of the time, Kuno hung around in the background and was glad when the "the never changing schedule of our duties"[274] finally mandated that they depart.

On the return ride the lieutenant whistled one popular tune after another, and when he had anything to say to Kuno at all, it was only to make fun of the clumsy jumping and hopping about that had passed for dancing or to disparage the Yankee girl who put on airs like she was the poster child for the saints even though she possessed a razor sharp tongue. "In the end, I prefer the creolized Gulf States," he said, referencing the names of the daughters of the Delaroche house. "To be sure, they gossip and chatter a lot about trivial things, and they all like to *flirt*, but they don't get bent out of shape with every little off-color remark or gesture."

When Kuno chivalrously attempted to defend his friend, the lieutenant directed his misanthropic mood, now worked into a frenzy, against him, and he retreated into a sullen silence.

Kuno received no further invitations to accompany the lieutenant to Fairview although he could see that the he had undertaken several pleasure outings in that direction. Their friendship seemed to have suffered a serious blow. DeBray remained in a foul mood and his jokes no longer seemed so friendly and harmless. Kuno, also now out of sorts, began to make a point of avoiding him as best he could, while gravitating more to the company of the sergeant. An explanation for the lieutenant's sudden mood swing, however, was not long in forthcoming.

One afternoon the following week while Kuno was on duty, the lieutenant rode off once again. The next morning a thick fog blanketed the landscape. Sergeant Shoots, who fancied himself a great fisherman, had asked Kuno to come along with him on a fishing outing.

"When the fog lifts, and that will be around ten o'clock, the fish in all the ponds with standing water will begin to bite, fish whose mouths are otherwise glued shut. I've seen the proof of it enough at Zabrce[275] and Himmelwitz,[276] and it's just the same here in America. I can't take any of the *cowboys* along because they spoil the fishing with their constant banter. Go and get you a pass from the lieutenant."

Kuno was agreeable and headed straightaway for the officers' tent. He was not a little astonished to hear as he approached the company chief singing very reverently—his voice was unmistakable—"Nearer my God to Thee." He was even more surprised to see a copy of the Bible lying open on the camp table, and his amazement approached incredulity when the lieutenant, instead of responding to his request for a pass, took his hand instead and shook it vigorously, and announced:

"Kuno, I have been a real jackass, and I hope you won't hold it against me that I have acted so nasty towards you lately. The truth of the matter is I have been very jealous of you when, in reality, I should have realized all along that she was only interested in you because you are such an unusual type in whom everybody takes an interest. And now congratulate me, because yesterday Ruth

"Man on horseback." Friedrich Richard Petri papers, [detail from 11949],
The Dolph Briscoe Center for American History, The University of Texas at Austin.

Mullins promised to become Mrs. Ruth DeBray as soon as I change my errant ways. If you were a good Christian, I would ask you to kneel down with me and join me in prayer, beseeching Him that I may bring this transformation about quickly and that, in order to be worthy of such happiness and bliss, Heaven will welcome me, the unworthy ne'er-do-well Clarence DeBray, into the fold. And now, in God's name, be on your way fishing, and rejoice along with me that I have found my saving angel."

OTHER THINGS KUNO EXPERIENCED DURING WARTIME

On the way to the fishing hole, Kuno's thoughts went this way and that through his head. He had never enjoyed reading novels and everything the German poets wrote about love had always seemed a bit over-the-top and idiotic to him. And now he had the example before him of a cheerful and accomplished man of the world succumbing so readily and haplessly to such a passion. And then, how could it be possible for these two people, who at root were so utterly different, to unite as a married couple; his jovial, easy-going friend and the ear-nest and pious Ruth? The thought, however, that the handsome lieutenant had been jealous of him, a young man completely inexperienced in the ways of the world, amused him greatly in his quieter moments.

He was not able to indulge himself with these thoughts for too long. The sergeant had taken it upon himself to hold a little lecture on strategy. They were passing through two rose hedges that marked the boundary of a neighboring plantation when Shoots suddenly stopped and remarked: "Look here, that reminds me of Frogtown on the upper Mississippi where I demonstrated to the esteemed officers that a good Prussian non-commissioned officer knows more about the art of war than most Confederate *captains* and *colonels*. Our regiment was part of an advance scouting party during the great *cavalry raid*, and our mission was to locate and confiscate the enormous quantity of supplies that the Yankees had stockpiled for the coming attack on Vicksburg.[277] In order to get it done, we had to maintain a fast pace. In the afternoon, we came upon a small nest of a dozen or so houses and a courthouse in the middle. We passed through the town only to find out that a couple of hundred Yankees were in front of us. We had the *river* to our right and a *swamp* to our left and the Yankees, who understood their business well, had blockaded the road with bales of cotton and large logs next to a gin and mill in order to defend their position. The road was a sunken trace of thick red mud with hedges, like these, to either side. It was a dire situation calling for cool heads and seasoned advice, but our good *colonel's* only response was to rail to the heavens and curse a blue steak. Finally, our Captain Smith, who now thanks be to God has been assigned *detached service*[278] where he will not be able to sacrifice men needlessly, ordered that we should charge down the road at a full gallop, dismount in front of the barricades, and put the Yankees to flight. It was complete idiocy and unnecessary sacrifice. In the deep *mud* we could only advance slowly and before we could reach our objective they would have shot down at least half of my brave boys, and behind the cotton bales were Missourians, who knew how to shoot. I was so galled by the thought that I told the *captain* like it was. At first, he *kicked* and didn't want to hear that what he had ordered was utter folly. Finally, however, when the *colonel* became insistent and hinted we were losing our nerve, I told the *captain* to give me thirty men and I would take care of it. We sneaked off to the right down to the *river* and then crept forward along the bank using the large *cottonwood* trees for cover until we came up behind the gin. The Yankees had not given us much credit for good sense and hadn't posted pickets to cover their flanks, and as soon as we got in position, we began to give them a good peppering. They returned fire but wasted their powder because they couldn't see anything to shoot at but gun barrels, and then our second *detachment* took them under a crossfire from the right, and how they jumped and squirmed, and then the *captain* came charging to the front with the rest of the men, and in a couple of minutes it was all over. We took the whole lot prisoner and our path was then open. We had to release them because we couldn't deal with prisoners, but at least I got a good canteen and a breech loading rifle out of the affray. We didn't lose a single man and only two had glancing wounds. The next morning we arrived at Holly Springs and from all the enormous stockpile of supplies we captured there nothing remained, because anything we couldn't cart off we burned. If it hadn't been for me, General Grant might have taken Vicksburg six months earlier, and if Pemberton had known half as much as me then he would never have got caught on the nest."[279]

At this the gutsy sergeant laid out his plan of battle using his feet to energetically delineate troop positions and movements in the sand while Kuno listened with due respect to this extraordinary presentation.

Shoots was also right about the fishing. The fish in the small bayou aggressively went after the bait after the heat of the sun had burnt away the fog, which delighted the sergeant to no end. Through his facility at fishing he hoped to relieve the monotony of the daily fare of his men. In two hours they were able to catch eight large *catfish* that weighed in total nearly forty pounds. In addition, they pulled in several trout and gaspergou[280] from the clear waters. That evening there was a great feast that brought in many compliments to the sergeant.

As they were making ready to depart from the fishing hole, they heard the pure voice of a child singing:

"Wo ist denn mein Schatz geblieben?
Ist nicht hier? Ist nicht da?
Ist wohl in Amerika."[281]

[Where the heck is my loved one at?
Not here, not there
Probably in America.]

Both of the fishermen listened up upon hearing the familiar rhymes. And then when the same voice took up the popular folk song, *"Muß i denn, muß i denn zum Städele hinaus,"*[282] they had to get up and try to find out who it was singing such songs in the middle of nowhere. Using all their talents for stalking, they silently approached the voice and lo and behold they discovered a small Negro boy with a bucket full of crabs next to him stretched out on the limb of a tree belting out German tunes at the top of his lungs.

"How in the world does the *nigger* come to be singing German songs?" asked the sergeant in amazement. When the two showed themselves and addressed the boy in English, his first inclination was to take to his heels, but when Kuno called out to him in German, he approached them cautiously and soon they had an answer to the riddle.

When yellow fever broke out in Louisiana in the late fall, the owners of the little black boy, a German tailor in Opelousas, fled with his family to the border with Arkansas where they found lodging in a small village. There the tailor, Schneider by name and a cheerful Swabian, succumbed to the disease nevertheless, leaving his wife and children in great distress. The small black Hans found himself in this dire situation to a certain degree protector of the family because he was good at catching fish, crabs, and rabbits with which to help feed the family. Hearing this, the fishermen gave him two nice trout and sent him on his way back home. Shoots, however, could not stop wondering on the way back about how bizarre a situation it was that a *nigger* could sing and speak German just as good as any regular human, while in Kuno's breast the familiar songs had awoken memories of his faraway Texas home.

A few days later the order came to march back to Texas. The officers had expected this for a long time now since for all intents and purposes the southern and middle regions of Arkansas as well as northern Louisiana had been swept clean by Wharton's cavalry division.[283] The whole region was sparsely settled, the inhabitants largely impoverished and in terrible straits, and the number of livestock greatly reduced. The scarcity of fresh meat had been covered some-what by wild game but fodder for the horses was no longer to be found since the cultivation of grains in this area was close to nonexistent. There was only one choice: change quarters or lose horses, of which many were in such bad condition that they could barely support their riders. Already two regiments had departed. Company A had fared better than most because there were several large plantations in the area, and Madame Marcelline had generously offered with open hands more than had been demanded.

But even here, the corn sheds were near to empty, and it was clear to see that the owners would have trouble enough getting their own draft animals through the winter. At other locations, however, the people had been less willing to share. Things were bad enough for them and the promises of the Confederate government, or the offer of their paper currency, if even available for payment at all, were no longer believed or willingly accepted. The foraging details had to range ever further afield and yielded less and less.

Kuno had only taken part in one of these forays and it remained an unpleasant memory for a long time. The *farmers*, who only a few months before had welcomed the *greycoats* with open arms as friends and protectors, and had said to them: "Take what you want; what is ours is yours," had, in the meantime, changed their minds. Many resisted or were otherwise uncooperative, while others had obviously hidden their livestock and grain, and where that was clearly the case, the foragers unashamedly took everything they could lay their hands on while getting an earful from the non-too-happy victims. Among others, they confiscated a rather nicely fattened heifer from a widow, who had tried to drive them away by sic'ing her hounds on them and then heaped scorn on them as "Confederate robbers."

Kuno was given the task of driving the animal back to the gathering place while his comrades rode off in search of more prizes but he arrived at the rendezvous without the animal. He offered the excuse that underway the animal had made a break and gotten away, and he refused to say anything more about the loss. The widow, to be sure, had been extremely rude and uncooperative, but he had also observed that she as well as her children, who were barefoot and only partially clothed, looked anything but plump and well-fed. His comrades may well have guessed the real reason the animal had gotten away, but they were not angry about it; the sergeant, on the other hand, was not very happy, and made the point of excluding Kuno from all future foraging *details*, for when it came to provisions, he knew no mercy.

Before breaking camp Lieutenant DeBray made one farewell visit to Fairview and asked Kuno to accompany him with the proviso that he would do him a great favor if he would keep the young cousins and the grandmother occupied so that he would have the opportunity to have a good heart-to-heart with *Miss* Ruth. Kuno, however, took little pleasure in the thought that he was to perform decoy service, especially after his friend's confession, which would naturally render him very self-conscious in the presence of Ruth. He excused himself, therefore, and the lieutenant must have covered the situation quite tactfully for he returned as blissful as a newlywed. He relayed the best wishes of all the ladies and handed over to Kuno a petite letter. In it, Ruth reaffirmed, "her sisterly affection for her nice young German friend," and expressed the hope that he would continue as friend and confidant of Lieutenant DeBray. Their continued association, she was quite certain, would continue to exercise a salutatory and moderating influence upon one who had enjoyed way too much freedom in his formative years and, in consequence, had been exposed to all sorts of temptations at an early age, and upon one who still had difficult battles to fight in this regard. He complied with these wishes in full, as will become evident.

The next morning the tents that served so long as headquarters were struck and on the morning of January 2nd they were the last of the entire regiment to cross over onto Texas soil. Two days later they took up quarters in a new camp in Upshur County.[284] From this point the regiment picked up and moved from time to time ever further into the interior of Texas, as fresh requirements for food and fodder dictated. They found themselves camped among the red, iron-ore hills of Cherokee County[285] where, after a bitterly cold February, the first timid shoots of green began to emerge in March and, finally, they set up camp on the west bank of the Brazos River in Burleson County[286] where they were finally formally discharged from military service in May. In the *camps* prior to the general discharge, however, the men were drilled more often and more rigorously than had been the case for a long time, and not only as *company drills*, but larger exercises at the regimental and battalion level were also organized and carried out.

Sergeant Shoots, who by his own declaration had placed so little value on such drills, nevertheless, swelled with satisfaction at being able to put to good use all of his formidable Prussian experience, but on more than one occasion was aggravated to the breaking point by the accursed *cowboys* who continued to show up for duty unprepared and in an unmilitary frame of mind. Discipline was also enforced more strictly during this period, and any outside observer would have come away with the opinion that the troops were preparing for an extended continuation of the war. And, indeed, they were.

But the better informed among them knew better. They could see clearly that the last lingering prospects for victory had faded as one after another, first Atlanta, the great armory of the Confederacy, then Savannah and Columbia had fallen into the hands of the enemy; that Hood's army was now defeated and practically annihilated; that most major ports were either blockaded or occupied; that Lee's 40,000 brave but undernourished forces, reduced on a daily basis by constant fighting, could not hold out much longer against Grant's 150,000 well-supplied and armed soldiers; that Richmond was doomed to fall.

But there were still enough optimists among those who clung to the iron-clad belief that Lee and Johnston would still be able to unite their weakened armies and beat back Grant with new victories, and then turn upon Sherman, who had been laying waste the south Atlantic states for months now, and destroy his army. The great majority of the population, including the soldiers, believed otherwise. They hoped for no further miracle, and longed fervently for peace. Nevertheless, energetic steps had been taken in preparation for another large offensive. This was to begin once the horses had been restored to serviceable condition, or had been replaced, and enough provisions had been gathered and stockpiled to support a large push to the North from Texas.

With the continued blockade of the Mississippi, the plan was to march across Arkansas and Missouri, penetrate Kansas and, in this manner, bring relief to their hopelessly encircled comrades in Virginia and Tennessee since the enemy would be compelled to withdraw large numbers of troops and material to meet the emerging threat from the west. It was an audacious plan, but at the most it would have increased the number of legendary *raids* by one, but otherwise accomplished little.

Kuno did not take part in most of the exercises because he was engaged for most of the time as a courier for Brigadier General Hardeman[287] and, thereby, avoided much of the monotony of camp life. He had this to thank primarily to the warm recommendation of his *captain*—he had received this promotion just after the New Year—and, secondly, to the stamina of his trusty paint. The duty required him to put up with much greater hardships due to wind and weather than was common to camp life, but that mattered but little to him. He came in contact with many high officers and occasionally took quarters in the homes of rich and well-connected people, with whom the generals and colonels were accustomed to taking their lodgings. This constant interaction also gave him occasion to hone his social skills and broaden his knowledge of American English, an advantage not to be underestimated. In later years, he often thanked his lucky star that he had been brought into the service against his will just for this reason.

Because of confusion in the forwarding of the mail due to constant change of location, he received scant news from home. The first letter arrived in February. It was from his mother and its contents showed clearly that it had been preceded by many other letters and that his letters had safely arrived at their destination, but most of the replies to the same had gone missing. The mother still expressed hope in the eventual victory of the South and gave expression to her conviction that her youngest son would bravely do his part to bring this about. The following passage in her letter gave him pause for much reflection:

"Herr von Seiffert; who has taken up residence with the Lüttenhoffs since exiting the miserable forest to join us at Possum Creek, came by to pay us a visit yesterday, and pressed us for details concerning your well-being. He was quite astonished that neither you nor Hedwig betrayed a word about your encounter with him and his deceased friend in the woods. I really was hurt by the fact that my youngest son kept silent about such a thing to his mother. The word here is that he will become a teacher

"Well then, I guess Scharfenegg has finally found the peace that eluded him for so long on foreign soil, and Seiffert has now hung his hat in Possum Creek and intends to become a schoolmaster . . . ," thought Kuno to himself.

In the second half of February, General Hardeman gave Kuno a letter to deliver to General Kirby Smith,[288] overall commander of the Trans-Mississippi

Department, who was in Shreveport, Louisiana. An ice-cold norther had followed a spell of unusually warm spring weather and laid down a layer of ice on all the trees and bushes. His journey led him through an area almost completely devoid of human habitation and it was so bitterly cold that he had little interest in camping out in the open air. After the sun had gone down, the deep silence of the forest was disturbed by the rich, sonorous voice of a man singing *"Wer hat dich, du schöner Wald, aufgebaut so hoch da drüben?"*,[289] and the solitary rider thought he had never heard anything more beautiful. Deeply moved, he stopped in order to listen until the last tones had disappeared. He then continued in the direction of the singing until he saw a crackling campfire in front of him, and soon he was hailed by no other than the unflappable Ferdinand Klösel, who put his massive arms around him as soon as he dismounted and gave him a bear hug, like a father would a long-lost son, and then led him to the fire where he could thaw himself good and proper. He then produced his field canteen to take care of internal warming. Gathered around the fire Kuno discovered half of Company F, with David Abrahamson in charge. The other half under Captain Krusius' command had already departed at noon with orders to join the regiment in Cherokee County. A portion of the regiment had remained behind in order to follow up with the wagons and cattle as soon as the ice melted.

When this story is over, I intend to be a cattleman rather than a farmer, Klösel insisted, because in this miserable stretch of East Texas I have gotten a thorough schooling in the trade, and in the end it's much easier than plowing and hoeing. And, by the way, it's not such a bad life either, at least here the horned critters are not so dog-scrawny like the ones in Arkansas. But enough of my gossip; you, my poor young man, are a veritable ice cube, and I know a good medicine to stave off a cold.

Kuno gladly accepted the invitation to spend the night with his friend, and soon enough the medicine made an appearance in the form of a stout punch whose main ingredient was plum brandy which Klösel had scored on one of his exploratory details from a farmer who had brewed it for himself.

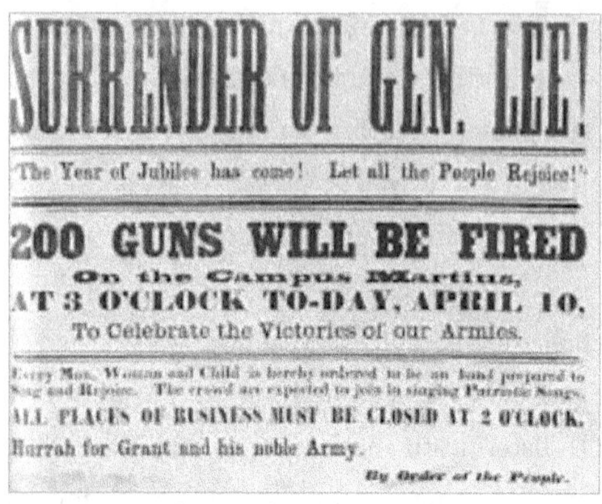

The men enjoyed singing and passing the cup around until well past midnight when they finally lay down to sleep. Kuno resumed his ride at the first light of dawn. He was in a happy mood and fully convinced that a German felt most at home and jovial when in the company of other Germans.

In Shreveport Kuno had the opportunity to observe the workings of a very large base camp. After he had delivered his letter to the commander, he was directed to return for an answer the next day. But this changed in consequence of a large Council of War that had just begun.[290] Accordingly, he would return to Texas in three days but now as guide for a staff officer who would be conveying important documents to General Hardeman and other Texas generals, documents of such importance that they could not be entrusted to a young courier alone.

In the headquarters Kuno also made the acquaintance of two German officers and came away with the distinct impression that the officers here were much less optimistic than their counterparts in Texas. The final collapse of the Confederacy was openly discussed and most agreed that it was probably a matter of weeks; at the most a question of months. He heard bitter complaints about the ineptness of the state governments; about serious shortages in basic supplies; about fraudulent suppliers who left the soldiers to starve while amassing as much cotton as possible, which they accepted in payment from the government; and cotton was, for all intents and purposes, as good as gold.[291] Later, it came to light that the overall commander, General Smith, had already made contact with Emperor Maximillian in Mexico as early as February and offered his services should the Confederacy go down in defeat.[292]

Translator's Note

The following section is termed "The Breakup," a term used by historians to refer to the events immediately preceding and following the surrender of General Robert E. Lee and his Army of Northern Virginia at Appomattox Court House on April 9, 1865. The author begins this section with a short overview of the "breakup" to set the context for the subsequent story. His overview, although cursory, is quite accurate, showing that Trenckmann was an astute and knowledgeable student of not only the Civil War but its aftermath as well.[293]

Lee's surrender set into motion a chain reaction of events that quickly took on a life of its own. The various Confederate governments and military commands west of the Mississippi River had been forced to operate more or less independently of Richmond after the fall of Vicksburg in July 4, 1863, and they responded to the implications of Lee's surrender differently. Several die-hard Confederate Generals, such as General

Kirby Smith, overall commander of Texas, Louisiana, and Arkansas, and General Hardeman, commander of the Fourth Texas Cavalry, deluded themselves at first that the war could be continued in the Western Theater and, accordingly, took steps to reorganize and motivate the men to renewed struggle. But as the rank and file, who had suffered unthinkable deprivations and had not been paid in months, got wind of Lee's (and Johnston's surrender) the armies of these generals began to dissolve like snow before a warm spring thaw.

What resulted was not an orderly process, a fact that many Southern historians have attempted to downplay for many years. Where bands of returning soldiers congregated, such as in Galveston and Houston, they often turned into disorderly mobs, breaking into governmental storehouses and helping them-selves to food and clothing that had been stockpiled there. In some places the looting turned into riots where private businesses where attacked and plundered as well. The worst examples were in Houston and La Grange, the county seat of Fayette County, just to the west of Austin County. After first helping themselves to governmental stores, returning elements of Walker's Texas Cavalry plundered and looted the predominantly German businesses in the town, hauling off over $30,000 worth of booty and threatening to burn down the town if anyone opposed them.

The situation in Texas was compounded by the fact that Texas had contributed a disproportionate share of cavalry units to the Confederacy, and most who served in cavalry units had initially contributed their own horses and tack. In the course of the war, many of these units had been converted to infantry. This did not sit well with the rank and file, leading in a few cases to outright mutiny. But due to inability to replace horses lost to enemy action, or to want and disease, even those units that did remain organized as cavalry often became **de facto** *dismounted units. As these ex-cavalrymen returned, many on foot, the "breakup" in Texas often took on the aspect of a massive and involuntary reallocation of horses and mules, since the returning cavalrymen felt justified in appropriating whatever horses and mules they could manage to steal.*

But not all Confederate units dissolved in such an unorderly fashion. Kuno finds himself attached to the Fourth Texas Cavalry under General Hardeman, whose men affectionately refer to him as "Ol' Gotch," in this final stage of the war. Kuno contrasts

the orderly standing down and disbandment of the men under Hardeman to that of
other units. Many years later, Hardeman helped to found Texas A&M College and
Trenckmann graduated as valedictorian of the first class. It is quite possible, therefore,
that Trenckmann had had the opportunity to meet the old soldier at some point.

The author touches on all these aspects of the breakup to set the stage for Kuno's
return to his old home at Possum Creek.

THE *BREAKUP*

What had to happen, happened. On the first of April, 1865, General Grant's strategy, buttressed by limitless means, achieved the goal that he had worked towards for a full year. General Lee's thinner and ever weakening lines of de-fense, which had to be extended further with each passing week in order to avoid being completely encircled and entrapped, were finally broken. The battle was continued for one more day, and though utterly hopeless, many still fought with the reckless courage that comes from despair, and then came the order to withdraw from the fortified positions around Petersburg and Richmond in a last gasp effort to save what little was left of the once mighty "Army of Northern Virginia." President Jefferson Davis and his cabinet hastily fled the city, fiercely contested for over four years now, as fires raged unchecked and thieves and marauders plundered at will. And then came the awful retreat where the great commander, magnificent as ever, bringing into play all his formidable military skills, marshalled his reduced army of now twenty or thirty thousand *greycoats*, who, despite so much suffering and deprivation, still retained the cohesion, courage, and fighting spirit that had led to so many victories in the face of superior odds in the past, for one last attempt at a breakthrough. It seemed as if they might succeed against all odds, but a subaltern had neglected to remove and stockpile the needed provisions at the Amelia courthouse where they were desperately needed to resupply the starving army.[294] The supplies fell into the hands of the well-nourished Federals, and Lee was forced to delay his withdrawal by a day as his men collapsed from hunger and exhaustion. The Federals blocked their retreat; Grant and his army stood before them. By the eighth of April they were completely surrounded near Appomattox courthouse. With a mere two thousand cavalrymen, the shriveled remnants of their former brigades, and riding horses so worn-out they were barely capable of a trot, Gordon and Fitzhugh made last desperate attempts to open an escape route between the Federal lines, charging the overwhelmingly superior force with the same élan that had characterized a hundred previous fights.[295] The enemy momentarily wavered, but only to tighten the noose tighter around those who were not lying bleeding in the sand—and then, the white flag of surrender was unfurled and many a gray haired soldier, who had long since forgotten what it was to shed tears openly, cried as the *Stars and Bars* was lowered before the *Stars and Stripes*.

From that point events cascaded from one to the next in quick succession. On April 14, President Lincoln was assassinated by the fanatic John Wilkes Booth and with his death all prospects for a compassionate policy of reconciliation that could have quickly healed the wounds of war were dashed; a policy which, without a doubt, this great man would have championed. On the May 26 Johnston's army laid their weapons down; on May 4, Major Dick Taylor's army in Alabama followed suit. At the beginning of May General Pope, the overall commander of Union forces in Louisiana, opened negotiations with General Kirby Smith, and also with the Texas government. But it soon came to light that Pope actually was not authorized to either impose demands or offer concessions. Confederate soldiers began to leave their units and, in a few places, they actually mutinied before being formally mustered out of the service. The army, in fact, dissolved on its own.

Things were different in the camp of General Hardeman.[296] News of Lee's surrender arrived at the end of April was at first greeted with skepticism, and while many had anticipated as much, others declared outright that it was a nasty lie, spread by the deceitful Yankees. But the full truth of it soon became clear enough. When news arrived of the assassination of Lincoln, a few individuals wanted to celebrate, but their jubilation dissolved soon enough before the consternation of the more thoughtful among them, who realized how ominous this evil deed was for the South.

Just as the contempt that had been heaped upon the Yankees four years ago had, by and by, changed into a kind of begrudging recognition of an honorable opponent; an opponent with whom they had often stood eye to eye in battle, so too had blind hatred for the Foremost man of the Union transformed little by little into a complex emotion in which respect, admiration, and fear all blended.

And after it became known that Johnston had also laid down his arms, a few hotheads—referencing the fact that Texas had maintained itself as a republic for many years—openly called for Texas to join with southern Arkansas and western Louisiana to continue the fight until the North was compelled to rec-ognize the "legitimate institutions of the South." But they too quickly fell silent and prepared for the inevitable.

Already soldiers, individually or in groups, the majority barefoot, ragged, and in wretched condition, began straggling back from the east side of the Mississippi from where they had received discharges, or had deserted, or had been released from years of captivity in Northern prisoner of war camps. They all had one wish: "To return home to be among their own," and in their single-minded determination to do just that, they took little interest in communicating the true scope of the South's debacle to the soldiers under Hardeman, who still stood organized and armed, as if the war might continue.

Then came the news that 400 men had attempted to mutiny in Galveston[297] and that thereafter men from all branches of service were withdrawn from that city and sent to Houston where, completely free of all discipline and authority, they took to the streets and rioted, plundering all the warehouses where the Confederate authorities had stockpiled food and clothing and, in other areas, even attacking private businesses.

General Hardeman still hesitated in the expectation that he would receive further orders from his superiors. But when news arrived of the civil disorder and disgusting looting by disbanded soldiers in Houston and La Grange,[298] he realized that he had to act before his *boys* also took "French leave." He made it known that each soldier would receive as his own property one of the young mules that had been collected and trained for the transportation corps over the past several months, a small recompense for the fact that most had received neither pay nor clothing for over a half-year, or longer.

Among the soldiers a mood of controlled excitement prevailed. Everyone looked forward to the return trip home but in spite of impatience the men said to themselves: "*'Old Gotch'*[299] will know when the time is right, and we will not leave until he gives us the word." In the last week of May the brigade gathered under weapons for the last time on the parade field. All the companies were woefully undermanned since hundreds had been granted passes to return home to re-outfit themselves since they literally had no more clothing left on their bodies to hide their nakedness. But because there was no longer any purpose to it, most of these men never returned. Consequently, many companies only counted twenty or thirty men, but those who did remain seemed all the more determined to comport themselves as good soldiers to the very end.

A number of the higher officers held speeches: some short and fiery; others long-winded and boring. At Hardeman's special request, Captain Krusius was also obliged to give a speech, "because our German comrades have shown themselves to be such brave soldiers and trustworthy comrades from Val Verde to this day." Though his remarks were brief, he spoke so sincerely and to the point that *Company* F took pride in their leader and *Long Mike* regretted it for a long time that he was away on a detail dealing with mules during the ceremony and could not be present for this strong showing on the part of their captain.

A Confederate major, a handsome, well-proportioned man who had participated with Lee in the terrible battles around Petersburg, gave a moving description, delivered with polished rhetorical skill, of the surrender of Lee at Appomattox; the final curtain call of the great national drama. He praised the courage of the Southern soldier in flaming words and the unforgettable glory these soldiers had earned at such terrible costs; the one fruit to offset the sting of defeat. In concluding, he implored them to keep alive the memory of their heroic deeds and never forget their fallen brothers, and to take pains to ensure their stories were passed on to their children and grandchildren. Rousing cheers greeted the conclusion of his magnificent speech.

Then General Hardeman spoke. This brave soldier did not possess the rhetorical skills of his predecessors and, visibly affected by the deep emotions of the moment, began his speech haltingly and softly, but he got hold of himself soon enough, and spoke directly to the situation. He thanked them for the loyal and faithful service they had given to their country and their willing obedience to their officers. He expressed the expectation that they would conduct their affairs as honorably in peacetime as they had soldiers in battle, and concluded with the words:

"What will happen now, in our Southland, I cannot say. We are the defeated and must bear this sad reality like men. But also, when peace comes, which by and by will return to our downtrodden land, it is important that we remain comrades, loyal to one another, and stand as one whenever we find ourselves or our homeland threatened or imperiled. In a few minutes you will be dismissed and no one will be around to give you orders anymore; you will be free to do and act as you please. Then forget not the last wish and request of the man who has served as your leader, who has done his best to do right by you; who henceforth will be only another discharged soldier among many. And my wish is this: return to your homes where your loved ones are awaiting you, but return not like an aroused and angry *mob*, but rather like disciplined soldiers still under your former officers, and conduct yourselves in such a manner that no one, not one wife, not one man, not a single child will have cause to raise complaints against soldiers from this brigade. And now, farewell *boys*, and may God bless you!"

"Hurrah for *Old Gotch*!" arose spontaneously from the throats of hundreds of soldiers followed quickly by the rousing *Confederate yell*, at core an appropriated Indian war cry, but a yell which had startled and frightened the enemy during many an attack. Hardeman's Brigade then stood down; one of the last large organized military units in Texas to do so. The men hastily prepared to return home with one exception, and this was a soldier named Jack Duff. Duff was generally regarded as one of the most devil-may-care men in *Company A*, a true virtuoso in risky exploits and also a master in all known games of chance; a good comrade and a model of manly strength and vigor.

At the moment, however, he lay on a bed in a log cabin only a few hundred paces removed from the parade ground, as pale as wax and short of breath, and his sergeant, who had tended to him for weeks as affectionately as any mother, had just closed the eyes that were now staring blankly into the distance when Kuno, returning from the parade ground, quietly entered the room. The soft-hearted old soldier, tears streaming down his cheeks, whispered softly to Kuno, as if afraid of waking the dead, "Jack is dead; he did not need to lay down his weapons. Before I came in and just as you all yelled '*Hurrah for Old Gotch*,' he raised himself and yelled out quite loud, '*Hurrah for Dixie!*' and then once again as softly as a breath, '*Hurrah!*' and when I fastened him by the shoulder he sank back down, and as I looked on, he took one final breath and was gone. And now summon the others from your *mess* so that we can make the necessary preparations. I promised Jack this morning that if he died I would take him to be buried in New London where he grew up under the big walnut tree where his father and mother are buried."

Kuno, deeply moved, hurried off to do as he was bidden. Since returning from his last mission the previous week, Kuno had taken his turn at the bedside of his deathly ill comrade on several occasions. Duff had fallen ill on an expedition to gather fodder for the horses a couple of weeks previous, but had remained in the saddle until the supplies had been delivered. But then he suddenly fell unconscious and soon lay in a fever induced delirium in which he either believed he was driving cattle or was fighting Indians or Yankees.

Often those tending him could barely restrain him and keep him in bed during these episodes. The regimental doctor, who was not exactly a model of erudition, diagnosed his condition as a nerve fever, and declared that there was nothing to be done about it except to diligently keep watch over him and tend to his needs, which was certainly the right thing to do, all the more so because there were no drugs present to treat fevers in the regimental apothecary. And, in truth, a more conscientious and dedicated care than he received from his comrades he would not have received in even the best hospital. Thanks to his robust constitution, he survived the first fever attack, regained consciousness and began to cheer up his caregivers with practical jokes and tomfoolery. But then he suffered a relapse because of a large slab of bacon that his good friend and cousin Conolly had slipped to the convalescent at his bidding who, in the meantime, had developed an enormous appetite. Once again, his condition worsened to the point of death, and when the fever finally subsided, he seemed utterly depleted and his strong constitution finally broken. He lay there in an agitated state half awake, half asleep and must have sensed that the end was near when he made his request concerning his burial.

At the end of an hour the deceased lay dressed in the nicest uniform that could be found in a hastily cobbled together wooden coffin over which the much tattered and shot up regimental flag was draped. Many officers and men from the regiment came by to pay their final respects to the man who had earned such a reputation for bravery and playful good-naturedness. After a short meeting, it was decided that the brother-in-law of the deceased, Pat Conolly, the sergeant, and Kuno Sartorius would transport the body as quickly as possible to New London to be buried. Captain DeBray, whose father lay on his death bed, quickly departed with his company to the south, all the remaining companies took their leave soon thereafter, and all, in accordance with the wishes of their commander, in good military order. The men of Captain Krusius' company, for example, parted ways only after arriving at the house of their commander at Amictia and after joining him in a large feast of barbequed beef.

An hour before sundown the small funeral procession was also ready to depart. The coffin lay upon a transport wagon pulled by the best mule team of the regiment with Conolly in the driver's seat, while Kuno and Shoots drove the four mules ahead of them that were due to the deceased and to the driver. Before their departure from the by now almost completely deserted camp, the military mail arrived which included letters for both Kuno and Shoots. The sergeant's letter bore German postmarks and a border decorated with images of mourning, and brought the news that his mother-in-law had departed from this earthly existence. Kuno's letter came from his mother, had been underway for weeks, and brought the good news that everything and everybody was well at home. They had a distance of fifty miles to cover and in consideration of the warm weather, haste was necessary. The team pulled well and the two riders had to take pains to keep up with their stubborn prize mules. Luckily the moon was bright and the night cool. Underway the sergeant, who had passed a good portion of the time sunk in his own thoughts, suddenly exclaimed to his young companion:

"So, Kuno, it suddenly occurred to me what the future now holds for me: I need to get a job, work hard, and get enough money together in order to buy passage back over. The old dragon—God rest her soul—is dead, and so it is time to go back to Germany. I was always a good soldier with no bad marks on my record, so I think I should be able to rejoin my old regiment with no problems.

The confidence of the brave old soldier was not built on sand. In anno sixty-six he fought in the Battle of Königsgrätz,[300] lost an arm, and lived out his years as an honorable signalman for the Prussian railroad.

Before daybreak the men took a short pause in order to rest the animals and prepare a light breakfast for themselves. They resumed their journey at first light and by ten o'clock in the morning had arrived at their destination, a small *backwoods* farm on the right bank of the river not far from New London. Along with his small wife, old man Duff, uncle of the deceased and a genuine *squatter*, welcomed their nephew Conolly and his party and without much in the way of excess sorrow, went about the business of preparing for the burial of the dead man. Several neighbors helped to lower the coffin into the ground along with the flag, as previously agreed to, and the three comrades together with the uncle, employing his long-barreled hunting rifle, fired a farewell salvo over the grave of the last victim of this war. The three ex-Confederates then gladly accepted the invitation of the simple but upright old man to spend the night in order to recover from the exertions of their trip and get a good night's sleep.

The following morning Shoots rode on to New London in the hope of finding employment there, while Kuno, after taking heartfelt leave from his comrades, began the long journey home to his family and to Hedwig who was eagerly awaiting his homecoming at Possum Creek.

⊷✯⊶

Translator's Note

With the burial of Jack Duff and Kuno's homecoming to Possum Creek after his discharge from the army, part one, the Civil War Years, ends and part two, the Reconstruction years, commences. Due to the combined length of the two parts, the second part will be released as a separate book.

It would have been easy (and in some sense, natural) if Trenckmann had ended the tale with Kuno's homecoming from the army; Kuno returns to Possum Creek matured by his multiple experience of war and soldiering, a young man who now has a broader perspective on the world than that offered by the self-contained and innocent life he had previously known at Possum Creek in childhood. But his experiences also win for him a renewed appreciation for the men and women of Possum Creek. He now views his childhood playmate Hedwig through the eyes of a young man rather than a boy; the two fall in love and start a new life among the educated German farmers of Possum Creek, and are happy forevermore.

The story could easily have ended on this note, but did not because Trenckmann obviously felt like the "breakup" and the difficult Reconstruction years that followed were just as traumatic and determinative for the German settlers of Possum Creek as the war itself, posing fresh challenges to the old republican ideals of the Forty-Eighters. Consequently, he continues the story with our young hero still observing, learning, and growing; still seeking the balance between the dominant Anglo Texas and the more restricted German Texas world he had grown up in. This also gives the author more time to allow the relationship between Kuno and Hedwig to fully develop.

The response on the part of the educated German farmers of Possum Creek to Reconstruction, as portrayed by Trenckmann in the second book, turns out to be just as complex and nuanced as their response to the Civil War proper: there were those who were open in their support for the freedpeople and there were these who felt threatened by their new-found assertiveness. As with the Civil War, Kuno is forced to navigate his way through these conflicting opinions.

Coming to terms with emancipation, both for black people and white people, provides one of the major themes of Texas history for the latter three decades of the nineteenth century, for the whole of the twentieth century, and, one can argue, for contemporary society as well. The second book of Trenckmann's story offers one of the very few literary responses to this theme to be found in Texas literature dating to the immediate aftermath of defeat.

There is one final aspect to the story that gains in importance. Even as the great national drama of the American Civil War comes to an end and recedes into the past, new wars in Europe, especially the series of wars fought by the Kingdom of Prussia against Denmark, Austria and France, wars which paved the way for eventual German unification under Prussian leadership in 1871, continue to rivet the attention of the immigrant German communities in North America. These wars posed a particular dilemma for the **Lateiner** *of Possum Creek: on the one hand, most cannot help but feel pride in the astounding military successes of the Prussian armies in these conflicts; on the other hand, glorification of Prussia represents renunciation of the republican and equalitarian ideals that had motivated many of them to emigrate in the first place, for Prussia is an arch-conservative, aristocratic construct that stands in complete opposition on all fronts to the ideals of 1848. Indeed, this whole tale can be read at one level as the evolution of the ideals of 1848, as they collide, first, with the realities of the Texas frontier, and, secondly, with the rapidly changing political and social circumstances in Europe, which the German farmers avidly follow through the numerous German language newspapers that have proliferated throughout North America and Texas in the latter decades of the nineteenth century to find their way into even the remotest households. The author weaves the European events into his story to produce a surprising* **denouement** *of all the threads to the narrative. Kuno's military experience, it will be seen, makes him even more appreciative of the accomplishments achieved by his German countrymen on numerous fields of battle in Europe, but once again he finds himself torn between conflicting attitudes, and it all comes to a head in his relationship to Hedwig. Stay tuned for Book II of Trenckmann's* **The Forty-Eighters of Possum Creek; A Texas Story.**

APPENDIX

The Characters in W.A. Trenckmann's

Die Lateiner am Possum Creek as they relate

to the real-life inhabitants of Millheim

Virtually every character and event in the novel is built around memories of people and events from Trenckmann's childhood days at Millheim. The author purposefully (and understandably) shuffled descriptions and embellished events since many of his readers in 1908 would have had first-hand knowledge of Civil War Millheim and not a few emerge as characters in the novel, albeit in disguised form.

The following section relates the principal characters and situations to the real-life inhabitants of Millheim and the information is gleaned primarily from Trenckmann's memoir, "Experiences and Observations"; Adalbert Regenbrecht's article, "The German Settlers at Millheim"; Charles Nagel's book, *A Boy's Civil War Story*; and Flora von Roeder's book, *The Engelking Letters*. (See bibliography for further descriptions of these works.) The author gratefully acknowledges the research of James Woodrick who compiled this list and graciously agreed to share it.

1) THE REAL MILLHEIM SETTLERS

ANDREAS FRIEDRICH TRENCKMANN

Born in 1809 in the village of Wefensleben, a five hours' walk from Magdeburg. His father was a farmer. After a hard period of school—he had to spend all his spare time tutoring at the seminar in order to have enough to eat—he became a successful teacher. For a long time he was owner and director of a private school in Magdeburg. His first wife died young, leaving four sons and a daughter, his second died soon after the birth of a baby girl. He then married Johanne Jockush, eldest daughter of a long-established Magdeburg family, owners of a brewery which produced a light agreeable white beer. His oldest daughter became the victim of yellow fever soon after their arrival in Galveston. He was a serious man who believed state laws should be followed, thus he begrudgingly accepted the Confederacy. He had a good voice and loved to sing, but did so rarely. His guiding principle in life was the necessity of duty, and this he derived mainly through the teachings of the German philosopher Immanuel Kant. The reaction that set in after 1848 made Germany unbearable to him, although he stood in the good graces of the Prussian government, which gave him a recommendation when he emigrated, stating that he was a well-meaning democrat. He was chief of the civil guard during bloody street battles in Magdeburg in 1848 and had prevented the hanging to a lamppost of the hated governor, Count Haack.

The family emigrated in the spring of 1853 and bought an established farm from the poet Johannes Romberg in the wooded Bernard Valley in Colorado County; their neighbors were the Himly, Reichardt, and Litzmann families. Five years later they moved to on a larger farm at Millheim on which the former owner Wilms had erected a horse-and-mule-drawn grist mill and gin.

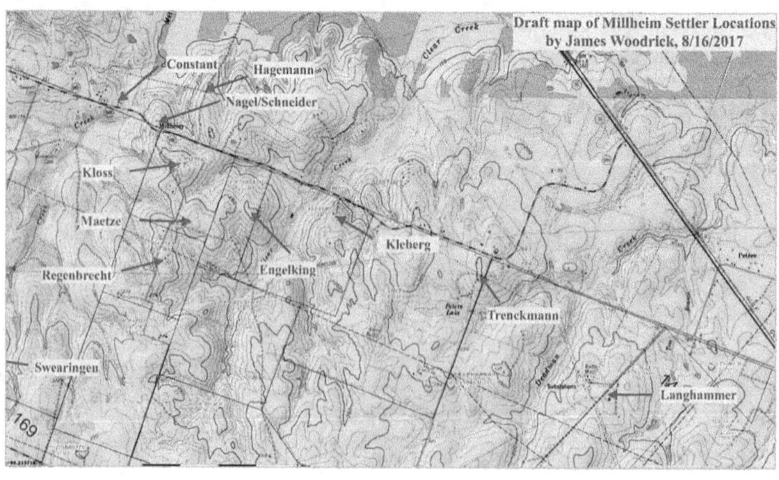

Regenbrecht said of him: "He voted against secession, but obeyed the laws of the *de facto* government of the Confederate States and did not object to the enlistment of two sons in the Confederate Army at the beginning of the war; one of whom, Adolph, was killed in battle."

Son Adolph had escaped from the hospital in Virginia in order to take part in the expedition into Maryland and with a great part of his regiment had fallen at the battle of Sharpsburg in Maryland.

Son Otto marched with Sibley's Brigade to New Mexico, then Louisiana, returned sound and unwounded. He married Marie Himley in 1872.

Son Emil was married and in Shelby when he joined Capt. Henry Wickeland's infantry unit, part of Waul's Legion, in July 1862. He participated in the Vicksburg campaign at Holly Springs, captured at Vicksburg. Returned home, moved to Shelby, taught school.

Son Hugo, youngest son from first marriage, reached draft age during war and was "recruited." He was opposed to secession and did not want to fight in war. He operated the gin, which exempted him from the draft for a while. He was drafted shortly before the war ended, served in the Brazos port of Velasco and died of malarial poisoning a year after the war.

Son Paul (two years older than William) died of anemia.

Whist was played at the Trenckmann house. W.A. remembered making *fidibi* to light the pipes of the whist players. He also said that whist-playing at the Trenckmann house solidified friendships with the Engelking and Regenbrecht families.

GUSTAV MAETZE

Born in Glogau, Silesia. Educated there, and at University of Breslau. Regenbrecht said of him: "After graduation he was appointed rector of the town school of Bernstadt. In 1848 he was elected a representative to the Prussian National Assembly. He joined the democratic wing of the Assembly. The royal government usurped arbitrary power. Therefore, the Assembly resolved that no taxes should be paid to the government. The resolution was not executed, because the people were tired of the frequent political disturbances and wanted peace and the government was supported by the army. The representatives who voted for said resolution, were prosecuted. E. G. Maetze escaped to Texas." After arrival he boarded briefly with Engelking and Regenbrecht, then bought his own farm and sent for his wife and two children from Germany. She died and he remarried; his new wife was a cousin of Mrs. Trenckmann. He was a highly respected teacher who earned his livelihood by this profession though he farmed on the side and enjoyed gardening. He was against secession but believed state laws should be followed. Thus, he accepted the Confederacy and served as a major in the home guard. His son Gustav enlisted in Sibley's Brigade. He was a good singer. He was active in politics and was elected county commissioner in 1856. Later he served as a senator in the Texas legislature.

His daughter Ida was classmate of W.A. Trenckmann. He mentioned in "Experiences" that he liked her as much now as he did them. Perhaps a model for Hedwig.

FERDINAND ENGELKING

Graduate of University of Bonn in law; served as a Prussian law clerk. Arrived 1840; married Caroline von Roeder in 1842 of the prominent von Roeder/ Kleberg clan and moved to Millheim. Continued to receive timely infusions of money from his mother in Germany. Built first school in Millheim on his farm. Operated mercantile store; farm secondary. Had one slave in 1860, bought another (female cook) early in the war.

Son Sigismund enlisted in 1861 with the First Texas Infantry, was severely wounded at Sharpsburg, captured and imprisoned. Father went to get him. Another son Fritz joined, served in Louisiana.

In "Experiences," W.A. Trenckmann stated that his family and the Engelkings and Regenbrechts were close friends because their fathers often played whist in the Engelking house, a scene that begins the novel.

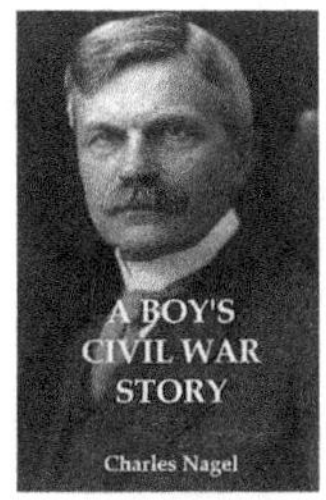

HERMAN NAGEL

A doctor, educated at University of Jena, Wurzburg, and graduated in medicine at University of Berlin. Was well known as a swordsman in university days; had scars on his mouth and temple from duels. Arrived Millheim 1855 where he made rounds on a mule. Nagel had a fancy buggy, odd springs sitting high on its axles. He also owned a piano and this made the Nagel house the meeting place for the singing society. His mother had lost her land in a fraud in Germany. Wife Marie Litzmann. Children Paul (b. 1851), Charles (b. 1849), and Helene (b. 1855). A strident opponent of slavery and secession. His oldest son Herman joined Confederate army in 1862 in Voigt's unit and was disowned by his father. With one brief exception, Charles never saw him again. Fled to Mexico with son Charles in 1863 to avoid forced conscription of both son and father; then to St. Louis. This escape became the basis of son Charles' book, *A Boy's Civil War Story*. Charles Nagel rose to become a prominent lawyer. He is credited with establishing the Chamber of Commerce and served in the Taft Administration as Secretary of Commerce.

LOUIS KLEBERG

Family famous in Texas history for subsequent King Ranch connection. Part of the extended Kleberg/von Roeder family which moved *en masse* to Texas prior to the Texas Revolution and which is credited with establishing Cat Spring, the second oldest German community in Texas. Short—5'6" at most—body somewhat deformed, had a large and impressive head. A man of great nerve and determination. Married a von Roeder. First German to settle in Millheim. New laws, perhaps justice of peace, did deed work for which he was sought by others. For the later immigrants he counted as an "old Texas hand." A model for Herr Grossenberg in the story.

ADALBERT REGENBRECHT

The model for Winzig in the novel. Father a professor of jurisprudence, rector of Univ. of Breslau, military hero, wealthy. In 1848 he was a schoolboy age 17; did not participate in revolution. Studied law for several years, then came to Texas, arrived in Millheim in 1856, boarded with Gustav Maetze, then Ernst Nagel. Bought farm in 1857. Large man, well over 6' tall, but thin—160 pounds. Married a Hagemann, early Millheim settlers.

Enthusiastically supported freeing slaves. Voted against secession. Did not want to fight against the Union nor to desert his family, finally let himself be persuaded to join the Confederate Army after he had been pursued for a long time and in danger of being shot. He said of himself:"Physically perfectly unfit for military service and opposed to the war, I succeeded in avoiding the service except that, although exempt as justice of the peace, I was compelled to go to the camp of instruction near Houston. After some weeks I was discharged by a writ of habeas corpus."Known to be forgetful.

2) THE MAJOR CHARACTERS IN POSSUM CREEK

HERR LÜTTENHOFF

Son of a small, impoverished farmer from Mark Brandenburg. Put himself through school tutoring other students; took position as assistant teacher in a city school in a mid-sized German city, found and married daughter of rather well-to-do baker. Opened own school which flourished; achieved modest level of prosperity. His actions in 1848 initially appreciated by local elite. As captain of the Home Guard, intervened to maintain order and suppress demonstrators. Disliked the response against the demonstrators and changed sides; joining ranks of tax protestors. Because he was son of a farmer he was better suited for rural life than most of his fellow *Lateiners*. Holds a little too stubbornly to agricultural practices advocated in German and English publications which were not necessarily suited to Texas. **[This is a clear description of Andreas Trenckmann.]** He is described as a tall man over 6' tall, broad-shouldered, mid-50s. Serves as surrogate teacher to his own and neighboring children since no suitable German teacher could be found in the small community. **[This sounds like F. Engelking before Gustav**

Maetze arrived in Millheim in the early 1850s.] He has a fourteen-year-old daughter Hedwig and an eight-year-old son Albert and a wife named Anna. [Albert and Hedwig Lüttenhoff probably based on Gustav Maetze's children.] He lives a mile away from Possum Creek. Uncompromising opponent of slavery; loyal supporter of the Union, even found himself in peril on occasion. [This is reminiscent of Dr. Nagel.] He felt, however, it was a duty to fight for country when called upon. He has a dark head of hair and a full beard. [This sounds like Regenbrecht.] Lüttenhoff's eldest son Erwin has adopted views of Southern Anglos and goes off to war against his father's wishes. He refuses his son a farewell and considers him banished from the family forever. [This part describes Herman Nagel, whose eldest son Herman joined Robert Voigt's unit in 1862. He never reconciled with family after the war.]

In the novel the second son Hugo shares the father's views on slavery; while in Hill Country buying sheep, he falls in with German firebrands who have mounted an expedition to flee the state and join up with Union forces in Mexico; he perishes in the battle of the Nueces (August 1862). [This appears to be an invention. No one from Millheim is known to be on the list of those killed in Nueces battle.] In the novel Lüttenhoff is Kuno's "beloved schoolteacher." [This has to refer to Gustav Maetze.]

HERR SARTORIUS

Rudolph Sartorius's family owned a large country estate, served as bureaucrats in Prussian Rhineland. Had decided to study law, but had a troublesome schooling. Married daughter of an impoverished German nobleman of ancient lineage. Found legal profession too dry, was infatuated with literature and decided to emigrate to Texas. Had ample means, settled at Possum Creek where he purchased a farm and large pasturage for the numerous livestock. Also had four slaves, one a cook with son Pompey. Not a good farm, ranch or slave manager. Gleaned agricultural knowledge from books. Would have been ruined except for a string of cash infusions from Germany. [This describes early Engelking in Texas, as told in *Engelking Letters*.] Had large cattle holdings. [Engelking had 800 acres but that was secondary to his store.]

Has a deep bass voice, can sing. Large statue, 6' tall at least, broad-shouldered, fit and trim, clean-shaven, dark black hair, in his late 50s. Closest neighbor to the Lüttenhoff family.

Has a slave named Sally. **[Sally was name of Trenckmann's servant, who, however, was a hired woman.]** Has a son Kuno, soon turning eighteen and facing induction in Confederate army; has promised his teacher, Herr Lüttenhoff, he will not go and will hide out in brush instead. His older brothers have already gone off to war. One became an officer and fell at Cedar Creek (October 19, 1864)—it is obviously late in the war. Later marries childhood friend/playmate Hedwig Lüttenhoff.

Sartorius settled in Texas much earlier than Lüttenhoff, and thus had come by the view that slavery was a necessary evil; had actually supported secession. **[This is either Ferdinand Engelking or Louis Kleberg, both of whom came in the early 1840s. Trenckmann came in 1858.]**

Has three sons and no daughters in the story; wife has become very frail in the story. **[This is clearly the Trenckmann family.]**

Oldest son off to war **[Adolph Trenckmann was killed at Sharpsburg]**, second son sits in prison in Ohio since fall of Vicksburg **[Sigismund Engelking was in Voight's unit, part of Waul's Legion as was Emil, captured at Yazoo City, in prison at Camp Morton, Indiana]**, youngest son getting ready to go; eighteen-year-old son is Kuno. **[Hugo Trenckmann]**.

KUNO SARTORIUS

Clearly modelled on Hugo Trenckmann, youngest son of Andreas Trenckmann from first marriage, reached draft age during war and was "recruited." He was opposed to secession and did not want to fight in war. He operated the gin, which exempted him from the draft for a while. He was drafted shortly before the war ended, served in the port of Velasco on the lower Brazos River and died of malarial poisoning a year after the war.

GROSSENBERG

Short, fat, drinker. A *Lateiner*. Came from family of bureaucrats. Soldier in Hussars, gambled away inheritance. Fell from horse, broke leg, crippled for life. Arrived Texas early 1840s after wandering for a period through middle and southern states. Gave music lessons to daughter of wealthy slaveholder and married her. Thus, came to own 1/4 league "on Possum Creek" and two slaves. Elected to be justice-of-peace. Wife and new daughter soon died. Brought unmarried sister Albertine to live there and manage household. He drank, forcing them to sell off assets to live. Knew legal system because he was familiar with land system, having been there a long time. Strongly in favor of secession. **[Strong reference to Louis Kleberg.]**

WINZIG

Opposite of Grossberg. Wore formal suit, coat and tie. A quintessential German academic type. Father was professor of philosophy at Univ. of Konigsberg. Fought in duels. Earned PhD, but unsuited for academic life. Mild speech impediment. Upon arrival, soon wed Minna, daughter of *Lateiner* on Possum Creek he stayed with. She had come to Texas as a child. Became dedicated farmer. Became known as a despised abolitionist. Had two small children. One of first to be conscripted to Confed. army. Resisted, placed in irons, nearly shot for treason, finally declared unfit for service. Elected constable of Possum Creek and Collinsville (Cat Spring) **[Clearly modeled after Adelbert Regenbrecht.]**

MR. PHILLIPS—WEALTHY PLANTATION OWNER

Anglo-American who owned a large plantation on Palmetto Creek; son Bobby (Robert Emmett) joined First Texas Cavalry, perhaps Sibley's unit. Slight built, not quite 60; had been to Germany and met the famous poet Johann Wolfgang von Goethe; liked his German neighbors but his son despised them.

Owned Acadia Plantation, eight miles from Possum Creek, which was grandiose and impressive. Stood on the highest hill before the Palmetto Creek bottom separated from the prairie by a small valley through which a small narrow and wooded stream flowed. A brick factory on the plantation had supplied materials for the houses. **[Description matches Bernardo Plantation, although it was further away than 8 miles and across the river, not overlooking Palmetto Creek.]**

BERTRANDS

Husband and wife of French descent who have moved to Millheim. Pretentious, opportunistic, scheming, duplicitous; Trenckmann paints them as the villains of the story. They own the mercantile store in Possum Creek whereas in the real Millheim, the only store was owned by Ferdinand Engelking. Trenckmann's novel is colored from beginning to end by events in Europe and especially the Franco-Prussian War of 1871, which enabled Germany to unite as one country with the King of Prussia becoming the German Emperor. With these astonishing turns of events still fresh in the minds of many of his Texas-German readers, the novel evinces an unmistakable anti-French bias, which most of his readers would applaud. The Bertrands, husband and wife, who appear to be completely invented by the author, are the clearest embodiment of this attitude. Trenckmann's prejudices in regard to French culture are a little bit surprising because he studied French culture and literature and was fluent in French.

ERNST EBERHARD COUNT OF SCHARFENEGG

One of the most fascinating and enigmatic characters in the novel. Influences Kuno to break his oath to his teacher to refuse service in the Confederacy. A long digression in the novel about his story. A rising star in the Prussian military from a distinguished family. Disgraced for offhand but disrespectful comments about Prussian King and, in consequence, drummed out of the army and banished from Germany and disowned by father. Entered the French Foreign Legion, served in Algiers, fought in Crimean war, returned to France, renounced an inheritance, went to Mexico in 1863, finally came to Texas with his comrade and only friend, Eginhard von Seiffert. Broken in health by his many adventures, dies in the forest, a man "without a country," the worst of all fates. **[Who was this? Was he invented by Trenckmann or is he based on a real character? We do not know.]**

1   Walter L. Buenger and Walter D. Kamphoefner, *Preserving German Texas Identity: Reminiscences of William A. Trenckmann, 1859-1935,* (College Station: Texas A&M University Press, 2018).

2   "Weihnachten in trüber Zeit," supplement to the Bellville Wochenblatt, 1894. Translated by Anders Saustrup as "Christmas in Troubled Times," (Winedale: The Friends of Winedale, 1976).

3   Biesele, *The History of the German Settlements in Texas,* 54, 55; For short biographical sketches of all the principal families, see: *The Cat Spring Story,* Publication of the Cat Spring Agricultural Society, San Antonio: Lone Star Printing Co., 1956.

4   Biesele, *The History of the German Settlements in Texas,* 54, 55.

5   Charles Nagel, *A Boy's Civil War Story,* 55.

6   "The German settlers of Cat Spring who were so greatly interested in agriculture, education, literature, music, and art, manifested little interest in religion." (*The Cat Spring Story,* 55.)

7   Turnverein Millheim

8   Rudolph L. Biesele, "Latin Settlements of Texas," *Handbook of Texas Online,* accessed January 10, 2015. *https://tshaonline.org/handbook/online/articles/uel03.*

9   Clara Trenckmann Studer, "Trenckmann, William Andreas," *Handbook of Texas Online,* accessed January 10, 2015. *https://tshaonline.org/handbook/online/articles/ftr08.*

10   Ibid.

11   Nagel, *A Boy's Civil War Story,* 16.

12   This began to occur with increasing frequency during the jingoistic anti-German hysteria that characterized the First World War and thereafter.

13   Regenbrecht, Ibid., 30.

14   Soon after the beginning of the Civil War it became evident that the Confederacy could not long survive without draft laws, which would place more men in the field and hold in the service those volunteers who had enlisted for short terms. To meet these ends, the Confederate Congress passed the first conscription act

on April 16, 1862. That act made every white male between the ages of eighteen and thirty-five subject to military service in the Confederacy for a period of three years unless exempted from service. Unfortunately, the law gave the President of the Confederacy, with a governor's approval, the right to employ state officers for enrollment of conscripts, which led to much abuse and discontent.

15   A. J. Bell to J. P. Flewellen, November 28, 1862, *Official Records*, Series I, Vol. XV, 887.

16   Bill Stein, "Distress, Discontent, and Dissent: Colorado County, Texas, during the Civil War," in Howell, ed., *The Seventh Star of the Confederacy*, 301–316.

17   Amberg et al to W. G. Webb, January 3, 1863, *Official Records*, Series I, Vol. XV, 929.

18   The Battle of Nueces took place August 10, 1862, between (largely) German Unionists from Fredericksburg and Comfort who were attempting to flee Texas and make their way to Mexico and a pursuing Confederate force under Lt. C. McRae. A desperate battle took place between the approximately sixty Unionists and the larger Confederate forces on a remote bend of the Nueces River many miles to the south and west of the German settlements. After several hours fighting, the surviving Unionists withdrew from the battlefield leaving the seriously wounded behind. These were subsequently executed contrary to the rules of war and their bodies left unburied.

19   "Roman à clef," *Wikipedia*. Accessed November 3, 2017, at *https://en.wikipedia.org /wiki/Roman_%C3%A0_clef.*

20   The form, made popular by Johann Wolfgang von Goethe, with the publication in 1795 of *Wilhelm Meisters Lehrjahre* (Wilhelm Meister's Coming of Age), is more common in German literature than in English and French.

21   In the real Millheim, Constant Creek flowed in from the south and bisected the community. The historic Trenckmann farmstead was to the east of Constant Creek and south of its confluence with Mill Creek (Palmetto Creek) in the novel. Their closest neighbors were the Kleberg and Engelking homesteads. (See illustration.)

22   Trenckmann often interjects American words or phrases like "cross-timbers" into the text. The translation indicates this by placing the word or phrase in italics. Dr. Hubert Heinen of the University of Texas has analyzed this practice in "The Literary Use of English Words in W. A. Trenckmann's *Die Lateiner am Possum Creek*." *Journal of the German-Texan Heritage Society* 7.1 (1985), 28–37.

23   *Factotum*: A Latin word used in German for a know-it-all.

24   Palmetto Creek: It becomes clear in the course of the narrative that Palmetto Creek may for the most part be understood as Mill Creek, which was originally named Palmetto Creek during the colonial Mexican period, whereas Possum Creek stands for present Constance Creek which flows just to the west of the present Millheim Harmonie Hall. At other places in the narrative, however, Palmetto Creek appears to stand for the Brazos River.

25   Norther: A weather event peculiar to Texas, usually in the fall and winter. Often preceded by warm, balmy weather and southern breezes, the wind shifts suddenly and violently to the north with a precipitous drop in temperature, sometimes as much as fifty degrees in an hour. Many German immigrants from the period

commented on this phenomenon. The Texas German poet Johannes Romberg even wrote a poem dedicated to it. (see: Romberg, "Ein Nordwind in Texas," *Gedichte von Johannes Romberg* (Wagner: Leipzig, 1900), 134.)

26   Bowling alley: The German immigrants brought with them a style of bowling alley (*Kegelbahn* in German) that used seven wooden pins and a smaller wooden bowling ball. A few of these German style bowling alleys, which require nothing in the way of machinery, still exist in Texas. One of the more famous ones is at the small community of Fischer.

27   This fictional controversy echoes the true-life controversy over the naming of the community.

28   Skunk: interestingly Trenckmann uses the Texas German word for skunk, namely *Stinkkatze* as opposed to the standard German word *Stinktier*.

29   The quote, which reads in German, "Wer sich grün macht, den fressen die Ziegen," is attributed to Johann Wolfgang von Goethe (1749–1832), who counts as the premier representative of German poetry. The saying appeared in a poem from 1828, "Ein Meister einer ländlichen Schule" (Master of a Country School). (" Wer sich grün macht, den fressen die Zieger," *Aphorismen.de*. Accessed May 17, 2017, at *http://www.aphorismen.de/zitat/239*.)

30   Whist: a classic English trick-taking card game that was very popular in the nineteenth centuries. The game called for four people, divided as partners. Although extremely simple on the surface the game, nevertheless, called for strategy and concentration.

31   *Fidibus*: German student slang for twisted bits of paper or split pieces of kindling used to light pipes.

32   It was common practice at the time to have the kitchen in a separate building. This kept the heat of cooking out of the main house in the summer but also reduced the risk of a catastrophic fire.

33   Nimrod: In the Bible, a mighty hunter and king of Shinar who was a grandson of Ham and a great-grandson of Noah.

34   *Festina lente*: Latin for "hasten slowly," or "haste makes waste."

35   *Loquor*: Latin for to say, speak. We find the root in the English word "loquacious."

36   The house matches a style of log construction common throughout the Southeastern United States during the nineteenth and early twentieth centuries. It was variously referred to as a dogtrot, breezeway house, dog-run, or possum-trot house. The house also resembles the house of Ferdinand Engelking, a prominent resident of Millheim. (See Appendix).

37   *Weekly Telegraph*: The *Telegraph and Texas Register*, later variously known as the *Weekly, Tri-weekly*, or *Daily Telegraph*, was the first newspaper in Texas to achieve a degree of permanence. The paper was begun on October 10, 1835, at San Felipe de Austin by Gail Borden, Jr., Thomas H. Borden, and Joseph Baker. During the Civil War a shortage of paper led the editors to print on whatever was available. ("Telegraph and Texas Register," *Handbook of Texas Online*, accessed October 14, 2014, *https://tshaonline.org/handbook/online/articles/eet02*.)

[38] The Battle of Cedar Creek, fought October 19, 1864, was the culminating battle of the Valley Campaigns of 1864 during the American Civil War. Confederate Lt. Gen. Jubal Early launched a surprise attack against the encamped army of Union Maj. Gen. Philip Sheridan, across Cedar Creek, northeast of Strasburg, Virginia. After initial successes, a Union counterattack routed Early's army and the final Confederate invasion of the North collapsed. The Confederacy was never again able to threaten Washington, D.C., through the Shenandoah Valley, nor protect one of its key economic bases in Virginia. The stunning Union victory aided the reelection of Abraham Lincoln and won Sheridan lasting fame. ("The Battle of Cedar Creek," *Wikipedia*, accessed May 8, 2017, *https://en.wikipedia.org/wiki/Battle_of_Cedar_Creek.*)

[39] Early: Jubal Anderson Early (1816–1894) was a lawyer and Confederate general in the American Civil War. He served under Stonewall Jackson and then Robert E. Lee for almost the entire war, rising from regimental command to lieutenant general and the command of an infantry corps in the Army of Northern Virginia. He was the Confederate commander in key battles of the Valley Campaigns of 1864, including a daring raid to the outskirts of Washington, D.C. In the last months of the war, however, he only commanded a skeleton force. ("Jubal Early," *Wikipedia*, accessed October 23, 2014, *https://en.wikipedia.org/wiki/Jubal_Early.*)

[40] *Hectatombs*: In ancient Greece, a hecatomb was a sacrifice to the gods of 100 cattle. In practice, however, the word often denotes any large sacrifice or slaughter.

[41] "Zwei Grenadier zogen nach Frankreich" (Two foot soldiers headed for France): A poem by the German poet Heinrich Heine (1797–1856) that treats two soldiers returning to France from captivity in Russia after Napoleon's disastrous Russian campaign. As the soldiers make it to Germany they learn of Napoleon's final defeat and are crushed by the news. The poem appeared in 1822 and was often put to music.

[42] The family name Sartorius is a Latinized form of *Schneider* (tailor) or its North German synonyms *Schröder* or *Schrader*. Interestingly, the name, which is fairly uncommon, also appears in another work of Texas German literature, namely *Texas Fahrten* (Travels in Texas) by Hermann Seele, translation, introduction, and notes by Theodoer Gish (Austin: Nortex Press, 1985).

[43] The Prussian legal system was heavily influenced by Roman jurisprudence and tradition.

[44] *Referendar*: In Germany, a graduate in law who seeks a legal career must embark upon a period of practical training. During this internship, he is referred to as a *Referendar*.

[45] *Assessor*: In German legal tradition, one who has completed his internship (see previous note) and passed the first state exam is termed an *Assessor* and is qualified from this point on to pursue a career in the civil service.

[46] Literature: By the 1840s a large and impressive literature about Texas had become available in Germany; most of it favorable. For a bibliography of this literature, see: Detlef Dunt, *Journey to Texas, 1833*, ed. James C. Kearny (Austin: University of Texas Press, 2015), 175–182.

47 Brockhaus: The Brockhaus name in Germany is equivalent to the Webster name
    in America. The *Brockhaus Enzyklopädie* has been the standard German-language
    encyclopedia since the first edition was published by Löbel and Franke in Leipzig
    1796–1808 under the title *Conversations-Lexikon.*

48 Mark Brandenburg: The Margraviate of Brandenburg was a major principality
    of the Holy Roman Empire from 1157 to 1806. Brandenburg grew rapidly in
    power during the 17th century and inherited the Duchy of Prussia. Although the
    Margraviate of Brandenburg ended with the dissolution of the Holy Roman Empire
    in 1806, it was replaced with the Prussian Province of Brandenburg in 1815, which
    became the most powerful German state in the nineteenth century. The Kingdom
    of Prussia achieved the unification of Germany and the creation of the German
    Empire in 1871. (*Wikipedia*, "Margraviate of Brandenburg," accessed May 24, 2017,
    https://en.wikipedia.org/wiki/Margraviate_of_Brandenburg.)

49 Tax protest: In the latter stages of the 1848 Revolution, that is in November and
    December of that year, there were many protest actions of varying degrees of
    effectiveness called throughout the several German states. I have not found
    documentation about this particular action, but I have no doubt that it alludes
    to a real protest.

50 In this description, Herr Lüttenhoff calls to mind Gustav Maetze, who served
    for many years as teacher to the children of Millheim. Trenckmann, however,
    is very careful not to make his characters readily identifiable since at the time
    of publication, 1908, many people who were native to Millheim and lived during
    the Civil War period were still alive and might have been flattered or offended.

51 Nueces River: The author is alluding to the battle that took place August 10, 1862,
    between (largely) German Unionists from Fredericksburg and Comfort, who were
    attempting to flee Texas and make their way to Mexico, and a pursuing Confederate
    force under Lt. C. McRae. A desperate battle took place between the approximately
    sixty Unionists and the larger Confederate forces on a remote bend of the Nueces
    River many miles to the south and west of the German settlements. After several
    hours fighting, the surviving Unionists withdrew from the battlefield leaving the
    seriously wounded behind. These were subsequently executed contrary to the
    rules of war and their bodies left unburied. Lüttenhoff is accurate in saying that
    the Germans had been betrayed by one of their own but incorrect in saying that
    all the Unionists perished: in fact, over half of them escaped. A monument in
    Comfort, Texas, entitled *Treue der Union* (True to the Union) commemorates the
    fallen Germans and is said to be the only monument of its kind that dates to the
    immediate post-war period in the South. Much has been written about the battle
    and controversy still swirls around the question: was a rebellion brewing among
    the German Unionists on the vulnerable western frontier of the Confederacy
    that justified such a harsh response or were the Confederate authorities merely
    delusional and paranoid? For one of the best overviews of the battle and vast
    literature that has grown up around it, see: Mary Jo O'Rear, "Reckoning at the
    River: Unionists and Secessionists at the Nueces, August 10, 1862," in Kenneth

Howell, ed., *Seventh Star of the Confederacy*, (Denton: University of North Texas Press, 2012).

[52] Supporters of secession: Ninety-nine votes were cast against secession and only eight for at the Millheim-Cat Spring box. (Regenbrecht, Ibid., 30).

[53] Steel, stone, and sponge: In the days prior to safety matches, nearly everyone carried these objects in order to start a fire. The first commercially available, nonpoisonous matches did not become available until well after the Civil War.

[54] Prince Metternich: After the final defeat of Napoleon by the Grand Coalition in 1814 the heads of the five reigning dynasties and representatives from 216 noble families began to converge on Vienna. The resulting Congress of Vienna dictated a political structure for Europe that endured for nearly sixty years that upheld many late-feudal privileges of the aristocracy while vigorously suppressing any democratic or liberal tendencies. The fires of German nationalism, which had been ignited during the Napoleonic wars and which found a strong base of support in German student fraternities, regarded Metternich as the arch-enemy to their aspirations.

[55] Camp Magruder: There were actually several camps that went by this name. This one appears to be encampment of Southern forces somewhere east of Minden, LA, during the winter of 1864–65. Records indicate as many as 15,000 men lived in this camp who were prevented from joining forces east of the Mississippi because of the Union blockade. (Agan, *Echoes of Our Past: The Civil War Years in Minden*, 84).

[56] Andreas Hofer, an innkeeper by trade, was the leader of the Tyrolean Rebellion against the French and Bavarian occupation during the War of the Fifth Coalition in 1809. After Emperor Francis I of Austria had signed the Treaty of Schönbrunn, Hofer fought a losing battle. Betrayed and captured, he was executed by personal command of Napoleon at Mantua in Italy on February 20, 1810, by the French forces. A song about him became popular German folk song and, since 1948, the official anthem of the current Austrian State of Tyrol. ("Andreas Hofer," *Wikipedia*, accessed January 5, 2018, *https://en.wikipedia.org/wiki/Andreas_Hofer.*)

[57] Two opposites: Sartorius is alluding to their names, which translate as "Big Mountain" and "Tiny."

[58] Hussars: Light cavalry with origins in Hungary, Croatia, and Serbia. They had become a common feature in Western Europe by the 18th century. Their uniforms, however, continued to reflect their Eastern European origins.

[59] *Grand seigneur*: Trenckmann uses the French term for a man of the world.

[60] Quarter of a league: A league was 4,428 acres; hence, 1,107 acres.

[61] *Maître de plaiser*: French for "master of ceremonies."

[62] University of Königsberg: An obvious allusion to the fact that the famous German philosopher Immanuel Kant (1724–1804) spent most of his academic career at the university in the East Prussian capitol of Königsberg.

[63] *Koryphaen*: Derived from the Ancient Greek word for "head," the word is sometimes used in learned discourse in German with the meaning of "luminary" or "expert."

[64] *Mensur*: Traditional kind of fencing practiced by student fraternities in the German speaking areas of Europe. It is a strictly regulated sword fight between two male

members of different fraternities with sharp weapons. Participation in such fights was a requirement in many of the fraternities and considered to be a showcase of character. Only on rare occasions did these largely ceremonial duels result in death or serious injury but very often produced scars to the cheek or forehead that were considered badges of honor.

65   Conscription: A system of compulsory national conscription for military service, now known as the draft, was first employed by the South during the American Civil War. The Union quickly followed suit but the vast majority of Union troops remained volunteers. Because the Confederacy had a much smaller population than the Union, Confederate President Jefferson Davis proposed the first conscription act on March 28, 1862; it was passed into law the next month. There were many abuses and resistance became both widespread and violent, with comparisons made between conscription and slavery. ("Conscription in the United States," *Wikipedia.* Accessed April 24, 2017, at *https://en.wikipedia.org/wiki /Conscription_in_the_United_States.*) In Texas, martial law was declared in both the south-central counties of Colorado, Fayette and Austin (large German populations), and in the Hill Country German counties because of widespread resistance to the new conscription laws. The Battle of the Nueces, mentioned above, can be seen as the most dramatic manifestation of this resistance.

66   Collinsville: Can be read as present Cat Spring. Cat Spring counts as the second oldest German community in Texas behind Industry. It was first settled in 1834 by a group of German immigrants from the duchies of Oldenburg and Westphalia led by Ludwig Anton Siegmund von Roeder and Robert Kleberg. The earliest agricultural society in Texas, the Cat Spring Agricultural Society, was formed in the town in 1856 by W. A. Trenckmann's father, Andreas Trenckmann. Millheim and Cat Spring are often considered sister communities. (Charles Christopher Jackson, "Cat Spring, TX," *Handbook of Texas Online.* Accessed June 19, 2017, at *https://tshaonline.org/handbook/online/articles/hnc24.*)

67   *Tante Bos:* An affectionate nickname given to a German newspaper of the time, but the translator has not been able to determine which it was.

68   Falada: In the Grimm Brothers' fairytale "The Goose Girl," the princess's horse, named Falada, can talk.

69   Enfield muskets: Not to be confused with the Enfield rifles first introduced in 1895 that became the mainstay of the British Army for the first part of the 20th century. The English company produced muzzleloaders during the Civil War that became the mainstay of Southern forces. Many considered them superior to the muzzleloaders used by Union forces.

70   American black ducks are large ducks with a profile nearly identical to mallards. They have rounded heads, thick bills, and bulky bodies. Like other dabbling ducks they sit high in the water with their tails high. They are native to eastern North America and their range includes south-central Texas.

71   During the so-called Runaway Scrape, the wild and panicked retreat of Anglo settlers before the advancing Mexican armies of General Santa Anna after the

twin disasters of the Alamo and Goliad in March–April 1836, most settlers joined the general retreat. A German family, however, the family of Conrad and Maria Theresia Jürgens, who had settled near Post Oak Point, a small farming community on the banks of Post Oak Point Creek, a tributary of the San Bernard River, three miles south of Industry in far western Austin County, decided to stay put. They were raided by Indians who captured the wife and the two children while Jürgens escaped and joined a group of settlers who had camped near Mill Creek bottom. Mrs. Jürgens was later ransomed at a Red River trading post, but the Indians did not release the boys. She gave birth to a daughter, Jane Margaret (who later married H. D. Jordt), while she was with the Indians. H. D. Jordt was the son of Thomas Detlef Jordt (aka Detlef Dunt) who wrote the first emigrant guide published in Germany by someone with actual experience of Texas. (See: Kearney, et al, *Detlef Dunt's Journey to Texas in 1833*; for the Jürgens capture see: "The first German woman in Texas," Louise Ernst Stöhr reminiscence, reproduced in *Journey to Texas in 1833*, 126–139; also, Arliss Treybig, "Juergens, Conrad," *Handbook of Texas Online*. Accessed May 21, 2017, at *https://tshaonline.org/handbook/online/articles/fju09*.)

72   Conscript hunters: Member of the home guard whose duty it was to enforce the conscription laws. They were widely disliked because of their excesses and were often referred to derisively as "heel flies." The term, which is taken from a type of fly that attempts to lay its eggs on the heels of cattle—and hence a great annoyance—was common at the time but popularized in "Heel-Fly Time in Texas," an autobiographical work of J. Warren Hunter first published by the *Frontier Times* in 1931.

73   Yaupon: *Ilex vomitorus*, an evergreen brush common to the post-oak savannah of south-central Texas. It is often cultivated as an ornamental plant because of the red berries it produces in the fall and winter.

74   Christoph von Schmid (1768–1854) was an ordained priest, an educator, and a German writer of children's stories with an underlying Christian message. His stories were very popular and translated into many languages.

75   Pietism is considered the major influence that led to the creation of the "Evangelical Church of the Union" in Prussia in 1817. The King of Prussia ordered the Lutheran and Reformed churches in Prussia to unite; they took the name "Evangelical" as a name both groups had previously identified with. This union movement spread through many German lands in the 1800s. Pietism, with its looser attitude toward confessional theology, had opened the churches to the possibility of uniting. The unification of the two branches of German Protestantism sparked the Schism of the Old Lutherans. Many Old Lutherans formed free churches or immigrated to the United States and Australia, where they formed bodies that would later become the Lutheran Church of the Missouri Synod and the Lutheran Church of Australia, respectively. (Many immigrants to America who agreed with the union movement formed German Evangelical Lutheran and Reformed congregations, later combined into the Evangelical Synod of North America, which is now a part of the United Church of Christ.)

76 Freethinkers and *Lateiner* are often used as synonymous and interchangeable
terms, but this is not quite correct. *Lateiner* suggests education at a university level,
but many educated Germans of the period felt liberated and emboldened by the
spirit of German critical philosophy that began with Immanuel Kant (1724–1804)
and continued through Georg Wilhelm Friedrich Hegel (1770–1831). This spirit,
as they understood it, was incompatible with traditional Christian assumptions,
especially in respect to the divinity of Christ and the infallibility of the Bible. In
the 1840s, many had fallen under the influence of the German philosopher Ludwig
Feuerbach (1804–1872), himself a student of Hegel. In 1841 Feuerbach published
a devastating attack on orthodox Christianity entitled *Das Wesen des Christentums*
(The Essence of Christianity). Feuerbach's criticism can be summarized in the
following formulation:

Christianity has set for itself the goal of fulfilling the unfulfillable hopes
of mankind, but for precisely this reason, has left the achievable aspirations of
mankind unaddressed: it has compromised our earthly existence through the
promise of eternal life; it has undercut faith in our own abilities through faith in
God's ability to intervene; it has weakened our belief in a better life here on earth
through belief in a better life in heaven. Christianity has given to its believers
what they imagine they want, but just for that reason, has not given them what
in reality they need in their earthly existence . . . the necessities of life without
which a satisfying human existence is not possible. (Ludwig Feuerbach, "Positiver
Atheismus," repro'd. in *Der deutsche Vormärz* (Stuttgart: Reclam, 1974), 170–172.
[Translation by author])

Several of the prominent *Freidenker* who emigrated to Texas routinely referred
to themselves as *Feuerbachianer,* or "Feuerbachytes." (see Soergel, *A Sojourn,* 92, 93.)
Added to this was the wide-spread conviction that the Christian church in Germany
was a willing partner to the all-pervasive *Obrigkeit* (governmental authority) under
which many chafed. (See Nagel, *A Boy's Civil War Story.*) To be sure, German
freethinkers established several of the *Lateiner* settlements in Texas, noted for
their absence of churches. This was certainly the case for the Cat Spring/Millheim
communities. The Cat Spring Agricultural Society centennial commemorative,
published in 1956, does not mince words: "The German settlers at Cat Spring,
who were greatly interested in agriculture, education, literature, music, and art
manifested little interest in religion." (*Cat Spring Story,* 20, 99–100; *Cat Spring
Minutes,* 29.) The constitution of the first public school excluded religious instruction
from its curriculum. Although most of the *Lateiner* tended to be Freethinkers, there
were a few exceptions, most notably Reverend Louis Cachand Evrendberg at nearby
Cummins creek community. To quote Kamphoefner and Buenger, *Preserving Texas
German Identity,* 6: "It is apparent that William Trenckmann, perhaps even more
than his father, shared the irreligious outlook of his community . . . . The dozen
or so references Trenckmann makes to churches are often pejorative, associating
them with prohibition and the Ku Klux Klan."

77 *"De Brevitate Vitae"* (Latin: "On the Shortness of Life"), more commonly known as *"Gaudeamus Igitur"* ("So Let Us Rejoice") or just *"Gaudeamus,"* is a popular academic commencement song in many Western countries, mainly sung or performed at university graduation ceremonies. Despite its use as a formal graduation hymn, it is a jocular, light-hearted composition that pokes fun at university life.

78 Mustang wine: Wine made from the native Texas grape often called "Mustang grapes."

79 This is a quote from Friedrich Schiller's famous play, *Wilhelm Tell*. Schiller's play became a touchstone for German nationalists in the nineteenth century who aspired to see a Germany united under a liberal constitution. The full quote in German reads: "Ans Vaterland, ans teure, schließ dich an, / Das halte fest mit deinem ganzen Herzen. / Hier sind die starken Wurzeln deiner Kraft; / Dort in der fremden Welt stehst du allein, / Ein schwankes Rohr, das jeder Sturm zerknickt." [Embrace the Fatherland, the precious Fatherland / Embrace it body and soul / Here lies the strong roots of your strength / There in a foreign land you are alone / a weak stalk, that any storm can break]. (Friedrich Schiller, *Wilhelm Tell* II, 1 / Attinghausen.)

80 Blue cat: The blue catfish, *Ictalurus furcatus*, is the largest species of North American catfish, reaching a length of 165 cm (65 in) and a weight of 68 kg (150 lb) and common throughout the South. They are usually found in deeper waters and are caught on trotlines with baited hooks. Although they can grow to be much larger, an eight-pounder is considered an ideal size because the meat tastes better at the smaller weights.

81 Saxon dialect: Germany has many dialects which persist to the present. Upper Saxon German (German: *Obersächsisch*), not to be confused with the Low Saxon dialect group in Northern Germany, is an East Central German dialect spoken in much of the modern German State of Saxony and in the adjacent parts of Saxony-Anhalt and Thuringia.

82 Old Fritz: affectionate nickname for Frederick II (1712–1786), who was King of Prussia from 1740 until 1786. His most significant accomplishments during his reign included his military victories, his reorganization of Prussian armies, his patronage of the arts and the Enlightenment in Prussia, and his final success against great odds in the Seven Years' War. Prussia greatly increased its territories and became a leading military power in Europe under his rule. He became known as Frederick the Great and was affectionately nicknamed *Der Alte Fritz* ("Old Fritz") by the Prussian and later by all German people. ("Frederick the Great," *Wikipedia*. Accessed May 22, 2017, at *https://en.wikipedia.org/wiki/Frederick_the_Great.*)

83 Jena: Battle of Jena, also called Battle of Jena–Auerstädt, (Oct. 14, 1806), military engagement of the Napoleonic Wars, fought between 122,000 French troops and 114,000 Prussians and Saxons, at Jena and Auerstädt, in Saxony (modern Germany). In the battle, Napoleon smashed the outdated Prussian army inherited from Frederick II the Great, which resulted in the reduction of Prussia to half its former

size at the Treaty of Tilsit in July 1807. ("Battle of Jena," *Encyclopædia Britannica Online*. Accessed May 22, 2017, at *https://www.britannica.com/event/Battle-of-Jena*.)

84 Ligny: The Battle of Ligny (June 16, 1815) was the last victory of the military career of Napoleon Bonaparte. In this battle, French troops of the Armée du Nord under Napoleon's command, defeated part of a Prussian army under Field Marshal Prince Blücher, near Ligny in present-day Belgium. The Battle of Ligny is an example of a tactical win and a strategic loss, in that the bulk of the Prussian army survived and went on to play a pivotal role two days later at the Battle of Waterloo, reinforced by IV Prussian corps that had not participated in the battle at Ligny. However, had the French army succeeded in keeping the Prussian army from joining the Anglo-allied Army under Wellington at Waterloo, Napoleon might have won the Waterloo Campaign. (*Wikipedia*, "Battle of Ligny," accessed May 22, 2017.)

85 "Lichterfelde Kaserne, southwest of the Berlin downtown area, was an old Prussian cadet training school. The Nazis took it over in 1933, and it became the headquarters of Hitler's bodyguard regiment, the Leibstandarte-SS "Adolf Hitler." Later, newer buildings were built to serve as the headquarters for the Leibstandarte.

86 The Guards Cuirassiers (German: *Garde-Kürassier-Regiment*) were a heavy cavalry regiment of the Royal Prussian Army. Formed in 1815 as an Uhlans regiment, it was reorganized as a cuirassiers unit in 1821. The regiment was part of the Guards Cavalry Division and fought in the Second Schleswig War, the Austro-Prussian War, the Franco-Prussian War and World War I. The regiment was disbanded in September 1919." ("Guards Cuirassiers," *Wikipedia*. Accessed May 22, 2017, at *https://en.wikipedia.org/wiki/Guards_Cuirassiers_(Prussia)*.)

87 Königsberg: The historical name for the present-day city of Kaliningrad. Königsberg was founded in 1255 on the site of the ancient Old Prussian settlement Twangste by the Teutonic Knights during the Northern Crusades, and was named in honor of King Ottokar II of Bohemia. A Baltic port city, it successively became the capital of their monastic state, the Duchy of Prussia (1525–1701) and East Prussia. Königsberg remained the coronation city of the Prussian monarchy, though the capital was moved to Berlin in 1701. It was the easternmost large city in Germany until it was captured by the Soviet Union on April 9, 1945, near the end of World War II. ("Königsberg," *Wikipedia*. Accessed May 22, 2017, at *https://en.wikipedia.org/wiki /K%C3%B6nigsberg*.)

88 Frederick William IV (German: Friedrich Wilhelm IV.; 1795 – 1861), the eldest son and successor of Frederick William III of Prussia, reigned as King of Prussia from 1840 to 1861. Also referred to as the "romantic on the throne," he is best remembered for the many buildings he had constructed in Berlin and Potsdam, as well as for the completion of the Gothic Cologne cathedral. In politics, he was a conservative, and in 1849 he rejected the title of German Emperor offered to him by the Frankfurt parliament, considering that, by rights, parliament had no authority to make such an offer. In 1857, he suffered a stroke, and was left incapacitated until his death.

89 The German word was *Quatsch*.

90 In March 1848, crowds of people gathered in Berlin to present their demands in an "address to the king." King Frederick William IV, taken by surprise, yielded verbally to all the demonstrators' demands, including parliamentary elections, a constitution, and freedom of the press. He promised that "Prussia was to be merged forthwith into Germany." On March 13, the army charged people returning from a meeting in the *Tiergarten* (Berlin Zoo); they left one person dead and many injured. On March 18, a large demonstration occurred; when two shots were fired, the people feared that some of the 20,000 soldiers would be used against them. They erected barricades, fighting started, and a battle took place until troops were ordered thirteen hours later to retreat, leaving hundreds of dead. Afterwards, Frederick William attempted to reassure the public that he would proceed with reorganizing his government. The king also approved arming the citizens. On March 21, he proceeded through the streets of Berlin to attend a mass funeral at the *Friedrichshain* cemetery for the civil victims of the uprising. He and his ministers and generals wore the revolutionary tricolor of black, red, and gold. After Polish prisoners were liberated, they paraded through the city, acclaimed by the people. They had been jailed as suspects in planning a rebellion in formerly Polish territories now ruled by Prussia. The 254 persons killed during the riots were laid out on catafalques on the *Gendarmenmarkt*. Some 40,000 people accompanied them to the burial place at Friedrichshain.

91 Mierolawski: Ludwik Mierolawski (1814–1878) was a professional revolutionary for most of his life. He first made a name for himself in the 1830 in the unsuccessful November uprising by Polish patriots against Russian rule. Although only a teenager, he acted as standard-bearer in the uprising and attracted much attention. Thereafter, he emigrated to France but remained in touch with democratic and nationalistic aspirations across Europe. Prussian authorities imprisoned him after the March 1848 uprising in Berlin but the following year he was summoned to lead the military forces of the Baden revolutionary government. He was very clever at resisting the Prussian military forces sent to crush the revolutionary government, but in the end his outnumbered and outgunned forces were compelled to surrender. He is sometimes referred to as the Polish Napoleon because of his tactical adeptness in the face of superior forces.

92 Marabouts at Zou-Zian In December 1849 French forces laid siege to the Algerian stronghold of Zaatcha. The Marabouts (Muslim religious leaders), one of which named Bouzian (Zou-Zian) had called for a religious war and put up a fierce resistance, but after their positions were overrun, the French soldiers went on a rampage slaughtering all men, women, and children without exception.

93 Kabyles: The Kabyle people are a Berber ethnic group native to Kabylia in the north of Algeria, one hundred miles east of Algiers. They represent the largest Berber-speaking population of Algeria and the second largest in Africa. The area was gradually taken over by the French during their colonization beginning in 1857,

despite vigorous resistance. (*https://en.wikipedia.org/wiki/Kabyle_people; https:*
//de.wikipedia.org/wiki/Belagerung_von_Zaatcha?

94   Crimean War: The Crimean War, (1853–1856) was a conflict between Russia
and an alliance composed of France, Britain, the Ottoman Empire, and Sardinia.
Russia eventually lost. The decline of the Ottoman Empire, and the unwillingness
of Britain and France to allow Russia to gain territory and power at Ottoman
expense was the root cause of the war.

95   China campaign: Actually Indo-China and specifically Vietnam. In September
1858, fourteen French gunships with 3,000 soldiers attacked the port of Da Nang,
Vietnam, and occupied the city, causing significant damage in the process. This
marked the beginning of the French colonization of Indo-China.

96   Goela [sic]: El Goléa is an oasis town located almost at the center of Algeria.
It is the gateway to the Sahara Desert to the south.

97   *Kommerzienrat*: An honorary title bestowed upon distinguished members of the
business community, especially if they had contributed to the commonweal.

98   *Coleurstudent:* A student at a German university who belonged to one of the
prestigious fraternities. The term refers to the fact that members of German
fraternities traditionally sported caps and sashes with distinctive and splashy
color combinations.

99   *Mont-de-piété*: French for pawn shop.

100 *Seine-Babel*: This rather curious and outmoded expression alludes to the common
conception of Paris held by many Germans of the period that the city was a kind
of modern day Tower of Babel where many nationalities mixed and many languages
could be heard.

101 *Pont de invalids*: Lowest bridge spanning the Seine River in Paris.

102 *Glühwein*: A typically German winter drink where spiced wine is served hot.

103 The *Chasseurs d'Afrique* (literally, Huntsmen of Africa) were a light cavalry corps
in the French *Armée d'Afrique* (Army of Africa). First raised in the 1830s from
regular French cavalry posted to Algeria, they numbered five regiments by World
War II. For most of their history they were recruited from either French volunteers
or French settlers in North Africa doing their military service. In addition to
numerous campaigns in North Africa, these colorful regiments also served in the
Crimean War, Franco-Prussian War, Indochina, France's invasion of Mexico and
both world wars.

104 In 1862 a combined Spanish, English, and French expeditionary force invaded
Mexico. The ostensible purpose was to collect loans that the Mexican government
had repudiated. The Spanish and English were limited in their goals, but the French
were more ambitious and eventually set up a short-lived client state under Emperor
Maximilian I.

105 Forey: Élie Frédéric Forey (1804–1872) was commanding general of the French expeditionary corps to Mexico in 1862. His troops landed in September 1862 in Veracruz,
captured Puebla In May 1863, and after a protracted siege, Mexico City as well.

106 Juarez: Benito Juárez (1806–1872) was a national hero and president of Mexico (1861–72), who for three years (1864–67) fought against foreign occupation under the emperor Maximilian and who sought constitutional reforms to create a democratic federal republic.("Benito Juárez," *Encyclopædia Britannica Online.* Accessed May 22, 2017, at *https://www.britannica.com/biography/Benito-Juarez.*)

107 New London: There is a town in far Northeast Texas (Rusk County) by this name, most noted for a gas leak explosion in 1937 that killed in excess of 300 people, but this is obviously not intended. "New London" in the book is most likely either present Columbus or La Grange, which would have been the closest towns of consequence at the time on the Colorado River.

108 *Maidli*: The word is Alemannic dialect for *Mädchen,* or young girl, and is spoken mainly in Switzerland.

109 Jenny: A female mule.

110 The Landau is a four-seated and four-wheeled coach with a leather strap suspension. The rear seats face one another in a parallel configuration. It was usually a convertible with a cover that could be put up and down. This type of coach was developed in France in the seventeenth century but by the eighteenth and nineteenth centuries was recognized as a status symbol among the upper classes of Europe.

111 Meyers *Konversationslexikon* of 1905 describes the Chignon as a "hair style resembling a bag-like bulge on the back of the head and fastened with a comb."

112 Crinoline was originally a stiff fabric with a weft of horse-hair and a warp of cotton or linen thread. The fabric first appeared around 1830, but by 1850 the word had come to mean a stiffened petticoat or rigid skirt-shaped structure of steel designed to support the skirts of a woman's dress into the required shape.

113 *Interpellate* is a rather obscure word narrowly associated with governmental and diplomatic language. It suggests a formal interrogation (as of a foreign minister) concerning official policy or personal conduct. The word also exists in German in verbal form as *interpellieren,* which Trenckmann uses. It is a word of obvious Latin derivation that only educated Germans would ever have used or even understood.

114 Scores of temporary camps and bivouac sites existed across Texas during the war. Camp Hardeman was situated near Independence, TX, about twenty miles from Millheim.

115 The German word used was *krummschliessen.* This refers to an extreme form of punishment used in the Prussian army whereby one wrist of the offender was chained to an opposing ankle.

116 Blackjack: *Quercus marilandica* is a small oak tree with very large leaves that often have a dark hue to them especially in the late summer and early fall. The name derives from this fact as it refers to the oversized ears of a mule (jack). The trees have a wide range in the eastern and central United States and often are found together post oaks (*Quercus stellate*).

117 Tarot: a group of card games that originated in Italy and spread to most parts of
    Europe. Tarot is a game of suits and trumps and may have introduced the concept
    of trumps to card games.

118 Krähwinkel: This name, which translates literally as "crows' corner," suggests
    something like "boondocks" in English. The German playwright August von Kot-
    zebue (1761–1819) first popularized the term in his play, *Die deutschen Kleinstädter*
    (1801), in which he satirized German village life. The Austrian actor and dramatist
    Johann Nestroy revived the term in 1848 with his burlesque musical *Freiheit in
    Krähwinkel* (Freedom in Krähwinkel). In Texas, however, the term had come to be
    applied among south-central German speakers to the small German settlement of
    Frelsburg in northern Colorado County, and this is most likely the settlement to
    which Trenckmann alludes. Trenckmann actually taught at Hermann's Academy, a
    private German school located at Frelsburg for a couple of years.

119 Galop: As with the galloping of horses, a lively dance, introduced in the late 1820s
    to Parisian society and made popular in Vienna, Berlin and London. The galop was
    a forerunner of the polka, which was introduced in Prague ballrooms in the 1830s
    and made fashionable in Paris in the 1840s.

120 Bertran de Born (1140–1215) was a baron from the Limousin in France, and one of
    the major troubadours of the twelfth century. Political intrigue associated with the
    Third Crusade is at the heart of his poetry. His œuvre consists of about 47 works.
    Several melodies survive and some of his songs have been recorded.

121 Henri-Gatien, Comte Bertrand (1773–1844), was a French general whose career
    was closely bound up with that of Napoleon, who honored him in 1808 with the
    title of Count and at the end of 1813, with the title of Grand Marshal of the Palace.
    He accompanied the Emperor to Elba in 1814, returned with him in 1815, held
    a command in the Waterloo campaign, and then, after the defeat, accompanied
    Napoleon to St. Helena.

122 Roundelay: Also called roundel; a slow medieval dance performed in a circle or a
    song in which a line or phrase is repeated as a refrain. Trenckmann uses the Polish
    word *Kuplet,* but it refers to the same thing.

123 Tarantella: a group of various folk dances characterized by an upbeat tempo, usually
    in 6/8 time, accompanied by tambourines. It is among the most recognized forms of
    traditional southern Italian music. ("Tarantella," *Wikipedia,* accessed July 4, 2018.)

124 *Brockenszene* in *Faust*: The *Brockenszene,* or "mountain cliff scene," is the concluding
    act in Johann Wolfgang von Goethe's monumental tragic play, *Faust,* Part II,
    completed in 1831. It is a tempestuous scene with smoke and fire, the devil and
    chorus of angels. In the scene, Faust emerges victorious over Mephisto.

125 Moravians: The settlement included a few families of Czech (Moravian) nationality.

126 Paul de Kock (1793–1871) was a popular and prolific French author of stories of
    middle-class Parisian life. The 1905 *New International Encyclopædia* describes his
    stories as rather vulgar, but not immoral, demanding no literary training and
    gratifying no delicate taste.

127 Joseph Marie Eugène Sue (1804–1857) was a popular French novelist of the period who was known for his socialist and anti-clerical novels. He also established the genre of the serial novel, which became very popular and widely imitated at the time.

128 *Gymnasium*: In Germany the upper or preparatory school necessary to attend a university. The curriculum was (and still is) heavy on languages.

129 *Lourdaud*: French for "oaf" or "lout."

130 *Triumphator*: In ancient Rome, the term used to refer to returning generals who had achieved great victories against the barbarians.

131 Aristocratic origins: It was universally believed at the time that certain physical traits characterized the aristocracy, namely refined facial features with obligatory aquiline noses, tall and slender bodies, and small feet and hands.

132 The word used in the German was *standesgemäss* (class-appropriate). Very rigid social distinctions prevailed in Germany during this period, and strict conventions governed how one dressed and behaved in society. The nobility was especially meticulous in observing these conventions Frau Sartorius continues to embody these notions even in Texas.

133 German has formal and informal forms of address, which do not exist in Standard English. Lüttenhoff has suddenly switched from the informal *du* to the formal *Sie* in his reply to Kuno, which carries the unmistakable message that their formerly close and familiar relationship is now a thing of the past.

134 Pietism was a movement within Lutheranism that began in Germany in the late 17th century and reached its zenith in the mid-18th century, but declined during the nineteenth century. Because of its mystical bent and emphasis on the individual's religious experience, authorities often viewed Pietism as anarchic and an affront to the established order (*Obrigkeit*).

135 Journeyman: Germany had, and still has, a centuries-old tradition of guilds (*Zunftwesen*) for trades such as shoemaking with the traditional three-part progression of apprentice, journeyman, and master. At the journeyman stage, one was expected to travel around and get the benefit of other workshops and masters.

136 Wanzleben and Halberstadt: Towns in the German state of Saxony-Anhalt.

137 Prince Eugene of Savoy (1663–1736) was a general of the Imperial Army and statesman of the Holy Roman Empire and the Archduchy of Austria and one of the most successful military commanders in European history.

138 Initially the Confederacy attempted to meet its manpower requirements through militias and volunteers. This proved woefully inadequate. On April 16th, 1862, the Confederacy extended the terms of enlistment to three years and also made all white male citizens between the ages of eighteen and thirty-five subject to conscription. In 1863 and again in 1864 the age range for enrollment was extended from seventeen to fifty.

139 Foot towels: Soldiers on both sides were issued woolen socks. Wool is inherently less sanitary than cotton, but cotton socks were unknown at this time. It could be that many eschewed woolen socks and adopted the practice of wrapping their

246

feet in cotton towels or rags, both for comfort and sanitation, especially during the summer months.

140 Shirtfront: The German word used was *Vorhemd*. This is an article of formal clothing that was popular in the latter half of the nineteenth century. It consisted of cardboard covered with cloth, often lined, that was decoratively embroidered, and worn between the shirt and a vest and attached by strings in the back.

141 Barked up the wrong tree: The German phrase used was *in die unrechte Schmiede kommen*, an antiquated phrase that literally means "gone to the wrong smithy" and that has no exact English equivalent.

142 First Texas Cavalry Regiment: There were at least three units that used the name First Texas Cavalry. One can be dismissed because it was a Union force composed of Texans, largely Texas Germans, who supported the North. The second unit by that name was established early in the war as the First Texas Mounted Rifles by Ben McCulloch but by the latter stage of the war had been reorganized as the First Texas Cavalry under Colonel Augustus Buchel, a native of Hesse and veteran of the Hessian, Turkish, and American armies. (James A. Hathcock, "First Texas Cavalry," *Handbook of Texas Online.* Accessed October 06, 2015, at *https://tshaonline .org/handbook/online/articles/qkf12*). During this time frame, namely winter of 1864–5, Buchel's First Texas Cavalry was stationed at Hempstead in Ft. Bend County about thirty miles from Millheim.

143 *Kandidat*: The term usually refers to a university student who has completed his comprehensive exams but not yet completed the doctorate; i.e., an advanced student. But in this case, it seems to mean a theology student who has completed all the requirements to be a pastor and who now awaits a pastorate.

144 Mule rabbit: What is commonly called a "jack rabbit" and so-called because of the long, mule-like ears. Jack is another name for a mule.

145 Phillips Plantation: The Phillips Plantation is fictional but appears to be a composite, modeled both on the historic Ellersly Plantation, which was located on the west side of the lower Brazos River eight miles from the coast, and also on Bernardo Plantation, which was located on a high bluff on the Brazos River four miles south of the site of present Hempstead in Waller County. The description of the layout of the plantation matches descriptions of Ellersly with the one exception that the Ellersly manor house was constructed entirely of bricks whereas Bernardo was made of wood. In respect to Ellersly, the *Handbook of Texas* states: "The plantation house was located in a grove of live oaks between two roads, and the entrance gates were flanked by hand-hewn oak posts topped by carved replicas of a spade, a diamond, a club, and a heart. The two-story house was constructed of slave-made bricks. It had twenty-one rooms, and galleries with pillars extended the length of the house on the west and south. The stairs and bannisters were made of mahogany, and the ceilings were plastered and decorated with intricate medallions. The fireplaces and mantels were made of marble, and the floors were carpeted. The furniture was either walnut or mahogany. Atop the house was a laboratory with a telescope. All in all, Ellersly was considered the finest home in Texas before the

Civil War." (Claudia Hazlewood, "Bernardo Plantation," *Handbook of Texas Online*. Accessed December 8, 2015, at *https://tshaonline.org/handbook/online/articles/acb01*. René Harris, "Ellersly Plantation," *Handbook of Texas Online*. Accessed December 8, 2015, at *https://tshaonline.org/handbook/online/articles/ace02*.)

[146] Catalpa: *Catalpa bignonioides*, A medium-sized tree to 50 feet in height and 1 to 2 feet in diameter, with a dense, oval crown. It is widely planted as a fast-growing yard tree in the eastern third of Texas.

[147] Silver poplar: *Populus alba*, commonly called abele, silver poplar, silver leaf poplar, or white poplar, is a species of poplar, most closely related to the aspens. It is native from Morocco and the Iberian Peninsula through central Europe to central Asia and was widely planted in the New World as an ornamental.

[148] Dutchmen: Americans often referred to Texas-Germans as "Dutchmen." This is because *Deutsch*, the German word for "German," sounded like "Dutch," a word they knew. Depending on context, it was sometimes, but not always, a pejorative term.

[149] Darky; coon: There are many terms for black people used in this text that would be considered offensive to modern sensibilities. There has been no effort to sanitize these in the translation. The author is reflecting attitudes that were current even among ostensibly progressive-minded people at the time. In general, the decade before the outbreak of World War I saw a revision in attitudes about the Civil War, with a more sympathetic interpretation of the South and Southern attitudes and a more patronizing and demeaning attitude about black people. It was the heyday of the black-face minstrel shows that cast Negros as ignorant buffoons. Thomas Dixon's wildly popular novel, *The Klansman*, appeared in 1905. It reinforced racial stereotypes while praising the Ku Klux Klan. The novel inspired *The Birth of a Nation* (originally called *The Clansman*), a 1915 American silent film epic drama, directed and co-produced by D. W. Griffith. The book and the film are said to have inspired the reincarnation of the Ku Klux Klan in 1916.

[150] First Families of Virginia (FFV) were those families in Colonial Virginia who were socially prominent and wealthy, but not necessarily the earliest settlers. They descended from English colonists who primarily settled at Jamestown, Williamsburg, and along the James River and other navigable waters in Virginia during the seventeenth century. These elite families generally married within their social class for many generations and as a result most surnames of First Families date to the colonial period. ("First Families of Virginia", *Wikipedia*. Accessed January 25, 2017, at *https://en.wikipedia.org/wiki/First_Families_of_Virginia*.)

[151] Johann Wolfgang von Goethe (1749–1832) is Germany's foremost man of letters, with contributions in all genres, but he was also a man of the world interested in science, art, music, and politics. After taking up residence in Weimar in 1775, he served as a minister for the Duke of Saxe-Weimar with various responsibilities. Weimar, while he lived there, attracted many men and women of letters and intellectual distinction and, despite its small size, became the intellectual hub of the nation.

152   The German term employed was *Kunst-Banause,* which is a pejorative term derived
       from Ancient Greek for someone who has no interest in art and culture.

153   Caesar's *Commentarii de Bello Gallico* has been a mainstay in Latin instruction for
       centuries because of its simple, direct prose. Ariovistus was a leader of the Suebi
       and other allied Germanic peoples in the second quarter of the 1st century BC.
       They were defeated, however, in the Battle of Vosges and driven back over the
       Rhine in 58 BC by Julius Caesar.

154   Major Bolton: In *Weihnachtsfeier in trüber Zeit* (Christmas in troubled Times),
       Trenckmann mentions a plantation owner named Bouldin whose slaves peeked
       into the window in amazement at the family celebrations during Christmas 1863.
       The man was Col. William Graves Bouldin and his plantation was in Chappell Hill.
       Trenckmann probably substituted *Bolton* for the real name *Bouldin.* A true tale of
       land swindling and chicanery affecting many of the German residents of Millheim
       forms an unmistakable backdrop to the Bolton story. One of the most extensive
       court cases involving disputed land claims in Texas took place in Austin County and
       involved many of the early Millheim settlers. A lawsuit, Hill v. Portis, was finally
       decided by the Texas Supreme Court in 1868 after years of protracted litigation with
       the result that many Millheim Germans who had bought land in the Mill Tract in
       the 1840s summarily lost title to their land without compensation, although many
       later redeemed them and remained in the area, allowing the Millheim community
       to thrive. (James Woodrick, private communication, "The Millheim Land Swindle.")

155   From the subsequent narrative, it becomes clear that Pine Valley can be read as the
       stretch of the river bottom on the right side of the Brazos River from the old crossing
       at Washington-on-the Brazos to present Hempstead in Waller County. Many large
       slave plantations had located here in the antebellum era.

156   Northern forces blockaded all the major ports of the South during the Civil
       War. Mexico remained neutral during the conflict and such cotton as could be
       transported overland could be exchanged for Mexican gold.

157   Kuno was looking for the road from San Felipe to Washington-on-the-Brazos
       (via Chappell Hill). His first effort at crossing was most likely the so-called
       Lawrence Crossing near the tiny community of Peters where present Hwy. 36
       between Bellville and Sealy crosses Mill Creek. He then backtracked upstream
       for ten miles where the present Mill Creek road crosses Mill Creek. The area today,
       as then, is heavily wooded. Once he crossed the creek and got out of the creek
       bottom, he then attempted to strike a course back to southeast to intersect the
       San Felipe/Washington road, but got lost.

158   *Ritterburg* (knights' castle or fortress): an ironic allusion to the cabin where the two
       titled Germans had holed up who had rescued Hedwig.

159   Hoe cake: Hoe cake is the Southern name for a johnnycake, which is a flatbread
       made from cornmeal. It probably originated with Native Americans.

160   In this section of the narrative, the author inserts many anglicisms that subse-
       quently became fixtures of Texas German. In this sentence, the American English
       verb *fix* is presented as the Germanized past participle *gefixt.*

161 *Möris*: Trenckmann is alluding to Saint Maurice (also Moritz, Morris, or Mauritius), who was the leader of the legendary Roman Theban Legion in the third century, which was composed entirely of Christians. According to legend, the whole legion was put to death by the emperor Maximian when they refused to worship pagan Roman gods or slaughter fellow Christians. He was the patron saint of several professions, locales, and kingdoms. He is also a highly revered saint in the Coptic Orthodox Church and Oriental Orthodox churches.

162 Major road: There were several old roads that dated from the Mexican era that come into play in the story, namely the Old San Felipe Road, Gotier's Trace, and Goacher's Trace (not to be confused). The road Kuno was looking for was most likely Goacher's Trace. James Woodrick, a historian who has researched the old roads, writes: "The second 'Goacher Trace' was laid out by James Gotier in about 1835 from Bastrop to his camp and newer home on Rabb's Creek in modern Lee County south of Giddings….Later this road was extended to connect with the La Bahia road near Burton, then to Washington-on-the-Brazos…" (James Woodrick, "The Gotier Trace," *The Wendish Research Exchange.* Accessed February 12, 2017, at *https://wendishresearch.org/2016/02/08/the-gotier-trace-by-james-woodrick/*.)

163 Leesburg: Most likely present Washington-on-the-Brazos.

164 New Mobile: Most likely present Hempstead.

165 Pine Valley: Most likely right side of the Brazos River between Washington-on-the-Brazos and Hempstead.

166 Hog-wallow prairie: Heavy black land prairie with clay underneath. The clay swells and contracts according to the moisture content creating an undulating appearance, as if rooted by hogs. Several German travelers of the period commented on the phenomenon. Joseph, Count of Boos-Waldeck, wrote in 1843: "Now it was time to begin the plowing. But it turned out to be undoable with the few oxen we had because of the heavy, 'hog-wallow' prairie…" (Boos-Waldeck Bericht, May, 1844, Solms-Braunfels Archives, transcripts, XXX, 44.)

167 Rafts, or massive logjams, often formed on the Central Texas rivers. The most famous of these rafts formed at the mouth of the Colorado River and existed throughout the colonial and republican periods of Texas as a formidable barrier to navigation. It was reputedly over eight miles long and was not finally cleared until ca. 1850.

168 Large slave plantations typically hired an overseer to manage the day to day tasking of the slaves.

169 *Rebbe*: Yiddish for "rabbi."

170 *Gannef*: Yiddish for "thief."

171 Mändelchen: German diminutive or affectionate form for Amanda.

172 Hops and malt: From the German saying that a certain point in the process of brewing beer, if a mistake has been made, putting in these ingredients will serve no purpose.

173 The German term used is *Freund Hein*.

174 *Fenz*: The two standard German words for fence, *Mauer* and *Zaun*, both have
     associations that do not relate well to the Texas experience. As a result, Texas
     German immigrants quickly adopted and Germanized the American word
     fence as *die Fenz*. Trenckmann uses this word as if it were a normal German
     word and does not set it off in quotes as he does with other American words,
     which is a clear indication that the word had already been incorporated into
     Texas German by this date.

175 This alludes to a documented encounter between several German women and a
     recruiting officer that took place in Industry, TX, another predominately German
     community only a few miles upstream from Millheim, in 1862. The irate wives
     drove away a recruiting officer with pots, pans, and kitchen knives. The officer
     pulled his pistol, but fortunately had the prudence not to use it.

176 Seppl: In German, the diminutive and affectionate form for Joseph.

177 *Kanzelredner*: This term, which translates as "podium-speaker," refers to a preacher's
     ability to hold a public sermon.

178 *Kultusministerium*: Highest state office responsible for education.

179 Krähwinkel: See note 119 above.

180 Deferments: The first mandatory conscription laws were passed by the Southern
     States during the Civil War, and were controversial form the beginning. The
     North quickly followed suit. The Texas conscription laws, passed in January and
     implemented in the spring of 1862, had many loopholes and deferments, some
     of which were sensible and necessary, while others were skewed in favor of the
     slave-holding class, and occasioned much discontent. In this regard, the provision
     that owners of at least twenty slaves received an automatic deferment was especially
     egregious, and gave rise to the saying, "A poor man's war for a rich man's nigger."
     Gins and mills for grinding grain, processing cotton, and sawing lumber were
     indispensable for daily life, so the authorities found it necessary to grant deferments
     to the owners and operators of these establishments.

181 Croesus: Croesus (595–c. 546 BC) was the king of Lydia, renowned for his wealth,
     who, according to Herodotus, reigned for fourteen years: from 560 BC until his
     defeat by the Persian king Cyrus the Great in 546 BC.

182 Low German or *Plattdeutsch*: Low German refers to the dominant dialect of North
     Germany. The designation "low" is not a value judgment, but rather alludes to the
     fact that the dialect was (and is) spoken in the North German lowlands as opposed
     to High German, which originated in the mountains of South Germany and present
     Switzerland. High German began as a series of regular shifts in the consonant
     system, separating High German from all the other Germanic languages, including
     the Scandinavian languages and English. This process began between the sixth
     and ninth centuries and spread slowly northward and eastward. Largely due to the
     extraordinary influence of Martin Luther's translation of the Bible in 1529, High
     German edged out Low German to become the dominant dialect in Germany. By
     this period of the nineteenth century, practically all speakers of Low German had
     studied and could speak High German, but the reverse was not true.

183 Devil's revenge: Trenckmann has Kägel speaking in Low German in this section and there is no obvious way for a translation to convey this. "Devil's revenge" is my translation of the Low German *Dübels Räk*; High German *Teufels Rache*, literally "devil's revenge."

184 *Rot*: As with *Fenz*, a Germanization of the English "road."

185 *getrietet*: i.e. "treated," a past participle formed by Germanizing the English "treat"

186 Battles in Vienna: This refers to the events of October 1848 when Vienna was first occupied by revolutionaries and then bombarded and defeated by combined Austrian and Croatian forces. Many leaders of the popular uprising were subsequently executed. The gains of the March Revolution were largely lost, and Austria began a phase of both reactionary authoritarianism—"neo-absolutism" —as well as liberal reform. ("Vienna Uprising," *Wikipedia*. Accessed March 2017, at *https://en.wikipedia.org/wiki/Vienna_Uprising*.)

187 The German saying is: "Das vergossene Blut schreit zum Himmel."

188 The German saying is: "Es ist nichts so fein gesponnen, es kommt einmal ans Licht der Sonnen."

189 Sanctimonious yammering: In German *Salbaterei*.

190 *meinden*: Germanization of the English verb "mind"

191 *"Three cheers and a tiger"*: The phrase, almost entirely forgotten today, apparently originated in 1822 among the Boston Light Infantry. It was, however, apparently, widely used and known during the Civil War. The three cheers stood for three "hurrahs"; the "tiger" called for a growl at the end of the cheers. (William Shepard Walsh, *Handy-book of Literary Curiosities*, 1,053.)

192 *ge-seeft*: "saved"

193 Johann Heinrich Daniel Zschokke (1771–1848) was a Swiss civil servant, reformer, and author. He was originally from North Germany, but spent most of his life in Switzerland. He wrote extensively on many subjects and in several genres. In the very popular *Stunden der Andacht* (Hours of Devotion), he expounded the fundamental principles of religion and morality in a rationalistic spirit

194 The German word is *Krispinsjünger*. Crispinus (English: Crispens), an early Roman Christian martyr, is the patron saint of shoemakers; his day is October 25.

195 This would be the Bernard Prairie that stretched between the Brazos and Colorado River drainages.

196 In German, *ehrlich* means "honest" or "trustworthy."

197 Pin oaks: Local name given to a species of water oak that are common along streams and riparian habitat of Central Texas. Deer and wood ducks prefer the acorns of the pin oaks to all other mast.

198 Prairie chickens: The Attwater prairie chicken is a subspecies of the greater prairie chicken that is native to coastal Texas and Louisiana in the United States. At one time, it was extremely abundant, existing by the millions on the Gulf prairies of Texas and Louisiana; an easy meal for the early pioneers. Now, due to loss of habitat, it is highly endangered. In 1972 the federal government set up Attwater

Prairie Chicken National Wildlife Refuge in Colorado County, to prevent the extinction of the bird.

199 White flag: White tail deer, native to this area, when startled, use their notably white tails (underneath side) to signal danger to their fellow deer.

200 Backstraps: The tenderloins of deer, universally referred to as "backstraps," are considered to be the best cut, followed by the hams, or haunches.

201 Bank's advancing bluecoats: Nathaniel Prentice Banks (1816–1894) was an American politician from Massachusetts and a Union general during the Civil War. Banks replaced Benjamin Butler at New Orleans as commander of the Department of the Gulf. He was charged with administration of Louisiana and gaining control of the Mississippi River. After the fall of Vicksburg, he launched the Red River Campaign, a failed attempt to occupy eastern Texas that prompted his recall.

202 Split rail fence: This was the most common way to erect a fence in this part of the state prior to the introduction of barbed wire, which did not occur until the early 1880s. The fences were made by splitting the trunks of post oak trees, which have a straight grain and hence split easily, and which are found in abundance in the area. The split wood was divided into rails and stakes and the whole thing could be put up in a way that interlocked and held itself up without rope or nail. Because of the extraordinary expense in time and labor needed to erect such a fence, much of the prairie land remained in the public domain during this period and open range convention applied. Accordingly, it was the responsibility of the landowner to fence other people's livestock out rather than to fence your own livestock in.

203 Grass burs, also called sticker burs, are a veritable plague in the sandy parts of Texas, and are well-known to anyone who has ventured out barefoot in the summertime. The sticker comes from a lateral and low-growing grass-like weed, of which there are three common types. The burs are actually spiny seeds that mature in the summer, just in time to torture tiny feet. Sandburs prefer the sandy soils and all three common kinds thrive in Texas.

204 Black heads: Probably the Ring-necked Duck, *Aythya collaris*, a large duck common to North America, the Ring-necked Duck is fairly common in freshwater marshes, ponds with dense vegetation on the shores, and small lakes. During winter, it frequents the coastal marshes and sometimes the estuaries in Texas.

205 Small water hen: the author is obviously referring to the American coot (Fulica americana), also known as a mud hen. Though commonly mistaken for ducks, American coots belong to a distinct order and are considered to be inedible.

206 Black jacks: *Quercus marilandica* (blackjack oak) is a small oak, one of the red oak group. It is native to the eastern and central United States, from Long Island to Florida, west as far as Texas, Oklahoma, and Nebraska.

207 Dewberries: The dewberries are a group of species in the genus *Rubus* closely related to blackberries. Dewberries are common throughout Texas and most of North America, but are especially prevalent in South-Central Texas, usually along fencerows. The berries, which mature in late April to May, are sweet and edible, and can be eaten raw, or used to make cobbler, jam, or pie.

[208] Rider: split rail fences were stacked in such a way that two horizontal rails fit into the "x" formed by the upright posts. The bottom one was termed the rider.

[209] Rüdesheimer: Rüdesheim is a famous wine-making area on the Rhine River in Germany. The region is about thirty-eight kilometers long and two to three kilometers wide on both sides of the Rhine. Viticulture has been practiced here since Roman times. The region is considered to have the most favorable geographical and climatic conditions for the production of wine in Germany. Many different varieties of grape are cultivated there.

[210] For a good first-hand description of camp life and the necessity for foraging, see: Brown, Journey *to Pleasant Hill: The Civil War Letters of Captain Elijah P. Petty.*

[211] Linden in Cass County: Interestingly, at this point in his narrative, Trenckmann switches to real names for the places mentioned. Linden is the county seat of Cass County in far northeast Texas. The county is located at the point where Texas, Louisiana, and Arkansas meet. Interestingly, at this stage of the narration, the author begins to use real place names instead of made-up ones.

[212] Bell County is located in Central Texas south of Waco. Belton is the county seat.

[213] Shoemaker's horse: The author uses the German expression, "auf Schusters Rappen kommen," which means literally to ride a shoemaker's horse, meaning, of course, to walk.

[214] Macek and Saha: the names are both Czech. The author alludes on several occasions to the Czech immigrants who had settled in and amongst the Germans in Austin County.

[215] Pan Meik: Czech for "Good Mike."

[216] The character that the author introduces here is one of the most interesting in the novel and, quite clearly, calls to mind Shakespeare's Falstaff.

[217] Amacitia: A fictional name for the German settlement of Latium in neighboring Washington County. The unincorporated town is on Farm Road 389 near Pond Creek about twelve miles southwest of Brenham in the southwest corner of Washington County. It was one of five *Lateiner* colonies founded by German political refugees in Texas after 1848. Early German settlers included artist Rudolph Melchior, who decorated the Winedale Inn, and civil engineer Hermann R. von Bieberstein, later a prominent Texas surveyor. After the war, many Czech families moved into the area. (Carole E. Christian, "Latium, TX," *Handbook of Texas Online.* Accessed April 20, 2017, at *https://tshaonline.org/handbook/online/articles/hnl15.*)

[218] Dueling scars: As mentioned in an earlier note, formalized dueling with swords was widespread among students of German university fraternities. The duels were conducted according to strict protocols and were rarely fatal but often resulted in scars to the face that were considered to be badges of honor. The German slang term for these scars is *Schmisse.*

[219] The author uses the word *Klitsche*: an archaic East Middle High German slang term for a small, run-down farmstead.

220 Blücher: Klösel is referring, ironically of course, to the Prussian Field Marshal, Gebhard Leberecht von Blücher, who together with the English under Wellington decisively defeated Napoleon at the Battle of Waterloo in 1815.

221 I have translated the German term *Ausreißer* with the American term "AWOL" a term with which anyone who has ever served in the American military will be familiar. It stands for "Away without Official Leave." Apparently, the term first gained currency during the Civil War, so is appropriate for the text.

222 Twist of tobacco: a rope-like piece of tobacco twisted together and either bitten off or cut and used as chewing tobacco.

223 Greybacks: Confederate paper currency was universally referred to as "greybacks" in contradistinction to "greenbacks," or Union paper money.

224 Mishmash: As mentioned in note 23 above, the author often has his characters mix English words and even whole phrases into the speech of his characters. Of all the characters, Long Mike takes this to the extreme, which prompts the comment in the text from Ferdinand Klösel. "Mishmash" is my translation for *Kauderwelsch*.

225 Perique is a type of tobacco from Saint James Parish, Louisiana, known for its strong, powerful, and fruity aroma. When the Acadians made their way into this region in 1776, the Choctaw and Chickasaw tribes were cultivating a variety of tobacco with a distinctive flavor. A farmer named Pierre Chenet is credited with first turning this local tobacco into what is now known as Perique in 1824 through the labor-intensive technique of pressure-fermentation. Perique is used as a component of various blended pipe tobaccos, as many people consider it too strong to be smoked pure. ("Perique," *Wikipedia*. Accessed April 21, 2017, *https: //en.wikipedia.org/wiki/Perique.*)

226 Ft. Lynn was located in Miller County Arkansas. There is now a town there by that name. It was probably more of a temporary and rather insignificant fortified encampment than a fort proper for there is very little mention of it in standard reference works.

227 Sabine Pass: Sabine Pass is the natural outlet of Sabine Lake into the Gulf of Mexico. It borders Jefferson County, Texas, and Cameron Parish, Louisiana. Two battles took place at Sabine Pass during the Civil War. The Second Battle of Sabine Pass took place on September 8, 1863, the result of a failed Union Army attempt to invade the Confederate state of Texas during the American Civil War. It has often been credited as the most one-sided Confederate victory during the War. ("The Second Battle of Sabine Pass," *Wikipedia*. Accessed April 21, 2017, *https: //en.wikipedia.org/wiki/Second_Battle_of_Sabine_Pass.*)

228 Walker's Cavalry Division: Actually, Walker's Texas Division, which included both infantry and cavalry units. The only division in Confederate service composed, throughout its existence, of troops from a single state, it took its name from Maj. Gen. John George Walker, who took command from its organizer, Brig. Gen. Henry Eustace McCulloch, on January 1, 1863. During its existence, it was commonly

called the "Greyhound Division," or "Walker's Greyhounds," in tribute to its special capability to make long, forced marches from one threatened point to another in the Trans-Mississippi Department. The division saw a lot of action in Arkansas and Louisiana and is credited with keeping southern Arkansas and eastern Louisiana in Confederate hands during the war. (Lester Newton Fitzhugh, "Walker's Texas Division," *Handbook of Texas Online.* Accessed April 21, 2017, *https://tshaonline.org /handbook/online/articles/qkw01*; for contemporary accounts of the division, see; Blessington, *The Campaigns of Walker's Texas Division by a Private Soldier;* and Brown, ed., *Journey to Pleasant Hill: The Civil War Letters of Captain Elijah P. Petty.*)

229 Clodhopper: The author uses the word *Klutentreter,* a pejorative term for a farmer, but he is clearly referring to Union troops.

230 Mother-in-law: This refers to the first sergeant of the company, as will be explained in the course of the narrative.

231 Perleberg: The capital of the district of Prignitz, located in the northwest of the German state of Brandenburg. The town today has about 12,000 inhabitants. ("Perleberg, Germany," *Wikipedia.* Accessed April 23, 2017.)

232 Strict Prussian regulation and *Hardee's Tactics*: William Joseph Hardee (1815–1873) was a career U.S. Army officer who sided with the South and became a general in the Civil War. In 1855, while an instructor at West Point, Hardee published *Rifle and Light Infantry Tactics for the Exercise and Manoeuvres of Troops When Acting as Light Infantry or Riflemen,* popularly known as *Hardee's Tactics,* which became the best-known drill manual of the Civil War, widely used on both sides. ("William J. Hardee," *Wikipedia.* Accessed May 24, 2017, at *https://en.wikipedia.org/wiki /William_J._Hardee.*) According to Prussian military regulation, the position of "attention" required a soldier to stand very stiff with the hands cupped, pointed, and touching the seams of the trousers, hence the phrase, "on the pants seams."

233 The officer described in the text appears to be modeled after Gustav Hoffmann (1817–1889), early German settler, Confederate officer, and state representative. He was one of the original settlers of New Braunfels, Texas, where he was elected the first mayor in June 1847. Hoffmann had military experience in Prussia, and with the outbreak of the Civil War he raised a company of cavalry from Comal County that joined Henry H. Silbey's brigade in October 1861 as Company B, Seventh Regiment, Texas Cavalry. Comal County, interestingly, was the one predominantly German county in the state with a majority vote for secession. Hoffmann participated in numerous battles and was seriously wounded during the assault on Fort Butler in June 1863. He became full-time commander of the Seventh Texas Cavalry toward the end of the war. Hoffmann returned to New Braunfels and in 1872 was elected a representative to the Thirteenth Legislature. He later moved to San Antonio, where he died on March 10, 1889. (Martin Hardwick Hall, "Hoffmann, Gustav," *Handbook of Texas Online.* Accessed April 26, 2017, at *https: //tshaonline.org/handbook/online/articles/fho14.*)

234 Moltke: Helmuth Karl Bernhard Graf von Moltke (October 1800–1891,) served as a German Field Marshal and Chief of Staff of the Prussian Army for thirty years.

He was instrumental in Prussian victories in three wars that paved the way
for German unification under Prussian leadership in 1871, namely the War
with Denmark (1864), the Austro-Prussian War (1866), and, most importantly,
the Franco-Prussian War (1870–71). He is considered one of the greatest German
military figures of all times.

235　Brigadier-General Mullins: No record found of a Confederate general by this name.

236　Camp Sidney Johnston: named after Confederate general Albert Sidney Johnston
(1803–1862) who was killed early in the Civil War at the Battle of Shiloh. The author
is mistaken on this point: Fort Albert Sidney Johnston was not located at Yellow
Bayou, but rather in present Shreveport, Louisiana. Remnants are said to exist
in a small park located at present-day Clay and Webster Streets.

237　Yellow Bayou: Located in East-Central Louisiana on the west side of the Atchafalaya
River about sixty miles north of Baton Rouge, Yellow Bayou, a place more than a
town, was the site of the last battle of Major General Nathaniel P. Banks' ill-fated
Red River Expedition. During his retreat following the battles of Mansfield and
Pleasant Hill, Banks reached the Atchafalaya River on May 17 south of Yellow
Bayou. Upon learning that a Confederate force under Major General Richard Taylor
was camped nearby, Banks ordered an attack. The contest see-sawed and both
forces finally withdrew from the field, but military historians consider the battle
a tactical Union victory for the simple reason that Bank's army survived to fight
another day.

238　Confederate forces launched an invasion of New Mexico from San Antonio in
late 1861 with an eye on capturing all of the American West for the Confederacy.
It was an extraordinarily audacious effort because of the vast distances and
inhospitable terrain involved. The army, composed entirely of Texans, was
assembled in San Antonio by Brigadier General Henry Hopkins Sibley during the
summer of 1861. Many of the recruits came from the south-central Texas counties
of Austin, Washington, Fayette, and Colorado, and were largely volunteers. The
Seventh Mounted Infantry was a component in this army and included many
Texas German soldiers. Trenckmann's older brother, Otto, participated in the
expedition. After initial successes at El Paso and Val Verde, the army was forced to
withdraw after the Battle of Glorieta Pass on March 28, 1862. Although technically
a Confederate victory, Union forces managed to seize and burn the Confederate
supply wagons, compelling the Confederate forces to retreat. After a long and
difficult retreat across the badlands of the *Jornado del Muerte* wilderness in southern
New Mexico and then across the Trans-Pecos desert, the force was reorganized
and transferred to Louisiana. For a good description of the campaign see: Jerry
Thompson, ed., *Civil War in the Southwest: Recollections of the Sibley Brigade*, College
Station: Texas A&M Press, 2001.

239　Battle of Mansfield: In the spring of 1864 Union forces stationed in New Orleans
and at Vicksburg launched the so-called Red River Campaign. The objective was to
capture Shreveport, the capitol of Louisiana located in the northwest corner of the
state and thus bring all of Louisiana and southern Arkansas under Union control

and then to threaten invasion of Texas from the east. The Battle of Mansfield, Louisiana, (April 8, 1864) was the first major battle during the Red River Campaign. Confederate forces under the command of Major General Richard Taylor routed Union forces commanded by General Nathaniel Banks. The Confederate forces included a large contingent of Texas units including (by now) Brigadier General Thomas Green's Texas cavalry division (see subsequent note), which included the 7th Mounted Infantry, commanded by Colonel Gustav Hoffmann, who serves as a model for Captain Krusius in the narrative.

[240] Battle of Pleasant Hill: After defeat at the Battle of Mansfield (see note above), Union forces under General Banks withdrew about forty miles to the south near the community of Pleasant Hill where they intended to make a stand. Confederate forces were aggressive in pursuing the Union forces and launched an attack without first gaining solid information as to the deployment of the Union forces. Because of this, the resulting battle was a tactical victory for the Federals, but a strategic loss since the Union army retreated following the battle, the Red River Campaign collapsed, and Louisiana (except for New Orleans) remained under Confederate control for the duration of the war.

[241] Colonel Thomas Green: At the Battle of Val Verde in February 1862, due to some indisposition—some say he was drunk—General Sibley was forced to turn over command of his forces to Colonel Thomas Green in the middle of the battle. Initially a stalemate, it appeared after several hours of fighting that the outnumbered Confederate forces were in a hopeless situation with Union forces to their front and on both flanks. Green, however, rather than surrender or retreat, rallied the Confederate forces to an attack. After some hesitation, the Confederates took up the attack with enthusiasm and routed the Union army, who fled across the river in disarray. The Union forces were compelled to withdraw into Fort Craig to the south while the Confederate forces resumed their march north toward Albuquerque and Santa Fe.

[242] Büchel: Marinus Cornelius van den Heuvel was a Dutch immigrant, equally fluent in Dutch and German, who settled on Mill Creek in Austin County before the Civil War. He organized and enrolled a company of Texas Germans at Shelby, Austin County, on September 1, 1861. Captain Heuvel was shot through the right eye and killed at the Battle of Val Verde while leading his company on a charge against a plum thicket where Union forces had fortified their positions. Van den Heuvel serves as a model for Büchel. (op cit., Thompson, *Civil War in the Southwest*, 34. 155)

[243] As mentioned in a previous note, General Sibley was forced to turn over command of his forces to Colonel Thomas Green in the middle of the battle. The general was ill but also apparently quite inebriated.

[244] Angely's "Paris in Pommern": Louis Jean Jacques Angely (1787–1835) was a German playwright, actor and director of French Huguenot descent, who wrote *Possen* (farces) and vaudeville musicals after French models, which he adapted for German audiences. He was very popular in smaller second-tier theaters throughout Germany. *Paris in Pommern* (Paris in Pomerania) was a one act comic musical

written in 1839. It included the character of Heyman Levi, an itinerant Jewish salesman who, in the play, is asked to judge which among farmer's three daughters is the ugliest, which puts him in a particular dilemma himself. The play casts Levi in a sympathetic but stereotypical light.

245 In English translation, "Sitting deep in the cellar next to a barrel of wine," a popular drinking song of the nineteenth century, written by Karl Müchler. ("Im tiefen Keller sitz ich hier," *Volkslierarchiv.* Accessed May 28, 2017, at *https://www.volksliederarchiv .de/im-tiefen-keller-sitz-ich-hier/.*)

246 Actually, "The harp that once through Tara's halls," an Irish love song either written or compiled by Thomas Moore in the first part of the nineteenth century. ("Harp That Once Through Tara's Halls," *Irishsongs.* Accessed May 28, 2017, at *https://www .irishsongs.com/lyrics.php?Action=view&Song_id=141.*)

247 "Comin' Thro' the Rye" is a poem written in 1782 by Robert Burns (1759–96). The words are put to the melody of the Scottish Minstrel, "Common' Frae The Town." This is a variant of the tune to which "Auld Lang Syne" is usually sung—the melodic shape is almost identical, the difference lying in the tempo and rhythm. ("Comin' Thro' the Rye," *Wikipedia.* Accessed May 28, 2017, at *https://en.wikipedia .org/wiki/Comin%27_Thro%27_the_Rye.*)

248 Corn dodgers: A small cornmeal cake either baked or fried or boiled as a dumpling and a Southern specialty similar to Johnny cakes.

249 Walker's Texas Division was the only division in Confederate service composed, throughout its existence, of troops from a single state.

250 Bodkin beard: In German a *Knebelbart,* a style of beard where the hair on the chin is the predominant part, often fashioned into a pointy shape of medium length. Fashionable in the nineteenth century.

251 *Himmelkreuzdonnerwetter*: A strong German expletive, literally "heavenly-cross-thunderweather," but spelled phonetically to indicate that the sergeant was rolling his Rs.

252 Częstochowa is a medium size city in southern Poland on the Warta River. It has been situated in the Silesian Voivodeship since 1999, and was previously the capital of the Częstochowa Voivodeship. ("Częstochowa," *Wikipedia.* Accessed May 1, 2017, at *https://en.wikipedia.org/wiki/Cz%C4%99stochowa.*)

253 Rosenberg: There are actually several small towns by the name of Rosenberg in Germany. It is not clear which one he means.

254 Grimms' Fairy Tales: A collection of German fairy tales first published in 1812 by the Grimm brothers, Jacob and Wilhelm, and commonly known in English as Grimms' Fairy Tales. The influence of these books was widespread and worldwide. Walt Disney Productions produced and released an animated musical fantasy film based on "Snow White and the Seven Dwarfs," in 1937. The movie made the Grimm brothers a household name in America.

255 Pinchen: This is a diminutive (or affectionate) form of a first name, but it is not clear what name it refers to; perhaps a Polish name.

256 Gross-Krotoschau: This is the German designation for Krotoszyn, a town in central Poland. Historically, it belonged to the Kingdom of Poland, but in the nineteenth century after the Partitions of Poland, the town was located in the Prussian province of Posen.

257 Tacitus (AD 56–c. AD 120) is considered to be one of the greatest Roman historians. Among his other works, Tacitus wrote of the Germanic tribes north of the Rhine and may actually have visited there. His account, given in *Germania* (in *De origine et situ Germanorum*) provides our most complete description of the Germanic North that we have from classical times.

258 Bill Bee and the soldiers are putting on an amateur version of a minstrel show. Offensive to modern sensibilities, the stock minstrel show had already developed as a recognized form of American entertainment by the Civil War and reached its height of popularity in the period from 1850 until 1870. It is generally recognized as the precursor to vaudeville and was equally popular in both Northern and Southern theaters. Over time "minstrely," as it was termed, developed a stock, three-part format: the march-in, various skits and musical presentations, and a short one-act play depicting life on a Southern plantation. The second part always included a stump speech, or sermon, during which the performer spoke in plantation Negro dialect as he lectured. The character he portrays pretends to great wisdom and intelligence, but his mangled speech and hilarious malapropisms always cast him in a preposterous light. Minstrel shows, quite obviously, served to reinforce racial stereotypes since they portrayed black people as dim-witted, lazy, buffoonish, superstitious, and happy-go-lucky.

259 Different pronunciations: Students of Latin in England (and America) were taught to pronounce the vowels differently than in the European countries.

260 Houston College: There is no record of a college by this name that dates to *antebellum* Texas. There were many private schools and colleges founded in the period between statehood and the outbreak of the Civil War, but few survived as originally organized. It is possible, therefore, that such an institution did briefly exist, but has now been forgotten. Sam Houston Normal Institute (now Sam Houston State University) was established in Huntsville in 1879.

261 Pony: A translation or study aid

262 Horace: Quintus Horatius Flaccus (65 BC – 8 BC), known in the English-speaking world as Horace, was the leading Roman lyric poet during the time of Augustus. The most frequent themes of his Odes and verse Epistles are love, friendship, philosophy, and the art of poetry. (*Wikipedia*, "Horace," accessed May 3, 2017)

263 Poker, Seven up, and Monte: These are all popular card games that lend themselves to gambling. Poker is more a generic term for several different card games used for gambling. Three-card Monte–also known as "Find the Lady" and "Three-card Trick"–is a confidence game in which the victim, or "mark", is tricked into betting a sum of money, on the assumption that they can find the "money card" among three face-down playing cards. It is the same as the shell game except that cards are used instead of shells. Seven Up, also known as "All Fours," "High-Low-Jack" or,

is an English tavern trick-taking card game that was popular as a gambling game until the end of the nineteenth century. ("Poker," "Seven Up (game)", and "Monte," *Wikipedia*. Accessed May 12, 2017.)

264 Songs: "The Little Brown Jug" and "Bonnie Blue Flag" are both well-known songs of Civil War vintage. The Texas Ranger song is less clear. He is probably referring to the song that begins with the lyrics: "Come all you Texas Rangers, wherever you may be . . . " This song appears to date to the period, or even earlier.

265 The text often refers to the county seat of the county where Possum Creek was located, but never mentions it by name, either made-up or real. Bellville was, and still is, the county seat of Austin County.

266 Lightning rod: Benjamin Franklin invented the pointed lightning rod conductor in 1749 as part of his research into electricity. Lightning rods became a decorative and utilitarian fixture on many houses in the nineteenth century and, in many cases, sturdy enough for a person to be able to scale the part that went down to the ground.

267 Stonewall Jackson: Thomas Jonathan "Stonewall" Jackson (1824–1863) was a famous Confederate general during the American Civil War. He was mortally wounded by friendly fire while scouting enemy positions during the Battle of Chancellorsville in May 1863. Prior to the war, Jackson taught at the Virginia Military Institute in Lexington, Virginia. ("Stonewall Jackson," *History.com*. Accessed May 13, 2017, at *https://www.history.com/topics/american-civil-war /stonewall-jackson.*)

268 "Spoons" Butler: Benjamin Franklin Butler (1818–1893) was a high-profile American politician and businessman from Massachusetts who received a political appointment to the Army during the war. In May 1862, he commanded the force that captured New Orleans. While serving as military governor, he put into place sanitation policies that had a dramatic effect on reducing the incidence of yellow fever in the city. This did not, however, endear him with the citizens of New Orleans. He refused to tolerate acts of defiance against his men, especially by the Southern ladies of the city, and he also cracked down on the flow of contraband in and out of the city. He was nicknamed "Beast Butler" or alternatively "Spoons Butler," the latter nickname deriving primarily from an incident in which Butler seized a set of silverware from a New Orleans woman attempting to cross the Union lines. ("Benjamin Butler," *Wikipedia*. Accessed May 15, 2017, at *https://en.wikipedia .org/wiki/Benjamin_Butler.*)

269 Tête-à-tête: In this context, a piece of furniture that became popular in the nineteenth century with an S-shaped, serpentine form that encouraged two people, often courting couples, to face each other and engage in conversation without actually touching. Tête-à-tête literally means "head-to-head" in French, and this configuration allows for just that.

270 Written as a minstrel tune by Stephen Foster in 1851, the song, usually under the title, "The Old Folks at Home," became one of the most popular songs of all time in terms of sheet music sold and even was adopted as the official state song of Florida,

although in 2008 its lyrics needed to be rewritten to be more in tune with the times. This is because the original song is sung from the standpoint of a slave who longs to be back on the plantation. The song is a nostalgic romanticizing of slavery and plantation life.

271 Sarah Flower Adams was a well-known British actress who turned to writing poems and hymns after health issues ended her acting career prematurely. She wrote her most notable hymn "Nearer, My God, to Thee" in 1841. The hymn was originally set to music written by her sister, Eliza Flower, but is usually sung to another tune, "Bethany," written by Lowell Mason in 1856, and it is this version that is most familiar to listeners today.

272 New Orleans was captured and occupied by Union forces relatively early in the war (April 1862) and was the major port occupied by Union forces along the Gulf coast. The city, therefore, was spared the blockade that affected the rest of the South with access to goods from both Europe and the North for the duration of the war. The result was that the large porous city became a mecca for smugglers dealing in contraband on the black market. This frustrated General Butler, commander of the occupation forces in the city, who put in place vigorous measures to stem the flow of contraband and in the process earned the undignified title of "Spoons" after he confiscated silver spoons from a Southern lady who had attempted to smuggle them across the lines under her petticoats.

273 The Virginia reel is an English/Scottish folk dance that dates from the seventeenth century. The dance was most popular in America from 1830–1890. The Quadrille is a dance performed by four couples that was fashionable in late eighteenth- and nineteenth-century Europe and its colonies and it is related to American square dancing.

274 "The never changing schedule of our duties": a quote from the German poet Friedrich Schiller. In German: *"des Dienstes ewig gleichgestellte Uhr,"* from *Die Piccolomini*, which is the second part of Schiller's *Wallenstein* trilogy.

275 Zabrze is a city in Silesia in southern Poland, near Katowice. It is located in the Silesian Highlands, on the Bytomka River, a tributary of the Oder.

276 Himmelwitz (Polish: Jemielnica) is a village in Strzelce County, Opole Voivodeship, in south-western Poland. Before 1945 the area was part of Germany. The district is dotted with many small ponds and lakes.

277 Although there is a community by the name of Frogtown in Mississippi, there is no record of a Civil War action having taken place there. The episode at Frogtown, described by Sergeant Shoots, appears to have been invented by the author, but set in the context of the historical Holly Springs raid that took place December 20, 1862. Under a plan conceived by Colonel Griffith of the Sixth Texas Cavalry, General Earl van Dorn led a surprise raid against the Union garrison guarding an enormous stockpile of supplies at Holly Springs, Mississippi, located in the very north of the state. After driving the Yankee defenders away, his forces helped themselves to much needed supplies and destroyed what could not be appropriated. This was a

costly surprise to General Grant, thwarting his first attempt to capture Vicksburg, Mississippi and a great morale boost for the Confederacy.

278 Detached service: Civil War era terminology that correlates to modern TDY, or temporary duty. Individual soldiers, or even whole units, were often detached and assigned temporarily to other units to augment their strength as the need arose.

279 Lieutenant General John C. Pemberton (1814–1881) was in overall command of Vicksburg, the vital Confederate fortress city that guarded passage on the Mississippi River. Outnumbered and woefully lacking in supplies, he put up a stubborn defense against General Grant's superior forces but in the end was trapped in the city with a force of over 20,000 men and forced to surrender in the summer of 1863. When Sergeant Shoots alludes to Pemberton being "caught on the nest," he is referring to Pemberton's inability to escape the encirclement and preserve his army.

280 Gaspergou: A Southern Louisiana Cajun name for a fresh water drum fish.

281 This is a well-known children's ditty that is used to learn the numbers. It actually begins with counting off the numbers up to the number seven.

282 *"Muss i denn"* is a traditional German song in the Swabian German dialect. The present form dates back to 1827, when it was written and made public by Friedrich Silcher. It is about a soldier having to leave the woman he loves and vowing to remain faithful until he returns to marry her. The song became famous beginning in the mid nineteenth century. ("Muss i denn," *Wikipedia*. Accessed June 2, 2017, at *https://en.wikipedia.org/wiki/Muss_i_denn*.)

283 The author is referring to the Sixth Texas Cavalry which was nominally under the command of Col. Sul Ross but at the time of surrender in May 1865 was commanded by Col. Jack Wharton. The Sixth participated in the Holly Springs raid, mentioned above, and, in general, saw heavy action throughout the war. Only 160 men of the original 1,700 remained at war's end to be paroled. (Jennifer Bridges, "Sixth Texas Cavalry," *Handbook of Texas Online*. Accessed June 2, 2017, at *https://tshaonline.org/handbook/online/articles/qks13*.)

284 Upshur County: Upshur County is in northeastern Texas located in the Piney Woods vegetation zone. Camp Tally, a Confederate training and recruitment center, was located near Coffeeville. (Mary Laschinger Kirby, "Upshur County," *Handbook of Texas Online*. Accessed June 2, 2017, at *https://tshaonline.org/handbook/online/articles/hcu01*.)

285 Cherokee County

286 Burleson County is in southeast Texas with the town of Caldwell as the county seat. The Brazos River forms the eastern boundary of the county, hence a large portion of the county was, and is, devoted to corn and cotton production in the Brazos River Valley. The county is now part of the College Station-Bryan, TX Metropolitan Area.

287 William Polk Hardeman (1816–1898) served with distinction during several campaigns during the Civil War, including the New Mexico and Red River campaigns, eventually rinsing to the command of the Fourth Texas Cavalry. After successful campaigns at Yellow Bayou and Franklin, Hardeman was promoted

to brigadier general. (Nicholas P. Hardeman, "Hardeman, William Polk," *Handbook of Texas Online*. Accessed June 2, 2017, at *https://tshaonline.org/handbook/online /articles/fha58*.) Hardeman was one of the founders of Texas A&M College and it is quite possible that Trenckmann, as the first valedictorian of the first graduating class at A&M, had met Hardeman personally at one point or another. He is portrayed very sympathetically in the novel.

[288] Edmund Kirby Smith (1824–1893), a West Point graduate, already had a distinguished military record behind him from various Indian wars and the Mexican War when the Civil War broke out. On October 9, 1862, he was given command of the Trans-Mississippi Department. General Kirby Smith was almost the last Confederate general in the field, but in a hopelessly isolated situation, he finally surrendered to Gen. Edward R. S. Canby, on June 2, 1865. (Thomas W. Cutrer, "Smith, Edmund Kirby," *Handbook of Texas Online*. Accessed June 2, 2017, at *https://tshaonline.org/handbook/online/articles/fsm09*.)

[289] Literally, "Who built you up so high over there, beautiful forest?" The song is from a poem, *"Der Jäger Abschied"* (The hunters' farewell) by the German Romantic poet, Joseph von Eichendorff (1788–1857). His works were (and continue to be) very popular in Germany. Many of his poems were set to music and made their way into popular usage.

[290] Council of War: Although timing and place are not quite correct, Trenckmann is alluding to a series of historical meetings, or councils, generally referred to as the "Marshall Conferences" that brought together political and military leaders to debate wartime challenges of the Confederate states west of the Mississippi and to forge a unified strategy to deal with these challenges. General Kirby participated in three such councils. The last council, precipitated by the surrender of all Confederate land forces east of the Mississippi and the dissolution of the Richmond government, took place in May of 1865 just prior to the final capitulation, which occurred in June. (Allan C. Ashcraft, "Marshall Conferences," *Handbook of Texas Online*. accessed June 3, 2017, at *https://tshaonline.org/handbook/online/articles/nhm01*.)

[291] With the collapse in value of Confederate currency, the South had to come up with creative ways to pay for the provisions and armaments necessary to sustain the war effort. Cotton was essentially the only thing of value in the South. As a result, Gen. Kirby Smith authorized the creation of a cotton bureau within the Trans-Mississippi Department in 1863. The new arrangement required planters to sell a certain percentage of their cotton crops to the bureau at a discounted price in Confederate currency; and under threat of condemnation of their total crop, most complied. But, in point of fact, much of the cotton was often withheld from market and stockpiled, with the government issuing IOUs, or cotton deposits, based on the stored cotton, to pay for needed supplies. These deposits became the *de facto* currency of the Confederacy west of the Mississippi River. (Jack Becker and Matthew K. Hamilton, "Wartime Cotton Trade," *Handbook of Texas Online*. Accessed June 3, 2017, at *https://tshaonline.org/handbook/online/articles/drw01*.)

292 The relationship of die-hard Confederates—and General Kirby Smith certainly counted as such—to Emperor Maximillian and the developing Civil War in Mexico is quite fascinating. In May 1864, an Austrian Archduke, Ferdinand Maximillian, arrived in Mexico to become emperor of the so-called Second Mexican Empire. This was not a move welcomed by the mass of the Mexican people and, under the leadership of Benito Juarez, they revolted and a Civil War ensued that resulted in the overthrow and execution of the emperor in 1867. This all developed during the final phase of the American Civil War, when cooler heads in the South realized that defeat was inevitable. Many die-hard Confederates and panicked slaveholders hoped that they might be able to reconstruct some semblance of the hierarchical slave society they had known in the South in a Mexico ruled by Maximillian and his aristocratic supporters. With the final capitulation of the western theater many hundreds of ex-Confederated did, in fact, relocate to Mexico where they set up several colonies and settlements; most short-lived. Many, like General Kirby Smith, volunteered to fight for Maximillian and his aristocratic backers in pursuit of their delusional goal.

293 Breakup: For a succinct scholarly treatment of the "breakup," see: Clampitt, "The Breakup," *SWHQ*, Vol. 108, No. 4 (Apr., 2005), pp. 498–534.

294 Farmville, Virginia, was the object of the Confederate Army's desperate push to get rations to feed its soldiers near the end of the American Civil War.

295 Maj. Generals John Brown Gordon (1832–1904) and Fitzhugh Lee (1835–1905) had the honor (or foolishness) of leading their men in the last charges of the Army of Northern Virginia.

296 "General Hardeman participated in the New Mexico campaign. He was twice wounded at Val Verde and commanded the force that defeated a larger Union attack in the defense of Confederate supplies in Albuquerque. He participated in Gen. Richard Taylor's Red River campaign, which turned back the numerically superior army of Union general Nathaniel P. Banks, and eventually rose to the command of the Fourth Texas Cavalry. After successful campaigns at Yellow Bayou and Franklin, Hardeman was promoted to brigadier general.

After the surrender of Gen. Robert E. Lee at Appomattox, Hardeman, like his cousin Peter Hardeman and thousands of other Confederates, became an exile. He joined a company of fifteen high-ranking officers, eluded Gen. Philip H. Sheridan, and escaped to Mexico. There he served briefly as a battalion commander in Maximilian's army and became a settlement agent for a Confederate colony near Guadalajara. In 1866 he returned to Texas, where he served as inspector of railroads, superintendent of public buildings and grounds, and superintendent of the Texas Confederate Home in Austin. He died of Bright's disease on April 8, 1898, and was buried at the State Cemetery in Austin." (Nicholas P. Hardeman, "Hardeman, William Polk," *Handbook of Texas Online*. Accessed June 10, 2017, at *https://tshaonline .org/handbook/online/articles/fha58.*)

297 On May 14, 1865, approximately 400 Confederates in Galveston attempted to organize a mutiny. For a full description of the situation as well as the subsequent troubles in Houston, see: Clampitt, "The Breakup," 507.

298 For a description of the La Grange riot, see: Clampitt, "The Breakup," 517.

299 Old Gotch: Trenckmann is correct in attributing the affectionate nickname "Old Gotch" to General Hardeman. (Nicholas P. Hardeman, "Hardeman, William Polk," *Handbook of Texas Online*. Accessed June 10, 2017, at *https://tshaonline.org/handbook/online/articles/fha58*.)

300 The unification of Germany in 1871 was made possible by the diplomatic and political genius of Prussian Chancellor Otto von Bismarck and the military brilliance of Prussian Field Marshal Helmuth von Moltke. The road to unification required three wars: a short but bloody war with Denmark in 1864; the so-called Seven Weeks War fought between Prussia and Austria in 1866; and the Franco-Prussian War of 1871. The Battle of Königsgrätz (July 1866) was the opening battle of the Austro-Prussian conflict, and resulted in an overwhelming Prussian victory. It was the first battle in which von Moltke put into practice his new military tactics, often summarized by the phrase: *"getrennt marschieren; gemeinsam schlagen."* (march separately; join in battle together). In practice, this meant using the railroads to move and supply armies in a coordinated and efficient way that had never been done before. The lessons learned during the war with Austria were brilliantly employed by the Prussians in the subsequent Franco-Prussian War of 1871, also a resounding victory that paved the way for Germany to unite under Prussian leadership.

I. GERMANS IMMIGRATION IN TEXAS IN THE 19TH CENTURY

Benjamin, Gilbert Giddings. *The Germans in Texas: A Study in Immigration.* Austin: Jenkins Publishing Co., 1974.

Biesele, Rudolph Leopold. *The History of the German Settlements in Texas.* Chapter VIII, 161-177. 1930. Reprinted, Ann Arbor: McNaughton & Gunn, 1987.

Jordan, Terry G. *German Seed in Texas Soil: Immigrant Farmers in Nineteenth-Century Texas.* Austin and London: University of Texas Press, 1966.

Jordan, Gilbert. "German Texana." In *Eagle in the New World: German Immigration to Texas and America*, edited by Theodore Gish and Richard Spuler, 85-101.

Jordan, Terry G. *Immigration to Texas.* Boston: American Press, 1980.

Kearney, James. "Introduction." In: *Friedrichsburg: Colony of the German Furstenverein* by Friedrich Armand Strubberg, Austin, Texas: University of Texas Press, 2012, 1-28.

Kearney, James. *Nassau Plantation: The Evolution of a Texas-German Slave Population.* Denton, Texas: University of North Texas Press, 2010.

Tiling, Moritz. *The History of the German Element in Texas 1820-1850.* Houston: M. Tilling, 1913.

II. MILLHEIM, AUSTIN COUNTY, SOUTH-CENTRAL TEXAS GERMAN SETTLEMENTS

Biesele, Rudolph Leopold. "The German Settlements on the Lower Brazos, Colorado and Guadalupe Rivers." In: *The History of the German Settlements in Texas.* Chapter VIII, 161-177. 1930. Reprinted, Ann Arbor: McNaughton & Gunn, 1987, 42-65.

The Cat Spring Story, Publication of the Cat Spring Agricultural Society, San Antonio: Lone Star Printing Co., 1956.

Engelking, Ferdinand. "The History of Millheim." Supplement to *Bellville Wochenblatt,* 1899. See Kollaschny, 59.

Goeth, Ottilie Fuchs. *Memoirs of a Texas Pioneer Grandmother.* Irma Goeth, trans. Guenther. Burnet, Tx.: Eakin Press, 1982.

Hermes, Wm., Sr., "Erlebnisse eines deutschen Pioners in Texas," *La Grange Deutsche Zeitung,* August 19, 1915, 11, col. 2.

Kearney, James. *Nassau Plantation: The Evolution of a Texas German Slave Plantation.* Denton: University of North Texas Press, 2010.

Kollatschny, Herbert. *The Settling of Cat Spring and Early History of Austin County.* Sealy, TX: Wittnebourg Printing, 2012.

Nagel, Charles. *A Boy's Civil War Story.* St. Louis: Eden Publishing House, 1935.

Regenbrecht, Adalbert. "The German Settlers of Millheim (Texas) before the Civil War." *SWHQ.* Vol. 20, No. 1, (July, 1916), 28-34.

Richter, William and Anne Lindemann, editors. *Historical Accounts of Industry, Texas, 1831-1986.* New Ulm, Texas: New Ulm Enterprise Press, 1986.

Sörgel, Alwin H. *A Sojourn in Texas, 1846-47: Alwin H. Sörgel's Texas Writings.* Translated by W.M. Von-Maszewski. San Marcos: German-Texan Heritage Society, 1992.

Stöhr, Louise. "Die erste deutsche Frau in Texas" [The first German wife in Texas]. *Der deutsche Pionier* 16, No. 9 (Dec. 1884); 372-375, translated and reproduced in: Kearney, et al, *Journey to Texas in 1833* (Austin: University of Texas Press, *2012*), 126-130.

Studer, Clara Trenckmann. "Trenckmann, William Andreas," *HBT Online,* accessed August 14, 2017,

von Hinüber, Caroline Ernst. "Life of German Pioneers in early Texas," *Texas State Historical Quarterly,* vol. 2, no. 3 (January 1899), 227–232.

Von Roeder, Flora von. *The Engelking Letters; A Collection of Letters Written by or Pertaining to Ferdinand Friedrich Engelking, 1810-1885.* Translated and edited from the German by Flora von Roeder. Edited and set by Stephen A. Engelking. Tuningen, Germany: Published by the Hugh and Helene Schonfield World Service Trust, 2012

Von Roeder, Flora von. *These are the Generations.* Houston: Baylor College of Medicine, 1978.

Von Roeder-Moeckel, Olga Johanna. *Story of von Roeder and Ernst Families.* Self-published pamphlet in the Texas Room under Austin County, Nesbitt Memorial Library, Columbus, Texas.

Von Rosenberg, Charles W., comp. *Ancestral Voices. The Letters of the von Rosenberg and Meerscheidt Families, 1844-1897.* Self-published, n.d.

Woodrick, James Victor. *Austin County: Colonial Capitol of Texas.* Austin: Self-published, 2007.

York, Miriam Korff. *Friedrich Ernst of Industry.* Nixon, Tx: Giddings Printing, 1989.

III. GERMAN LATEINER COMMUNITIES IN TEXAS

Biesele, Rudolph. "The Texas State Convention of Germans in 1854," *SWHQ* 33 (April, 1930).

Fischer, Ernest G. *Marxists and Utopias in Texas.* Burnet: Eakin Press, 1980.

Nagel, Charles. *A Boy's Civil War Story.* St. Louis: Eden Publishing House, 1935.

Ransleben, Guido E. *A Hundred Years of Comfort.* San Antonio: The Naylor Co., 1974.

Regenbrecht, Adelbert. "The German Settlers of Millheim before the Civil War." *The SWHQ* 1 (July, 1916), 28-34.

Reichstein, Andreas V. *German Pioneers on the American Frontier: The Wagners in Texas and Illinois.* Denton: University of North Texas Press, 2001.

Reinhardt, Louis. "The Communistic Colony of Bettina." *Quarterly of the Texas State Historical Association* III (July, 1899), 33-40.

Trenckmann, William A. "Austin County." Beilage zum [Supplement to] *Bellville Wochenblatt*, Bellville, Texas, 1899.

IV. BOOKS, ARTICLES, ARCHIVAL COLLECTIONS, DISSERTATIONS: TEXAS GERMANS IN THE CIVIL WAR

Althaus, Voy Ernst. *Dark Blue Down South: A Story of the Central Texas Germans and the United States First Cavalry during the Civil War.* Self-Published, 2012.

Bailey, Anne J. *Invisible Southerners: Ethnicity in the Civil War.*

Baum, Dale. *The Shattering of Texas Unionism: Politics in the Lone Star State during the Civil War Era.* Baton Rouge: Louisiana State University Press, 1998.

"*Bekanntmachung über Sklaverei*" [Proclamation on Slavery]. *Frankfurter Journal*, No. 196, July 17, 1844. [Reproduced in Solms-Braunfels Archives, V, 207, 208.]

Biesele, Rudolph. "The German State Convention of 1854." *SWHQ* 33, No. 4 (April 1930), 247-261.

Bishop, A.W. *Loyalty on the Frontier or Sketches of Union Men of the Southwest.* St Louis: A.F. Studley & Co., 1863.

Boethel, Paul C. *The Big Guns of Fayette.* Austin: Von Boeckmann-Jones Company, 1965.

Boethel, Paul C. *Sand in your Craw.* Austin: Von Boeckmann-Jones Company, 1959.

Buenger, Walter L. *Secessionism and the Union in Texas.* Austin: University of Texas Press, 1984.

Buenger, Walter L. "Secession and the Texas German Community: Editor Lindheimer vs. Editor Flake," *SWHQ* 82 (April 1979): 379-402.

Burrier, William Paul, Sr. *Nueces Battle and Massacre: Facts and Fiction.* San Antonio: Watercress Press, 2015.

Burrier, William Paul, Sr., ed. *August Siemering's Die Deutschen in Texas während des Bürgerkrieges: The Germans in Texas During the Civil War.* Edited by Wm. Paul Burrier, Sr., Researched by Anne Steward and Wm. Paul Burrier, Sr., Translated by Helen Dietert and Ronnie Pue. 2013

Downing, David C. *A South Divided: Portraits of Dissent in the Confederacy.* Nashville: Cumberland House, 2007.

Elford, Alison Clark. *German Immigrants, Race, and Citizenship in the Civil War Era.* New York: Cambridge University Press, 2013.

Elliott, Claude. "Union Sentiment in Texas, 1861-1865." *SWHQ,* Vol. 50, No. 4 (Apr., 1947), pp. 449-477.

Flach, Vera. *A Yankee in German America; Texas Hill Country.* San Antonio, Texas: Naylor Publishing Co., 1973

Grasshoff, Ray. *Man of Two Worlds: A German Family Confronts the American Dream.* Lulu.com, 2009.

Grear, Charles D. *Why Texans Fought in the Civil War.* College Station: Texas A&M Press, 2014.

Gurasich, Marj. *A House Divided.* Fort Worth: TCU University Press, 1994.

Heinen, Hubert. "German-Texan Attitudes toward the Civil War." *Yearbook of the Society for German-American Studies* 20 (1985): 19-32.

Hoffman, David R. "A German-American Pioneer Remembers: August Hoffmann's Memoir," *SWHQ* 102 (January 1959), 336-355.

Honeck. Mischa. *We are the Revolutionists: German-speaking Immigrants & American Abolitionists after 1848.* Athens: University of Georgia Press, 2011.

Huff, Leo E. "Heel-fly Time in Texas: A Story of the Civil War Period." *Frontier Times* 2 (April 1924(, 33-48; (May 1924), 33-48; (June 1924), 33-47.

Hunter, J. Warren. *Heel Fly Time in Texas.* Bandera: Frontier Times Press, 1931.

Joiner, Jerry D. "Defending the Lone Star: The Texas Cavalry in the Red River Campaign." In: Howell, ed, *The Seventh Star of the Confederacy: Texas during the Civil War.* Denton: University of North Texas Press, 2009, 189-207.

Jordan-Bychkov, Terry G., Allen R. Branum, and Paula K. Hood, eds.; Ellen Ohlendorf Schwarz, trans. "The Boesel Letters: Two Texas Germans in Sibley's Brigade." *SWHQ,* Vol. 102, No. 2 (April 1999), 436-483.

Kamphoefner, Walther and Wolfgang Helbich, eds., Susan Carter Vogel, trans., *Germans in the Civil War.* Chapel Hill: University of North Carolina Press, 2006.

Kamphoefner, Walther. "New Americans or New Southerners? Unionist German Texans." In: *Lone Star Unionism, Dissent, and Resistance.* Jesus D. de la Tejas, ed. Norman: University of Oklahoma Press, 2012, 101-122.

Kamphoefner, Walther. "New Perspectives on Texas Germans and the Confederacy." In: *The Fate of Texas: The Civil War in the Lone Star State.* Charles D. Grear, ed. Fayetteville: University of Arkansas Press, 2008, 105-119.

Kearney, James. "The Adelsverein, the Plantation and Slavery," in *Nassau Plantation* (Denton: University of North Texas Press, 2011), 183-206.

Kelly, Patrick J. and Rhonda Minten, eds. *Living on the Edge: Texas During the Civil War and Reconstruction.* Cognella Academic Publishing, 2015.

Kenzer, Robert C. and John C. Inscoe, eds. *Enemies of the Country: New Perspectives on Unionists in the Civil War South.* Atlanta: University of Georgia Press, 2004.

Küffner, Cornelia. "Texas Germans' Attitudes Toward Slavery: Biedemeyer Sentiments and Class-Consciousness in Austin, Colorado, and Fayette Counties," MA Thesis, University of Houston, 1994.

Kroulik, John. "Memoirs of John Kroulik as Recorded by him during the Civil War, 1864. [mentioned in *Historical Accounts of Industry, Texas, 1831-1986*, 13.]

Leuschner, Charles A. *The Civil War Diaries of Charles A. Leuschner.* Charles A. Spurlin, ed. Austin: Eakin Press, 2010.

Marten, James. *Texas Divided: Loyalty and Dissent in the Lone Star State, 1856-1874.* Lexington: The University of Kentucky Press, 1990.

O'Rear, Mary Jo. "Reckoning at the River: Unionists and Secessionists on the River, August 10, 1862. In: Howell, ed., *The Seventh Star of the Confederacy: Texas during the Civil War.* Denton: University of North Texas Press, 2009, 85-109.

Pickering, David and Judith M. Falls. *Brush Men and Vigilantes: Civil War Dissent in Texas.* College Station: Texas A&M University Press, 2004.

Randers-Pehrson, Justine. *Adolf Douai, 1819-1888: The Turbulent Life of a German Forty-Eighter in the Homeland and in the United States.* New German-American Studies (Book 22). Peter Lang International Academic Publishers, 2000.

Siemering, August. *Die Deutschen in Texas während des Bürgerkrieges.* Freie Presse für Texas. Reissued and translated under same title by William Paul Burrier, ed., and Helen Dietert, trans. Tamarac, FL: Llumina Press, 2013.

Smyrl, Frank H. "Texans in the Union Army, 1861–1865," *SWHQ* 65 (October 1961).

Stein, Bill. "Distress, Discontent, and Dissent: Colorado County, Texas, during the Civil War." In: Howell, ed., *The Seventh Star of the Confederacy: Texas during the Civil War.* Denton: University of North Texas Press, 2009, 301-316.

Stein, Bill. "The German Draft Revolt" in *The Journaof the, German-Texan Heritage Society*, Volume XIV, Number 3 (1992), pp. 221-224;

Robert Voigt, Diaries and Letters, Box 3K/123, [Dolph Briscoe Center for American History, The University of Texas at Austin].

Von-Maszewski, Wolfram M. *Captain Voigt's Company of Waul's Texas Legion.* Richmond, Tx.: Tortuga Press, 2017.

"Insurrection of Germans in Colorado County." In: *War of the Rebellion: A Compilation of the Official Records of the Union and Confederate Armies.* Series I, Vol. 15, 220.

Wurster, Ilse, Charles Kettner, ed. *Die Kettner Briefe: The Kettner Letters: A Firsthand Account of a German Emigrant in the Texas Hill Country (1850-1875).* Wilmington, DE, 2008.

V. CIVIL WAR MILITARY HISTORY RELEVANT TO THIS STORY

Agan, John. *Echoes of Our Past: The Civil War Years in Minden.* Self-published. August 4, 2010. [location of Camp Magruder]

Alexander, Thomas E. and Dan K. Utley. *Faded Glory, A Century of Forgotten Texas Military Sites, Then and Now.* College Station: Texas A&M Press, 2012.

Blessington, Joseph Palmer. *The Campaigns of Walker's Texas Division by a Private Soldier.* New York: Lange, Little & Co., Printers, 1875.

Boethel, Paul. *The Big Guns of Fayette*. Austin: Von Boeckmann-Jones Company, 1965.

Brown, Norman D., ed. Intr. by O. Scott Petty. *Journey to Pleasant Hill: The Civil War Letters of Captain Elijah P. Petty*. San Antonio: Institute of Texas Cultures, 1982.

Cutrer, Thomas W. *Theater of a Separate War: The Civil War west of the Mississippi River, 1861-1865*. (Chapel Hill: University of North Carolina Press, 2017.

Cutrer, Thomas W. "Waul's Texas Legion." *HBT Online*, accessed August 14, 2017.

Foote, Shelby. *The Civil War: A Narrative; From Ft. Sumter to Perryville*. New York: Vintage Books, 1958.

Hardeman, Nicholas. "Hardeman, P. William Polk." *HBT Online*, accessed August 14, 2017.

Lowe, Richard. *Walker's Texas Division C.S.A.: Greyhounds of the Trans-Mississippi*. Baton Rouge: Louisiana State University, 2004.

Lundberg, John R. *Granbury's Texas Brigade: Diehard Western Confederates*. Baton Rouge: Louisiana State University, 2012.

McGowen, Stanley S. *Horse Sweat and Powder Smoke: The First Texas Cavalry in the Civil War*. College Station: Texas A&M Press, 1999.

VI. THE HOME FRONT DURING THE CIVIL WAR AND THE "BREAK-UP"

Clampitt, Brad R. "The Breakup: The Collapse of the Confederate Trans-Mississippi Army in Texas, 1865." *The SWHQ*, Vol. 108, No. 4 (Apr., 2005), pp. 498-534.

Duty, Tony E. "The Home Front: McLennan County in the Civil War." *Texana* XII, 3, 197-235.

McCaslin, Richard B. *Tainted Breeze: The Great Hanging at Gainesville, Texas, 1862*. Baton Rouge: Louisiana State University Press, 1994.

Howell, ed., *The Seventh Star of the Confederacy: Texas during the Civil War*. Denton: University of North Texas Press, 2009.

Kelley, Patrick J., ed. *Living on the Edge: Texas During the Civil War and Reconstruction*. Cognella Academic Publishing, 2015.

Wahlstrom, Todd W. *The Southern Exodus to Mexico: Migration across the Borderlands after the Civil War*. Lincoln: University of Nebraska Press, 2015.

Wooster, Ralph A. *A Civil War Texas*. Austin: Texas State Historical Association, 1999.

VII. GERMANY IN THE NINETEENTH CENTURY; VORMÄRZ; REVOLUTION(S) OF 1848

Abel, Wilhelm. *Geschichte der deutschen Landwirtschaft vom frühen Mittelalter bis zum 19. Jahrhundert*. Stuttgart: Franz Steiner, 1978.

Brunn, Geoffrey. *Revolution and Reaction: 1848-1852*. New York: Van Nostrand, 1958.

Deutsche Chronik für die Jahre 1848 und 1849. Berlin: Druck und Verlag von A.W. Hahn, 1849.

Feuerbach, Ludwig. "Positiver Atheismus." In: *Vorlesungen über das Wesen der Religion*, (Stuttgart, 1908, 354-358), reproduced in *Der deutsche Vormärz* (Stuttgart: Reclam, 1974), 170-172.

Henderson, W.O. *The Rise of German Industrial Power, 1834-1914*. Berkeley: University of California Press, 1965.

Hermand, Jost, ed. *Der deutsche Vormärz: Texte und Dokumente*. Stuttgart: Phillip Reclam, 1974.

Kamphoefner, Walter. "Dreissiger and Forty-Eighters: The Political Influence of two Generations of German Political Exiles." In: *Germany and America: Essays on Problems of International Relations and Immigration*. Hans L. Trefousse, ed. New York: Brooklyn College press, 1980, 89-102.

Kiesewetter, Hubert. *Industrieller Revolution in Deutschland: Regionen als Wachstummotoren*. Stuttgart: Franz Steiner Verlag, 2000.

Kitchen, Martin. *The Political Economy of Germany, 1815-1914*, London: Croom Helm, 1978.

Kohn, Hans. *The Idea of Nationalism*. New York: Collier Books, 1944.

Kohn, Hans. *The Mind of Germany; The Education of a Nation*. New York: Charles Scribner's Sons, 1960.

Levine, Bruce. *The Spirit of 1848: German Immigrants, Labor Conflict, and the Coming of the Civil War*. Urbana: University of Illinois Press, 1992.

Lich, Glenn E. "Forty-Eighters." *HBT online*. Accessed January 3, 2017.

Mann, Golo. *Deutsche Geschichte des 19. Und 20. Jahrhunderts*. Frankfurt am Main: S. Fischer Verlag, 1964.

Meinecke, Friedrich. *Weltbürgertum und Nationalstaat: Studien zur Genesis des deutschen Nationalstaates*. München und Berlin: Druck und Verlag von R. Oldenourg, 1908.

Mueller, Jacob. *Memories of a Forty-Eighter: Sketches from the German-American period of Storm and Stress in the 1850s*. Cleveland, Ohio: Western Reserve Historical Society, 1996.

Wittke, Carl. *Refugees of Revolution: The German Forty-Eighters in America*. Philadelphia: University of Pennsylvania Press, 1952.

VIII. PLANTATIONS

Beazley, Julia. "Liendo Plantation," *HBT Online*, accessed November 09, 2015. Uploaded on June 15, 2010.

Bertleth, Rosa Groce. "Jared Ellison Groce," *SWHQ* 20 (April 1917).

Boddie, Mary Delaney. *Thunder on the Brazos*. Taylor Publishing Comp, 1978.

Claudia Hazlewood, "Bernardo Plantation," *HBT Online*, accessed November 09, 2015.

Creighton, James A. *Narrative History of Brazoria County*. Waco: Texian Press, 1975, pp. 221-224.

Curlee, Abigail. "A Study of Texas Slave Plantations, 1822–1865." Ph.D. dissertation, University of Texas, 1932.

Harris, René. "Ellersly Plantation," *HBT Online*, accessed November 09, 2015.

Holbrook, Abigail Curlee. "A Glimpse of Life on Antebellum Slave Plantations in Texas," *SWHQ* 76 (April 1973).

Platter, Allen Andrew, "Educational, Social, and Economic Characteristics of the Plantation Culture of Brazoria County, Texas", Doctoral Dissertation Education, University of Houston, 1961.

Strobel, Abner J. *The Old Plantations and Their Owners of Brazoria County.* Houston, 1926; rev. ed., Houston: Bowman and Ross, 1930; rpt., Austin: Shelby, 1980.

Woodrick, James V. *Bernardo: Crossroads, Social Center and Agricultural Showcase of Early Texas.* Manuscript, 2009.

Wooster, Ralph A. "Wealthy Texans, 1860." *SWHQ* 71 (October 1967).

IX. TEXAS GERMAN LANGUAGE

Boas, Hans. *The Life and Death of Texas German.* Durham: Duke University Press for the American Dialect Society, 2009.

Gilbert, Glenn G. *Linguistic Atlas of Texas German.* Austin: University of Texas Press, 1972. Terry G. Jordan, "The German Element in Texas: An Overview," Rice University Studies 63 (Summer 1977).

Heinen, Hubert. "The Literary Use of English Words in W. A. Trenckmann's *Die Lateiner am Possum Creek.*" *Journal of the German-Texan Heritage Society* 7.1 (1985): 28-37.

Schmidt, Dr Eugen. "Die Sprache der Deutsch-Amerikaner." in: *Freie Presse für Texas,* Vol. VI, N. 2 (summer 1904). 127, 128.

X. W.A. TRENCKMANN'S WRITINGS

"Weihnachten in trüber Zeit," supplement to the Bellville Wochenblatt, 1894. Translated by Anders Saustrup as "Christmas in Troubled Times." Winedale: The Friends of Winedale, 1976.

Die Lateiner am Possum Creek. Serialized in the *Bellville Wochenblatt,* Bellville, TX, starting December 25, 1907 (13) and continuing through the next forty-seven issues, concluding on November 19, 1908 (8).

The History of Austin County, Texas. Edited and published in 1899 as a supplement to the Bellville Wochenblatt. Translated by his children William, Else, and Clara. Stephen A. Engelking, editor.

"Erlebtes und Beobachtetes" W.A. Trenckmann's autobiography, which appeared in German in serialized form in *Das Bellville Wochenblatt,* Bellville, Texas, September 17, 1931, until February 16, 1933. Translated by his children in a private printing as "Experiences and Observations." Subsequently released in book form as *Preserving German Texas Identity: Reminiscences of William A. Trenckmann, 1859-1935.* By Walter L. Buenger and Walter D. Kamphoefner. (College Station: Texas A&M University Press, 2018. Pp. 224. Illustrations, appendices, notes, bibliography, index.)

"The Schoolmasters of New Rostock. Texan Folk Drama in Two Acts," Hubert Heinen ed. and transl. *Journal of the German-Texan Heritage Society* 8 (1986): 179-91.

"Frau Clara Reyes" Austin: *Das Wochenblatt,* November 16, 1934.

XI. MISCELLANEOUS

Members of the Texas Legislature, 1846–1980. Austin: Texas Legislative Council, 1980.

XII. NEWSPAPERS CITED

The Galveston Daily News, Thursday, September 7, 1922.
Bellville Wochenblatt, Bellville, TX, starting December 25, 1907 (13) and continuing through
the next forty-seven issues, concluding on November 19, 1908 (8)
Brenham Daily Banner-Press (Brenham, Tex.), April 5, 1923.
Frankfurter Journal. (Frankfurt Germany). No. 196, July 17, 1844.
La Grange Deutsche Zeitung, August 19, 1915, 11, col. 2.
Temple Daily Telegram (Temple, Tex.), Vol. 15, No. 251, Ed. 1 Thursday, September 7, 1922,
The Austin Statesman, March 7, 1923.
Seguiner Zeitung. (Seguin, Tex.), September 15, 1922.

XIII. COLLECTIONS:

Douai, Adolf. Papers. [Dolph Briscoe Center for American History Studies. University
of Texas at Austin.]
Robert Voigt, Diaries and Letters, Box 3K/123, [Dolph Briscoe Center for American History,
The University of Texas at Austin].
John Amsler and L. P. Amsler letters. [The Texas Collection, Baylor University, Waco,
Texas].
Solms-Braunfels Archives (transcripts). [Dolph Briscoe Center for American History
Studies. University of Texas at Austin].
The William A. Trenckmann Papers, 1859-1933. [Dolph Briscoe Center for American
History Studies. University of Texas at Austin].
Bellville Wochenblatt (microfilm). [Dolph Briscoe Center for American History Studies.
University of Texas at Austin]